FIRE
BLOOD

FIRE BLOOD

ELLY BLAKE

LB
LITTLE, BROWN AND COMPANY
New York • Boston

Little, Brown and Company
Hachette Book Group
1290 Avenue of the Americas, New York, NY 10104
Visit us at LBYR.com

First Edition: September 2017

Little, Brown and Company is a division of Hachette Book Group, Inc. The Little, Brown name and logo are trademarks of Hachette Book Group, Inc.

ISBNs: 978-0-316-27332-9 (hardcover), 978-0-316-27327-5 (ebook)

Printed in the United States of America

LSC-C

10 9 8 7 6 5 4 3 2 1

FOR MY MOM, NANCY,
WHO TAUGHT ME TO LOVE WORDS

ONE

I CIRCLED THE FROSTBLOOD WARRIOR, my boots kicking up dust from the drought-dry earth. One little mistake, one little lapse in focus, would mean defeat.

His left fist twitched before his right came out with a cyclone of frost. But I knew all his favorite tricks, his feints and false moves. I twisted to the right, throwing a plume of fire from my palms.

My vision clouded. A sudden memory took me: *my hands, red with fire, stretched toward the icy throne of Fors—the timeless symbol of Frostblood rule—its wicked, gleaming shards mocking my paltry fire. I couldn't melt it. I couldn't defeat the curse inside it.*

But then another's frost joined my fire, not extinguishing but creating a blinding blue flame that poured toward the throne, softening its edges, dulling the sharp points, making the ice weep in defeat. I could hear King Rasmus's delighted laugh as the Minax broke free from the throne's dying heart, as the shadow creature crept against my skin, seeking entry, promising the joy of a thousand sunbursts and the absence of pain or weakness ever, ever again.

I snapped back to the present, stumbling as an icy blast hit me in the chest. I rolled and regained my feet, but my sight remained foggy, the memory far too real. The skin near my ear where the Minax had marked me burned, and I cried out.

"Ruby!"

Hands cupped my shoulders. I had an urge to knock them away and run.

Arcus's voice murmured, deep and even, designed to soothe but sharpened by a hint of distress. "Slow your breathing. It will pass."

It's not real it's not real it's not real.

My heart pummeled my ribs. My throat thickened. "I can't breathe."

Arcus's hand moved to my sternum, pressing gently, his long fingers splayed against my neck. "Slow and steady. Everything is fine. I'm here. You're safe."

Gradually, the soft words and touch made their way past the fear. I blinked until the royal gardens came into focus and I smelled the perfume of roses and summersweet. Tapered yews stood sentinel around the wide clearing, and beyond that, taller leafy sycamore and birch trees bowed over the evergreens like gentlemen over the hands of ladies. The heat of the late-summer sunrise calmed me, along with the occasional rustle of leaves brushed by the hand of Cirrus, the west wind.

I turned my head and was ensnared by icy-blue eyes under a brow drawn tight in concern. Arcus's skin had lost some color. I reached up and slid an unsteady palm along his cold cheek, smiling when he didn't flinch as my fingertips touched his scars.

"Your episodes are growing more frequent," he said.

I shrugged, the movement jostling his hand, which still rested over my collarbone, the heel of his palm against the upper curve of my breast. We both seemed to realize it at the same time. A flush scorched my cheeks. His lids fell, hiding his eyes as he moved the hand to my upper arm.

There were unspoken boundaries we hadn't crossed yet, though I hadn't decided if that was due to Arcus's self-control or the fact that our moments alone were brief and often interrupted.

"Have you found out anything more about the curse?" he asked.

"Not yet." Brother Thistle and I had spent many hours in the castle library combing through books on the Minax—the haunting, shadowy creature that Eurus, god of the east wind, had trapped in the frost throne. Eurus's curse corrupted any ruler that held the throne, inciting war and tyranny, which fed the curse further. The more violence and death, the stronger it grew.

The Minax had found an easy target in Arcus's younger brother, Rasmus, a young man who was too fearful and too angry to fight it. Under the influence of its silky promises and opium-like alleviation of pain and fear, King Rasmus had sent his soldiers to hunt and kill Firebloods, and most of my kind had been murdered in raids. The strongest were brought to the capital city, Forsia, where they'd died in the king's arena. As far as I knew, I was the only Fireblood in the kingdom who'd survived, and with help from Brother Thistle and Arcus, I'd melted the throne. We'd assumed the curse would be destroyed as well.

We'd been wrong.

Now Brother Thistle and I were trying to find a way to stop my visions and stop the creature itself.

I absently rubbed the carelessly stitched line on my little finger. It itched when I was upset, a reminder of my time in the Frostblood arena, what I'd had to do to help Arcus take his rightful place as king. But with the Minax still out there, inhabiting other bodies and biding its time, I wondered if destroying the throne had done more harm than good.

Arcus watched me for a minute, then took my hand and drew me through a barely perceptible opening between evergreens and onto a winding path. "I want to show you something. Close your eyes."

I let him lead me over what felt like flagstones and spongy pine needles until the path changed to gravel that crunched under our boots.

"All right. You can open them."

He kept hold of my fingers as I opened my eyes to see plants, flowers, shrubs, and small trees surrounding us. "Everything is white," I breathed, moving toward a planter bursting with alabaster-stemmed flowers, petals aglow with reflected sunlight. I reached out and my finger felt biting cold. "They're made of ice!"

Arcus came up behind me, his chest lightly touching my back. His hand brushed mine as he cupped the flower I'd touched. "Do you like them?"

Petals like white wood shavings rose above gently curling stems, and shrubs flaunted leaves in the most delicately crocheted lace. Tall, feathery fronds drowsed over tightly woven packs of icy rosebuds, like parents watching over a bed full of sleeping children. Miniature trees with translucent trunks etched in a frosty wood-grain pattern sported flat, veined leaves and peach-shaped globes. Ice crystals hung like frozen tears from every branch and stem. The twisting, ethereal shapes clinked together in the morning breeze.

"It's lovely." I turned to Arcus. Some fierce but gentle emotion sparkled in his eyes.

"I hoped you'd like it," he said softly. "Though it's not the most logical gift for a Fireblood."

Vulnerability hovered in his expression, and the reason for it hit me. "You made all this?" I examined the garden with awe. There were layers and layers of swaying flowers, carefully rendered shrubs, and elegant trees, all surrounded by a curving, four-foot-high ice wall. "By yourself?"

He nodded, lips twisting in a slight grimace. "It frustrates Lord Ustathius to no end to find me here instead of in the council chambers. I told him this helps me think."

"And does it?"

"Yes. It helps me think of you."

His tenderness softened the last of the tension from my body. His arms came around me and mine curved around his back, our lips touching with careful pressure, as if we were made of the same gauzy frost as the ice petals and could crack if we pressed too hard.

My Fireblood skin gradually warmed his, and the shocking cold of his lips gentled mine into cool softness. The kiss was smooth, seeking. His freshly shaven jaw was like silk, lightly scented with his soap, with hints of his own unique scent that I found more heady and pleasing than a handful of fragrant wildflowers.

Moments were lost in feeling, the tinkle of ice making strange music all around us. Arcus's hand came to my cheek, his other arm pressing me closer, his mouth demanding more. He tasted of the mint tea he drank every morning, and his hair was thick and satiny under my fingers. My control unwound like a spool of fabric rolling across the floor. Heat flared, and drops of water rained from the trees onto our cheeks. He smiled against my lips, his fingers brushing droplets from my brow and nose.

I pulled away just far enough to meet his eyes. "I'd have been happy with a single flower."

"A single flower would melt in an hour or two," he said, his voice huskier than usual.

I quirked a brow teasingly. "You think it would last a whole hour in my hands?"

His teeth flashed before he stole another quick kiss, his arms tightening around my waist. "I know you need to escape the palace sometimes, and I wanted you to remember that frost is not just harsh and unforgiving. It can be delicate and welcoming. It can bend. It can learn the shape of things and melt and freeze again in a different form."

Warmth filled my chest at his caring perception. He was right that I often wanted to escape the Frostblood Court. The courtiers stared and sneered and talked about me openly whenever their new king wasn't present, questioning his judgment in letting a "wild Fireblood" peasant live in the castle. I feared I was becoming a liability in his struggle to unite the new additions to the court who had supported Arcus in the rebellion with the entrenched members of the court who had been close to King Rasmus. Their new king not only tolerating but showing favor to—possibly even courting—a Fireblood was apparently one step too far.

But Arcus's words reminded me that he wasn't his court, that he would adapt when I needed him to, that he accepted me as I was, even if no one else did. It touched me more than I could say. I wished I could find the words to tell him, but lately that seemed impossible.

Feeling came easily. Putting those feelings into words was increasingly difficult.

As Arcus watched my face, he grinned at whatever he saw there, his masculine beauty kick-starting my heart. His smiles turned his face from austere to radiant. My hands wound around his neck, my fingers diving into the hair at his nape. He pulled me snugly against him and his lips brushed my cheek, then moved down to find the pulse point at the side of my neck.

A loud cough broke the silence. I pulled back, but Arcus's lips followed me, staying glued to the column of my neck, breaking away only when I pushed against his chest. He branded my cheek with a final kiss and turned leisurely, his arms still locked around my waist.

"Lord Ustathius, you have the most unfortunate timing of anyone I've ever met. Whatever you wish to discuss, I'm sure it can wait."

He started to turn back to me, but the sour-faced advisor coughed again, somehow injecting the sound with both apology and censure. "I'm afraid it can't, Your Majesty. There's an urgent matter."

Arcus gave a frustrated sigh, his eyes hooding. "How many urgent matters can there be?"

"A great many," said Lord Ustathius, his gray eyes as serious as a thunderhead, ample warning that he was about to launch into one of his familiar lectures. "When you are simultaneously bringing armies home, establishing diplomatic talks with neighboring countries, and trying to win the hearts of your people, there will be no end to the demands on your person. Commitment. Sacrifice. Selflessness. These are all required if your ambitious plans are to have—"

"Any reasonable hope of success," Arcus completed. "Yes, my lord advisor, you have drilled that concept so thoroughly into my head that I hear the words in my sleep. However, I must have a breath of air now and then or I will go mad. Surely you don't begrudge me exercise."

"Is that what you call it, Your Majesty?"

My cheeks grew hotter.

Arcus squeezed my hands comfortingly. "What is the crisis this time?"

"A messenger from Safra has arrived and he insists on taking a reply from your hand only. Also, I have called an emergency meeting of the council to discuss caring for the wounded who are returning from the wars. The flood of refugees arriving in Forsia is increasing daily, and we need to address their needs for healing and shelter."

Every word seemed to add a weight to Arcus's shoulders. He sighed heavily as he looked back at me.

"I'm sorry," he said quietly.

I shook my head. "You're needed. I'm lucky to see you at all."

His mouth tightened, puckering the scar on his top lip. "I wish it weren't so difficult. Meet me here at dawn again tomorrow?"

"Only if you can manage it."

"Wouldn't miss it." He looked at me carefully. "You're sure you're all right?"

"Of course. No more visions."

He returned my smile, but tension had gathered in his eyes. With a final squeeze of my hand, he turned and strode toward the castle. Lord Ustathius started to follow him, then stopped and turned back to me.

"What is it?" I asked. I still felt vulnerable, unguarded—both from the vivid memory of the Minax escaping from the throne and from Arcus's kisses. I took a calming breath, hoping to find some control over my heat, which had risen, as it always did, with strong emotions.

Despite his distrust of me, Lord Ustathius's tone was steady. "You do him no favors by taking his attention from his duties as king."

"I don't force him to spend time with me."

"But you encourage it. Perhaps you should think about what he is trying to achieve. It would be better for him, and for the kingdom, if you weren't here to complicate matters."

His candor silenced me for a moment before I found my voice. "You think I should leave? For the good of Tempesia?"

"And for the good of the king. He has a new life now and his attachment to you wins him no esteem with the court."

It was as if he'd seen the vulnerable place in my heart and he'd aimed an arrow right for it. "I'm well aware of the court's lack of esteem."

Lord Ustathius's expression softened into something like sympathy, which somehow felt more deadly than his censure. "Let him look to the future. Let him choose what is best for him as he grows into the king he is meant to be."

"And by 'choosing what's best,' I suppose you mean your daughter?"

He lifted his chin slightly. "You cannot fail to see Lady Marella's virtues and accomplishments. Any man would be fortunate to have her hand in marriage, particularly a king who needs strong allies in the court."

I looked down, struggling against the jealousy that tightened my chest. The worst part was that I knew he was right. Marella was a Frostblood noblewoman—poised, intelligent, charming—a perfect helpmate who would smooth Arcus's path as king in countless ways. I was a Fireblood peasant from nowhere, with a heart full of flames and the distrust of the entire Tempesian population. I couldn't be more ill-matched to the Frost King if I'd been created as his opposite by a mischievous god.

"I don't say this to hurt you," Lord Ustathius continued. "But I know you must see it, too. It does no good to deny the truth."

"The truth," I countered, "is that I don't make my decisions based on what the court wants. I'll stay here as long as King Arkanus wants me to." I lifted my chin and forced myself to hold his cold, burning gaze.

"Then best of luck to you, Miss Otrera," he said finally, his tone conveying clearly that he viewed me as a foolish child. "I fear you are climbing much higher than you were meant to. Like Pragera, who tried to climb Mount Tempus to reach the home of the gods and was doomed to plummet eternally as punishment for his hubris."

"In the Fireblood version," I said, "Cirrus takes pity on him and gives him wings as he falls."

"Then let us hope your version is the correct one. You are closer to the edge than you think."

"Another court dinner, my lady?" Doreena asked as she fastened the buttons at the back of my gown—a fussy, high-waisted affair made of ocher silk.

"Imagine my excitement," I grumbled, trying not to fidget. "Arcus seems to think that rubbing me in the court's noses will endear me to them. In the same way, I suppose, that stepping in horse droppings increases one's appreciation of horses."

Doreena laughed in her quiet way. "Such sarcasm. Have you been taking lessons from Lady Marella?"

"You know that's the one thing she doesn't need to teach me."

She continued to smile. "Well, you are neither a horse nor its..." She cleared her throat to avoid the rest, which just showed that Doreena was more refined than I'd ever be. "And you are quite endearing, my lady. Before you protest, you *are* a lady, because the king says you are. You wear fine dresses and have a beautiful room. Accept your place, else the court will never accept you."

As if it were that easy. However, she had a point about the room. Red brocade curtains fell in thick folds, creating a snug cocoon around the four-poster bed. An arched mullioned window, complete with a window seat, faced a garden bursting with flowers and topiaries. An overstuffed wingback chair nestled between a fireplace and a mahogany bookshelf crammed with books. Arcus had chosen the room, placing me in the wing used by the royal family. I sensed he was trying his best to make me as comfortable as possible in a place he knew felt very far from home.

Wherever "home" was. Even if people had returned to

my village now that the raids against Firebloods had ended, it wouldn't be the same without Mother there.

Grief stabbed me, a twisting knife in the dead center of my chest. Mother had died trying to protect me from the Frost King's soldiers, from the captain who'd blithely killed her and burned our village. If she were here, no doubt she'd tell me to try to fit in, to make allowances for people's prejudices, to hide the heat that makes them all so uncomfortable. But that's exactly what I'd been trying to do for weeks.

I tugged at the frothy lace that dripped at my wrists, hiding my pain with petty complaints. "Could you please tell the seamstress I don't need so much lace at my collar and cuffs? Marella's gowns are always sleekly tailored, but this woman seems determined to make me look barely old enough to cut my own meat."

Doreena's gaze swept over the dress. "You look very pretty, my lady. Perhaps you're nervous."

I stifled the urge to argue. Now that she was my lady's maid, I was glad Doreena felt freer to tell me what she thought. And she was right. I *was* nervous.

"I hate facing all those snobby nobles. They stare at me like I'm about to burst into flames at any second. Last night Lady Blanding looked me in the eye as she spilled wine on my dress! I could have happily set her hair on fire."

Doreena came to stand in front of me, regarding me seriously with her owlish brown eyes. She still had the look of a woodland creature, ready to startle and bolt at any sudden movement.

However, she'd been the first person to show me kindness here, and considering Rasmus had been king at the time, that had taken courage.

"You must not lose your temper," she advised, not for the first time. "That's when you fail to control your gift. And that's exactly what they want—to prove that Firebloods are dangerous and that you're unsuitable for court. They want the king to see you as they do: a threat."

To some degree, I understood their hostility. After centuries of wars, broken treaties, and retaliation, Frostbloods and Firebloods had learned to regard each other with bone-deep distrust. I looked at my hands, small and sun-browned and innocuous-looking, but with the ability to wipe out a battalion of soldiers if I wanted. No wonder the court feared me. Sometimes I feared myself.

I met Doreena's pleading gaze. "It's hard to grin and pretend I don't notice their insults."

"You don't have to grin. Just don't light them on fire."

I grunted noncommittally. "I make no promises."

On the way to the dining hall, a draft from the open door of the former throne room chilled my arms into gooseflesh. I'd avoided this room in the weeks since I'd melted the throne, but tonight I was drawn to the stark emptiness, the eerie peacefulness of dust motes tracing lazy curlicues in the twilight. At sunrise, the mosaic floor tiles would flash with vivid color, but now it all looked washed in gray. Stale and abandoned.

Arcus no longer used this as the throne room—it held the echo of too many horrible memories. Instead, he'd placed a simple ice throne, square cut and modest, in a receiving room on the ground floor.

My soft-soled slippers made no sound as I approached the spot where the massive frost throne had sat for centuries.

According to myth—or history, if you believed the stories were true—the ice throne had been the handiwork of Fors, the god of the north wind. Not satisfied with merely creating Frostbloods, he'd also given them an enormous throne of ice to strengthen the powers of their monarchs. A particularly useful gift considering the regularity of the wars against Firebloods.

Not to be outdone by Fors, his twin sister, Sud, goddess of the south wind, had created a throne of lava to enhance the powers of her precious Fireblood rulers.

When their brother Eurus, god of the east wind, had tried and failed to create his own race of people, he'd ended up instead with voracious shadow creatures that killed Frostbloods and Firebloods indiscriminately. So the wise and peace-loving Cirrus, goddess of the west wind, had finally plunged into the fray, sweeping the thousands of shadowy Minax underground to a place called the Obscurum, sealing it behind a Gate of Light that no mortal could breach. Then the siblings' mother, Neb, had decreed that none of her children could interfere in the mortal world any longer, which meant the Gate should stay closed forever.

Eurus was tricky, though. He'd saved two of his favorite Minax from exile, hiding one in the Frostblood throne and the other in the Fireblood throne. The Minax, with their ability to possess people, provoked the kings and queens into increased enmity and hatred, causing war and mayhem and the deaths of many more Firebloods and Frostbloods.

After centuries of bolstering Frostblood rule, the throne of Fors was gone. All that was left from where it had once sat was a discolored area of tile, round and shiny black, a stain that could never be scrubbed away. Much like the scar near my left ear, which the Minax had given me in this very room after it escaped from the melted throne.

My fingers moved to stroke the heart-shaped mark.

As soon as I touched it, I was plunged into another vision, dark and deep.

I stand in a cavernous room with black stone pillars straining up into looming darkness. I move over the floor, not walking but gliding like a ragged exhalation, as if I'm made of air. By tiny degrees, the outline of a heavy black shape sharpens into an unkempt, asymmetrical rectangle chiseled out of night.

It's a throne—wide enough to fit ten men, yet only one small figure sits on it, feet dangling high above the floor. Greenish light reflects off the figure's onyx crown, which is gnarled and pointed, like twisted antlers interlocking and curving up almost a foot in height. The figure's head is bent a little, as if the crown is too heavy for the delicate stem of its neck. Closed lids open to reveal yellow eyes pinning me where I hover several feet away. I sweep downward in a misty approximation of a bow, then straighten.

"Come closer," the figure says, the voice soft and female.

I long to obey, to slide underneath her skin to feel her power.

"You have the stone?" she asks.

I hand it to her. As she takes the stone, fire glows around it, lighting the room. A triumphant smile breaks over her face, and the sight spills something like happiness into my soul.

"You've done well," she says. "You will be rewarded."

She beckons. Joy lights my mind.

As I seep into her fingers, I gaze at her face, where strands of inky hair cling to her cheeks and chin.

Suddenly, I was back in the throne room, struggling to draw my next breath. Pain bit into my palms. I opened my fists. My fingernails had scored angry red crescents into my skin.

I scrubbed my hands against my face, trying to rub away the horror of recognition.

When I'd moved toward the queen with the twisted black crown, the face she'd worn was my own.

TWO

I LONGED TO RUN FROM THE THRONE room, to get as far away as fast as I could, but I was conscious of the guards in the hallway. Instead, I pinched my earlobe and gave myself a stern lecture. *Get ahold of yourself, Ruby. You can't go tearing around the castle like a wild boar.*

I needed Brother Thistle. With his knowledge of history and myth, he might have some theory of the vision's meaning. As Arcus's closest confidant ever since their time together at Forwind Abbey, he often dined with the king and court. I straightened my spine and made my way to the dining hall on unsteady legs, taking a moment to smooth my features into a placid mask before entering.

A carnival of torches glowed from black metal sheaths, tilting away from the ice-covered walls. Candles winked like lightning bugs atop icicles that dripped from a massive chandelier. The scent of roasted meat clashed with the ladies' flowery perfumes.

Arcus sat at the head of the table, at ease in a midnight-blue doublet, his mahogany hair adorned with the plain silver band that he wore as a crown during formal occasions. I scanned the table for Brother Thistle and felt a swoop of disappointment when I realized he wasn't among tonight's guests. No doubt he'd found some excuse to remain perched over books in the castle library like a broody hen roosting among her eggs. I half turned to the door, but Arcus noticed me and stood.

I was trapped. I couldn't leave now without appearing rude.

The rest of the men stood as well, some of them readily, like Lord Manus and Lord Pell, new additions to court. However, they didn't hold the lands and resources that others did, like Lord Blanding and Lord Regier, bastions of King Rasmus's old guard. Arcus needed them on his side to maintain the kingdom's strength and unity.

These older noblemen rose more slowly and reluctantly at my arrival.

Arcus motioned to a chair of carved ice covered in a white fox pelt at his right. A chill slid up my back as I moved forward and sat in the familiar chair. The seat at the king's right was a place of honor, but it was also where King Rasmus had forced me to dine with him—a tradition for champions who had won in his arena. I'd had the dubious honor of being the first Fireblood to win against his Frostblood champions, something that had drawn his attention in ways I'd rather forget. The memory of the former king hung in the air like smoke in a windowless room.

The noblemen rustled back into their seats, the rotund Lord Blanding with a satisfied groan. Lady Blanding patted her elaborately piled gray hair and sniffed loudly before turning to Lady Regier. "I always fancy I smell singed meat when the Fireblood girl is near," she said in a booming whisper.

The lovely Marella, who sat on the other side of the table, caught my eye and tilted her head to indicate Lady Blanding. "I always fancy I smell mothballs when the old crow dines with us."

Lord Manus snorted, then covered the sound with a cough.

"Marella," I whispered, sending her a stern look. The last thing I wanted was for her to draw attention to me.

The aquamarine feather on her headband curved delicately over her braided wheat-gold hair as she leaned toward me. "Don't worry. She can't hear a thing unless you're shouting in her ear. I could tell her to jump off the eastern cliffs and she'd just compliment my gown."

Her less-than-innocent grin drew an answering smile from Lady Blanding, who said, "You look absolutely divine tonight, Lady Marella. Your seamstress has outdone herself. And how jaunty that feather is."

"Thank you, Lady Blanding," said Marella with a dip of her chin. "Your hair looks like a wasp's nest."

I had to bite the inside of my cheek to keep from laughing. Lady Blanding smiled warmly and sipped her wine.

Lord Ustathius, who sat at the king's left hand, glared at his daughter. “You insult one of the king’s court, and by association, the king himself.”

“She can’t hear me,” Marella replied calmly, nodding as a footman piled her plate with slices of thinly shaved roast beef.

“The rest of us can,” he replied. “You owe the king an apology.”

She arched a brow at Arcus. “Shall I grovel on my knees, Your Majesty, or would hand-wringing suffice?”

Arcus’s lips were slightly compressed, as if he held in a smile. “To be honest, I see no reason for you to apologize, as you were defending one guest from another. But if you’re desperate to atone . . .”

“I am. Aren’t I, Father?”

Lord Ustathius’s brow lowered ominously.

“Then you must grant me a favor,” Arcus continued. “I’ve invited several ambassadors and heads of state to a ball to help seal our tentative peace accords. I would like your help planning the details of the affair.”

I tried to stifle the feeling of envy at Arcus turning to Marella for help and not me. It wasn’t Marella’s fault that she was raised to be the perfect lady. It was logical for Arcus to ask her. But it was one more reason that Lord Ustathius was right—his daughter was far more suited to stand at Arcus’s side than I was.

“Tentative peace accords, indeed,” said Lord Regier, the proud angle of his chin providing an unwelcome view up his generous nostrils. “We have received only the vaguest of agreements from the kingdom of Safra, despite the fact that we know they can’t hold out much longer. Rumor has it that eastern commerce suffers greatly from lack of trade with us. And our southern provinces, which should be offering allegiance to the new king, are still insisting that they reject Frostblood rule! Never mind that the traitors live on Tempesian land that we generously allow them to cultivate. And to add to their insults, they have offered rewards to anyone who produces the king's head on a pike!"

"They have every reason for defiance," said Lord Pell, conviction in his blue-gray eyes. "The southern provinces have always welcomed immigration from Sudesia. As a result, most of the Firebloods—and the raids against them—were concentrated in the south. You can't blame the provinces for hating King Rasmus. But their dignitary will certainly feel differently about the new king."

"There's nothing certain about it," Lord Regier replied. "I might remind you that they harbored the very Fireblood rebels responsible for the death of His Majesty's own mother and for the horrendous attack that resulted in our king's scars."

Silence fell.

Even if he wasn't bothered by the insensitive remark about his scars, I ached for what Arcus must be feeling, having his mother's death brought up so casually, and by such a buffoon. His mother had been killed by Fireblood rebels during the time when Arcus's father, King Akur, had taken land away from the southern provinces. The southerners had naturally rebelled, including a significant number of Firebloods. Not only was his mother killed by these southern rebels, an assassination attempt had also been made on Arcus.

"That's all in the distant past," said Arcus tightly. "It's time to establish a dialogue with the provinces. We've sent a messenger to invite their dignitary to the ball."

Lady Regier chuckled. "You'd have some illiterate farmer dusting up the great hall?" She shuddered theatrically.

Arcus stared at her until her smile faded. "I will welcome an important leader whom I hope will become a valued ally." He paused before adding, "I've also sent an invitation to the queen of Sudesia."

My breath caught as gasps reverberated around the table. *The Fireblood queen.*

"You've invited our greatest enemy to our capital?" Lord Blanding stood, dropping his napkin onto the table. Though his words were directed at Arcus, he glared at me. "Have you forgotten that Sudesia supported the southern rebellion?"

"We don't know that for certain," Lady Manus interjected, regarding him steadily with her cobalt eyes. "And it wasn't much of a rebellion, was it? King Rasmus made sure of that by killing half the population of the Aris Plains."

"A gross exaggeration." Lord Blanding gave her a disgusted look before turning back to Arcus. "You go too far, Your Majesty. I cannot help but conclude that such a rash decision was brought about by your affection for this...this girl." His small mouth pursed in outrage, the tension in his jaw making his jowls shake. I stared back until his eyes slid away.

"Sit down, Blanding," said Lord Manus coolly. "Do you really think the queen will agree to come? His Majesty sent the invitation as a sop to mollify the southern provinces." He turned to Arcus. "At least, I'm assuming that was the strategy? Show good faith to the Fireblood queen in the hopes that the provinces will come to the table to talk?"

"I invited the queen of Sudesia because I hope she'll attend." Arcus's eyes returned to me. "Your attendance at the ball would also be welcome, Lady Ruby. It would be good for the ambassadors to see how Frostbloods and Firebloods are mending ties."

I didn't relish the further attention a ball would bring, but I was willing to do what I could, even as a sort of informal ambassador. I was elated that he actually wanted to mend ties with Sudesia, the Fireblood homeland, a place I had wondered about for as long as I could remember. He gave my hand a squeeze and let go before we made the table truly uncomfortable. I dropped it in my lap, smiling my approval. Something like hope fluttered in my chest.

Lord Pell began to laugh. "I always said you were a raging optimist, Arcus. If the Fire Queen attends your ball, I'll wear my smallclothes on my head."

"Well!" Lady Blanding nearly howled. "What a revolting image!"

Arcus stifled a smile and turned back to Marella. "Are you up to the task of throwing a ball, my lady?"

My chest tightened again, but I forced a small smile when Arcus glanced at me. I would not allow myself to be petty. Marella was the best person for the task.

"I'd be delighted," said Marella. "It's been ages since we had a proper ball here. I look forward to experimenting with Cook on new dishes. And my dancing skills have been growing quite rusty. I'm sure to break toes."

"Well, you'll have time to practice beforehand. I've set the date for the autumnal equinox."

"How festive! Isn't that when the peasants dance around the fire to thank the gods for the harvest?" She looked at me expectantly, presumably because I was the only person of low birth at the table.

It seemed like a lifetime had passed since I'd attended the festival in my village, though it was less than a year ago. My throat tightened when I remembered that I'd had my first kiss that night from a village boy named Clay. He'd died in front of me in the Frost King's arena only a few weeks ago. I nodded while taking a sip of wine to cover the fact that I couldn't speak.

"It might be fun to incorporate some of the peasants' traditions," Marella added, oblivious to my discomfort. "But perhaps we don't want any bonfires in the great hall. The chandeliers *are* made of ice."

If I hadn't been upset, I might have remarked that she'd better not invite *me*, then.

After a few minutes, the conversation returned to the state of the kingdom.

"If Cirrus would just give us some rain," Lady Regier complained with an aristocratic sniff, "and if those laborers would just work a little harder, we would have all the grain we need."

"The problem isn't lack of hard work," Lord Manus corrected, "but lack of men and women to plant and till and harvest. My wife spoke correctly when she said the Aris Plains have been torn apart by our former kings."

Most of Tempesia's crops came from the swathe of land called the Aris Plains in the southern provinces. King Akur had taken land from independent farmers, awarding it to Frostblood nobles in exchange for funding and troops. The southerners hadn't given up the land willingly. Battles over the contested fields had prevented planting two years in a row and significantly taxed the kingdom's grain reserves, which still hadn't recovered. After Rasmus took the throne, the Fireblood citizens in southern Tempesia were hunted and murdered during his raids. It was no wonder the remaining people who lived in the southern provinces hated the Frostblood aristocracy, even if a new king had taken the throne.

"If the southerners had just accepted their fate as serfs under Frostblood rule," said Lord Blanding, "there would have been no fighting and no shortage of crops." He took a swig of wine from his goblet and set it down decisively, as if the matter had been settled once and for all.

My stomach roiled with hatred for the former king and anyone who had followed him, Lord Blanding included. I suddenly found I couldn't sit at the table a moment longer.

I stood. Arcus immediately rose, and the other men followed suit as before.

"I'm afraid I'm a little tired. Good night." With a quick curtsy in Arcus's direction, I turned away.

"Well, how abrupt," said Lady Blanding as the guards opened

the dining hall door for me. "But what can you expect from a peasant of the wrong blood?"

As the doors shut, it wasn't her words that struck my heart with a painful blow but the silence that followed. Arcus hadn't said a word to defend me.

"You'll ruin your eyes reading in the dark," I said testily, still fuming as I entered the castle library. Brother Thistle sat hunched over a yellowed tome lying open on a round marble table, his beard tucked into the neck of his monk's robe to keep it out of his way.

The library was in the newer east wing, with walls of paneled wood. Bookshelves running four stories high stood sentry on either side of a wide central aisle. Spiral staircases grew like twisted trees crowned by raised walkways with intricately carved railings. No ice covered the walls. The room was kept dry and well aired, protecting the thousands of books. I could happily lose myself among the seductively infinite stacks, if only I had time to read for pleasure.

Instead, I'd been helping Brother Thistle search for information on the Minax and taking short breaks to receive his instruction on how to speak Sudesian, the language of the Fireblood islands to the south. My grandmother had spoken Sudesian to me when I was young until my mother had made her stop, not wanting me to inadvertently reveal our heritage and my powers to anyone in the village. I'd had no idea that Arcus was considering making peace with the Sudesians when I'd first asked to learn the language, but now it seemed oddly prescient.

As I neared the table, Brother Thistle lifted a hand in a distracted greeting, not bothering to raise his head. He was a scholar, historian, and expert in ancient languages, but he was also a powerful Frostblood. Normally, a coating of frost covered everything he touched, but somehow he restrained his gift around his beloved books. It still amazed me, his level of control.

"How do you do it?" I found myself asking.

"Do what?" he muttered, not looking up.

"Repress your frost." I had learned to control my gift to some degree, but nothing like the iron-willed dominance the Frostblood master exerted over his own power. *Can you repress your ability, girl?* That had been one of the first things he'd asked before rescuing me from Blackcreek Prison, where I'd been held for months after the Frost King's soldiers raided my village. I'd answered no then. My answer would be the same now.

He finally looked up. "As I have told you many times, Miss Otrera, if you wish to fit in here, you will have to learn how to dampen your heat. Have you been keeping up your mental practice?" He meant the meditation he'd taught me at Forwind Abbey, the mountain monastery where I'd lived for months while learning how to master my fire so I could destroy the throne.

"Sometimes." In truth, it made me uncomfortable to repress my heat, and it was tiresome to continually fail. "But it hardly matters now. With Arcus on the throne, Firebloods are no longer forced to hide their heritage."

Not that any Firebloods were left in Tempesia, aside from me.

I'd hoped some had survived Rasmus's raids, but despite Arcus's efforts to coax them out of hiding, none had been found yet.

"You will have to be more diligent than that," Brother Thistle admonished.

His censure always put me on the defensive. "I'll never be a Frostblood, icily perfect with my emotions buried under mountains of restraint. Sorry to disappoint."

"You don't need to deny your gift. But neither do you have to remind the court of your opposing nature at every opportunity."

The comment stung. Brother Thistle had been one of the very few people who had always accepted me. "No matter what I do, they'll never forget what I am."

Idly, I made twin flames sprout like wings from my open palms, then pushed my hands together, extinguishing them.

Returning his attention to his book, he asked, "What has upset you?"

Perversely, the fact that he read me so easily made me reluctant to admit to it. "Besides living in an ice castle that's warmer than its inhabitants? Besides my very presence making it difficult for Arcus to keep his court loyal?"

He gave me a swift glance. "You are pale. Have you had another vision?"

He was too observant. "This one was... disturbing."

I related the details and watched his brows rise in surprise as I told him that I'd recognized myself as the queen on the throne.

"Well, what do you think?" I asked with forced lightness. "Prophecy or madness?"

His fingers drummed the table. "I considered the possibility that Sage is sending you visions to warn or guide you, as we now believe she did before—when you were lost in the blizzard near Forwind Abbey, and when you needed help to fight off possession by the curse."

"Warn me?" My voice was a little higher than I'd intended. "But I thought Sage was prevented by the gods from sharing her prophecies."

The woman known as Sage was a healer who had nursed the goddess Cirrus back to health after she exhausted herself creating the Gate of Light and two sentinels to guard it. In thanks, Cirrus had given Sage the sun-drenched crystal used to create the Gate. The light from the crystal flowed into Sage's veins, gifting her with a long life and the ability to see the future—knowledge she'd been forbidden by Cirrus from sharing.

Brother Thistle patted my hand, a reassuring gesture that nevertheless made me jump at the shock of his cold skin. "And that is why I dismissed the idea. I now believe your visions relate to the fact that you are the only person to throw off possession by the Minax."

I grimaced. He made it sound like I'd been fortunate. It didn't feel like something to celebrate, especially with the Minax still out there somewhere.

"Perhaps you are open to a connection with it," he continued, "and it can send you these images at will. Or perhaps you are seeing things it does not wish you to see: memories or dreams."

"You think a Minax dreams?"

He opened his palms. "It is possible."

I shifted uncomfortably. I didn't like the idea that the Minax shared human traits. "Have you found anything about how to stop the visions?"

He cleared his throat, his demeanor clouding over with the intense look he always wore when immersed in research. "Well, Vesperillius, a scholar from the Northern Pike Mountains, claimed to be tortured by visions of the Minax after touching the frost throne. After searching for years for a cure, he went on a trip to Safra and, on the advice of a local shaman, drank the venom of a tree snake. The visions stopped immediately."

"Lovely. I'm sure I could choke down some venom."

"Vesperillius died three days later."

I grimaced. "Maybe not tree snake venom, then." I finally voiced the question I'd asked myself so many times over the past weeks. "What if I'm possessed and we don't know it?"

He reached out and took my hand, turning it palm up so my wrist, with its fat, red vein, was on display. The vein at Brother Thistle's wrist was equally thick, only blue. The sure sign of the Fireblood or Frostblood gift.

"You show no signs of possession," he said. "Your veins have not changed to black, nor do you display a desire for blood or chaos."

He said it gently, aware the trauma was still fresh. In the king's arena, the rules of the games had forced me to kill, but the Minax's influence had made me enjoy taking lives. I remembered with ringing clarity what it felt like—the ecstasy, the lack of fear or remorse, the temptation to let the Minax inhabit me permanently. I almost hadn't been able to resist.

"No more than usual," I agreed drily. "Although I *have* fantasized about setting Lady Blanding on fire."

He waved a hand. "Everyone has fantasized about setting Lady Blanding on fire."

That drew an unwilling smile.

"I did, however, find one text that suggested a way to"—he picked up a book on his left, offering it to me—"destroy the Minax."

I immediately opened the book and shoved it onto the table to read. In my haste, I knocked a round glass paperweight onto the rug.

Brother Thistle flashed me an irritated look and bent to pick up the paperweight, a momentary lapse in his self-control causing the glass to fog with a layer of frost. "One of the prophecies of Dru suggests that, aside from their creator Eurus, only a Minax can destroy another Minax."

Excitement sparked through my veins. This was the breakthrough we needed!

"The only other Minax that hasn't been sealed behind the Gate of Light is in the fire throne in Sudesia. So"—I paused as the pieces fit themselves together in my mind—"we have to go there."

"It is not that easy to travel to Sudesia. The kingdom is a labyrinth of rocky islands and narrow channels that only experienced sailors could hope to navigate. We simply don't have that knowledge after so many years without trade between our kingdoms. And the Strait of Acodens, which is the most straightforward and safest way there, is guarded by Fireblood masters."

"Well, aren't there maps? Nautical charts that show a less conspicuous route?"

"Perhaps. If they survived King Rasmus's purging of Sudesian writings from his library. Which I haven't found evidence of yet."

Frustration ate away at my already thin patience. "You can believe in a hundred moldering prophecies, but you can't conceive of us finding a way to sail to another kingdom? How hard could it be?"

"Will you instruct me on sea travel now, Miss Otrera?" His patience was clearly starting to wear, too. "You have never even set foot on a ship."

"Well, we can't just throw up our hands and do nothing. The Minax promised to come back for me, and I don't know... I don't know if I can fight it off a second time."

A tense silence followed. He knew better than to offer me false reassurance. I made sure my voice was steady before speaking again. "Arcus sent an invitation to the Fire Queen. We can ask for her help."

Brother Thistle looked up in surprise. "I am amazed he would think of mending ties with Sudesia." He shook his head. "Sudesians are not known for their forgiving natures. Much as you won't want to hear it, he likely sent that messenger ship to its destruction. She would never agree. It was a gesture. No more."

He fussed with the items on the table—the paperweight, a quill, a strip of linen that marked his place in a book. "Even if we could safely travel to Sudesia, what would you do? Melt the throne in order to free the fire Minax? The prophecy says that the Child of Light will melt a cursed throne, and it made sense to me that a Fireblood was necessary for that task. But... the prophecy does not mention both thrones. We do not know if you are powerful enough to melt the fire throne."

Brother Thistle believed prophecies about a Child of Light who would stop the release of the Minax from where they were trapped underground. He was convinced I was that illustrious but unlikely person.

There was also a Child of Darkness, one who would try to release the Minax rather than prevent it. If Brother Thistle had theories about who that was, he hadn't shared them with me.

"Another issue," I couldn't resist adding, "is the small fact that I'm *not* the Child of Light."

He waved the protest away, as he'd heard it so many times. "The fire throne is made of lava rock. The temperature required to melt such a thing would be... inconceivable. Only a Fireblood master could hope to try, and you are far from a master."

"Thank you," I said, dry as Safran desert to cover the fact that the comment stung. I'd been learning to control my gift for months, but I knew I was far from a master. And I had no one to teach me any more than what Brother Thistle already had by adapting his Frostblood techniques to my fire. I longed to find out what I could achieve if given the proper training.

"But aside from that," he continued, "it took an opposing force to destroy the frost throne. Perhaps it would take a Frostblood to destroy the fire throne."

The solution to that seemed obvious. "Then we bring you and Arcus to Sudesia."

"How do you think the queen would receive us after King Rasmus massacred all the Firebloods in Tempesia? As far as she is concerned, they were still her people, and we are the enemy. Furthermore, what would we do if the fire throne were destroyed?" Brother Thistle asked. "The fire Minax would be released and Sudesia would be at its mercy, just as Tempesia is at the frost Minax's mercy."

"Then we need to find a way to trap it and bring it here to destroy the frost Minax! Maybe there's a way to control it." I made the task sound simple when I was really just spinning ideas out of vague hopes. I cast a glance at the piles of books on the table and stacked nearby on the floor. "Have you found anything helpful at all?"

He made a vague gesture of denial. "Nothing, aside from what I have told you. However, there is a book that other volumes refer to as the authority on the thrones and their curses. I was certain it was here in the king's library. Have you seen *The Creation of the Thrones* by Pernillius the Wise?"

I couldn't help chuckling. "Pernillius? I think I'd remember such a ridiculous name. Ask Marella. She shares your passion for putrefied history. Or is it petrified? Perhaps both. It's all so very, very old."

My teasing grin earned one of his signature scathing glances. "I have asked her, of course. She has not seen it. It must have been lost. Or perhaps Rasmus had it burned."

My hopes for a quick answer died a quick death.

"If only Sage would appear and give us instruction," I mused. The last time I'd seen her was the moment I'd destroyed the frost throne. She'd been frustratingly silent since. In darker moments, I worried the visions of the Minax were a sign that my connection with Sage had been severed.

"That would be very helpful," Brother Thistle agreed. "Until then, we continue our research."

"What should I read tonight, then?" I asked, shaking off the dismal thoughts. "Since I've been so cruelly denied the wisdom of Pernillius."

He tapped a book with a red cover. "This one."

I took the book to a table and opened it, scanning for some mention of the thrones until the words swam before my eyes. Hours later, I had found nothing of use, and I still couldn't stop thinking about Brother Thistle's revelation: Only a Minax could destroy another Minax.

And the other Minax was in the land of Firebloods.

THREE

FOR FIREBLOODS, AUTUMN MEANT a period of weakening and loss, when an attentive summer sun turns fickle, playing a coquettish game of hide-and-seek until winter falls over the land with all the subtlety of a blacksmith's hammer.

Thus, when the equinox dawned cloudless and bright, I had no urge to celebrate the day, least of all by attending a ball full of highborn strangers who would sneer and whisper about me behind their hands. If Arcus hadn't expressly asked me to go, I would have found some excuse to stay in my room reading.

"You're brooding again, my lady," said Doreena, laying a chemise, petticoats, corset, and silk stockings onto a chair. "You'll give yourself frown marks."

"Tempus forfend. What will the court say if I'm wrinkled as well as dangerous?"

She smirked. "They will say you make a very severe queen."

"Doreena." I gave her a narrow-eyed look. "Please stop saying things like that."

"But it will happen. Someday."

"When volcanoes erupt with snow."

She lifted her sharp little chin. "Everyone in the servants' hall talks about how much the king moons over you."

"Hmm. And what exactly do they say?" Despite myself, I felt a flicker of hope that they might be supportive.

She paused. "Opinions vary."

The flicker of hope died. "That's your delicate way of saying that no one is happy about it."

"Some are!"

I gave her a knowing look. "You?"

"Well... yes."

I had to laugh at her apologetic expression. "Don't worry, Doreena. You're worth ten supporters. With you on my side, I can conquer kingdoms."

Her lips curved shyly. "Or at least one king."

By the time I stood in the doorway of the ballroom, most of my bravado had fled. I'd faced trained killers in King Rasmus's arena, with an entire crowd howling for my blood. But somehow the thought of all these eyes on me, the hum of murmured hatred buzzing in my ears, was threatening in its own right. I might not end up bloody on the floor, but I wouldn't escape unscathed.

Marella had outdone herself decorating the ballroom. The icy pillars had been carved with elaborate designs, and the chandeliers wept with hundreds of icicles that managed to look elegant and dangerous at the same time. Thick velvet curtains in rich jewel tones framed soaring windows. Rectangular wooden tables groaned under silver platters laden with savory appetizers and frosted cakes.

"Lady Ruby Otrera," a man announced in ringing tones. All eyes turned to me, some curious, others openly hostile. I searched for a familiar face, feeling a pulse of relief when I spotted Marella moving toward me. She wore an emerald ball gown that complemented her porcelain skin. Gold lacing crisscrossed the bodice, and gold sunbursts edged her wrists and hem.

"Ruby," she said warmly, "don't you look lovely! Turn around so I can see the back."

I did a quick twirl. For once, the seamstress had shown restraint. There were no ruffles on the deep red dress, just a simple square-necked bodice that hugged my waist before flaring into a full skirt covered with a layer of red tulle. Doreena had asked the gardener for a crimson lily, which she'd pinned into my ebony hair.

"So do you," I replied. "That color suits you."

"All colors suit me," Marella replied, her grin irreverent.

A jowly middle-aged nobleman approached, raising a goblet of wine in greeting before bowing deeply to Marella. "My dear Lady Marella, why don't you introduce me?"

She inclined her head. "Lord Prospero, this is Lady Ruby."

My brows drew together. I was no lady. I wished they wouldn't try so hard to pass me off as one.

Rather than bowing, Lord Prospero merely inclined his head. "So, you are the Fireblood of such renown. How kind of the king to show you such... hospitality." His eyes swept me up and down. "Charming."

It wasn't lost on me that he kept a few feet of distance between us. I performed a quick mental check, making sure my body temperature was close to normal, at least for me. Nerves made my gift harder to control, and the last thing I wanted was to embarrass Arcus in front of his guests. Or worse, hurt his chances of getting the court and the dignitaries to sign the peace accords. I needed them all to see that I wasn't a threat, that I was about as volatile as cooled porridge, that peace was possible and Firebloods were not to be feared. Much as it irked me to admit it, even just to myself, a part of me craved the court's approval.

The nobleman turned his attention back to Marella. "What a divine job you've done with the ballroom. The pride of the kingdom, I dare say. You show the indisputable beauty and power of frost." His eyes met mine in something like challenge.

"Marella is very talented," I agreed neutrally.

"But surely you must acknowledge the strength of ice," he said. "You can build an entire castle from it." He gestured to the pillars.

"The original castle is made from stone," I pointed out.

He gave me a pitying look as if I'd said something embarrassingly naive. "The newer additions are made of pure ice."

"I'm afraid I tend to avoid those wings." I tried to relax my tense jaw while scanning the crowd for one of the footmen bearing trays of ice wine. At least if I were holding a glass, I'd have a reason not to grab Lord Paunch by the collar and ask him what he thought of the power of fire. One of the footmen caught my eye, mostly because he was openly staring at me, then snapped his head forward. Something about his thick blond hair and the square shape of his face seemed familiar. But Lord Prospero interrupted my thoughts with a dismissive laugh.

"Well, of course you do. You'd end up soaked to the skin from all that melted ice. I imagine your kind doesn't like to get wet. In fact, I've heard Firebloods avoid bathing more than absolutely necessary."

I heard Marella's indrawn breath.

Do not react. Do not let him win.

He smirked. "Or perhaps that's true of peasants in general." His contemptuous drawl snapped the last thread of my patience.

I took a step closer. "Actually, I love baths. Provided they're nice and *hot*."

I curled my hand in front of his face, allowing a searing flame to leap up in my palm. Like all Tempesian aristocrats, he was a Frostblood, but I didn't think he was a very powerful one. His cold didn't permeate the air the way Arcus's or Brother Thistle's did. I saw fear in his eyes, but instead of taking pity on him, I let the flame grow. He reared back, the flames dancing in his constricting pupils. It was so satisfying to remind one of these overstuffed lords that I was no longer a prisoner who existed for their entertainment.

Marella's forced laugh broke the tension, like a fingernail popping a soap bubble. "Oh, Lady Ruby, you certainly know how to take a joke too far. Put your fire away before you mark up my dress. The seamstress would never forgive me if I ruined her creation only minutes into the ball."

I exhaled slowly, lowering my cooling hand to my side.

Lord Prospero regained his equilibrium enough to lift his drink in a shaky salute. "Enjoy your time here. While it lasts." And he pointed himself toward the dessert table.

When I turned back to Marella, she regarded me with a speculative expression. "You enjoyed that, didn't you?"

I swallowed and shrugged. I *had* enjoyed threatening him. More than I wanted to admit.

"They will always bait you," she said, "but that doesn't mean you have to swallow the hook so eagerly."

"I don't know why I let him get to me."

"Because," she mused, tapping a finger to her lips, "you're a fox among wolves."

I considered the analogy. "You'd describe yourself as a wolf?"

"Wolves are lovely, agile creatures with killer instincts," she said, a twinkle in her violet eyes. "I don't mind the comparison."

"Well, everyone here thinks *I'm* the wolf. Though sometimes I feel more like a rabbit."

Just then the hair on the back of my neck lifted. I turned my head to see the same blond footman staring at me with a strangely intent expression. As I tried to puzzle out where I'd seen him before, he sidled over and spoke to another footman hovering by a group of courtiers. The two then broke off and moved into the crowd, trays of ice wine held aloft. Something about the group of courtiers held my attention, though. They stood too close, heads bent as if to better hear one another whisper, and they kept darting glances around the ballroom.

"A wolf among bears, then," Marella said, drawing my gaze back to her. "A Firebeak among frost beasts. Something like that. In any case, you'd be wise not to make more enemies than you need to. Arcus can only protect you so much, and only weeks ago you were still fighting in the arena."

As if I needed a reminder of how thoroughly I was hated. "And you think introducing me as a lady will make any difference to the people who were cheering for my opponents?"

She gave me a scolding look. "Oh, Ruby. How you get caught up in unimportant details. Everyone else here has a title. It does no good to remind them of all the myriad ways you don't belong. Now, just enjoy yourself, would you? Look, it's time for the first dance."

Lord Regier stood on the dais in front of the musicians at the far end of the room and said a few welcoming words. "And now, His Majesty, King Arelius Arkanus, will start the dance with a lady of his choosing."

Arcus appeared from the throng, his eyes roving over the crowd before settling on us. He looked devastatingly regal in a midnight-blue velvet jacket over a white shirt, though his shoulders were a little too broad for him to ever look truly elegant. Fawn trousers hugged his thighs above high, polished black boots. His dark hair was brushed back and he wore the silver band on his brow.

I glanced at Marella. She held herself with easy poise, but her skin was flushed, and a pulse beat visibly in her neck. A sign of nervousness or excitement.

Of course, I realized with a dip in my stomach. He was coming to ask her for the first dance. She was the official hostess, after all. Dancing with me would only further divide him from his supporters. I stepped back to make room for him to sweep her into his arms.

He bowed to her, but extended a hand to me.

"Trying to escape?" he teased, his eyes like sun-bleached cobalt as they took leisurely inventory of my appearance. Though his skin radiated cold, his gaze was somewhere between warm and melting. "I don't fancy your chances of running in that dress."

I glanced at Marella. "But—"

"Don't keep them all waiting," she said, smiling widely. If I hadn't known her well, I would have missed the stiffness of her jaw, the tightness of the muscles around her eyes.

"Quite right, Lady Marella." Arcus tucked my arm into his, steering me to the center of the floor. The music began and he started to move smoothly in time, pulling me along with him.

"You might have given me some warning," I muttered, wishing we were alone so I could actually enjoy the feeling of his hand on my waist, the other hand loosely clasping mine. "I don't know how to dance."

"No one can see your feet. Just stay close to me."

He moved with confidence. I felt as stiff as a wooden doll.

"It feels like you're bracing for an attack." Arcus's breath tickled my ear, his smiling lips brushing my temple. "This isn't sparring, you know. I'm not going to kick your feet out from under you."

"Good thing, Your Highness," I replied with an eyelash flutter, "or my dress might fly up around my ears, and wouldn't *that* be a scandal."

His lips twitched, the scar pulling taut in that way I found endlessly endearing. "And then there's the matter of me having to duel with anyone who dared to stare at you. Which would be every man here."

"They'd only stare because they're afraid of me. They're all waiting for me to melt something."

"Ah, but, Lady Ruby, you already have," he said, letting go of my waist to spin me in a quick circle. As I came back around, his hand returned to steady me. "You've melted my icy heart."

I laughed, surprised at both the sudden spin and the remark. The glittering candles, the scent of freshly cut roses in crystal vases, and Arcus's cool breath on my cheek as he said sweet things in my ear all made me feel giddier than usual. Warmth stole into my limbs, and I let myself relax into the rhythm, forward and back and turning, my dress billowing out behind me.

"I didn't know you liked this sort of thing," I said a little breathlessly. "Dancing and ballrooms."

"Neither did I." His tone matched the heat in his gaze, while his hand at my waist moved to my back to press me closer. His firm touch and the dazzling light in his eyes sent sparks up my spine.

"If you keep raising my temperature, I'm going to melt your chandeliers," I warned.

"I shall just make new ones." He wiggled his fingers toward the ceiling as if conjuring ice.

Despite the disapproving stares, I realized I was actually enjoying myself. If the king wanted to dance with me instead of Marella or some other Frostblood lady, his court would just have to accept it. After all, they couldn't control how he felt about me. Or how I felt about him.

I let myself bask in the appreciative heat of his gaze, imagining how I could slide my palm up to cover the ridged skin of his cheek, then trail my fingers over his perfectly sculpted lips with their tempting imperfection. What would the court do if I had the temerity to kiss the king in front of all of them? The ladies would all faint, no doubt.

I wasn't sure I cared.

"If you keep looking at me like that," he said in a low rumble that sent shivers over my skin, "perhaps *I'll* melt the chandeliers."

"Hmph." I shook my head slightly to clear the image of our fused lips. "That'd be a story for the history books."

He laughed. Our eyes met and clung. As we executed a perfect turn, for a second I was flying.

The spell was broken as Lord Regier invited everyone to join the dance. As couples filled the space, I had to focus on keeping up with Arcus's steps without colliding with anyone else.

"Any word from the Sudesian queen?" I asked hopefully, for perhaps the hundredth time since he'd announced the ball.

Something flitted across his expression—disappointment maybe, or regret. "You're hoping she'll show up at the last minute? It's unlikely."

I nodded, feeling foolish.

"I'm sorry," Arcus said in a low voice.

"It's not your fault," I said brightly, resurrecting my smile. "You invited her, and that's what counts."

He nodded and pulled me a little bit closer.

A minute later, Marella and her dance partner came alongside us. "I hate to be a nuisance," she said with a charming half smile, "but I do believe I've earned a dance with the king. I did work myself to exhaustion organizing this gala, after all."

"My dear lady," Arcus replied with amused tolerance, "if you are so exhausted, dancing will hardly help."

"But, my dear king, I live to dance. Or have you forgotten?"

I blinked at her coquettish tone, my chest clenching with jealousy.

Marella winked at me and leaned close to whisper, "I need an excuse to get away from Lord Trilby. His hands are like sparrows in winter. They keep migrating south."

My jealousy faded. I didn't blame her for wanting to escape, and luckily, when we went to change partners, the young noble blanched and claimed to need refreshment.

Arcus was already laughing at something Marella had said as I steered myself toward the dessert table. I selected a powdery bite-size cake and popped it into my mouth. Custard filling exploded against my tongue. *This wouldn't be a bad way to spend the rest of the ball*, I decided, choosing several more sugary confections to sample.

"The Frost Court certainly adores its sweets," said a low, mocking voice with a slight accent. "And you are clearly no exception."

I turned and found my gaze ensnared by a pair of golden-brown eyes. The young man's face was sharply cut, his cheekbones high, his chin on the stubborn side. His expression was arrogant, but it was the color of his hair that made me stare. The wavy locks were a strange mix of light brown, auburn, gold, and ginger, as if each strand had been painted a slightly different hue by an indecisive hand. He was dressed in formfitting trousers and a simple gray tunic, but the silver embroidery on the edges was of the finest quality.

He regarded me with a level gaze. I realized I must be covered with powdered sugar. Heat covered my skin.

"Your statement tells me two things," I said, trying to sound composed as I surreptitiously dusted my fingers together, creating a little winter scene with the fall of snowy sugar. "One, you're not from the Frost Court. The court never analyzes or questions itself. It just . . . *is*."

"Astute. The Frost Court perceives itself as the pinnacle of taste and civilization. But the way you say that makes me think *you* are not part of it, either."

A few minutes ago, I had taken Marella to task for calling

me a lady. Suddenly, I didn't want to admit to this stranger that I didn't belong.

"Two," I counted, ignoring his observation, "you don't like sweets."

His lips quirked. "Now, that is a leap of logic. Simply observing that others like sweets does not mean I don't like them myself."

"It's implied," I answered. "If you liked them, you'd simply select one and eat it."

"Like you've been doing, little bird?"

I blinked up at him, trying to decide whether to address the fact that he'd been rude enough to point out I was about to gorge on cakes or the unsanctioned use of a nickname. Before I could decide, he spoke again.

"Perhaps I have a weakness for a certain variety of sweet." He moved infinitesimally closer. "The kind that is not found on a dessert table."

The air suddenly felt trapped in my chest. Was he flirting with me? No one flirted with me. The court hated me. But then, he wasn't from this court.

"Who are you?"

The tension at the edges of his lips spoke of suppressed amusement. "You've deduced that I'm neither a member of this court nor a lover of cake. Why not guess my identity as well?"

I examined him carefully, taking in his confidence, his air of entitlement, his easy grace. He had an accent, but the noble speech was still clear. Perhaps he was the Safran ambassador, whose coveted signature on the peace accords could reopen trade to the east. But no, the Safrans dressed in robes, not breeches.

"You're from the South," I said, an easy guess, since most everything was south of the capital.

"Vague," he replied. "But accurate."

"Fine, then, I'll be specific." His clothing was a recognizable style, making it likely he lived in Tempesia. And he'd agreed he was from the South. The farthest south within the kingdom was the Aris Plains. Which left only one option. "You're the dignitary of the southern provinces. Though you're rather young for that, aren't you? Not much older than me, I'd say. Perhaps you're the son or younger brother of the dignitary."

His smile grew. "Oh, little bird," he said smoothly, "I am second to no one."

I huffed at his arrogance. "So you *are* the dignitary?"

He inclined his head.

"Arcus was afraid you wouldn't come." I'd been so fixated on the Fireblood queen, I'd forgotten to ask if the dignitary had replied to the invitation. So this was the elected leader of the southern provinces, the group of people who wanted self-governance within the kingdom. It was brave of him to show up. Some of the court would probably hang him for treason if they could.

His brows rose, and I realized I'd used the nickname "Arcus" instead of "King Arkanus."

"A last-minute decision," he replied. "Who could resist a glimpse of the king's famous Fireblood champion?"

"I'm not his champion."

"Don't waste your time on false modesty, little bird. You were the first Fireblood to win in the king's arena. A story to inspire bards and troubadours! The Fireblood peasant girl, hidden away in a mountain village until her mother's death drove her to revenge. Destroyer of thrones. Killer of kings. And somehow, instead of facing execution for these crimes, she won the affection of the new Frost King and resides comfortably in his castle. I won't make you blush by repeating the reasons they say he keeps you so close. Even if I can see quite clearly why those rumors are likely to be true. Your neck is far too lovely to be split in half." He smiled as he watched my reaction—I struggled against a rush of angry heat—and he held up his palms. "Don't blame me, Lady Ruby. I only repeat what I hear. You're a legend, though perhaps more hated than admired in this court."

Normally, I'd have told him what he could do with his thoughts on my so-called legendary status and my place in the court, but I didn't want to do anything that would ruin Arcus's chances for gaining a signature on his treaty. I swallowed my angry retort and scanned the room for an escape.

"It's rather stuffy in here," I said, aiming for a tone that conveyed regretful but firm dismissal. "I think I'll take a stroll in the garden. If you'll excuse me."

"I'll accompany you," he said smoothly.

Annoyance flared, which for some reason made him grin.

"Hoping to escape me, were you? As I came all this way to speak to you, it would be rude of you to ignore me. After all, your king is hoping your presence here aids his campaign to unite his broken kingdom."

"I wouldn't call the kingdom 'broken,' and even if it were, I wouldn't be the one to unite it."

A twitch of his eyebrow gave the impression of disbelief. "It's a sound strategy. Using your...friendship...to convince his detractors that he's different from his brother. If his companion is a Fireblood, he can't be *all* bad. Isn't that the current propaganda being churned out by the Frost Court?"

"It's not propaganda. And he doesn't need me to convince people of that."

"On the contrary, you're the reason I'm here. And perhaps the Safrans would say the same. You'd make a far more effective ambassador than the imbeciles the king appoints to speak for him."

"He has to work within the confines of the court," I said, offended at the implication that Arcus chose his representatives poorly. "Why am I defending him to you? Go speak to him yourself, if you're so skeptical. And leave me in peace."

He laughed. "Perhaps you're no ambassador after all. No dignitary can afford to trample on diplomacy with such abandon. But surely you've been instructed to help mend ties with the southern provinces?"

Arcus had said my presence here would help. He needed the peace treaties signed if he was to bring his troops home to their fields and villages. If I could help him do that, I should swallow my pride and keep my temper.

"I would be pleased to have you accompany me," I said with a sigh.

"Ah, now see? That wasn't so bad."

As we turned toward the doors leading outside, someone sniffed loudly behind us. I turned and found myself face-to-face with a fox—a white frost fox pelt curled around the shoulders of a noblewoman.

"How fitting," said Lady Blanding, somehow managing to look down her nose at me, even though we were about the same height. "The Fireblood peasant and the illiterate provincial, cozy as two rats in a barrel. They say a rodent will always manage to find more of its own kind."

"Madam," said the dignitary, "the only rodent I see is above your shoulders."

"This is no rodent," she retorted, smoothing the white fur with bejeweled fingers, her voice high with outrage. "My stole was made from a pure white frost fox, a gift from my husband before the species was hunted nearly to extinction."

"I wasn't referring to the fox," he replied, each word enunciated, his gaze steady. When she finally took his meaning, her eyes turned to steel.

"My husband and I are powerful people," she said, her voice as frigid as the pillars. "If I thought you deserved it, I might have argued for your salvation. As it is, I leave you to your fate."

With a final outraged glance, Lady Blanding whirled and stomped away, her gray hair wobbling like a tower of curdled whipped cream. The back of her head sported a comb in the shape of a fox head, its diamond eyes staring lifelessly at me.

"Is that typical of your interactions with the Frost Court?" the dignitary asked.

"Pretty much," I answered, still smiling at the look on Lady Blanding's face when she'd realized she was being insulted. "I've never enjoyed it quite so much, though."

"I believe we were going to get some air?" At my nod, he started to reach for my arm but checked the movement. Instead, he motioned outside. When we had crossed the threshold, the footmen shut the doors sharply behind us.

He chuckled. "I find it amusing that they keep the doors closed. Are they worried about letting in a draft?"

I stared. "That is strange, actually."

"We shouldn't squander such a thoughtful gift," he said silkily. "What should we do with all this newfound privacy?"

Instead of answering, I strode purposefully down the path into the ice garden, my slippers crunching over the gravel, my skirts rustling like autumn leaves. The air altered as we moved farther from the ballroom, cooling and crisping, the scent of expensive perfumes replaced by pungent hints of pine, oil from hanging lamps, and the minty breath of drowsing pennyroyal. I inhaled deeply, enjoying the chill but also using my gift to push out a layer of heat beneath my thin gown.

"I don't know what you think we're doing out here," I said as the dignitary ambled alongside me, "but I'm here to talk about you signing the peace treaty."

"And yet you're all alone," he said, as if he thought me too innocent to appreciate the possible danger. "What would stop me from deciding I didn't want to talk at all?"

"My fire would stop you," I said seriously, halting and turning to him. "And I wouldn't hesitate to use it."

He made an amused sound. "I'm afraid that isn't as intimidating as you'd like it to be, Lady Ruby. Not with me."

"You're not a Frostblood."

"Definitely not."

"Then you *should* be intimidated."

The edge of his mouth tensed, as if he fought a smile. "Because your 'Arcus' will have me dealt with if you ask him to?"

I angled my chin up. "If anyone can heal the wounds opened by his brother, Arcus can. And yes, I call him 'Arcus' because that's how I first knew him, well before he became king. His sense of honor runs deep and he has never let me down. You can trust him."

"You truly believe what you're saying, don't you?" he asked with a hint of wonder. And perhaps pity.

"Of course I do. And so should you. The sooner the peace accords are signed, the sooner we can begin healing Tempesia."

"And where do you fit into this . . . healing?"

I shrugged. "Doing whatever I can, I suppose."

"But what do *you* want? What do you want for yourself?" The question was strangely intense.

I hesitated. I could have kept my distance with some vague answer. But I sensed it was a serious question, and that he was still deciding whether to trust me, and by extension, trust Arcus. The trouble was, I didn't really know what I wanted. When I tried to picture my future, my mind clouded, as if I were looking at a glass ball filled with smoke. I needed to destroy the Minax, to stop the visions and get my mind back again, but I couldn't tell him that. So I told him a different truth.

"I want the kind of peace we had before King Akur, when trade was open between provinces. Between kingdoms. With Sudesia, where my mother came from."

Something flared in his eyes, bright and fierce. "Do you truly believe that's achievable in your lifetime?"

"Don't you?"

He wore an enigmatic smile. "I commend you for dreaming big."

"By all means," said a voice from somewhere in the darkness of the garden. "Let the fools dream of peace. I, for one, would prefer to make our enemies pay."

FOUR

THREE LANTERNS WENT OUT, ONE after the other, leaving only the nearest one casting a small circle of light around a shadowy figure. It was the footman I'd seen staring at me earlier.

"We had all kinds of elaborate plans to isolate you, Firefilth," he said, "and then you wander out here." He turned a menacing look on the dignitary. "We didn't expect *you* tonight, but we'll take the good fortune bestowed by Fors."

Though the dignitary hadn't changed position, tension radiated from him. "The god of the north wind has nothing to do with my presence here."

"Who are you?" I asked the blond man.

His grin widened. "I've been told I bear a resemblance to my brother. Surely you haven't forgotten *him*."

In the space of a breath, it all snapped into place. The sandy-blond hair, the familiar arrogant grin. I would never forget the man he resembled—the man who'd killed my mother. "You're Captain Drake's brother."

"Oh, so the lady does remember. And do you also recall his wife and daughter, watching from the crowd, sobbing their eyes out as you took my brother's life in the arena?"

I swallowed. "I do."

"Not that you care, but Ilva died within a week of her husband. They say it was a fever, but I know the truth. Grief killed her. Then my poor orphaned niece sent me a message that my brother's killer was being treated as a lady and living in the castle. Fortunately, there's a sizable group of people who want to get rid of you. I only had to join their ranks and wait for an opportunity."

In seconds, we were surrounded by half a dozen masked figures holding swords. Two of them held up hands coated in frost.

"Run," I whispered. "I'll hold them off."

My companion scoffed. "I was about to say the same to you."

I threw him a glance from the corner of my eye. "The peace talks depend on you. Go."

"I'm not here to sign any treaties. Shall we, then?"

The dignitary raised his palms and, in a gesture that held me immobile with stupefied shock, sent twin streams of vivid orange flames toward the sculptures and trees and shrubs made of ice, sweeping back and forth in a searing arc that sent our attackers shouting and stumbling and running for cover. The ice melted into a rushing stream that flowed onto the gravel path, sloshing over my toes and into my thin slippers. I continued to stare at the dignitary—the Fireblood—only the crash of my heart assuring me I hadn't actually turned to stone.

"Don't worry," he said to Drake. "That was just a little stretch. I have plenty left." He beckoned them forward with a bend of his fingers.

"Where the blazes did you come from?" Drake snarled. "There are no Firebloods left in Tempesia, aside from her. My brother made sure of that. I'd stake my life on it."

I was almost tempted to thank him for asking. I was wondering the same thing.

The Fireblood laughed. "A foolish bet, since it's obvious you've already lost. Though I'll gladly collect your forfeit." Cupping his hands together, he slowly pulled them apart to create a dense ball of flame that grew in size and intensity. Most of the attackers turned and ran, their boots sliding on the wet ground. Only the two Frostbloods remained with Drake, all three of them lifting their palms toward us in readiness.

"My brother didn't have the gift," said Drake, "but I do. Finally, it's a fair fight."

"Hardly fair when you outnumber us three to two," I pointed out, my voice unsteady. I still couldn't believe I was standing next to another Fireblood. *Be amazed later. Fight now.*

Drake shrugged. "I was never very good at arithmetic." He yelled an order, and a low, protective wall of frost formed. Then a blast of ice slammed toward us. My hands were ready, but the attack still knocked me off my feet. The dignitary, or whoever he was, managed to remain standing.

Drake was right; a Fireblood of his caliber would never have escaped Rasmus's notice.

"Who are you really?" I asked, pushing to my feet.

"My name is Kai," he answered.

"That's not what I—"

Another wave of frost knocked us back, turning to smoke and steam as it met our fire.

"Form a shield," Kai said, demonstrating by making a swirling lozenge of fire that grew in size. "Hold it steady. With me."

I watched and mirrored him. When the two masses of flames combined, light blinded me. I felt my way through the move, forcing the fire into an ever-larger oval.

"Stand your ground," he told me. "Now push forward on my mark. Hold. Hold. Now!"

We slammed the pulsing fire shield ahead in unison and heard surprised shouts as we broke through their icy wall and the thuds of bodies as they hit the earth. As my vision cleared, I saw figures on the ground, unmoving. I sucked in a breath and stepped toward them.

"Leave them," said Kai, grabbing my arm. I shook free and ran the rest of the way to the attackers, pulling off the first Frostblood's mask.

It was Lord Regier. He wasn't breathing. I found no pulse at his throat.

The other mask revealed his wife, Lady Regier.

"Oh Tempus," I said. "They're from Arcus's council. He'll be devastated."

I took her wrist, feeling a faint pulse. Kai shouted a warning and ran toward me, but he halted abruptly at the same moment the sharp edge of a steel blade bit into the skin at my throat.

"Stand slowly," Drake ordered from close behind me.

I did as he asked, barely breathing as his other arm cinched tight around my waist.

"You kill her, I kill you," said Kai. "Very simple. Let her go."

"I swore to Fors that she would die today and I've never broken an oath. Now you, on the other hand, the Blue Legion wanted you dead for daring to come here. But if you leave without signing the treaty, they might let you live."

"Well, normally, I would be only too willing to save my own precious skin," said Kai with alarming calm—alarming to me, at least, since I was fairly sure I couldn't summon my heat without Drake slicing me first. "But it happens that there is something I want rather badly—and it hinges on keeping this girl alive." He spread his hands in an apologetic gesture. "So I'm afraid I'll have to ask you again to let her go."

Drake shook his head, the motion making the knife saw gently back and forth against my neck. I didn't dare bat an eyelash at the sting.

"You can do your best to kill me once she's dead," Drake said, "but an oath is an oath. She dies now." His lips touched my ear as he whispered, "This is for my brother, Firefilth."

His arm tensed, and for a second I thought the last word I ever heard would be "Firefilth," and the last thing I ever saw would be a very annoyed-looking Fireblood with hair that refused to be anything but vivid orange, even in the dim light of a nighttime garden.

But then the vivid orange spread and lit the sky in a whip of flame that curled above and behind me, and the tension in Drake's arm became a tremble in the rest of his body. He fought back, his chest coating with frost as he tried to ward off the fire, but the heat intensified and he screamed.

And then my hands, which had been pressed against his arm, suddenly found they had pushed free, and I was stumbling forward onto my hands and knees, getting thoroughly soaked in an icy pool of water.

I stayed there, just trying to catch my breath. I'd been about to die, and then I hadn't.

Fire had saved me. And it hadn't been my own.

I finally looked up to see Kai shaking his head, no longer just annoyed but properly furious. "And how long do you think I can stay here now that I've killed a Frostblood, hmm? They'll be out looking for me in droves!" He spat a few words in what I could have sworn was Sudesian. From the tone, I was pretty sure he was cursing.

"I was just nearly killed," I pointed out shakily, rubbing my throat. "And you're angry that I've spoiled your visit?"

He made a furious gesture toward Drake's body. "This didn't go at all the way it was supposed to. I didn't know you had assassins trailing at your heels." He punctuated his thoughts with a few more foreign words. If anything, they sounded angrier and filthier than the previous curses.

"Well, I'm so sorry my attempted murder inconvenienced you." I struggled to stand and slipped back down onto one knee. Rather than helping me up, he pulled at his cuffs and brushed dirt from his tunic, as if fixing his appearance even mattered right now. "If you don't want to be inconvenienced further, I suggest you leave before anyone comes. The king's guards might have a few questions about how the southern dignitary happens to be a *Fireblood*. Considering they thought I was the only one left in Tempesia."

He gave me a pitying look. "I'm clearly not the southern dignitary. Though the disguise was rather amusing, I admit."

"Who, then?"

"I gave you my real name." He took my upper arms and hauled me to my feet. "But I'm not from the Aris Plains. I'm from Sudesia." My body went rigid. His eyes sparkled. "Yes, we have ships, you know."

"But the blockade—"

"The provinces are still friendly to us and find ways for our ships to pass through. Not often, mind you. But enough that we heard tales, even before we received your king's invitation, of the Fireblood girl who destroyed the frost throne. I had come here to..." He paused and shook his head in frustration. "Never mind that. All my plans are in tatters, but I can still help you. Consider this your formal invitation: Come to Sudesia with me."

I tried to remember how to exhale. That was about the last thing I'd expected him to say.

"Why would I go anywhere with you?"

"Let me spell it out, then: They don't like you here. They tried to kill you once, and they will try again. I'm offering safety. Freedom. Not to mention knowledge and training that you're sorely lacking. Your mastery of your gift is on par with my six-year-old niece. A Fireblood school could do wonders for you."

"If you think insulting me will—"

"More important," he interrupted, "you mentioned that you want to see peace and harmony in this godsforsaken iceberg of a kingdom. Let me assure you, the emissary of the Aris Plains will never sign any treaties unless my queen sanctions it. The provinces' ties with Sudesia go back centuries. If you come to Sudesia, perhaps you can propose some kind of agreement."

In spite of myself, I was intrigued. Though I had no time or space to weigh the odds that he was telling the truth.

"Why are you offering this?" A gust of wind made the few remaining ice trees shiver and chime.

He grabbed my hand. The shock of his skin! The first person I'd known whose temperature matched mine. I was only numbly aware as he slid a ring onto my finger.

"Think of this as a ticket onto my ship. Meet me at the port in Tevros within the week. You could hold the key to peace in these soft little hands." He caressed my palm with his thumb, then grinned unrepentantly as I yanked it away. "Forgive me, but I don't care to wait around to be questioned by the king's soldiers.

You'll find me in a tavern called the Fat Badger near the wharf. If you don't show up, I'll assume you prefer assassination to my offer."

Then he dashed toward the perimeter of the garden, climbed a tree, and hopped as nimbly as a jackrabbit over the wall.

I wasted a few seconds staring after the Fireblood stranger, then realized how incriminating it would look if I were discovered with three injured or dead Frostbloods. I took my skirts in hand and splashed through the melted remains of ice flowers. How was I going to explain what happened? Would anyone believe me? If the court was looking for a way to show that I was a threat, I had practically gift-wrapped myself for them.

When I neared the door to the ballroom, muffled screams came from inside. I forgot everything but the need to make sure Arcus was safe. I grabbed the handle and yanked. Locked. I moved to the right, where light spilled through one of the windows.

And saw chaos.

Gone was the civilized mingling of Frostblood nobility with foreign ambassadors, the tilts of heads and the flutter of fans and the waltzing flare of skirts. In their place was well-dressed warfare—the heft of steel and the blast of frost wielded with animalistic ferocity, the combatants wearing ball gowns and brushed velvet instead of armor. Frostblood against Frostblood.

My eyes roved frantically, searching for Arcus. I couldn't find him. I threw myself against the window, but it held firm. I searched the ground and, in a few seconds, found a large enough rock to hurl at the glass, which exploded as it shattered. I used another rock to clear the jagged bits at the base, then slid through, only half aware of a stray piece slicing my palm.

I scanned the scene. Some of the guests were at the doors, pulling desperately on the handles and calling for help. Others were slumped on the floor, unconscious or dead. For a second, I wondered if Kai had been complicit in what was clearly a coordinated attack, then dismissed the idea instantly. He'd fought the attackers off with me.

I finally spotted Arcus, standing on the edge of the dais where the musicians had played a waltz only a half hour before. Lord Pell fought alongside him, but they were outnumbered by four other Frostbloods: two men and two women, all of them dressed as servants or guards. I rushed forward and blasted an attacker in the back, who screamed and went down, his black doublet in flames.

As the others turned and threw out their hands, my second blast of flame meeting their frost, my eyes cut to Arcus. Even outnumbered, it was strange that he hadn't won this fight. His gift was spectacular. But then I realized one of his hands was pressed to his chest near his shoulder. His face was paler than usual, his expression pinched with pain. Blue blood seeped between his fingers. He'd been stabbed.

I saw red.

Rage boiled my blood, lending me strength to bring down another of his attackers. Then Arcus shouted a warning, his gaze fixed behind me. I whirled. Three Frostbloods dressed as servants converged on me, two throwing frost and one wielding a sword. I heard Arcus call my name, but I was too busy dodging the sword and throwing flame at the attacker's feet, forcing him back. As I twisted to avoid a stream of frost from the side, ice caught me from behind, sending me to the ground.

"Kill the king and his Fireblood harlot, and rise, Blue Legion, rise!" the swordsman snarled.

Shock at his words held me immobile for a fraction of a second, but it was long enough to lose the opportunity to use my fire. I rolled out of the way as his sword tip crashed against the floor.

I found my feet, only to be grabbed from behind, but an elbow and a fist soon dislodged the hold. A few seconds were spent in intense concentration as I threw out fire to keep the attackers, at least six now, from getting close. But there were too many, and I was grabbed on either side, no matter that my sleeves were on fire from my own flame. A sword rose over my head.

And clattered to the ballroom floor. The servant's blue eyes blinked in shock, blue blood sliding from both nostrils as he crumpled. Lord Pell, standing behind the man, yanked his blade from the body. My other attackers were completely immobile, as if someone had stopped time. I glanced at the two Frostbloods holding me, a man and a woman, both encased in ice, their hands frozen around my arms. The fire on my sleeves was out, my dress in blackened tatters at the edges.

My head jerked up to check on Arcus. He stood on the dais, his hands thrust out. He had frozen my attackers in a single burst of frost. There was murder in his eyes, and for a fraction of a second, I saw his brother in him. The rage and hatred, the thirst for death. As if the Minax preyed on him now, twisting his fears and hurts and dusting away his pain to make him into someone who was incapable of mercy. I honed in on Arcus's eyes, half expecting them to be pure shining onyx. But they were still blue.

He blinked, his eyes focusing on me. He mouthed my name. And then he swayed, his eyelashes fluttering.

I pushed out heat into my arms, broke free of the ice, and ran to him, stepping over bodies along the way. I reached my arms up and caught him as he fell, giving a surprised *oof* as I was crushed under his muscular bulk.

"Arcus," I groaned. How ironic to survive the fight only to be flattened under the unforgiving weight of the person who had saved my life. A hysterical giggle bubbled up but came out as a strangled gasp. The laughter fled as I realized he wasn't moving. "No," I whispered, struggling to free myself.

Hands slid around Arcus's arms and for a second I panicked, expecting more enemies, but it was Lord Pell and Lord Manus, both of them bloody and stern-faced, gently pulling Arcus to his feet and holding him between them.

I sucked in a relieved breath and stood, moving my hands to Arcus's cheeks. "Wake up, please. Arcus, please." My words were whispered prayers, frantic and raw in my burning throat.

His eyelashes fluttered open. "Thank Fors you're all right," he mumbled, his mouth twitching up at the corner.

I turned to Lord Pell, drawing myself up. "He needs a healer *now*!"

Arcus laughed weakly. "You give orders like a queen." His eyes slid over me as Lord Pell and Lord Manus moved toward the ballroom doors, which now stood open.

"You're unhurt?" Arcus slurred as I followed him toward the exit.

I scanned for Marella and Brother Thistle, relieved that neither were among the prone forms on the floor. "I'm fine."

"I got blood all over your gown," Arcus said rather irrelevantly.

"It doesn't matter." I noticed a bearded man in robes who must be the Safran ambassador—alive and unharmed, talking with a few other delegates. Thank Sud. His murder would have meant war.

"If my blood were red like yours it would match your dress," Arcus rambled. "You should have worn blue. Oh, stop spinning, I don't want to dance."

I looked at him sharply, then met Lord Manus's eyes. "He's delirious."

"Couldn't find you," Arcus muttered, his eyes closing. "Worried."

Lord Pell chuckled, though I heard the tension in his voice. "The king nearly lost his mind when he couldn't find you during the attack, Lady Ruby. I've fought alongside him in battle and I've never seen him so close to wetting his pants."

"Quiet, Oliver," Arcus murmured.

"You were outside?" Lord Pell asked me as we reached the doorway.

I told a brief version of events about Lord and Lady Regier, Drake and his revenge, and what he'd said about the Blue Legion.

"You fought them all off by yourself?" Lord Manus asked.

The guards crowded around us now, offering help. I wasn't about to say anything about Kai. There were too many people here. "The king needs to be in bed."

A crooked smile spread over Arcus's face and his eyelids fluttered open. "Why, Ruby, I didn't know you were so eager to get me into bed. Wish I'd known sooner."

Lord Manus's cheeks darkened with the blue-tinged Frostblood version of a blush. I was sure my complexion was thoroughly pink.

"Come now, friend," said Lord Pell, motioning the guards to help carry their king, "before you give the guards far too much to talk about."

Arcus muttered something barely audible and stumbled, but the steady hands of his men were there to carry him. I had never seen him look so weak.

"What a night," said Lord Pell as we moved into the hallway toward the stairs. "The glorious dawn of our peace talks has ended in attempts on our lives."

"The dignitary from the Aris Plains!" Lord Manus exclaimed, as if just remembering. "We couldn't find him!"

"He was with me in the garden," I said now that we had more

privacy, although I couldn't quite bring myself to admit that he wasn't the dignitary at all. "He ran off during the attack."

"Well, we'll have to find him and grovel on our knees for all this. Thank Fors he wasn't killed. The assassins seemed to be targeting delegates, particularly the ones who've shown a willingness to sign the peace treaties. Which is probably why Arcus threw himself in front of the dagger meant for the Safran ambassador. Typical. He's calm and focused when defending himself, but he's a fiend when he's protecting someone else."

"He's going to be all right, isn't he?"

"The healers will tell us more shortly. Though it probably didn't do much good when he yanked out the blade so he could search for you."

I groaned. "I'm going to kill him. And then I'm going to find out the names of every man and woman who had a hand in this attack and"—there were so many things I'd like to do, and they all involved my fire—"express my extreme displeasure."

Manus chuckled. "Leave that to me. Your job is to go make him rest, since I doubt anyone else could."

FIVE

I SAT ON ONE SIDE OF ARCUS'S BED, and Brother Thistle sat on the other. A fire had been lit, though somehow the heat didn't penetrate the massive space. Plush royal-blue curtains covered wide windows that looked down on the castle courtyard. All the luxuries of the king's bedchamber—carved wardrobes, thick rugs, wingback chairs with delicately curved legs—were painted a soft yellow by the glow from candelabras.

I watched helplessly as the healers, a man and woman with similarly long, serious faces, checked the king's pulse and washed and dressed his wound.

It was deathly quiet after they left. Arcus lay in the bed, silent and still, his skin almost as bleached as the sheets, the covers pulled over his bare chest up to his bandaged shoulder. When I touched his cheek, he was frighteningly cold, even for him.

"Will he recover?" I asked, as if the monk, with all his scholarly knowledge, would know the answer to that question, too.

"He must." Brother Thistle's expression was openly worried as he stared at Arcus. He loved him like a son, that was clear. Surely we would make Arcus better with the force of our affection alone.

"Where were you when it happened?" I asked.

"I left the ball early and returned to the library." He offered it like a confession.

"You couldn't have known. This is more my fault than anyone else's." A wave of guilt swept through me. The so-called Blue Legion, apparently a network of bitter nobles, all hated the king because of me. Or at least what they perceived as my influence over him.

"The timing was deliberate," I observed.

"Of course."

"And the targets were anyone who supported the peace accords."

"That much is clear."

"Who is behind it?"

He rubbed his temples. "I fear there are many more suspects than we'd first thought."

I told him what Lady Blanding had said, her veiled threats that she had decided to leave us to our fate, and my suspicion that she'd known about the coming attack.

He didn't look surprised. "Arcus has promised to give the

Aris Plains back to the farmers of the southern provinces once he assures peace. I was surprised that he didn't see more direct opposition from his court, many of whom were given that land by Akur and Rasmus. Now we know why."

I feathered my fingertips over Arcus's bandage, the cold seeping into my skin. I sent a pulse of gentle heat into his shoulder near the wound, hoping it would help the healing process somehow, even just a little. "What happens now?"

"I truly do not know. His court is divided. He has friends—most notably Lord and Lady Manus and Lord Pell—but they alone don't have the land or connections to have great influence. And many who do, like my cousin, Lord Tryllan, choose neutrality over risk. They wait to see which way the wind blows before taking sides." He paused. "At any rate, we must form a new plan. No one will sign accords with a monarch whose reign appears so tenuous."

"His court is divided because of me," I said dully. "His reign is tenuous because of me. What can I do to help him?"

"You were with the dignitary from the southern provinces when you were attacked, were you not?"

If I could trust anyone, it was Brother Thistle. I told him everything.

"Remarkable! What would the Sudesians want with you?"

"I have no idea."

"Well," he mused, "if they meant you harm, the Fireblood could have just killed you himself. Perhaps you are celebrated as a hero for destroying the frost throne and helping overthrow King Rasmus."

"So I should trust him? Should I go if it will help Arcus achieve peace?"

Emotions chased one another across his face: curiosity, doubt, uncertainty, excitement. He shook his head. "We cannot act rashly."

"But we do need to act."

"More than you know." His tone was resigned.

"Why? What don't I know?"

There was something overly careful in his expression, as if he were preparing for my reaction. "Murders have risen tenfold in the villages within a few days' ride from here. In each case, the *murderer* has died of seemingly natural causes shortly after, but the blood found in the body is always black. I believe the Minax is possessing people, moving from village to village."

The pain of betrayal sent wild heat through my chest. "*How* could you not tell me before now?" I had a terrible thought. "Did you and Arcus not trust me? Did you think I would... that I was so corrupted by the Minax that you weren't sure whose side I was on?"

After all, the Minax's possession had been like an opiate, erasing all worry and fear. Brother Thistle knew how I'd struggled not to let the creature consume me.

"Of course not! Arcus insisted you were worried enough already without the burden of more guilt. He said you would blame yourself for releasing the Minax."

He was right about that.

"So it's out there possessing people." I clenched my hands

together. "Making them kill each other and feeding on the grief that follows."

"Perhaps, but I think its intentions go beyond that. Recently, our Frostblood general in the Aris Plains ordered his soldiers to attack a peaceful province with no command from the king nor a strategic goal in mind. They simply began cutting people down. I do not think it a coincidence that peace is always out of reach; the Minax thrives on war. If this goes on, we will continue to decimate one another with no end in sight. Arcus has sent his best trackers after it, but what would we do if we catch the person who is possessed? If we imprison or kill its host, the creature will merely choose another."

It seemed hopeless. Too many factors we didn't understand or couldn't control. "But we can't do *nothing*. The Minax is out there... slaughtering people, turning them against each other. Innocent lives." I gasped, my chest so tight I could barely breathe.

Brother Thistle spoke softly, calming me. "You are right. We cannot afford to ignore this opportunity or the knowledge we now possess on how to kill the Minax. Do you remember the book on the thrones I mentioned? The one that is no longer in our library?"

I nodded. "How could I forget Pernillius?"

"There were two copies, one for each Frostblood and Fireblood monarch. One for each throne. The secrets in it were considered dangerous, so it was kept under lock and key in King Akur's time. I"—he cleared his throat—"managed to obtain it once...."

"You mean you stole it?" I grinned in admiration.

"Yes, well, *borrowed* is a more accurate word. I held the book only briefly, before Lord Ustathius discovered I had it and took it back. That book"—he turned and peered at the shelves as if he might summon the volume with the power of his will—"is where I first learned of the prophecy of the Child of Light and the destruction of the throne. I am certain that it contained knowledge of the destruction of the Minax. Since the day I returned here after King Rasmus banished me, I have scoured the castle to no avail."

"Maybe Lord Ustathius still has it," I suggested.

"I questioned him. He says he barely remembers the book, although he does enjoy thwarting me. We had a sort of informal competition for the king's ear many years ago."

"So another copy lies in Sudesia," I said, drawing his attention back to the point at hand. "But on which island?" I'd seen the maps showing islands clustered together like pieces of broken slate tossed to the ground.

"I assume it is kept in the capital, Sere, where the queen lives, as well as being home to the school for Fireblood masters."

It was the closest thing to hope I'd felt in weeks. "But... Arcus will never agree to my traveling to Sudesia. He'll say it's too dangerous. And even if he would allow it, you know he would send warships and soldiers to accompany me. We might as well declare war."

"We need that book," he said. "I'm convinced it has the answers we seek."

I saw my own certainty reflected in Brother Thistle's eyes. There was no alternative: I had to go. But we couldn't tell Arcus.

Even as worry and guilt churned in my stomach, I couldn't help a surge of excitement at the prospect of boarding that ship. Sudesia was a land of warmth and fire. I had longed to know where Firebloods came from, the customs and practices of a place that seemed mysterious to me now but was home to my ancestors. Home to my mother before she'd come to Tempesia, though she'd never told me why. Maybe in returning to her homeland I would find that part of myself that echoed with empty longing since the day she died. "When I get there," I said, "*if* I get there safely . . . where should I start?"

"There is a library in the school for Fireblood masters that is second to none, and older even than ours. If you can find the ancient text, or perhaps a scholar with an obsession for esoteric knowledge, there lies our last hope of finding out how to destroy the Minax."

"Then you should come with me. No scholar is more obsessed than you."

"I highly doubt your Sudesian friend would allow me on his ship."

"Why shouldn't he? After all, if it weren't for you, King Rasmus would still be on the throne."

"If it weren't for *us*." He reached out and patted Arcus's hand where it lay limply on the covers. "Whatever our mistakes, we did accomplish that."

I covered Arcus's other hand with mine. We sat like that

quietly for a minute, the three of us connected. We'd been through so much together. I didn't want to leave them. The thought alone made it feel like a steel clamp was squeezing my heart.

"But it does not matter that I helped you," he continued. "The Sudesians would see me only as a Frostblood. An enemy."

"Then I'll go alone," I said softly. "But how can I leave Arcus like this, wondering if he'll recover? He'll worry about me."

"I will tell him our plans as soon as you're gone. He will be angry, but he will forgive me. Try to send us a message when you arrive in Sudesia. Perhaps if the southern provinces are aiding the passage of Sudesian ships, they would also be willing to let messages pass."

"I will. And I'll find the book."

"Do not tell the queen your intentions. If she is under the influence of the curse, she will protect the throne at all costs. Your best chance is to ingratiate yourself with her and the Fireblood masters. If they see you as some sort of hero for destroying the frost throne, you might be welcomed."

I noticed a thin coating of frost covering the monk's chair, a sign he was losing control of his gift and more anxious than he let on. And no wonder. There were so many hopeful assumptions in our plan. And so much on my shoulders. It was dizzying. For a minute I just gripped my hands together and breathed deeply until I regained my composure.

"So if you think about it," I said, "not only will I be searching for the book, I'll be trying to mend ties between our kingdoms, which is just what Arcus wants. In that light, I could be called a sort of unofficial ambassador on behalf of the Frostbloods." I caught his eye and we both smiled at the irony, though his smile didn't reach his eyes. "Really, Brother Thistle, who would have thought?"

"As much as I cringe to think of sending you on a mission of diplomacy," he said, "you are our best hope for peace. And our only hope for destroying the Minax."

We discussed the plan until my eyes grew heavy, and Brother Thistle left. Arcus's bed was so large that I was able to curl up at the foot quite comfortably. Exhaustion took over and I drifted off immediately, opening my eyes only when I heard Arcus asking for water. Dawn seeped through the crack between the curtains, laying a yellow stripe across the floor. I hopped from the bed, shivering in the morning chill. I poured water from a crystal pitcher and held the cup to Arcus's blue-tinged lips.

He struggled to lift his head. I slid one hand behind to help him, my heart contracting at the sign of weakness. Even in the battle for the throne, he hadn't been hurt like this.

He took a sip and nodded, settling against the pillow as I put the glass back on the table.

"I didn't expect you to be here," he said, his voice rough from sleep.

I smiled, light-headed with relief that he was awake and lucid. "At your service."

“I need to be ill more often,” he said. “My own personal—”

“If you say ‘servant,’ I’m leaving.” The truth was, he could say whatever he wanted and I wasn’t going anywhere. I would savor these last few moments with him.

One eyebrow rose. “I was going to say ‘healer.’ ”

“Ah.” I smoothed my fingertips over his forehead and he closed his eyes with a sigh. “That’s acceptable. Although I have no idea what to do other than keep you in bed.”

A mischievous grin spread across his face.

I narrowed my eyes at him. “And don’t say anything about *how* I’m to keep you in bed. You already embarrassed me in front of Lord Manus. I’ve never seen a Frostblood blush so much.”

He huffed a small laugh. “I’m sorry I don’t remember it, then.” He glanced around. “Was Brother Thistle here last night? I have a vague memory of hearing your voices.”

A pulse of alarm jolted through me. How much did he hear?

“We were discussing who could be behind the attack. What to do next.”

His eyes fluttered closed. “And? What did you come up with?”

“Nothing definite as yet.” I hated to lie to him. It was harder than I thought it would be. I continued stroking his forehead, then trailed the back of my hand against his cheek.

“Ouch.” His hand came up to grab mine. I blinked in surprise to see the ring Kai had given me on my finger. I’d forgotten all about it.

“Where did you get that?” he asked. “This filigree is so

intricate. It reminds me…" His brows pulled together. "It reminds me of a ring that has been passed down in my family. It was from Sudesia. But it has a sapphire. And thicker here."

"Oh?" I didn't know what else to say. If I told him about the ring, I'd have to tell him everything.

"Ruby." His voice was hard. "What aren't you telling me?"

"You've been keeping things from me, too," I countered quickly, pulling my hand from his. "The Minax? The murders?"

A flicker of guilt passed over his expression. "That's different. I was trying to protect you."

"Well, so am I."

His glance fell back to my hand. "Where did you get the ring?"

I sighed, resigned. "From the southern dignitary." I paused. "Only he wasn't who he claimed to be. As it turned out, he was a Sudesian."

His eyes pierced mine. "How the blazes did he get into the ball?"

I fiddled with the ring, watching as it caught a band of sunlight. "I don't know. He must have had someone vouch for his false identity. Anyway, he came to the ball to… to see me."

"To see you?" His volume rose with each word. "What for?"

I told him what Kai had said, leaving out the part about the people of the southern provinces helping him through the Frostblood blockade. If Arcus knew that, he'd be forced to deal with it.

"So this stranger claims to be a Sudesian and he's offering you passage across the sea." He was angry. "Why? What do they want with you?"

I shrugged. "Perhaps it's an interest in peace, which he thinks could be achieved through someone like me negotiating. But I didn't get to ask further questions. After the attack, he ran off."

"Not exactly the mark of an honest man. He could have made the offer directly to me."

"He doesn't trust you. Surely that's not a surprise. All the Sudesians know is what your brother has done to the Firebloods in Tempesia. And we'd just been attacked."

"For all we know, he was in on the attack."

I shook my head. "That makes no sense. Kai fought the attackers off with me."

"Kai," he spat. "You're on a first-name basis with him?"

I stiffened. "When Drake had a knife to my throat, Kai saved my life."

Arcus's face lost color. "Drake had a knife to your throat?"

I pulled back the collar of my robe to uncover the tender skin Drake had scored with his blade. "I would have died if not for Kai."

He swallowed and was silent for a minute. His expression didn't change, but his eyes showed fury and fear as they rested on the wound. Then his nostrils flared. "You wouldn't have been out there in the first place if not for him. What was he planning? To kidnap you? Who knows what would have happened if—"

"If those handy Frostblood assassins hadn't come along? Are you even hearing yourself? This could be the only way to repair ties with the southern provinces *and* find a way to destroy the Minax. Which, in case you've forgotten, is turning people into murderers. What if it's planning to come back for me as it promised?" I gestured to my heart-shaped scar. "What if the visions, which are only getting *worse*, are a precursor to possession? What if *I* become the next murderer? I can't just sit around waiting and wondering, not if I can do something to protect the kingdom, to protect *you*." I was half-breathless after rushing to say my piece. I took a steadying breath. "Brother Thistle knows of a book—"

He waved a hand. "I know about his blasted book. Don't you think I've been searching for it, too?"

"Then you know how important it is. Perhaps, if I can somehow learn how to bring the fire Minax back to Tempesia, we can find a way to destroy both creatures at once! So, fine, I'll admit that we don't know much about Kai. But considering what's at stake, and what we stand to gain, it's worth the risk."

" 'Worth the risk.' As if it takes much of anything for you to put yourself in danger."

"It's not safe here, either."

"It will be," he swore. "I almost lost you! I'll be a damn sight more careful whom I trust now. And by the way, the Blue Legion, or whatever they call themselves, tried to kill me, too. Are you suggesting I also run to Sudesia?"

"You're so infuriating! Think, Arcus. *Why* do these nobles want to kill you?"

"Because I'm making changes. Because they'll lose the land my brother gave them. And because they want to hold on to old prejudices and hatred."

"Yes. Precisely. Rasmus spent two years twisting everyone and everything to suit him, no doubt with the Minax influencing every thought and decision. And now you're trying to untwist it all in a matter of weeks. It's one thing to get treaties signed, but it's another to... to parade a Fireblood in front of them all."

Arcus's eyes flared, then narrowed. "Be very, very careful, Ruby. If you're suggesting that I'm using you as some sort of... taunt..." His eyes burned with cold fire. "To imply that it's wrong for you to be here because of your heritage..." He shook his head. "You're a hypocrite."

"And you're a fool if you don't see what you're doing! My presence here is *hurting* you. And I can't stand it."

His eyes were made of cracked ice, his cheekbones and jaw carved from stone, the scars standing out as if a sculptor hadn't sanded the edges down yet. "I'll die before I send you away to satisfy their hateful expectations."

The vow sent a quiver of something painfully sweet through my nerves. "But, Arcus, if you die, what do you think will happen to me?"

His eyes closed slowly and stayed closed. He looked almost defeated, so unlike his usual self, and I remembered that his body was fighting a battle to heal.

"I'm sorry," I said, slumping onto the edge of the bed. "You're so tired. You're injured and you should be resting. We can talk about this later."

He shook his head, eyes still closed. "I can't trust you not to leave."

I hopped up again. "You're being so obstinate! This could be the *only way* to save us. I came here alone and fought in the arena and killed and almost died several times over. Now I'm supposed to live wrapped in lamb's wool so I don't get a scratch?" I realized I was trembling and my hands were balled into fists. If there was one thing I couldn't bear, it was confinement. I wouldn't let anyone stop me—not even Arcus. "No. I'm going. *I'm going.*"

His eyes snapped open. "*No*, Ruby. You're not."

"What are you going to do?" My voice rose to a shout. "Lock me in your keep?"

"If I have to!"

"Well, you *will* have to! Just like your brother did! And I swear, I'll never speak to you again. I vow it on my mother's life."

The words echoed and hung in the air like knives about to fall. My stomach lurched with a fear I hadn't felt for weeks. Regret sank heavy, sharp talons into my chest. Had I just said that? How had we gotten here?

"Go, then," said Arcus, his voice a bitter thread of sound. If the silence weren't so absolute, I wouldn't have heard him at all. The air reverberated with hurt. "Go to your people. Risk your life, if it seems that important to you. I won't be accused of keeping you somewhere you don't want to be. You'd only come to resent me. I refuse to be the source of your unhappiness."

"It's important to you, too," I said, my voice breaking. "I'm doing this for you."

He didn't move, didn't speak for several moments. "Tell

yourself that, if you must. Chase things you'll never find. Trust the lies of a stranger."

"I don't think he's lying, Arcus. I don't."

"I can't talk about this anymore. Just go."

Suddenly, tears were behind my eyes and I couldn't breathe. "I can't leave you like this, when you're so weak. Let me stay until you fall asleep again, at least."

"No."

"Then I'll send for Brother Thistle."

He scoffed. "I don't want to see him, either."

I could feel the change in him, the determination to shut us out. I told myself his anger was rooted in hurt, his cold rejection based in fear. Arcus had learned that caring led to pain. His mother had been killed when he was young. He'd loved his younger brother, Rasmus, but was forced to lead a rebellion against him to save the kingdom from the cursed king. When we'd lived at the abbey, he'd pushed me away—so fearful of his own feelings for me that he'd denied them for as long as he could. He was trying to protect himself by building walls, layer after layer of solid ice to keep out anyone who could disappoint or hurt him. If he kept it up, he would only succeed in isolating himself from the people who cared about him.

"Don't say that," I said softly. "You're like a son to him. He just wants to help. Don't punish him for agreeing with me."

"He can accompany you on your way to the port and then go to the abbey from there. I have enough enemies here."

Brother Thistle was hurt but resigned at being expelled from the castle like an unwelcome guest. He spent the days packing, lost in his private worries.

Marella, on the other hand, once I admitted my plans, pestered me for details until I told her how I intended to find Kai in Tevros and sail from there. She insisted on helping me pack, ignoring my protests that I didn't plan to bring more than a satchel I could carry easily. As she looked critically through my wardrobe, she offered advice about the route to Tevros and told cautionary tales about the dangers of trusting strangers, mostly involving loss of coin and life. I finally asked bluntly if she thought I was foolish to go.

Her violet eyes stayed steady on mine as she contemplated the question. My stomach tied itself in knots as I waited. Her opinion, I realized, had become important to me.

Finally, she looked away, stuffing a ball gown into my travel chest. I doubted I'd have any use for such clothing, but since I wasn't bringing the chest, I didn't bother to say anything. She seemed to enjoy packing, and I was touched that she wanted to help.

"Whether it's wise is irrelevant," she said, carefully folding a chemise I also wouldn't be bringing. She looked serious, almost melancholy. Very unlike her. Before I could ask what was wrong, she shrugged and grabbed another gown. "Sometimes there is no choice. We all have our role to play and this is yours. You must go."

I wished I could feel as certain as she sounded.

I tried two or three times a day to see Arcus, but the guards turned me away every time. Finally, on the third day, I threatened to burn the door down, speaking loudly enough for half the castle to hear.

Arcus's voice came through the thick oak. "Let her in."

I entered his room, all my bluster leaving as soon as I set foot on the plush carpet. The guard shut the door behind me.

Arcus sat propped up on his pillows and his face held more color, but the look in his eyes was blank. Empty. Focused on something behind me, as if I was a stranger who happened to walk between him and the person he was talking to. Apparently he'd spent the last three days reinforcing those walls.

I stood awkwardly for a moment. "How is your wound?"

"They say it's healing well."

I nodded. Everything about his voice, posture, and expression told me that I wasn't welcome. That he couldn't bear to look at me.

I forced the words out, one by one. "I came to say good-bye."

His eyes slid closed. If it weren't for the humming tension in every line of his body, I'd think he'd just fallen asleep.

"This is one of the hardest things I've ever had to do," I whispered, trembling.

He shrugged his good shoulder, an elongated motion that spoke of indifference.

Heat flared, instant and sharp, and it was a relief. I preferred anger to that killing uncertainty. "So you're not even speaking to me?"

His eyes met mine with an intense look that was both confused and angry. "I just don't understand why you're doing this. Why trust that stranger? You say you're doing this for the kingdom and for me, but admit it, Ruby—you're really doing this for you. You want to go to Sudesia, and you want to do it on your terms. This whole thing is damn selfish." The words were equivalent to a shove in the chest.

"You're being unreasonable," I argued. "You, who prides himself on reason."

"Except I've never been reasonable when it comes to you."

The bald statement brought me up short. If he'd said that to me a few days ago, I would have been delighted, buoyed at the thought that he felt too much for me to be logical. But now the words sliced my rib cage like a scythe. This might be the last time he admitted to feeling anything for me more than anger. Or worse, indifference.

In our shared history, I'd never truly let Arcus see how much I needed him. And he, in perfect pantomime, did the same. No one wanted to be the first to admit we felt more than we could handle.

And now, I was walking away.

A stabbing pain radiated from my heart, which seemed confused about whether to pour out heat or to stop beating altogether.

Was he right? Was I just looking for excuses to go to Sudesia?

No. I might be impulsive, but Brother Thistle wasn't. He had no agenda other than helping Arcus, helping Tempesia. He also cared about me and wouldn't risk my safety if he didn't think it absolutely necessary. We needed to take this chance.

And I had to try to pull Arcus back to me before I left.

I moved so close that my legs pressed against the side of the mattress. My hand came to rest on his arm, its muscles rigid with tension. The temperature dropped, giving him away. He wasn't as calm as he wanted me to believe. There were cracks in his defenses.

As I bent toward him, he turned his head away and my lips landed on his cheek. The world narrowed to the small patch of his skin where two opposing temperatures struggled for dominance: the insistent heat of my lips, the defiant cold of his cheek. Neither yielding. Neither moving. The breath in my lungs cooled.

The realization hit me like shards of broken glass: He was not going to acknowledge my caress. He was going to pretend I wasn't even here, denouncing me completely with his perfect stillness. It felt as if I were being slowly ripped in half. He was forcing me into a choice I'd had no intention of making: To save the kingdom, I would lose him.

My heart skipped a beat when he finally moved. His hand came out to cover mine, his skin colder than my northern village in the dead of winter. Relief flooded me at his touch, until I realized he was only peeling my fingers from his arm, one by one.

"Good-bye, Ruby." His voice was as empty as the abandoned arena, echoing with the ghosts of past pain.

The shock somehow released me from my paralysis. I straightened.

"Good-bye," I echoed, my blood heating with anger. His skin was marble, his eyes so pale they were light gray, almost colorless. *I know you care about me!* I wanted to shout. *Don't push me away!*

I needed to move. I focused on the muscles in my legs, telling them to turn me in the direction of the door. Ordering my feet to take me away. *Now, quick, before you scream and rage and make a fool of yourself.*

Then, just as I started to turn, his face twisted, as if something inside him had suddenly broken. His hands gripped my wrists and pulled, but I was already pitching forward, my hand clutching his shoulder. Our lips met with jarring force, the reverberation landing in my jaw. And then the angle righted itself as he tilted his head to welcome the invasion.

He was so cold against my tongue that I shivered. He tasted like a winter morning, of icy water and mint tea. I drank him in with thirsty sips and he nipped my lower lip in punishment and reward.

When his fingers dove into the hair at the nape of my neck and his open mouth slid to the sensitive spot under my ear, I forgot everything except need, scrambling to throw my leg over his hips so I straddled him, my chest leaning against his. It took a moment for me to recognize his sharp inhalation as pain. He was injured and I was hurting him.

I subsided instantly, crumpling next to him like a falling scarf, settling slowly into stillness. His hand grabbed mine and drew it to his mouth, continuing the kiss in a safer, softer way. His lips rested against my wrist, where the red vein still throbbed with passion, soothing the skin while the pulse beneath slowly returned to normal.

We stayed that way for a long time, silent except for breathing that went from ragged to even. I shifted so that my head was pillowed on a spot low enough on his chest that I didn't touch the bandage. His hand settled on my head, stroking my hair. My scalp tingled with pleasure. After a while, the silence thickened.

"Why do we always go back to hurting each other?" I asked in a small voice, hoping not to destroy the fragile truce.

He paused long enough that I started to worry. "Because we feel too much," he said roughly.

I nodded, my head still tucked against his torso, relieved and full of understanding. "You hate it. Feeling."

"No, I don't," he denied instantly. "I hate . . . being at the mercy of it. I hate when I can't tuck the feelings away because they're too strong."

I lifted his hand and played with his fingers, thinking how beautiful they were—strong and capable and dusted with fine brown hairs.

"You'd be better off with someone who"—I swallowed—"didn't make you feel so out of control."

"Maybe," he said after a moment, making my heart stutter sickly. "But I wouldn't choose that."

I said very quietly, "You might have to choose that."

He had a duty to his people, to his court, but I wanted to hear him say that he didn't want the perfectly bred Marella, that he'd rather have me. But that was unfair to ask of him now, when I was about to leave. I closed my eyes tight, tight, and tried not to think about how much easier that choice could be in my absence.

"We have to let each other go a little," he said very softly, as if reading my mind, confirming my worst fears. "We both know that the future... We might have choices ahead that we can't predict now. We have to allow each other to make them without blame."

He said it so gently, tenderly. Somehow that made it hurt more. Why did he have to be so reasonable now, when I'd finally surrendered to feeling? I couldn't hold back the tears, my body shaking a little as I tried to quell them.

"I don't want to let you go," he said unevenly, "but I'll go mad if I try to keep holding on. You are flame, Ruby, and fire can either be free or it will be smothered. The last thing I want..." His voice broke, and the sound was like a kick in my chest. "The last thing I want is to smother you."

I sat up and turned away fully so that my back faced him, not as a dismissal, but because I needed the space. I didn't want to think about how right he was. His hand came out and smoothed my back, first pushing my hair out of the way, then touching the base of my neck, his fingers lingering over each vertebra on the way down.

I turned back to him and grabbed his hand, pressing my lips to it, then resting my forehead against his knuckles. "I'm sorry. I'm so sorry."

He twisted so that his fingers touched my cheek and my lips rested in his palm. After a minute, he took a shuddering breath.

"Don't take this the wrong way," he said softly, "but I'm so tired. I just . . . I can't bear much more of this."

I knew he was injured and sore and exhausted, but it still hurt to be pushed away. I had to be mature enough to leave him. To stop begging him, in all my subtle and not-so-subtle ways, to give me reasons to stay. If I backed down now, I doomed us all with my cowardice.

But I couldn't help asking quietly, "If—when I come back, will there be any place for me? With you?"

His voice was broken granite. "Always."

Emotion filled my chest, so much I ached with it. I couldn't ask for more than that.

So I gave his hand a harsh, almost bruising kiss, stood, turned, and walked to the door. I didn't let myself look back. I knew I wasn't that strong. It felt like lead weights had been tied to my feet. I stepped from the room, shut the door, and moved carefully down the hallway, feeling as if I'd left behind some vital and irreplaceable part of myself in the room.

The sky was gray outside the windows. The light that flowed into the hallway was gray. Even my skin, when I looked at my hand that still wore the ring, looked a sickly gray.

But the ruby in the ring shone as if the very heart of fire lived inside of it. And my heart gave a struggling little pulse of heat in reply.

SIX

A BRINY TANG SALTED THE AIR LONG before I crested a ridge that overlooked the bustling port city of Tevros. A vast bay sparkled in the midday sun. Docks poked out from the wharf surrounded by a profusion of vessels, from humble fishing boats to fat merchant ships, all with blinding white sails.

I pushed a hand against my galloping heart. For a minute, the fog that had clouded my mind since leaving Arcus lifted. I'd once asked if he would show me the sea someday, a longing I'd had since childhood, when the farthest I'd traveled was to the next village. Arcus had agreed, but now I was seeing it without him. What would he have pointed out to me, if he were here? What might he see that I would miss?

Even with the rocky headlands jutting out on both sides, the sheer mass of water amazed me. Staring at it gave me a feeling of insignificance. Once aboard the ship, I would be nothing more than a grain of sand on a piece of driftwood, tossed about by that infinity of churning and thrashing.

I sighed and continued down a winding footpath. I tried, for the hundredth time, to rub the ache in my chest with the heel of my hand. It felt like a thorn was rooted there, a little to the left of my breastbone, somewhere soft and tender where it would fester. Each word Arcus had said to me in that final conversation kept echoing in my head, the feeling of our kiss imprinted on my lips and in my blood. *He said there'd always be a place for me.* I told myself that, especially when I started imagining the worst—that he might cut me out of his memories, unwinding the threads of shared experiences that bound us, and freezing out the parts of his heart he'd told me, in that tender moment at the ball, that I'd melted.

I took a shuddering breath and dropped my hand. Hearts didn't explode, no matter how much it might feel like it. The pain would ease, eventually. And I couldn't second-guess my decision to leave. It served no purpose.

It was a relief to finally be alone. Brother Thistle had accompanied me, using the ride to discuss details of my mission, right up to the crossroads a mile back, my fork taking me to Tevros, his to Forwind Abbey.

As I'd shifted some of my supplies to his horse, he'd dismounted and surprised me with a quick hug.

"Be careful." He'd put his hands on my shoulders and peered at me intently. "Do not take any foolish risks."

"You take the fun out of everything."

"You will be circumspect in all things. Cautious and calm. You won't lose your temper."

I glanced around. "Who are you speaking to? That certainly doesn't sound like me."

His thick brows moved together like storm clouds gathering above the pale skies of his irises. "I wish I could go with you."

"Well, since you can't, make sure you check in on Arcus, would you? I hate that he's alone with the Blue Legion still lurking around."

"Don't worry, I won't leave him for long. Just until his temper cools. And he has several allies he can trust. I made sure they would watch over him. Focus on your task. And keep safe."

I patted the back of his hand. "You too."

I'd sent my gelding with him, eager to be out of the saddle after three days' ride. We'd had a dozen guards nipping at our heels the whole journey, on Arcus's orders, but I'd managed to convince them to return to the capital this morning. The previous night, we'd gone to an inn and I'd paid for round after round of ale with the heavy bag of coins the royal purser had given me for the trip. The guards had slumped over their pommels as we rode from the inn to the crossroads, their bleary, bloodshot eyes scanning halfheartedly for trouble. Brother Thistle assured them they could leave me to my own devices.

We both knew a contingent of the king's guard would probably ruffle Kai's feathers. Better I go alone.

Tevros was nothing much to look at. If the gleaming harbor was its face, then the city was its backside, with a tightly packed center hemmed in by cramped and ugly houses perched like squashed hats on scrubby, sloping land. Soon, I was off the hilly footpath and weaving through the busy streets.

I didn't have much experience with cities. It was all so much to take in: noisily rattling carts and painted wagons, baritone-voiced sailors and well-dressed merchants, exhausted-looking parents herding inquisitive children, vegetable stands and storefronts and peddlers. And the smells of fish and sweat and flowers and piss and the sea.

As I passed a shadowed alley, there was a flash of movement, a brush against my leg, and I suddenly felt lighter on one side. It took a second to realize my money purse was gone.

Furious at how easily I'd been robbed, I followed the sound of running feet. When I turned the corner into another alley, I came up short.

There stood the familiar lean form of a ginger-gold-haired, olive-skinned, crookedly smiling man. He was holding a small urchin who thrashed and kicked, a money purse clutched in one small, dirty hand.

"Ah, now what have I caught?" Kai mused calmly. "A tiny fish. But you're too small for the dinner table."

"Let me go!" The voice was high and I realized the pickpocket was a girl, her eyes wide. "Or I'll...I'll tell the constable you're trying to kidnap me."

Kai chuckled. "You wish to clean out our purses, but we're not ready to part with all those shiny coins just yet."

"Just bumped into her by accident," the pickpocket said. "I didn't mean to—"

Kai tsked. "Don't debase yourself with lies, little fish. You're skilled at your vocation, and I appreciate skill. Why don't we test the dexterity of those clever fins? If you catch this coin as it falls, it's yours. If I catch it, we'll find that constable and see if he throws you back into the sea."

Kai took the purse, drew out a coin, and tossed it into the air. It arced high and descended. The girl's hand shot out and snatched it. She grinned, her face flushed with triumph.

Seeing her smile, a bolt of recognition shot through me: a sick little girl on a winter's night when I'd run away from the abbey and ended up at the camp of some refugees who had fled the Frost King's soldiers. The families had been on their way to Tevros to see if they could board a ship and make a new life somewhere else. But the girl had been ill with a fever and a cough. I'd tried to help by finding the right herbs to heal her before the adults had chased me off. I'd often wondered about her, hoping she'd recovered.

I took in the urchin's flushed cheeks and the thick hair escaping from her cap. Her eyes shone with health, no longer bleary with fever, but her face was leaner, her features sharper.

"Kaitryn," I said, remembering her name.

Her eyes widened further. She turned swiftly, but Kai's hand shot out to grab her elbow before she could bolt. "I believe the lady knows you, little fish," he said calmly.

"Kaitryn, it's me, Ruby." I stepped forward and smiled reassuringly. "I met you when you had a fever. You probably don't remember."

"I remember." She stared at me for a few seconds. "They said you were a Fireblood and you'd get us all killed."

My lips twisted. "Well, I hope that last part wasn't true." I continued to smile, wishing she didn't look so scared. Or was that resentment in her gaze? "I'm so glad you recovered and made it to Tevros."

"Tevros is a hole," she said bluntly. "There's hardly any work here, and no ships will take us anywhere without the coin. My parents spent all their money on herbs to cure my lungs. Then my father got sick. Least, that's what my mother calls it, but he changed into someone else overnight. Went wild for no reason. One day, he killed someone in a fight. Went to prison and died a week later."

I felt the blood leave my face. "Kaitryn, I'm so sorry." There was no doubt that her father had been possessed by the Minax. Which meant that in freeing it, I had ruined her family.

She shrugged off my sympathy, but the pain in her eyes was unmistakable.

I turned to Kai. "Give the purse back to her." He looked at me quizzically for a moment, then shrugged and offered it up.

Kaitryn's eyes went wide. "Really?"

"You need it more than I do," I said.

Her hand flashed out, and the purse disappeared quickly into some hidden pocket in her patched and baggy vest.

"This will keep us fed for weeks," she said, eyes bright. "Months."

"Listen, Kaitryn," I said impulsively, "I'm about to go on a voyage and I'm thinking life aboard a ship would be better than life on the streets. Why don't you come with me?"

She looked up at me, her eyes narrowed thoughtfully, but then a chorus of young voices came from the street and her eyes widened again. "One of the gangs. They don't like me poaching here. Time to go."

"Kaitryn, wait, I'd like to help you if—"

But she was as slippery as the nickname Kai had given her, a little fish that slid from his grasp and disappeared into the crowd. I rushed into the street, but she was gone.

"A friend of yours?" Kai asked as he followed me. I scanned the forest of heads, but Kaitryn was nowhere to be seen.

As we walked toward the wharf, I told him the barest details of my first meeting with Kaitryn, lengthening my strides to keep up with his.

"Ah, the little fish has had a hard time of it." I was surprised at his regretful tone, which made me like this arrogant stranger just a little bit more. "I would have offered her a place on the ship if she'd stayed."

"Really?"

He shrugged. "Why not? Either way, she's gone. Along with

your purse." He looked at me askance. "Did no one teach you to guard your gold?"

"I'm not used to having anything to steal. Speaking of, I believe this is yours." I slid the ring off my finger and he took it, our fingers brushing briefly. Though his skin was hot, I shivered slightly. It was still so strange to feel skin the same temperature as mine.

We turned a corner and suddenly we were on the timber-floored wharf set against a sparkling blue-green harbor.

I followed Kai through a moving maze of seafaring folk. They marched past carrying barrels or crates, sold fresh fish from rickety stalls, and played noisy games of dice. Here and there, families and sweethearts said good-bye before boarding ships. A young couple embraced, looking as if they never wanted to let each other go. I swallowed and turned away. I didn't need to witness anyone else's good-byes. I'd just endured one of my own.

We stopped at a scarred wooden door with a faded sign bearing what appeared to be a rotund weasel smoking a pipe.

"The Fat Badger," Kai said with a flourish. "Where no one asks questions as long as your pockets are deep. Lucky for you, I didn't give my money away."

"And how did you get your hands on Tempesian money?"

His brow twitched up. "Does it really matter?"

It didn't. He could be a thief or a charlatan, but he was still my ticket to Sudesia.

There were only a few quiet patrons in the tavern—a man and woman talking over a meal at a small round table, a few people at a long wooden bar. A pulse of cold air signaled that at least one of the patrons might be a Frostblood.

A strange feeling came over me—dizziness and a prickling on the back of my neck. "Not now," I muttered. This was no time to be thrust into a vision. But none came. Only an unsettled feeling, as if unseen bees hummed their way around the room, waiting for a chance to sting.

A stocky barmaid wearing a dirty smock over a heavily patched dress brought two bowls of stew to our table.

"Extra pepper, just how you like it," she said to Kai. "Do you need anything else, love? Anything at all?"

Kai grinned. "Not now, thanks, Inge." He gave her a wink, making her cheeks redden. I wondered if she knew he was a Fireblood. And whether it would matter to her either way, considering the strength of that blush.

"Tempesian food is so bland," Kai muttered as she left, poking at his stew with his spoon.

My mouth was too full to reply. A hot meal was welcome after the hard cheese, dried meat, and stale bread I'd eaten for the past three days.

Out of the corner of my eye, I caught the man at the small table staring at me. But when I lifted my head to meet his gaze, he wasn't looking at me at all. Then from my left, I saw heads from the bar angle toward me. But when I turned toward them, they were hunched over their tankards or chatting with the barmaid.

As I looked back at Kai, I saw that he held a knife, the serrated blade pointing toward me. I reared back.

But then I blinked, and it wasn't a knife. It was a spoon, frozen halfway to his lips. One of his brows lifted in inquiry. "Something wrong?"

The buzz in the back of my mind rose to a roar. It was joined by dark, tinny laughter that I knew, I knew, I knew.

Nononononono.

"We have to get out of here," I said. Or I tried to, but my tongue felt thick in my mouth, the muscles too tight.

"What?" Kai asked. "What did you say?"

"True vessel," said the resonant, bell-like voice that had once echoed from the throne. It was bigger now, stronger. But smoother, too. More controlled. More convincing as it chimed with soft words I longed to hear.

"Ah, how you hurt inside," it crooned. "Pain. Loneliness. Grief. Tearing you apart. So unnecessary. So wrong for you. For us."

I shook my head, breathing shakily. The Minax's mind touched mine, stirring up all my sadness and loss and siphoning it away. Replacing it with heady relief. When I glanced at the people at the bar again, they were all looking at me.

They all hated me. They wanted to kill me. They were rising from their seats, drawing knives from sleeves or pockets or boots. Moving closer.

"Ruby," a voice said, the accent pronounced. "Ruby! What's wrong?"

I turned to see Kai, and two images phased in and out, first a look of concern on his face, then a look of killing fury. His hand held a knife, then it didn't. Knife, no knife. Concern, hatred. Danger, safety.

And it was the arena all over again, the sense of life or death, the longing to live, the relief that darkness was taking over. Feelings no longer mattered. All the pain I'd felt over leaving Arcus conveniently faded away.

"They will kill you," said the voice in my head. "They are all against you. They will plunge their knives into your flesh and rejoice in your blood spilling on the floor."

Joyous darkness pulsed. How breathtaking, how enticing, how irresistible. Lost in its caress, I let it flow over me and envelop me like a sweetly clinging fog.

"We will destroy them. Trust only me."

The world lost color and I was filled with stark power. I could see my opponents' beating hearts. I fought against the impulse to cease that beating, grasping at sanity as I might grasp at the edge of a cliff to avoid plummeting to my death. But my enemies were all rushing at me now and it was live or die. Them or me.

"Ruby!" Kai yelled. "What are you—"

My hand, which no longer belonged to me, threw out fire. A man convulsed as heat filled his chest, his eyes rolling to show the whites. He fell and landed on his back, his head hitting the floor. His fingers twitched, his head turned to the side, and he was still.

Screams and chaos. A strobe of sunlight as the door opened. People rushing out. Someone's hands on my wrists, holding my arms to my sides. A voice shouting at me in another language.

And all the while the whisper in my head told me I'd done well, filled me with light-headed glee. Softened the edges of everything. And laughed.

I laughed, too. I couldn't stop.

Harsh swearing in my ear and hands on my upper arms, shoving me toward the door. I whipped around, gathered my heat, and focused on the beating heart of my captor. The Fireblood, his center pulsing white with heat.

He grabbed my wrists and squeezed. "So you're going to try to kill me, too?" He searched my eyes. "What's wrong with you? What happened in there? Ruby!"

His firm but gentle grasp, or perhaps the shock of his temperature being so similar to my own, somehow brought me back to awareness. Something frayed and snapped. The darkness faded, tendrils of shadow lifting into the air, leaving me bereft and grieving and alone. I sagged toward the floor.

Arms caught me in a tight hold, hauling me back up. I shook my head, trying to clear it.

Kai. That was his name. His face was flushed, his arms hot around me, his expression horrified.

"I—I didn't mean to . . ." I turned to look behind me. The bar was empty except for the barmaid and a woman wailing over the still figure of the man.

The man I'd killed.

"Sud, no. No!" I invoked the goddess of the south wind to help me. This couldn't be happening.

But then the man on the floor moaned and coughed. The

woman bent over him sobbed in relief. "Thank Fors you're alive," she said brokenly.

Relief overwhelmed me. But, oh Sud, what had happened? Had the man tried to kill me? Or was that all in my head?

"Call the constable!" the woman screamed. "That filthy Fireblood tried to kill my husband!"

Kai yanked me out the door into the confusion of the wharf. His hand was clamped on the back of my neck.

"Where are you taking me?" I asked, pulling against his hold.

He dragged me into an alley and pushed me up against the side of a building. "Why did you try to kill that man? Tell me!"

I shook my head violently. "He had a knife!"

"He was just *sitting* there! Did you recognize him? Did he hurt you before?"

"No." I was trembling all over. So cold. "It must have followed me somehow. I don't know."

"What? What followed you?"

"The *curse*. Please, please, just take me away before it comes back." And to my horror, I found I was sobbing.

There was a long silence. And then I was being pulled along the wharf to one of the creaking docks. A short, wide-shouldered man wearing a cap helped me into a rowboat and Kai climbed in after me. They spoke in lilting Sudesian, and the burly man began to row with steady strokes.

We moved into choppy water, around the headland, and into a cove. A ship nestled there, its front covered by the figurehead of a wide-eyed young woman with flowing carved hair that streamed onto the sides of the ship. She looked as startled and as lost as I felt.

A couple of sailors threw out lines and secured the rowboat, then tossed out a rope ladder. When I reached the top, I dropped to the floor—or rather, the deck. I'd read about ships enough to know that much. I listened to Kai shouting orders, then the creak of chain as they hauled up the anchor.

The wind caught the sails and spray arced over the ship's side, shockingly cold on my fear-heated skin. I pushed to my feet and scrambled to the railing. As we curved around the jut of land that bordered the harbor, the docks and wharf grew smaller and smaller and slipped out of sight. Eventually even the land was nothing more than a series of inky smears on parchment left by the fingers of a child.

I stood there for a long time and watched Tempesia fade from a violet-gray blur into the flat, blue horizon—leaving everything I'd ever known behind.

SEVEN

WHEN I WAS DONE HEAVING OVER the railing and my legs felt like wet straw, Kai led me to a small cabin where I promptly crawled into bed and fell asleep.

Sometime later, he came back wearing fresh clothes: fawn breeches, black boots up to the knee, and a loose-fitting white shirt. The lamplight made highlights and shadows out of his angular features and tinted his hair a deeper orange. He held a metal tray with a cup and a wooden bowl that steamed.

"Eat," he said, plunking the tray on a small table next to a chair, both of them bolted to the floor. "I think your sickness has passed."

The cabin was so small I could make it from one end to the other in a single leap. Not that I felt like leaping. Or moving at all. I considered pulling the covers over my head and going back to sleep. Instead, I forced myself to sit up.

"Thank you," I said quietly.

"It's just pottage with turnips. You won't thank me once you've tasted it."

"No, I mean thank you for bringing me aboard after..."

He leaned against the wall and crossed his arms. "If that man had attacked you, I would have fought alongside you. But he did nothing. You didn't answer me when I told you to stop. You were like a wild thing. An animal."

I shuddered. "I know."

His eyes were hooded. "You claim there is a curse."

I'd forgotten I'd said that. I flapped a hand in the air to cover my anxiety. "It won't make sense to you. You won't believe me."

He hesitated. "Your eyes are the color of honey in the sun, but when you looked at me in the tavern, the color was gone. Your terror was genuine. Tell me what scared you, and I will try to believe you."

To buy some time while I considered what to say, I took a bite of pottage and grimaced. If Kai thought Tempesian food was bland, I didn't know how he could stomach this. I put the bowl back on the tray. "It's a long story."

He folded himself into the chair next to the bed, crossing his outstretched legs at the ankle and folding his arms. "The journey is long. There is time."

Brother Thistle had cautioned me not to tell the queen my

reasons for coming to Sudesia. It stood to reason I shouldn't go around blabbing my plans to anyone else. Kai might seem like an ally, but I barely knew him. So I gave him an altered version of events.

"I had to fight for my life in the arena," I said, searching for partial truths that he would accept. "I had to kill people."

"Yes, I know this."

"Even though it was necessary to my survival, I sometimes feel the burden of what I've done. Sometimes I even feel like a... a dark presence has taken hold of me."

"What kind of presence?" he asked, leaning forward with his elbows on his knees.

"I have memories of those fights that are so real, it's as if I'm reliving them. For a few moments... sometimes... I can't tell what's real."

I watched his face, gauging his reaction. I had to be careful not to tell him things that would make him distrust me, but at the same time, a part of me wanted to unburden myself. Part of me still wanted absolution for what I'd done, even though I'd had no choice. The death of Clay—the boy from my village whose rebellion against King Rasmus had landed him in the arena—wasn't my fault, but it still haunted me. And the eyes of Captain Drake's wife and daughter as I stood over his bloodied corpse flashed into my mind at odd moments. I told Kai, and he listened quietly with a neutral expression.

"So you had a flashback in the tavern?" he asked.

"I . . . The man must have reminded me of someone I'd fought in the arena."

It hadn't been a flashback, though. The Minax had made me see things that weren't there. No wonder there had been so many murders. It must trick people into thinking they are under attack, filling their minds with hallucinations.

"But you said something had come for you. A curse. You begged me to take you away before it came back."

I grasped at the first explanation that came to mind. "There are times I believe I've been cursed for what I've done. And I want to escape that curse and start over."

There was truth in that. I wanted to be free of the Minax. I wanted to discover what my life would be like without the creature's consciousness affecting my thoughts and dreams, ruining my sleep and my peace of mind with guilt and disturbing memories.

His expression was serious, lips firm, eyes a little wary as he said, "And what happens if you encounter someone else who reminds you of an old opponent? Will you attack that person, too?"

I shook my head and spoke with conviction. "Those flashbacks are connected to Tempesia. When I'm in a new place, those memories will fade."

I hoped that was true, that I was leaving my visions behind. I was on a ship sailing south on the Vast Sea. Surely I'd be safe from the Minax with that much distance between us. And when I returned to Tempesia, I'd be armed with the knowledge, and hopefully the means, to destroy it.

Suddenly I felt lighter. Calmer.

"Are you sorry you brought me along?" I braced for him to tell me that I was too dangerous to be on his ship.

His eyes narrowed thoughtfully, but he didn't answer right away. I burrowed into the covers and watched the lantern light flicker against the ceiling.

He made a sort of thoughtful humming noise and stood up, stretching his arms, pressing his long-fingered hands against the low ceiling, then smoothing his shirt back into place and tugging on his cuffs. His keen gaze came to rest on me. "I'm not sorry I brought you. I understand wanting to leave your past behind. And you have survived things even I cannot imagine."

"Thank you," I said again, nearly weak with relief. "I know you could have taken me to the constable."

He leaned his leg against the bed and gave a wolfish half smile. "Do you really think I'd have taken my little bird to the constable?"

"I'm grateful to you, Kai. But I am neither yours nor a little bird."

"But you look like one. Lost and alone in your nest." He picked up a few strands of my hair and let them fall, laughing as I narrowed my eyes at him. "And it's so easy to ruffle your feathers."

"Don't make it sound as if you brought me along out of pity. I haven't forgotten that you told our attackers in the garden that I could help get something you need."

"They want you in Sudesia, and I'm bringing you. Why shouldn't I receive something in exchange for my trouble?"

"Who wants me?"

He hesitated. "Queen Nalani and her husband, Prince Eiko."

The prospect of the queen's attendance at the ball, though unlikely, had been monumental enough. The idea that she actually cared about my existence, had even sent someone to bring me to her kingdom, was too much to contemplate.

As a child, my grandmother had told me stories about the magnificent Queen Nalani, beloved by all Firebloods. In my daydreams, she was warm, unguarded, intimidating but fair. It was a fantasy, I knew, and yet a seed of that belief had remained. Whatever her failings, I was sure she wouldn't be like King Rasmus—a twisted and power-hungry warmonger.

Unless the other Minax was inhabiting her throne and warping her mind.

"What is she like?" I asked, fearing the answer.

"She's not someone you want as an enemy," he answered, then added with amusement, "Don't look so worried. She is a good queen. She cares about her people."

I let out a relieved breath. "What would she want with me?"

He shrugged. "Do you think she tells me everything?"

I lifted my brows. "Surely you can guess."

His lips quirked. "You're very modest for a Fireblood, you know. It's not that mysterious, Ruby. You destroyed the frost throne. You're a person worth knowing."

I tried to maintain my skepticism, but it was hard. I suddenly wanted to meet the queen more than anything. "How do you even know her?"

He narrowed his eyes thoughtfully. "My parents are . . . I suppose in Tempesian, the closest words are 'prince' and 'princess.' "

"You're related to the queen?"

"No, it's not like that. Each island is a principality, though the queen rules above all. My father is the prince of a small island."

"So why did she send *you*?"

"Because I've sailed the Vast Sea, I speak excellent Tempesian, and I have experience handling conflicts with Frostblood ships."

"I wasn't aware we were officially at war with Sudesia," I said doubtfully.

"We aren't. The conflicts have been more . . . opportunistic in nature. Merchant ships on their way back from the Coral Isles that were too heavy with cargo for their own good. I did them the favor of lightening their loads."

My mouth fell open. "You're a pirate!"

His eyes crinkled at the corners. "It's not piracy if it's sanctioned by one's own queen. 'Privateer' is the correct term, but I prefer to think of it as commerce. Unfortunately, the Tempesian navy has caught on and has made things rather difficult lately. All the merchant ships are heavily guarded now."

"Have you killed people?" I asked, trying to decide what I thought about this revelation. "If they resist?"

"Tempesian captains are surprisingly cooperative when their ships are threatened with fire." He moved to the door. "Get some sleep. Tomorrow I'll have one of my crew start teaching you Sudesian. It's time for you to learn your native tongue."

If he hadn't sounded so condescending, I would have admitted I'd been learning Sudesian for weeks with Brother Thistle. As it was, his tone put me on the defensive. "My native tongue is Tempesian."

He made a clicking sound of disappointment. "A Fireblood who speaks Tempesian is like a barking cat. A curiosity and perhaps rather amusing, but somewhat ridiculous."

"You're speaking Tempesian right now." I gave him a sweet smile.

"But like so many things, I do it exceptionally well." He eyed me with a suggestively raised brow. "Good night, little bird."

The world was tilting.

Dipping and rising and twisting in every direction.

And I was sliding off.

I grabbed at tufts of grass, my fingers burning as I tried desperately to hang on. Then the land froze under my palms, flat and smooth—merciless perfection without a single flaw or crack to hold on to. Above me, a velvet black sky.

Then the darkness of the sky shaped itself, forming pointed shoulders and a wickedly sharp crown. Shadow arms spread out to the sides, as if the night itself stood ready to embrace me—or devour me. I scrabbled at the icy ground until my fingers bled, which made the surface slicker, my slide faster. I could only watch as the world rose up and crashed down, the ground heaving to tip me right into the gaping maw of the monster.

A voice called my name. The scene in my mind faded as warm arms slid around my waist. Rain drove into my back like a thousand freezing needles. I opened my eyes and rubbed away the streaming rain. I was leaning over a railing while green-black water churned below.

It took a moment for my mind to clear. I'd been dreaming. Somehow I'd found my way on deck. And it had seemed as if I'd been about to throw myself over the side. I shivered violently.

Kai yanked me away from the railing as the whole world shook like a rattle in an infant's furious grip, everything creaking and groaning in protest. Another violent heave sent us both sliding along the main deck.

Bursts of lightning crawled across a midnight-blue sky befouled by a haze of sickly green at the horizon. The sails were furled but for one that juddered in the wind.

The ship rode up the incline of a wave in a long, ponderous slide, then perched atop the crest for a brief eternity before tipping over the edge, careening nose down to plow into the trough. I screamed as a mountain of water crashed over the bow and sluiced the deck, slamming into us so hard we hit the side of a raised deck. If not for that barrier, the water would have taken us with it as it swept over the edge.

As I wiped my streaming eyes, I saw that Kai held a rope in one hand, which I let him tie around my waist, his fingers slipping on the wet strands. He finished just in time for another slam of our bow into another nightmarish trough, another sweep of choking green water.

"Jaro looks tired. I need to take the helm!" Kai said before disappearing up the steps.

I turned to watch him approach the sailor who held the wheel. Lightning illuminated Kai as he relieved Jaro, his sodden white shirt glowing, his hair slicked against his skull and gleaming like polished mahogany, his normally bronzed skin bleached of color. The wheel bucked in his hands like a prize bull as we reached the crest of another wave. The lean muscles of his arms strained to keep it under control.

Another dive, another sluicing, another climb, and the older sailor who had been at the wheel appeared next to me. He had a broad face and thinning black hair sprinkled with silver; it was tied with a cord at the nape of his neck. His shirt and breeches had patches upon patches, all heavy and soaked. He pointed emphatically. "Go back in the cabin!"

But now that I was on deck, I didn't want to go back to the stuffy confines of the cabin. The sensation of being trapped still lingered from the nightmare. When I shook my head, the sailor gave an almost imperceptible shrug and braced himself next to me as the ship hit another trough, and another torrent of water scoured the deck.

Every once in a while, I forced my legs to support me so I could steal a look at Kai. His arms shook, his face was carved of granite, and his cheekbones stood out sharply beneath his skin. His eyes were forward, his focus unwavering. He fought to keep the bow pointed straight into wave after wave as the sea pummeled us with briny fists, until everything that existed in the world was wet and salt and aching cold.

It was futile, the ship's struggle against the sea. The storm seemed infinite, unstoppable. I feared that eventually Kai would make a mistake and we would be lost, spun to a splintering, churning death.

What would Arcus think if I never returned? Would he assume I'd chosen to stay away, that I'd forgotten him? The thought made my chest ache. Or would he know that I'd never leave him willingly? Then again, how would he know that? Despite his pleading with me to stay—or at least the closest thing he'd ever come to pleading—I'd left. That's all he would remember.

As always, my mind returned to practical matters. Arcus was far away and I was here. If there was any way to survive, I would find it. I wiped the mix of rain and sea spray from my eyes, first checking on the waves and sky, then Kai. He looked the same: still at the helm, still focused straight ahead.

But the waves were not as high, the wind not so fierce, the sky not quite as dark. Hours or eons after the onset of the storm, the dome above turned from indigo to pink-tinged gray. The crew spread out over the deck and scurried into the rigging, checking masts and yards and sails. Another sail was unfurled. Kai barked a tired command and received a reply. I turned to see him leave the wheel in someone else's hands, weaving a little as he stepped away.

I fumbled at the rope around my waist with numb fingers, cursing as they slid off. A shadow fell over me.

Kai didn't speak. He merely went down on one knee, pulled a knife from his boot, and began sawing at a section of rope. His hands trembled. Hours of holding the ship's wheel must have taken their toll.

As the rope fell away, he looked me straight in the eye, and I tensed, preparing for a tongue-lashing. Instead, his voice was calm.

"I see you've met Jaro. He's particularly fond of waifs and strays. He'll cluck over you like a mother hen, but at least he'll do it in Tempesian. He used to sail on a merchant vessel in my grandfather's time."

"My lady," said Jaro, stepping forward with a courtly bow. As he bent over, water ran from his hair down his forehead and dripped off the end of his nose. If I'd had the energy, I might have laughed at how incongruous it was: a grizzled sailor bowing like a courtier to a peasant who had tried and failed to be a lady.

"And, Ruby?" Kai said, meeting my eyes.

"Yes?"

"Next time, stay in the cabin."

EIGHT

BY THE END OF THE WEEK, I KNEW the mainmast from the foremast, the mainsail from the topsail, port from starboard, fore from aft, and the main deck from the quarterdeck. It reminded me of Forwind Abbey in the sense that everything had its place, though the names were different. Instead of kitchen, refectory, dormitory, cellarium, and reredorter, on a ship they were called the galley, mess, forecastle, hold, and head.

Jaro and his twelve-year-old daughter, a scrawny, perpetually active ship's girl named Aver, provided endless lectures on seafaring, including how to judge if the sails were balanced, how to navigate using an astrolabe, how to tie a multitude of knots, how to mend a sail or a rope, and how to protect a section of rope from chafing. If it had anything to do with a rope, Jaro knew about it. Sometimes, when he droned on too long, I wished he knew a bit less.

Jaro was delighted when he realized I already knew the basics of Sudesian. He included language lessons in each activity, teaching me Sudesian as he instructed Aver in Tempesian. Every word was repeated in both languages, and I was free to ask what words meant and encouraged to speak. He was a patient teacher, though he couldn't resist laughing at my more hilarious mistakes.

Every day, Kai conducted an inspection with the boatswain, a stern-faced woman named Eylinn. The crew snapped to attention, fixing anything that was out of place. It was clear they respected their commanders. Eylinn only spoke Sudesian, but she always nodded civilly to me.

After a couple of weeks, I concluded that time passed differently at sea.

Some hours moved slowly, inching along in dreadful monotony, like when I was helping with some mundane task such as peeling potatoes in the galley. That's when thoughts of Arcus would intrude, and longing would roar through my blood like a marauding invader, leaving me breathless and sick to my stomach. I tortured myself with memories: how giddy I'd felt when he'd danced with me at the ball, our searing kiss in the ice garden, the moment when he'd told me I'd melted his heart. All the times I'd thieved looks at him from some inconspicuous corner when he was occupied with the business of being king. And then, in sharp contrast, the agony of our last conversation would play itself over and over in my head in bits and pieces, moments of pain sticking in my mind like needles.

I wondered if he thought of me, or if he'd managed to obliterate me from his mind. When my homesickness was at its worst, I almost wished I could do the same.

On the other hand, some hours passed quickly, like in the evening when the weather was fair and the sailors had time to indulge themselves with music played on pipe or fiddle, with the rest of the crew adding lyrics to the tune. Some were jaunty, high-spirited reels that made me want to leap to my feet and dance, and others were mournful ballads that made my eyes fill with tears, even if I couldn't understand all the words. It was cathartic to cry, and though I tried to be inconspicuous, others were matter-of-fact when they broke down, as if tears were an accepted part of life. Sudesians were clearly more comfortable losing control in front of others.

Normally Kai didn't participate in these evenings. As captain, he kept himself aloof from his crew. But one night, about two weeks into the journey, he came to sit in the circle of lantern light on deck.

Jaro nodded at him. "A tale for us, Captain?" To me, Jaro added, "He tells a good story."

"What would you like to hear?" Kai asked with a smile.

After a brief and friendly argument among those present, with Aver weighing in most vocally, they settled on the story of Neb and the birth of her children, the wind gods. Kai wrapped his arms loosely around his bent legs and cleared his throat. Even though my Sudesian vocabulary was limited, I knew the old myths well enough to fill in the gaps.

“In the jagged and untamed youth of the world,” Kai began, his voice as deep and rich as honeyed cakes, “when Neb first opened her eyes, she found a blank land and a vast darkness overhead. Having nothing but herself, she pulled the teeth from her mouth and threw them into the dark one by one. They hovered there, becoming stars, even as new teeth grew.

“The smooth earth didn’t please her, so she pulled out a strand of hair and threw it to the ground. A tree grew in its place. Then she pounded the land with her fists until it splintered into mountains and valleys. She sat in the shadow of a mountain to rest, and her tired sigh became the air that stirs the leaves.” He exhaled and gestured to show the breath turning to air.

“But the spirits of the land that had slept under the surface were angry at being pummeled thus. One rock spirit rose up from the center of the earth, and he threw handfuls of stones at Neb. Though he raged, she saw in his eyes that the rocks covering his skin gave him pain, so she struck him on the shoulders, arms, and back until the stony armor fell from him, littering the world with boulders and pebbles. Neb put a hand to his shoulder. . . .”

I jumped a little as Kai laid a hand on my shoulder, the tips of his fingers inadvertently tickling the sensitive skin where shoulder meets neck. As he was merely adding actions to the story, I sat placidly instead of shrugging him off.

“She reveled in the feel of vulnerable flesh, like her own,” he continued, not looking at me, though I sensed his attention. “The rock spirit thanked her and said he’d been trapped in the earth for so long, he no longer knew his name. Neb named him Tempus, for he was the beginning and the end of time for her."

Kai squeezed my shoulder lightly before his hand slid away.

"And for a time, they were happy. Neb's belly grew round and her child was brighter than the stars. But Sun was an adventurous child, and one day she wandered too close to the edge of the world. She fell into the sky, tumbling out of reach, hovering eternally to shine her light on the land."

The ship rolled over a swell and the lanterns swung, then righted themselves.

"Sun would not come home no matter how Neb pleaded, and Neb could not fetch her daughter, who had become too bright and hot to touch. So Neb cried for the first time, her tears forming oceans, while Tempus's tears were molten rock, pouring into the center of the earth and spewing through cracks in the ocean bed to form new lands. In her grief, Neb pulled out her eyelashes, and where they scattered, plants and small animals came to life.

"Neb and Tempus retreated from each other," Kai continued, "she into the mountains and he below the rocky earth. But Neb was already carrying their second child, and her birthing cries drew her husband from his hiding place. Tempus held his newborn child and named him Eurus, giving him the name of the East, where the babe's lost sister rose into the sky every morning.

"Neb took leaves and branches and wove them into dolls as toys for her son. But in his boredom, he pulled them apart, and Neb had to keep making new ones. So instead, she gave him a fan made of palm leaves and Eurus used it to create the east wind."

Eerily, a breeze lifted the lax sails at that moment. Aver gasped and then laughed. Kai grinned at her.

"You see? Eurus himself enjoys our tale."

Jaro frowned and Kai chuckled. "Or perhaps it is Sud who tickles our sails as she waits for her turn in the story. Tempus and Neb had a third child, and they called her Cirrus. She was gentle and kind, and her laugh made the first music. The proud parents sat for hours pulling fruit from trees to feed her and watching their daughter wander over hills and valleys, delighting in everything she touched. She made the land more fertile wherever she stepped.

"But in their joy, they forgot about their second child. Eurus saw that their love for Cirrus was greater than their love for him. So he set a trap for his younger sister.

"'Follow me to the top of the northern mountain,' said Eurus, 'where our lost sister, Sun, tints the sky pink every night before sleep.' So Cirrus, eager to see the sister she had never known, followed her brother to the summit. When she reached out to try to touch Sun, Eurus used the palm frond to make a gust of wind. Cirrus lost her footing on the loose rocks and fell toward the ground far, far below.

"But it was all right," Kai reassured Aver, "because Sun saw her sister falling and bent her light in the north, making many colors dance across the sky as a warning to their parents. Tempus and Neb looked up to see their young daughter falling and threw her a palm frond. Cirrus caught the fan and used it to make a west wind that lifted her back to the top of the mountain.

"When they realized what Eurus had tried to do, Tempus and

Neb were furious. Tempus picked up his son and threw him as far as he could until Eurus fell to the rocky shores of an island."

Another gust of wind filled the sails harshly, as if a giant hand had punched them.

Jaro frowned and shook his head, but Kai continued his tale. "Eurus lived there for a timeless time, all alone, and when—"

"He deserved to be alone," Aver said, her face pinched in a scowl. "After what he tried to do to his sister."

"Indeed," said Kai. "He deserved to suffer for that."

Again, the wind swirled for a few seconds but then died completely. We all looked up to see the sails slack for the first time in weeks.

"It's bad luck to invoke the name of the east wind while at sea," Jaro whispered.

"You don't really believe that," I said, but I found myself nearly whispering, too. As if some unseen hostile ear might catch the words. After all, according to the legends, the god of the east wind was the creator of the Minax, and I certainly believed in its existence.

Jaro scrambled to his feet. "If the wind gods withhold their gift, we'll remain here, becalmed and helpless. It's no way for a sailor to die, starving at sea with—"

"That's enough, Jaro," said Kai, affectionate but firm. "We'll finish the tale another night."

Aver whined and pleaded for more, but he stayed firm. "Another night."

Aside from a few squalls, the weather was hospitable for the rest of the journey. When I emerged on deck one morning, about four weeks after sailing from Tevros, the islands had grown closer on our port side. A dark, rocky shoreline loomed ahead.

"Land?" I asked, leaning eagerly over the rail.

"The Strait of Acodens," said Jaro in his native tongue. My comprehension of Sudesian had become quite passable over the previous weeks. "This is where Fireblood masters guard the passage night and day, although Frostblood sailors never venture in this far—too many rocks and shifting sandbars for their big ships."

Tall, jagged cliffs blotted out the horizon. As we drew closer, the texture became clear: craggy and pockmarked, as if a bunch of rotted teeth had been jammed into the stone. A narrow ribbon of sea was threaded between two peaks, which leaned toward each other as they soared toward the sky. Outposts were set on ledges high above sea level. Figures in orange tunics moved into view. One of them called out, "Identify yourselves!" Kai gave his name and was greeted with friendly shouts.

It took a few minutes to navigate between the crags looming on either side. Sea spray arced over the deck as it roiled in the narrow gap. Any mistake in steering would result in a breach in our hull. It felt like the entire crew held their breath for the duration.

Once we'd passed through, the tension eased. It was clear from the grins on the crewmembers' faces that we were in the home stretch.

I leaned over the port railing and sucked in a lungful of humid air. The weather flaunted a welcome, sunny heat that made me want to stay on deck all day. It was the first time I'd felt truly warm outdoors. As we sailed south, I could feel the giddy power of the sun thrumming through my blood.

Over the next two days, the space between islands thinned, until we were hemmed in on both sides. Kai had the crew measuring the sea depth at regular intervals.

Then finally, late one day, there was a triumphant cry from Aver sighting the Isle of Sere, the capital. When she cried out the Sudesian word for home, it was one of the most joyous sounds I'd ever heard.

Home. The thought punctured something deep in my chest. I was in the land of my mother and my grandmother. I had longed to see it, even more than I'd ever admitted to myself. And I was here. I had made it.

The crew climbed into the rigging or pressed against the rails, whooping excitedly. A large island took shape, its wide bay backed by emerald hills, and behind that, the haze of several peaks topped with fluffy clouds that seemed to make the sky bluer. The bay was studded with white-sailed vessels bobbing in the turquoise water, mostly small boats, but some larger ships. Excited shouts from shore brought answering waves and smiles from the crew. It suddenly sank in that none of those waves or shouts were for me.

But even so, a kick of delight sizzled through my veins as I took in the sandy shoreline, the intensely green hills, the puff of smoke from a volcano that rose with haughty superiority above the other mountains. Everything looked so lush and jewel-bright, completely different from Tempesia and somehow *more* than anything I'd ever imagined.

If only Arcus were here to see it with me.

NINE

KAI WAS SILENT AS OUR CARRIAGE climbed the swell of a hill with sides draped in a cloak of green, a castle crowning its top. Thick walls connected four towers made of carefully fitted black stones. The style was heavy and square, without any spires or pointed roofs—more like Forwind Abbey than Arcus's ice castle. But though it appeared rather dark and forbidding at first glance, there was a stark beauty about it. The windows were all arched, the crenellations on the towers as delicate as lace edging. Low walls made from red and black stone bordered gardens bursting with impossibly bright flowers.

The dark stone edifice loomed, casting a deep shadow over the circular gravel drive. Trepidation quickened my breathing as the carriage rolled to a stop. I'd dreamed of this moment, but the reality held sharp edges and hidden dangers. The queen was no longer a figure of imagination, but a ruler with complete authority here. I'd put myself entirely in her power and had no idea what she wanted from me.

To cover my anxiety, I hopped from the carriage, ignoring Kai's proffered hand, and strode beside him to the open doors. Guards with silver-and-gold helms, each with an intricately worked halberd, stood at attention on either side of the entrance. Kai must have been well known, because they didn't even blink as we entered.

Shields and weapons covered the walls of the entrance hall. Richly carved tables in a reddish wood held porcelain vases with fragrant white flowers, their heavy blooms bowing their stems.

A courtier appeared and led us down a long sunlit hallway, up a set of winding tower stairs, and past two guards who opened a set of doors leading into a spacious room with a gilded chandelier and silver torches. A red-and-gold carpet echoed gold-fringed drapes the color of garnets, which bracketed doors open to a stone balcony. The breeze perfumed the room with heavy floral scents.

The room was sparsely furnished aside from two sturdy thrones, both of them gold and upholstered in red brocade.

No throne of molten lava. No dark, insidious presence lurking just out of sight. I didn't know whether to be disappointed or relieved.

A thin, dark-haired man in a red satin robe occupied the smaller throne. It had to be the queen's husband. Kai had mentioned him on the ship, but it took me a few seconds to remember his name: Prince Eiko. He faded into the background next to the queen. My attention grazed over him and honed in on her.

Hair as dark as polished walnut flowed in an elaborate braid over her shoulder. A strong, well-shaped nose dominated her face. An elegant neck curved into square shoulders, which were left bare above the bodice of a cherry-wine gown. Reflexively checking for signs of possession, I noted that it was impossible to see the veins at her wrists from several yards away.

Her fathomless eyes came to rest on me.

A thrill ran through me, sending jolts of energy through my body and lifting the hair on my arms. Dream had become reality. I stood only paces away from the queen of Sudesia, ruler of the Firebloods, descendent of the original ruler blessed by Sud.

And yet, it wasn't pure happiness or elation that I felt, but fear. Kai had said the queen had sent for me, but he wouldn't say why. Pestering him for answers had proved futile. I had come willingly, with an agenda of my own, but I was putting my safety completely in her hands. She had all the power here, and I had none.

She beckoned us forward.

Kai had taken my hand at some point and woven it through his arm. He led me to a spot several feet from the throne and stopped. He bowed low at the waist, and I sank into my best curtsy, the one Doreena had made me practice over and over before my first dinner with the Frost Court.

The queen just stared at me silently. I felt her assessment in my bones.

Her attention shifted to Kai. Her nostrils flared, and when she spoke, each word was like a stone dropping into a still pond. "What have you done?"

Kai took a breath before answering. "I did as you instructed, Your Majesty. I found a way to avoid the Tempesian blockade, and then I infiltrated the Frost Court to find her."

"And this is the girl?" She flicked her hand at me.

"Her name is Ruby Otrera," he replied evenly.

Her expression remained stony. "Your task was clear: Find the girl, relay my offer—that she would eventually receive an invitation to Sudesia if she served as my spy—and then leave her in the Frost Court."

My head whipped toward Kai. He'd been sent to recruit me as a *spy*? If he'd been looking at me, he would have seen the rage in my eyes, but he was looking down with uncharacteristic deference. "I did what I thought was necessary to save her, Your Majesty. Our . . . my plan was flawed."

I wanted to grab him and shake the truth out of him. Instead, I clenched my fists and stared, as the queen might reveal more if she thought I couldn't understand Sudesian.

"How so?" the queen asked coldly.

"She wasn't safe." His eyes flicked up to gauge her reaction, as if he knew this was an important card to play. "Frostblood assassins tried to kill her. They spoke of a group called the Blue Legion, whose aim is to return things to the way they were under King Rasmus."

She huffed. "I see no reason to believe that the new king is any different than the previous one."

Frustration burned in my chest. I yearned to shout that she had no idea what she was talking about, but instead bit the inside of my lip until the skin throbbed.

"We cannot trust her," the queen said.

"Your Majesty," said Kai softly, "I must remind you that she destroyed the frost throne and killed their king."

Not true. It had been Rasmus's obsession with the Minax that had led to his own death—not that correcting the Firebloods would win me any points.

The queen scoffed. "Yet she spared his brother, his successor. And then she remained in his court willingly. If she were a true Fireblood, she would have killed as many Frostbloods as she could before her own life was taken. Her only value to me was in her proximity to the king—a Fireblood spy in the Frost Court—and instead you offer me a girl with stale information."

"I may not have done what you expected, Your Majesty," Kai argued, growing more confident, "but I believe I have given you something more valuable. Instead of risking her life and the loss of an asset, we have her here. We can still use her knowledge against the Frostbloods: their strengths and weaknesses, the inner workings of their court, their plans."

Arcus's warning came back to me in a rush: that I shouldn't trust the lies of a stranger. A sense of betrayal built into white-hot anger in my chest.

The queen considered for a moment. "What are you hoping to gain from this, Prince Kai?"

He took a step forward, his back ramrod straight. "I want my second chance, as agreed."

"You forfeited that when you failed in your task. I should throw you in prison for your disobedience."

Kai's gaze shifted restlessly over me. Emotions flashed across his features—calculation, indecision, resolution—before he spoke. "The new king favors her. He... cares for her. You can use that to your advantage."

My indrawn breath fell sharply into the silence. Heat coursed through my veins, as if searching for a way out.

"How much?" she asked.

"A great deal," said Kai, avoiding my eyes. "She calls him by a pet name. And there are rumors that she is his mistress."

My hands itched to forcefully stop the words emerging from his lying mouth.

Kai continued. "There are also rumors that he intends to make her his queen."

Arcus never said anything like that! It was just talk among servants and courtiers and all the people who resented me and distrusted Arcus. My fury burned so hot, it was close to hatred. Kai was making a fool of me, treating me like a bargaining chip in some game I hadn't known he was playing. And I loathed myself for trusting him.

The queen had an arrested look as she examined me, as if seeing something she'd missed before. I kept my chin up, signaling my defiance. She didn't seem to notice. She was too busy calculating my value the way a money lender weighs gold.

"The king is in love with the girl who melted his throne?" She chuckled richly. "A comic playwright could not produce such outlandish farce. A Frostblood king led into foolishness by his emotions. It is beyond belief."

She bestowed her smile on Kai. "Perhaps I shall pardon you after all. If what you say is true, you've brought me a jewel in the king's crown, so precious to him that he will do anything to secure her safety. I might as well hold his icy heart in the palm of my hand."

At the mention of his heart, my restraint broke. I needed to release the pressure and heat that had built up in my chest, either with fire or words. Considering Brother Thistle's caution about my temper, words seemed safer.

"The king would *never* do anything to harm his people." I spoke in Sudesian, not caring if my speech was imperfect, only that she understood. My voice was low and seething, edged with warning. "You are wrong about him, Your Majesty."

Her brows rose. "So you admit you *are* special to him," she said, gazing at me as approvingly as if I'd just paid her a compliment. "How much are you worth, I wonder? Fifty ships? A thousand? Perhaps a message with our terms will yield some fruit."

She wanted to ransom me for *ships*? "He won't pay. You'll only provoke him." Whether that was true or not, I wanted her to believe it.

"So much the better. Whether he sends ships as payment for

your safety or he sends ships to attack, they would have to get through the Strait of Acodens. Our ships are smaller, but they are faster, more maneuverable. And we have fire. Much more deadly to a wooden vessel than frost is, my dear. Why do you think Frostblood raids on Sudesia have always failed?"

An invisible fist closed over my throat. Surely Arcus wouldn't cave in to her demands?

I'd been so intoxicated by the idea of finding my own people, I'd let myself believe I'd be welcomed with open arms. Instead, the queen was planning to use me to strike at Tempesia, which now suddenly seemed like home. If Arcus responded to her threats with aggression, there could be war. I felt so stupid—small and childish—for walking into their trap.

I knew Arcus, though. He'd think through every eventuality, calculate the danger, and choose caution. He would never risk so much or trust so blindly.

"He would never trade his people's safety for me or any individual," I said, trying to regain my composure, to sound calm and confident.

"He will," Kai countered. "I'd stake my life on it."

I clutched my hands together to keep from blasting him with fire.

"You clearly wish to protect the king," the queen observed. "Perhaps you plan to spy on me and take your information back to him."

"I am no spy. I am not your enemy." I realized my warning about provoking the king had been interpreted as a threat. I took a shaky breath and tried to repair the damage. "The king has no ill intentions toward you. In fact, he has drawn up a peace treaty—"

"Peace?" She leaned forward, her dark gaze so intent that I had an urge to take a step back. "When the Frost Court is wiped out, when Firebloods rule, when the last icy breath is expelled from the very last Frostblood, dissolving in air heated by the fire of *my* people, then, and only then, will we have peace. I vow to Sud that I will not rest, and my heirs will not rest, until that day."

The room had warmed, the air thick and cloying and humid. The queen's wrath was fearsome in its relentless heat. Even to me.

Her words were eerily similar to King Rasmus's, her urge to wipe out Frostbloods much like his campaign against Firebloods. Terrified of what I might find, I put out mental feelers, but I couldn't detect any hint of a menacing presence like the one in the frost throne. If the Minax wasn't causing her bloodlust, then perhaps the queen was even more dangerous than the king had been.

Nothing had gone as expected. I had crossed an ocean to get here, but I was no closer to completing my mission. The queen was furious, and she clearly wanted to take her anger out on me. The mention of peace had only incited her wrath.

I needed to regain some control. Brother Thistle had told me to ingratiate myself with the queen and the masters.

I took half a step forward. "I, too, burned for revenge against the Frostbloods, Your Majesty. I wanted to kill King Rasmus, and now he's dead. Surely that proves something to you? I've done nothing to act against you."

"You came from Tempesia without my permission," she replied coldly. "That is enough to earn you a place in my prison."

"She didn't know our rules, my queen," Kai broke in.

"But *you* did," Queen Nalani snapped. "Imprisonment might teach you about the value of obedience, a lesson you sorely need, Prince Kai."

"Very well, Your Majesty," he said quickly, "but I ask that you give Ruby a chance to prove herself. I beg you and Prince Eiko to consider the matter carefully before you decide."

The man sitting next to the queen—Prince Eiko—leaned toward his wife. "My dearest, I must agree with the boy." His eyes moved from her to me, his long, angular face drawn in serious, almost stark lines. His eyes narrowed speculatively, in a way that I didn't like. "She may be useful to us in some way that is yet unclear."

Queen Nalani turned to him. "What use is she to me here? If the Frost King cares for her, I could never trust her."

"Perhaps if you tested her abilities," Prince Eiko suggested, "you would find out whether she could serve you in some other capacity." Though he argued in my favor, the intensity in his voice was unnerving.

Queen Nalani's gaze shifted back to me. "What prevented you from killing the king's brother—King Arkanus? If you had done so, the succession would have been contested and it would have thrown the kingdom into chaos. Barring that, you could have been my spy. You would have served me better by undermining the Frost Court from within."

"I knew nothing of your wishes, Your Majesty," I said deferentially. It wasn't the time to argue. "Perhaps if you train me in your ways, I would know better how to please you in the future."

"Or how to stab me in the back." Her nostrils flared.

I swallowed the urge to argue. "My loyalty lies with you, Your Majesty. I hate the Frost Court and everyone in it." Except Arcus, I amended mentally.

I bowed my head, feeling Kai's stare on me. I was laying it on a bit thick, but this was no time to let pride or scruples get in the way of saving my own neck. And Kai's, too.

Prince Eiko leaned forward. "Why did you agree to come here, young lady? What did you expect to gain?"

I took a deep breath and met his eyes. "I have dreamed of coming here all my life. My grandmother told me stories of this land and its beauty, of the richness of its culture and its history." That much was true. "I longed to be where Firebloods are valued rather than reviled. I grew up hiding my gift. Then, when my identity was revealed, I was hated and feared. My life was worth nothing to the Frost Court." That was also true.

A silence fell. The queen's gaze seemed to soften. I had aroused her sympathy. I needed to continue while I held the advantage.

I had gathered from conversations on the ship that Fireblood masters were valued highly. Proving my usefulness seemed like a good way to start.

"Perhaps you could test me, as Prince Eiko suggested." I was careful to keep any hint of demand from my tone. "Prince Kai has explained that anyone can attempt the Fireblood trials, no matter their background. Would it be pleasing to you if I became one of your masters?"

A small smile played about her lips. "You speak too sweetly to be trusted, young lady. Though I appreciate how well you anticipate what I want to hear."

I clasped my hands in front of me and met her eyes squarely. "I admire you greatly, and I would do anything to gain your approval." It wasn't hard to say the words. There was truth in them, perhaps more than I'd like to admit to myself. I wanted to gain her trust, to be truly welcome somewhere. To belong.

She turned to her husband. "What do you think, Prince Eiko? What would I gain by granting this request?"

His reply was almost eager. "She managed to destroy the frost throne, which only a powerful Fireblood could accomplish. With training, she could exceed some of your strongest masters. Perhaps Sud has sent us this gift. We would be remiss not to consider such a possibility."

The queen's expression was smooth, but she seemed to weigh his words carefully. Finally, she transferred her attention back to Kai. "Speak, young prince. You always have much to say."

"I have seen her use her fire, and her gift is strong," Kai said. "She could be a valuable addition to the masters." He hesitated before adding in a low, almost urgent, tone, "And it might reveal things about her gifts that could be of great interest."

A crease formed between Queen Nalani's brows. Some silent message seemed to pass between her and Kai.

"And suppose she uses her training and knowledge against us?"

"We risk nothing, as she is here and can be kept contained," Kai answered.

"I would never use my knowledge against you or your kingdom, Your Majesty." No, I would use it to save Tempesia. I needed the knowledge of the masters. Once I found out how to destroy the Minax, I would leave.

She stared at me for a long time, then finally shook her head. "I cannot afford to take unnecessary risks." My heart sank as she continued. "Do not think you will be treated poorly, young lady. I understand that it was Prince Kai who brought you here. But I cannot trust you. You will be kept in my prison until I decide what to do with you."

A drop of sweat trailed down my back. I thought wildly for something that would change her mind. Prince Eiko looked unruffled by her verdict, but Kai showed his agitation with restless movements and quickened breathing.

"Your Majesty, please," Kai began.

The queen held up a hand. "Do not waste your breath, young prince. I will decide an appropriate punishment for your disobedience. Your family's loyalty alone is what saves you from imprisonment as well. You will remain in my castle until I decide what to do. Only a sign from the goddess herself would change my mind at this point."

As the queen frowned at him, a strong gust of wind blew through the balcony doors, lifting the gauzy curtains. The torches bent and flickered. The hot, humid air settled like a blanket over my skin.

The queen looked over in surprise. Prince Eiko turned to her and smiled. "I believe you have Sud's answer, my dear."

She paused for a long moment before nodding. "Indeed, it seems Sud has spoken. I am resolved, then." She had a more relaxed air, as if the tension of uncertainty had drained from her. "Ruby."

"Yes?"

"You will be admitted to the school for assessment and training. If the masters declare you a suitable candidate, I will allow you to take the trials. If you pass, you will be initiated as a Fireblood master and sworn to Sudesia. If you'd go to such lengths to embrace your heritage, that would give you a measure of credibility in my eyes. Perhaps I would even grow to trust you and allow you to live freely here."

The relief was so great, I had to lock my knees to stay upright.

"You risk your life at each stage of the trials. There are sacrifices you may be unprepared for." Her dark eyes held me spellbound. I had the uncomfortable sensation that she could see into my mind, that she was picking apart my motives and seeing the things I was trying to keep hidden.

"You will have to pledge yourself to me if you are initiated as a master," she added. "Your allegiance, your very life, will be mine."

As we left the throne room, Kai led me down the tower stairs and through a long arcade with sun-filled arches supported by thick, round columns.

When we were safely out of view of any courtiers or guards, I turned and gave his chest a shove. "A spy?" I could hardly even get the words out.

He crossed his arms and leaned against a column. "I never actually lied."

"You said the queen had sent for me!"

"I may have... bent the truth to ease your worries. And I knew the queen would welcome you once you were here."

His refusal to admit fault was infuriating. "And that was your idea of a warm welcome?"

"What harm has come to you? If you recall, I said you could train to be a Fireblood master. The queen agreed to let you take the trials. And quite easily, I might add."

"You forgot to mention she would essentially own me if I passed."

His brows rose a fraction. "Everyone knows that the masters are the queen's puppets."

"*I* don't know these things!" Suddenly, I was frustrated with myself for not pressing Kai for more information before and during our journey.

He glanced pointedly out the window at figures in the courtyard. A few curious faces were turned in our direction.

I raised my voice. "And I don't care who hears!"

"Then by all means," he said, more urbane than ever, "let us air your secrets here. I only thought you might prefer to speak of this in the privacy of your room. Go ahead, scream it all in front of the court. They do love a good show."

I sighed and lowered my voice. "Why bring me here if that's not what she wanted?"

"To save your life, for one thing. Not that you've shown a scrap of gratitude."

"Don't make it sound altruistic. You're trying to trade me for a second chance at something."

His chin lifted. "Some of us have to fight for the things that are offered so readily to others."

"Stop wallowing. You're a blasted prince, for Sud's sake."

A flush crept across his cheeks. "You know nothing of Sudesia. Nothing. And until you do, don't presume to judge me, Lady Ruby."

He made it sound like *I* was being unreasonable. I wanted to lash out. Unleash my fire on him. But he could do the same, and more. This was his domain, not mine.

And no matter how furious he'd made me, I was the fool who'd believed him.

He turned, continuing down the corridor at a quickened pace.

"Wait, Kai," I said, wrestling with my temper.

"What?" He didn't stop walking.

"Where is the throne?"

That brought him to a halt. He turned and regarded me with quizzical annoyance. "We just came from the throne room."

"I mean the throne of Sud. Black lava rock, running with molten lava. Massive and intimidating. Sound familiar?"

"That throne was destroyed in a volcanic eruption, along with the old castle and everything in it."

No. This couldn't be happening. I had counted on finding the fire Minax in the throne of Sud.

"When?" I asked.

He shook his head. "I don't know, before I was old enough to remember. Most of the island was evacuated for a time. Everything was rebuilt here. This is the only castle I remember."

I put a hand to my stomach, my shoulders hunched as if I'd just received a body blow. What a fool I'd been. Rushing to Sudesia with little more than a handful of stories and loads of assumptions.

"Ruby, are you all right?" Kai put a hand to my shoulder.

I straightened up, and his hand fell away. "I'm fine. Show me to my room."

It was time to start making new plans.

TEN

I SPENT THE NIGHT IN A GUEST ROOM decorated in blue and gold, with beaded throw pillows, painted vases filled with hibiscus, and lamps made of colored glass. The bed frame was heavy and intricate, with four polished wooden posts at the head and four posts at the foot, all rising to meet elaborate woodwork that ended in a sort of square border, draped in cream silk, at the top.

I lay on the bed but didn't sleep. My thoughts raced.

Despite the shocks and disappointments of the past day, not much had changed. The absence of the throne didn't alter my primary mission. I needed to find the book. It would reveal how to destroy the Minax, and I had to believe there was more than one way to do so. Finding the book meant gaining access to the Fireblood school, which meant taking the trials.

I might actually become a Fireblood master. Whether I was strong enough and powerful enough remained to be seen. But I couldn't fool myself any longer: On some level, I wanted this. I wanted to test my abilities and master them. To prove myself. To be more than I was.

The excitement lasted for a few seconds until I remembered what passing meant: pledging my life to the queen. Giving up my freedom. Following her orders.

I might never see Arcus again.

The Fireblood school was a squat, pillared building made of sun-burnished yellow stone. Vivid pink and red flowers in clay pots softened the linear facade with delicate leaves and round blooms. A gracefully arched doorway led into a courtyard where pairs of students moved in and out of view, their grunts and exclamations mixing with the dissonant music of wooden wind chimes trembling in a light breeze.

A tall man stepped through the doorway and bowed. He had a crooked nose that looked as if it had been broken and healed more than once, rounded cheekbones, and deep grooves carved between his brows. A streak of reddish orange ran through his dark hair, while a sprinkling of gray touched his temples. His hair had been scraped back and secured at the nape of his thick neck.

His eyes moved over me with a kind of focused assessment I'd seen on the faces of hostlers evaluating horseflesh. It was impossible to tell from his closed expression whether I passed muster. At least I'd braided my hair neatly, and a maid had washed my tunic and leggings before laying them out on my bed that morning.

"This is Master Dallr," said Kai, the first words he'd spoken since coming to fetch me for a tense and silent carriage ride. "He is the senior master and in charge of this school."

Master Dallr merely nodded and turned, leading us in. He and Kai exchanged pleasantries while I glanced around. Students from about ten years old to young adulthood were sparring in the large open courtyard, using only their hands and feet as weapons: kicking, punching, blocking, and flipping their opponents. They didn't use fire. After a few minutes, one of the masters—you could tell by her bright orange tunic, while the students wore sunny yellow—gave a loud whistle. Everyone moved back, forming a circle that left the center of the courtyard empty. Another master called out names and two students stepped forward. They bowed, took their positions, knees bent, fists at the ready, and at a command, began to move.

The opponents clearly weren't novices, but they weren't perfect. Some movements were quick and well executed, while others were ill timed or poorly aimed. The master in charge barked corrections and the students made the appropriate adjustments. Then the master said a word I didn't recognize and bolts of flame issued from the students' hands, meeting in the center and flowing toward the sky.

"What did he say?" I asked Kai, who sat to my right, cross-legged on the packed earth. In my curiosity, I'd forgotten I wasn't speaking to him.

"The commands are given in ancient Sudesian," he whispered, only a slight curve of his lips betraying that he noticed I'd broken my silence. "The first word meant 'release.' That next word meant 'spiral,' and this move now is called 'flick.' "

"It looks similar to Tail of the Dragon."

Kai looked intently at me. "That is the combination of spiral and flick. You know it?"

I nodded, absentmindedly making the motions in the air. Brother Thistle had taken great pains to teach it to me those many months ago when I'd struggled to gain even a basic command of my gift.

I noticed someone watching me and turned my head to find Master Dallr staring. "Perhaps our guest is keen to show us her skills in a practice match," he said. Before I could answer, he stood and whistled. The students immediately ceased sparring and bowed before running to sit at the edge of the circle.

"Prince Kai, if you would, please," the master said.

Kai glanced down at his red silk doublet and pristine black leggings.

I snorted. "Worried I'll ruin your pretty clothes?"

He sprang to his feet, his mouth assuming its typical smirk. "Not at all. I merely hope my skill doesn't blind you."

"Your doublet is doing that already."

His eyes crinkled, the gold flecks standing out against the brown, his irises carved from tigereye agate. "If only your attacks are as sharp as your tongue, Lady Ruby. Why don't you show us all what you can do?" He walked backward into the circle, arms spread wide in challenge, and raised his voice. "Behold! The girl who melted the frost throne will honor us with a glimpse of her greatness." And he topped the speech with a sweeping bow.

I looked around anxiously. I'd learned to fight from Brother Thistle and Arcus, matching their frost with my fire. I had no idea how to combat someone who shared my gift. But something about Kai's cocky grin made me determined to surprise him.

"All right. But what if we hurt someone?" I gestured to the spectators.

"We are all Firebloods here," Master Dallr replied. "And we will protect our students."

There were several masters spaced out at intervals in the circle, gazes alert, hands ready. I took a breath and returned Kai's bow before raising my fists.

"Begin," said Master Dallr.

The word still hung in the air as Kai punched out an experimental tongue of flame. I ducked and returned the favor, but missed him by inches. He had already swept a gout of fire at my feet. I jumped over the sheet of flame and sent my own at his chest. He ducked and somersaulted backward, his fists thrusting out twin jets as he regained his stance. One caught my sleeve, setting it alight. I dropped to the ground to put it out, then dodged another attack.

Kai's movements were fast, agile, and unpredictable. I found my mind shutting off and instinct taking over. Attack, jump, twist, duck, counterattack.

I threw out a wide swath of stinging flame. Too late, I realized my attack was curving toward the students. The masters positioned their palms facing me, their fingers pointed at one another, and redirected my fire in an arc around the circle, all hands receiving and shaping the flow of it. I hesitated, marveling at the way they had worked together, the fire controlled so neatly, when a burst of heat crashed into my shoulder, nearly knocking me down. I twisted and whipped out a spiral of flame, twitching it at the end like a whip.

"So you do know Tail of the Dragon," Kai said with a grin, even as a red welt bloomed on his cheek. "But do you know Sud's Hammer?"

A roughly hammer-shaped swirl of flame formed in his hand and came bearing down on me. I leaped out of the way as it slammed the ground, sending up a cloud of white dust.

"Or Fire Blade?" He swished twin razors of flame at me from both sides. With nowhere else to go, I threw myself on the ground, hands over my head. Kai's laughter drifted over me.

"Or Sud's Bowl?" he taunted. Heat surrounded me. I uncovered my head to see myself trapped under an inverted bowl of flame that burned so hot its center held tongues of blue.

It wasn't the blue of frostfire—not nearly so bright. But any hint of blue meant it was hot enough to injure me. Grandmother had once told me that blue flames meant burns even for a Fireblood. Kai's fire was strong, maybe stronger than mine. I needed a way out.

I gathered my heat and threw both arms up, punching a column of fire through the bowl. As I leaped out, Kai twitched to the right—I had noticed that he had a tendency to dodge that direction—and blinked in apparent surprise, giving me a moment before his hand came up to attack.

I sent fire arrows at his face. He turned nimbly and met my

arrows with heat that sent them off course, then clouted me in the chest with a thick bolt of fire.

As I flew backward, I fisted twin vortexes at him, not at where he stood, but curving toward where I anticipated he would move. To his right.

I heard the attack connect, and Kai fall, just as my back met the packed earth, the air leaving my lungs.

"Enough!" Master Dallr shouted. His shadow fell across my face as I gasped for breath. "You are untrained," he said quietly, "but you did not disgrace yourself. Your gift is strong."

It took me a second to realize that the master's hand was held out. I let him pull me up, just as Kai stumbled upright a few feet away, wiping his brow with his sleeve.

"I call this match a draw," Master Dallr said to the crowd. Young faces beamed at us, some of the students whispering and elbowing each other. It looked as if they'd enjoyed the show.

"Prince Kai," said the master, "if you and your guest would both follow me."

Kai was brushing dust off his now-ragged-looking doublet, his brows drawn tight.

"Are you more upset that you lost," I asked, gleeful that his cocky grin was finally missing, "or that I ruined your clothes?"

"It was a draw," he corrected as we followed Master Dallr through a shaded walkway and into the school. "And yes, I am upset that you ruined my doublet." He leaned toward me, his breath warm on my ear. "What are you going to do to compensate me for my loss? You don't have any Sudesian coin yet, so..."

His smile and the twinkle in his golden-brown eyes suggested several alternatives.

"Why did you wear it here if it's so precious?" I turned my gaze ahead, fighting the heat that rose to my cheeks. It was annoying how easily he could make me blush.

"I didn't expect to fight you. And when I did agree, I didn't expect you to be so good." There was unmasked appreciation in his tone. I smiled at that.

"You underestimated me."

"It won't happen again, little bird, I assure you."

We passed a black lacquered door with two burly masters positioned on either side. "What's in there?" I whispered to Kai.

"The masters' library," he whispered back. "Where all the secrets of the universe are found, or so they say. More likely it's full of rotted parchment. Master Dallr wears his key around his neck, the show-off."

My heart did a little reel in my chest. I was so close! Pernillius's *Creation of the Thrones* might sit only a few yards away, holding the answers to the Minax's destruction. Part of me wanted to rush the guards and break through the doors. But I'd likely just end up in prison. No, I needed to become a master so I had access to it for as long as I needed to find the right information.

At the end of the corridor, we entered a spacious room with arched openings to the corridor, the structure reminding me a bit of Forwind Abbey. But whereas the abbey was bleak and gray, the school's warm yellow stone seemed to soak up and reflect the slanting sunlight.

Master Dallr gestured for us to sit on jewel-bright cushions on the tiled floor as he took his seat in an upholstered chair with gilded armrests. It was clear from his saturnine demeanor that the school was his kingdom and this was his throne.

He studied me for a few moments before speaking. "The queen sent a message that you wish to take the trials."

"Yes." My pulse, just calming from the fight, picked up speed again.

"And you want this of your own free will?"

I met his eyes squarely. "Yes."

"Why?" he shot back, the question almost a command.

I paused. "I want to learn the skills you can teach me and gain control over my gift."

"And what will you do with that control and that skill?"

That was a harder question. I glanced at Kai, but he just looked forward resolutely, calmly. As if it was obvious. As if he'd been born knowing the correct answer to that question.

"I will use those skills to serve the queen," I said, aware of how vague that sounded.

"Forgive my candor, but you were not born here. Why do you wish to serve the queen? What would make you want to dedicate your life to serving her?"

Reasons flitted through my mind. What would convince the skeptical master? After a few seconds, he shook his head. "If you are to take the trials, you must know the answer deep in your bones. If you must think before answering, you are not ready."

The walls and floor radiated stored heat from the sun, and

my nerves further heated my skin. I hooked a finger around the damp strands of hair that had come loose from my braid and pushed them behind my ear. As I did so, Master Dallr's eyes fixed on the left side of my face.

"Where did you get that mark?" he asked abruptly.

Instinctively, my fingertips moved to cover the heart-shaped mark.

Dizziness hit. Everything slowed, sight and sound fuzzing, a tingle sliding up the back of my neck. As I blinked, the world shifted.

My hands gripped the railing of a ship as I stared into the churning froth that slid against the hull. My stomach roiled. I was so ill. So tired. Tired of fighting the impulses, the urge to hurt people around me, which stole my sleep and made me shut myself away for hours at a time until the feelings were under control. How much longer could I survive this? How much longer could I pretend? I swallowed and gripped harder, closing my eyes. I had to make it to land, at least. But even then, I had to hold on until I could—

A warm hand on my wrist made the image blur. A soft voice said my name. I blinked and shook myself. Master Dallr regarded me intently, his brows slightly furrowed. He had asked me a question. About my scar. I opened my mouth, but no words came out. His frown deepened. Kai watched me, too. I knew they were waiting for a reply. *The Minax marked me and told me I was its true vessel. It promised to return when I was filled with despair. I am the Child of Light or the Child of Darkness, or neither, and no one knows and I don't want to know. I never want to know.*

I couldn't say any of that. I could barely admit it to myself.

I was suddenly furious, with the Minax who kept sending me these bizarre visions and with myself for being unable to control them, to shut them out. This was my chance to enter the trials, and I was ruining everything, making the master doubt me. I needed an answer and it had to be the right one. The scar was from . . . from . . .

"A birthmark," said Kai smoothly, snapping time back into place. "She doesn't like to talk about it. Something about superstitions in Tempesia." He waved a hand as if dismissing the northern kingdom and all its silly beliefs.

I expelled a breath, grateful for the easy lie. "Yes. I was born with it. And you asked me why I would dedicate my life to the queen. I was never accepted in Tempesia." That much was true. "My true home is here, and my place is serving her. I want nothing else." I made sure to meet the master's eyes, unwavering.

His expression darkened and he went silent. "Very well," he said finally. "You may take the trials. You have a week to prepare."

Kai made a strangled noise. Master Dallr turned grim eyes on him.

"Master," said Kai respectfully. "A week? Most students have years."

"Indeed. And that is the challenge you have been set by the queen, Prince Kai," the master said. "You will train Ruby, and you may use the school as often as you wish. If she passes, you will be allowed to take your final trial a second time. I don't have to tell you that getting a second chance is unprecedented. The queen has been very generous."

I sucked in a breath, looking quickly at Kai to gauge his

reaction. So this was the reason he'd made the long voyage to Tempesia and risked the Frost Court: to trade me for a second chance at the trials. And he was getting what he wanted. I expected to see satisfaction, maybe elation, on his expressive features.

But if he was happy, it was hard to tell. He didn't move or speak for several seconds. It was unlike him to be at a loss for words. I touched his shoulder and his lashes fluttered as if he were coming out of a trance.

"I trust this is to your satisfaction?" Master Dallr asked drily, his mouth curving ever so slightly as he watched Kai's reaction. I wondered if it was the closest thing to humor that the master ever allowed himself.

A telltale pulse beat in Kai's neck. He stood and bowed low. "Extremely generous. Thank you."

We left the school, skirting groups of sparring students in the courtyard. Kai's hands were balled into fists.

I tilted my head up to speak in his ear. "You're pale as death. You look like you've eaten a bad fish."

Even my insult didn't jar him from his unaccustomed silence. He seemed to relax a little, though. By the time we reached the carriage, he'd regained his color along with his usual arrogant strut. When I was seated across from him, he knocked on the roof and we rolled away from the school. He stared at nothing in particular.

"What's wrong with you?" I leaned forward. "If I'm not mistaken, you were just given your second chance. I would have thought you'd be . . . oh, I don't know . . . happy?"

"I am happy," he bit out.

My eyebrows rose. "You seem like it."

"Conditions." He frowned. "I should have known she would add conditions."

"Why is it so important to you? Passing the trials?"

He shot me a burning glare, as if I knew the answer and was merely baiting him.

"What?" I gave him an open-palm gesture. "I wasn't born here. I don't know these things."

"Only a master can rule an island. Without passing the trials, I won't be able to succeed my father as ruler of our home."

"Oh." The pieces fell into place. "When did you take the trials the first time?"

He didn't bother looking at me as he answered. "Almost two years ago."

"What happened?"

He grimaced. "Revealing details of the trials is forbidden."

"So how are you supposed to train me if you can't tell me what to expect?"

He waved a vague hand. "I'll figure it out."

He was beyond frustrating. "Well, at least I know why you lied to me, essentially kidnapped me, and handed me to your queen like a wrapped present."

"You agreed willingly enough."

"Yes, we need to talk about all the *lies* you told to secure that agreement. For the record, I haven't forgiven you. I just put it aside because we had more important things to worry about today."

"Fine. I admit that I lied. But in the end, you're getting what you want, aren't you? The chance to learn how to master your gift? You were eager enough when you asked the queen to give you a chance at the trials."

"I don't like being lied to. Besides, she may be letting me take the trials, but I'm still under her control. I would rather have come here secretly."

He snorted. "Nothing happens on Sere without the queen knowing. You'd have been worse off if you'd tried to sneak in."

I folded my arms.

He stared at me for a few seconds. "All right, I'm sorry. I was desperate. And I didn't know you."

"You know me now." I stared at him. "Don't lie to me again."

"I promise," he said, fighting a smile.

"I don't trust you when you smirk at me like that."

"My enjoyment has nothing to do with whether or not I'm telling the truth. It's just that you're rather adorable when you're annoyed. Am I forgiven?"

The answer was easy. "No."

"You'll have to forgive me once you pass your trials," he said with confidence. "We'll train every available moment until you're as prepared as I can make you. Be warned, though. It won't be easy."

"I'm not scared of hard work."

"Good." He settled back and folded his arms behind his head. When he started to put his feet up on my seat, I knocked them off with my knee. It wouldn't do to let Kai have his way all the time. He would become truly impossible.

As we passed the wharf, my nose wrinkled at the scent of

hundreds of sweaty fishermen and laborers and ten times as many dead fish being gutted or dried or piled into baskets. In between shacks and fishmongers' huts, the sea sparkled with flecks of sunlight that winked like a thousand cold diamonds. It reminded me a little of Arcus's eyes when he was angry: sun-bleached blue lit with white sparks.

The bobbing ships made me think of the vision I'd just had in the Fireblood school. Whereas previous visions had been some form of memory—aside from the vision in the throne room, which was so strange it had seemed more like a nightmare—this recent one had felt real. Like a glimpse through a spyglass, as if I'd been watching something that was really happening. I had the sense I'd fallen into the Minax's mind for a few minutes. If that were true, it had found its way to possessing some hapless sailor and was currently on a ship.

What if it was on its way to Sudesia? Would it come all this way to find *me*, its true vessel?

If so, it only made my mission more vital.

I couldn't help but wonder what might happen to Kai once I escaped Sudesia. Would the queen turn on him and punish him for my disloyalty? Imprison him? Judging by our interaction in the throne room, she seemed as mercurial as the sea, capable of anything.

I watched Kai as he lazed on the carriage seat, staring out the window with a placid expression, as if he hadn't a care in the world. The only detail that belied the studied picture of ease was the hand resting on his knee. It was curled into a white-knuckled fist.

ELEVEN

"FORGET WHAT YOUR FROSTBLOOD monk taught you. *I'm* telling you to rein in your fire on the upswing and let it out at the end."

Kai demonstrated by snapping a fire whip, the crack reverberating off the walls of the school. We'd arrived at the end of a morning practice session, watching a few minutes of sparring before the students filed inside for meditation. The scent of flowers perfumed the oppressively humid air. A handful of masters watched us from discreet positions on benches or stools. We'd been practicing for an hour and Kai was already impatient. It didn't bode well for the rest of the afternoon.

"Fine." I swished the fiery rope into the air in what I thought were impressive trails of flame. I controlled it well, but even I could see that it didn't crack with the kind of force Kai had achieved.

He closed his eyes, his lips moving silently. Maybe he was begging Sud for patience, or more likely asking her to sweep me away with a strong wind that deposited me in a conveniently deep area of the sea. His initial optimism seemed to have worn off. He had to be so aggrieved that his second chance depended on me passing my trials.

Served him right for bringing me here in the first place.

"But yours has no *bite*." He cracked another fire whip over my head, making me cringe involuntarily. "Your way is a dull sword. A toothless snake. You need to fully realize each and every move. You won't pass the trials if you continue to—"

"I'm *trying*, Kai. I learned it one way and I can't just... undo that in my mind!"

He expelled a frustrated breath. "I don't have time to *un*teach you as well as teach you."

I shared his frustration. If I couldn't do this, all was lost. If my gift wasn't strong enough, or if I wasn't fast enough or clever enough to learn these lessons, everything I'd done since leaving Tempesia would be for nothing. My failure would mean the deaths of countless others if the Minax remained free.

Kai stared at his feet, his brow creased. This wasn't any easier for him, I realized. So much rested on our combined success. We were so similar, both ready to lose our tempers at the slightest provocation. But I also saw his vulnerability. As uncertain as he was of me, he must feel a little uncertain of himself, too.

"I want to learn, Kai." I waited until he lifted his head and looked at me before continuing. "But I'm having trouble understanding. Brother Thistle learned from watching the masters at a Fireblood school. It could have been this *very* school. How could his teaching be so different?"

He stared at me for a moment, his brow furrowed, then strode forward and grabbed my hands, turning them to face upward. I followed his gaze to my palms, which were dry and chafed and still smoking slightly from my last move. "The general principles he taught you are fine. But your monk is a Frostblood. He had to adapt these moves so they worked with ice, an element based in water."

He pressed my palms together and pulled them apart. "Ice breaks, loses its form. It's not as malleable, not as adaptable." He curled my fingers against my palms, making fists. "As a result, Frostbloods rely more on brute force, but Firebloods..." He opened my hand again, staring down at it for a second before lifting his head to meet my eyes. "Make a small flame, Ruby. Small."

I nodded and brought a flame to life in my palm. Kai held his fingers over it and, with a graceful manipulation as if he were sculpting clay, he made the fire twist and rise in little sections, its form almost like a castle. Or a crown.

"You're working with fire," he explained, "something that feeds on air and thrives on sharp bursts."

He made the castle-crown flare toward the sky, then smoothed his fingers against my palms, pressing until the fire died. Then he stroked my fingers until they stretched straight out. A tremor raced through my limbs.

"Fire is hungry, but it's also elegant." He turned my hands over again, lifting the right one and brushing his lips to the back as if he were a gentleman meeting me for the first time. A shiver rippled across my shoulders. "Wild *and* precise. Dangerous but beautiful."

He stared at me, his eyes bright and intense. The heat from his body, so close, pressed against me. It was like standing next to a bonfire. Even though I half suspected this was another excuse to flirt—for a second, I wanted to move closer. I was drawn by his heat, the sense of familiarity I'd felt from the moment he'd first touched me in the ice garden. Our similarity. How easy it was to understand him.

The impulses were distracting. But at the back of my mind, I saw another face—Arcus's cold blue eyes warming with approval as he trained me in Forwind Abbey, the tilt of his admiring smile when I surprised him with a move while we were sparring in the castle garden. The echo of him reverberated through the moment, breaking the spell.

I shook my hands free and stepped back. "I'm not sure I agree. Brother Thistle is plenty elegant in his use of frost."

"Perhaps." He sounded skeptical. "But you had nothing to compare him to. You have never seen Fireblood masters perform." He turned to two of the masters, a man and woman, and bowed respectfully before speaking to them in quick Sudesian that I couldn't catch. They nodded and came forward.

Kai pulled me to sit beside him on the packed dirt. "Watch."

The masters bowed to each other. Their loose breeches tapered tightly at the ankle. Their feet were bare.

I expected them to fight, but as soon as they started to move, I could see this wasn't a contest so much as a performance. As quick as hummingbirds, they punched, dodged, kicked, rolled, landed on their backs and pushed up, springing to their feet with impossible agility. Sometimes they used each other as props, linking arms or running up the back of their opponent before flinging themselves into a backflip, landing with effortless precision, then twirling and kicking, each movement blending into the next. If there had been music to accompany it, it would have been frenetic and lovely. It was a ruthless symphony of movement and sounds, the slap of bare feet on bare earth, the swish of a punch, the thud of a kick that just barely connected. They were so controlled, and yet they seemed to pour out everything, holding nothing back.

A shiver crept across my skin. It was the most spectacular display I'd ever seen. It was a fight, but it was also a dance.

Kai leaned close to whisper. "It is a thing of incredible grace, is it not? I have seen them many times and I never fail to be... overawed by the wonder of it. I don't believe you have ever seen Frostbloods move like this."

"This is what I'm supposed to learn?" I shook my head. If I had to achieve this level of skill to pass the trials, I was doomed.

I would never learn this. Not in a lifetime. And certainly not in a week.

The dance of aggression went on. I could see that the masters weren't really hurting each other. The punches stopped a hair's breadth from an opponent's nose, the kicks mostly for show. If one combatant had made a tiny error, he or she could have done serious damage. But there were no errors. No hesitations. No slips. Just a smooth, effortless homage to movement and possibility.

And then, the fire. They let loose streams of bright heat, feathery plumes that half blinded me. The plumes curved like wings, enveloping the masters with roselike petals of flame. Then all four hands sent fiery beams straight up to the sky, seeming to touch the sun.

The movements came faster, the twists sharper, the feats more daring, until the blur of motion only registered on some unconscious level. This must be the result of incredible raw talent mixed with years of grueling training. When they finally stopped, sweating, and bowed once more, I leaped to my feet to applaud.

Kai's hand touched my forearm and I saw that he was standing, too. He bowed and I followed suit. The masters returned the gesture, smiling brightly before returning to their seats.

Exhilaration sang in my blood, but I reminded myself I wasn't here to relax and watch a show, I was here to learn. "So that was a lesson in . . ." I trailed off.

"In beauty." Kai raised his face to the sun, showing me the classical lines of his profile. "In pride, artistry. You may not think it matters, and maybe it doesn't to your Tempesian sensibilities, but it does to us." He turned his gaze back to me, shining an even brighter gold, as if the sun had poured in and become trapped in his eyes. "The mastery of fire is not only about force. Beauty is inherent in every movement, if done correctly. The two are intertwined. At its best, fighting with fire is as lovely as a dance."

"Can you do that?" I motioned to where the masters had performed, a few scorch marks in the dirt the only evidence of their display.

"Of course," he answered haughtily, then chuckled at my expression. "I'm not that proficient, yet. We all have strengths and weaknesses."

He beckoned me to stand and join him in the circle again. He spread his feet and raised his fists, ready to spar.

"What's *your* weakness?" I asked curiously.

His expression cooled. "You're my apprentice, not my confessor. Try the move again."

"Strength? Agility? Speed?"

His jaw lifted. It seemed I'd nicked his pride. "None of those. Now, focus."

As he demonstrated the correct techniques, I watched with the hunger of a predatory bird, trying to imprint every nuance of his movements into my mind. It wasn't that I'd been doing things wrong, exactly. Just inefficiently, at least compared to him. Every shift of his feet, every extension of his arm, every breath and grunt and punch was designed to give maximum impact to the moves he executed. And execution was the perfect description. There was a ruthlessness to the way he moved, a threat in every aspect of his posture, from the cords standing out in his neck to the way his fingers curled as he let flames loose. If he'd been a genuine opponent intent on hurting me, I might have lost my nerve.

His attacks landed on me like hard slaps. Kai ordered breaks to let me catch my breath, but as the hours wore on, my limbs grew heavy. I realized that he'd held back before, giving me opportunities to strike. Now, he was relentless. I had to struggle every second to keep up.

"Defend!" said Kai for the hundredth time. I brought my forearm up a little too late, my foot slipped, and I was on my back. Kai's silhouette loomed over me.

My vision blurred. My scar burned.

"Get up," said Kai again, but his breath fell cold against my face and his voice was lower, graveled. The voice of another opponent in another fight.

"Wait," I gasped, fighting the sensation.

No, not now, not again.

Colors swirled and faded from the scene. Kai's heart pulsed white in his chest. The Frost King's arena loomed at the edges of my vision. I closed my eyes and scrambled backward, finding my feet and turning to stumble toward the gate that led out of the school, desperate to leave before the vision could take over.

A hand grasped my shoulder and spun me around. "Where do you think you're going? If you're even thinking of giving up—"

"I don't want to hurt you!" I said, twisting away.

He scoffed. "You were flat on your back."

"Just—give me a minute."

I breathed heavily, hands on my knees, waiting for the feelings to pass. The vision had never quite taken hold, but I experienced the same aftereffects. My skin was chilled. I trembled despite the heat. When Kai's palm slid gently to my upper back, I found myself turning to him, reveling in his warmth. I heard his surprised inhalation, and then his arms came around me, holding me with reassuring pressure. After a moment, he rested his cheek on my hair.

"I have you," he said softly.

And just like that, a shuddering breath expanded my chest and my eyes filled. Humiliation washed through me at the thought of showing my emotions so easily. I tried to push him away, but he held tighter. "Hush."

"I'm not a . . . child," I said between uneven breaths, embarrassed that he felt the need to comfort me. "I don't even know why I'm . . ." I gulped and blinked rapidly. Had it been the loss of control or the thought of hurting Kai that had bothered me so much? Or maybe the stress had been building more than I'd realized. Either way, I felt like a weak fool for allowing my tears to overspill so easily.

"Everyone needs comfort," he soothed, the words rumbling in my ear pressed against his chest. "You fight your emotions too much, Ruby. A Fireblood feels too much to suppress. You do yourself harm by denying them. Let them flow."

"Like you?" I sniffed and worked my hand into the space between my cheek and his chest to wipe my eyes. "Blustering and angry one second, then laughing and flirting the next?"

He chuckled. "I follow my nature. We all must do the same. Stop trying to shut down your feelings. Cry, Ruby. And when you're finished crying, do what you feel like. Nobody here will think less of you for it."

I raised my head a little to look at the masters, wondering if they were staring, expecting to see censure on their faces. Instead, they were unconcerned, one reading a book while two others spoke softly. One of them caught my eye and smiled. I turned my head back into Kai's chest, embarrassed. "That's not... acceptable where I come from."

He scoffed. "I've seen Frostblood culture. A bunch of walking snowmen, priding themselves on self-control. They're barely alive. What is the point of living if you can't let yourself feel anything?"

I thought of Arcus. Surely that didn't apply to him. He felt deeply; he just kept it hidden. That was one thing we'd always had in common, though I had a much harder time hiding my feelings than he did.

Maybe I didn't have to anymore.

My whole life had been spent trying to tamp down my feelings, keep them under wraps so I could hide my gift. It had been sheer necessity. A matter of life or death.

When I'd been discovered and my mother had been killed, I'd blamed myself for practicing my gift when she'd forbidden it. I'd drawn the soldiers' attention. Even now, when I let myself remember, I'd feel such terrible guilt it would overwhelm me.

"It scares me," I whispered. "I don't like to lose control."

His voice was low and firm. "If you would let yourself feel more freely, you'd find yourself struggling less. The volcano that pours lava continuously is less likely to erupt."

"Is that true?"

He grinned. "It sounds good, doesn't it?"

I couldn't help but chuckle. "That's all that matters to you, isn't it? Sounding good. Looking good. Feeling good. You don't worry about anything serious."

He tilted his head to the side, considering, then shrugged. "Worry causes wrinkles."

"Sud forbid." Smothering a smile, I faked a bored look of superiority, the kind Marella had perfected. "Neither your clothing nor your skin shall bear such shameful signs of wear."

He threw back his head and laughed, then gave me a little squeeze. "You're quite amusing when you're not lashing me with that sharp tongue. Although"—his eyes turned sultry—"I might not mind the violence of your tongue in the right circumstances."

I shook my head reprovingly, my lips twitching. "You're incorrigible."

He adopted a confused expression. "Is that a compliment or insult? I confess I don't understand your Tempesian values."

I finally let myself smile, noticing how his pupils flared in response. "Definitely an insult."

It seemed to take effort for him to pull his gaze away. "Very good. I see you've recovered. Come." He tugged on my hand. "You can knock me into the dirt. That should restore you completely."

We sparred for another two hours, but when the sun turned

pink with exertion from a long day of warming the earth, the students returned to the training yard, effectively ending our lessons.

Kai grinned as we trudged, dusty and exhausted, toward the waiting carriage.

"What are you looking so happy about?" I darted a suspicious glance at him.

"As I expected, I'm an excellent teacher." He turned his head to bestow his smile on me like a stray band of sunshine.

I blinked. "I suppose there's a compliment to me in there somewhere."

He punched my shoulder lightly. "You stopped fighting yourself and used your emotions to your advantage. Surely you felt the difference?"

I had. My attacks had been faster, more confident. I'd let myself enjoy the sensation of turning my anger and determination into flame. "I admit you're not a terrible teacher."

He stopped and grabbed both my hands, bowing over them extravagantly and brushing his warm lips over my knuckles. Before I could chastise him, he was helping me into the carriage. Moments before, I'd been his opponent, struggling to keep my feet as he hit me with attack after attack. In the space of a breath, he was treating me like I was a lady he was courting.

I shook my head as Kai settled into the carriage across from me, his long legs stretching indolently like a satisfied cat. Would I ever get used to his changeability? As much as he talked about feelings, it was hard to tell if he felt anything seriously at all. I had to remind myself that he was only training me so that he could have his second chance. I doubt he cared whether I passed or failed, aside from how it affected his own outcome.

If I died during the trials, would anyone here care?

I stared at the passing scenery: glimpses of the ocean between clusters of homes and vegetation and the wharf. A storm cloud hovered in the sky to the northeast. My thoughts turned to Arcus—the only person that I knew beyond doubt would protect me at his own expense.

Well, that had been the problem, hadn't it? He'd been risking his court's wrath to keep me near. And I'd cared enough about him to leave.

My chest tightened sharply. Would I ever see him again?

"You look sad," said Kai, his eyes glinting. "Chin up, little bird. You did well today."

"So you think I'll be ready?"

He didn't reply right away. I waited, wondering whether he would offer a platitude or an honest reply. Wondering which one I wanted.

His expression became uncharacteristically somber. "No one is ever ready for the trials."

"Even you?"

He hesitated. "Unlike the naive boy I was, I now know what to expect."

"I thought that was forbidden. Knowing what to expect."

His generous lips curved, his handsome face losing all traces of seriousness. "I'm the exception to all rules, Ruby. You'd best remember that."

TWELVE

DAYS PASSED IN A BLUR OF MUSCLE aches, frustration, and bruises, interspersed by glimmers of hope. I couldn't say Kai was patient, but he was determined and unwavering. He showed that he was capable of serious dedication. I knew that every time he attacked or blocked or surprised me, he was doing so because he wanted me to succeed. He wanted me to be ready. If I failed, so would he.

He'd taught me several new moves, he'd tested the strength of my fire by having me melt or burn myriad objects, and he'd made me meditate for hours to hone my mental control, not allowing me to move until I was frantic with the need to stretch or fidget. I didn't complain. I didn't argue. I learned quickly because I had to. I knew I was improving by the admiration I occasionally saw in his eyes.

One unexpected benefit of the long hours of training with Kai: We developed an easy harmony, the kind of meshing of gifts that the masters seemed to prize so highly. I started anticipating his moves before he made them, and he often predicted mine. It meant that neither of us won easily, although I sometimes wondered if Kai was still going easy on me to build my confidence. We became well-matched sparring partners, pushing each other to new extremes of skill and creativity. It made for a few spectacular fights, drawing the students and masters into appreciative crowds on more than one occasion.

We hadn't yet come close to the proficiency displayed by the senior masters, though. Many of the children even showed certain skills that already exceeded my own. Still, my gift was strong and growing stronger. Hope grew a little every day. I only wished hope equaled certainty. Even if I'd been the brightest pupil in Sudesia, there would be no guarantee I'd pass the trials. After all, even Kai with his staggering speed, agility, and power had somehow failed his first attempt.

Which meant I needed a backup plan.

Pernillius's book could very well be in the library at the school, but I wouldn't gain access to it unless I passed the trials. So I had to explore other paths to knowledge. I made a point of speaking to the masters during my breaks from training, hoping to find Sudesia's version of Brother Thistle. Surely one of them knew of a scholar whose favorite pastime was burying himself under piles of decaying volumes and musty scrolls. My tentative questions all led me to the same answer: Master Dallr was a keen student of history. He was the one to speak to if I had any questions on esoteric knowledge.

The problem was that Master Dallr had the friendly demeanor of a locked vault and the approachability of a sea-worn cliff. I could bash myself against his jagged exterior for hours on end and all I would get was a headache. Small talk yielded nothing. When direct questions about his love of history didn't work, I moved on to flattery. When that failed, I attempted charm, which was awkward for everyone. Kai winced at my eagerness. He began to tease me about hero-worshipping the legendary master, until I walloped him, flipping him onto his back in the school courtyard in a cloud of dust. He, of course, grinned.

The most I could glean from all my efforts was that the library did indeed house the most rare and valuable of the kingdom's manuscripts. And without exception, only the masters were admitted entry.

When the week of training was over, I was gripped by a sense of inevitability, underpinned by panic. I could no longer tell myself that I'd find the book without committing myself to any vows. Only as a master would I be trusted with the knowledge I needed.

The night before the first trial, Kai and I were invited to dine with the queen.

We entered the great hall, a spacious room on the second floor of the south tower with embroidered silk curtains in warm colors, and bronze hanging lamps with lacy openings that blazed with light. The highly polished wood table reflected the lamps, throwing an extra glow onto the colorful porcelain plates and glass goblets. Side tables topped in mosaic tiles were covered with fragrant dishes emitting the scent of roasted meat and unfamiliar spices. The queen sat at one end of the main table, and Prince Eiko sat at her right. Though the setting was rich and stately, the atmosphere seemed intimate. It struck me as less formal than dinners in the Frost Court.

With help from a lady's maid named Ada, I'd dressed in a white gown with gold lace covering the bodice—borrowed from the over-stuffed wardrobe of some Fireblood lady of the court. Kai, with clothing that had clearly been tailored just for him, was a study in masculine perfection in a cream doublet over fawn trousers and black knee boots. Queen Nalani wore a wine-colored silk dress and a heavy gold filigree crown, while Prince Eiko wore loose robes in navy blue. Her lips curved in the hint of a smile, but her expression remained as watchful as ever. I dropped into a curtsy, my palms damp against my skirt.

"You may rise, Ruby," she said in Tempesian, surprising me with both her fluency and her willingness to speak the language, presumably as a courtesy to me. "Good evening, Prince Kai." She invited Kai to sit at her left side and for me to sit next to him.

As Kai pulled out my chair for me, Prince Eiko stood politely. I took a second to examine him more closely. His sable hair was streaked with hints of white, his narrow but handsome face just beginning to soften at the jawline. My attention was arrested by his eyes, a bright shade of leaf green. They seemed to be fixed on the left side of my face, which made my scar feel unaccountably warm. I rubbed it briefly to ease the sting.

As he bowed, he towered over the table. I realized he was perhaps the tallest person I'd ever met, his height accentuated by his lean, almost skinny, frame. I curtsied again and took the seat that Kai held out for me, glad to have the table to hide the fact that I couldn't stop bouncing my knee. I didn't know why I was so nervous. The queen had decided to let me take the trials. As long as I didn't come at her with a fish fork, I didn't think she would change her mind.

A footman poured the wine, which tasted fruity and smooth but strong. I would have to be careful only to sip it. The queen and Prince Eiko made small talk with Kai as dinner was served, plate after plate of artfully arranged dishes laden with fish, sweet potatoes, pork, rice, and a variety of fruit. I took an experimental bite of a yellow fruit, blinking in surprise at the strong taste: both tart and sugary.

The queen chose that moment to turn her attention to me. "How is your training progressing, Ruby?"

"She learns quickly," said Kai before I could answer. "And she knows more than I expected. Perhaps almost as much as an initiate after two or three years of training."

My brows rose at that. He'd seldom praised me, not in actual words.

But the queen continued to look at me expectantly, obviously wanting me to answer as well. As if my answer mattered, which was an about-face from the last time we'd met. Yet her demeanor was surprisingly warm now. Perhaps this was the face she wore for social occasions. Or perhaps she wanted me to let down my guard. Did I dare to hope that I had earned some respect for doing well in my training? She had said her Fireblood masters were vital. If I passed, I would be important to her. To the entire kingdom. The idea sent a little buzz of satisfaction through me. I had to remind myself that I wasn't here to please the queen. I had my own agenda.

I patted the edges of my lips with a snowy napkin. "Kai is a good teacher."

"But not a patient one, I reckon," said Prince Eiko with a twinkle in his eye. "The young prince isn't known for his calm nature."

"A true Fireblood," said the queen proudly. "Though I have told him before that his impulsiveness could well be his downfall. As it has been before."

Kai inclined his head. "And yet, you've been gracious enough to allow me a second chance."

"Do not fail me this time," she said.

His face grew serious. "I won't."

A footman came forward and refilled our goblets, the crystal reflecting the glow from an enormous fireplace rimmed in black marble. It was strange to think that in northern Tempesia, the first snows would already be weighing down the pine boughs.

The queen must have noticed me staring at the fire.

"It's symbolic," she said, taking a sip of her wine. "A fire always burns in the formal rooms of my palace. Night and day, summer or winter, sun or storm. The flame eternal, like the spirits of the Fireblood people. Crush us, beat us, cut us down. We will not be extinguished. We live in the embers and rise again to consume our enemies."

"That's . . ." I searched for the right response. "Very apt."

"Do you believe it to be true?" Her warm dark eyes fixed on me.

"I hope so, Your Majesty. Though Firebloods in Tempesia were driven away or killed, I like to think we'll thrive there again one day."

"As it happens, I share your dream."

I froze with my goblet halfway to my mouth. "You want Firebloods to return to Tempesia?"

"My islands are many, but the total land is small compared to the kingdom north of the Vast Sea."

Prince Eiko swirled the wine in his goblet. "Tempesia has inferior soil and a harsh climate."

The queen inclined her head. "Except for the Aris Plains, which are fertile. When Firebloods began settling in Tempesia, it was still sparsely populated in the south. We brought our farming methods, tilling virgin soil and building homes. You know this, of course." She raised a brow at me.

"Yes, Your Majesty."

"We kept the early frosts from crops, effectively lengthening the growing season. We shared our shipbuilding, our navigation methods. We helped shape that kingdom and, for a time, we worked and lived with them in relative peace. Now they've taken our lands in the south and Firebloods were disposed of so the Frostbloods could reap the benefits of our labor. I will fight for our right to those prosperous lands once again."

It was unclear how she meant to fight for those rights, though. Sudesia, with its smaller population, couldn't possibly hope to take the lands by force.

Her lips curved. "You wonder why I'm giving you this history lesson?"

I did wonder, but it would be rude to admit that, so I practiced my diplomatic skills. "I find history fascinating. My mother and grandmother taught me some, but there's much I don't know. For instance, I don't know the history of the Frostbloods living in Sudesia. One of my"—I wondered what to call Brother Thistle, settling on the simplest description—"friends is a Frostblood who left here when he was a child."

Her expression cooled. The idea of a Frostblood as my friend probably stretched her imagination to its limits.

"In any case, let me return to my history," she continued. "Akur was crowned king, and some say he was driven mad by the murder of his queen by Fireblood rebels." She leaned forward. "He set out to destroy my people in revenge. So let me ask you this. Why did he not sail across the Vast Sea to conquer my lands?"

"Because of the Strait of Acodens," I replied.

"And the masters who guard it," she clarified. "They are the true jewels of the land. Never forget that, should you pass the trials, you will serve as my best defense against attack. Our power lies in unity, not as individuals. My people in Tempesia had no such protection."

"You still considered them your people?" I asked. "Firebloods who no longer live in Sudesia?"

"Firebloods have always been my people, whether they left Sudesia four days or four centuries ago." She gripped the stem of her goblet, her dark brows winging down over her fierce gaze. "We lost many ships, many loyal soldiers, in our attempts to save your compatriots from Rasmus's decree that they should be killed or brought to his arena. Though we were able to save some, most were lost. It is the greatest tragedy in the history of my people. And it happened during *my* reign. I will not rest until my people are in Tempesia again."

Her knuckles turned white, her fingers tightening until the crystal stem snapped with an audible crunch. I gasped aloud before I could stifle it. The look in her eyes was murderous.

A footman came and carefully whisked the broken pieces away. A full goblet soon replaced the broken one.

No one batted an eye. Perhaps the queen broke crystal on a regular basis.

Again, I wondered if the Minax was possessing the queen. I checked my senses for any sign of it, but found none—aside from a tingle on the back of my neck, which could merely be nerves. My eyes were drawn to her wrist to check the color of the vein, but her long sleeves kept me from confirming whether it was a natural red or the inky black of possession. I sipped my wine and tried not to show how much her unbridled fury had shaken me. She was passionate, but with that came unpredictable behavior. It was a reminder that my current freedom was based on her whims.

"You alone were blessed by Sud to survive the massacre of our people, Ruby." I met her eyes as she added, "Your mother, I heard, was not so fortunate."

I clasped my hands tightly in my lap, my stomach lurching. "That's right."

"I'm sincerely sorry," she said.

"Thank you." I cast my eyes downward. My hands were trembling and cold. This conversation had gone on far too long and I just wanted it to end.

"But let us turn to more pleasant matters." She sipped and asked smoothly, "Prince Kai, has your aunt found a suitable bride for you yet?"

Though a change in subject was welcome, it was startlingly abrupt. And it didn't seem like this was a pleasant topic for Kai. He had the look of a cornered rabbit as he replied, "Aunt Aila understands that I do not wish to rush into marriage. I am barely eighteen summers, Your Majesty."

It surprised me that we were almost the same age. All that restless swagger made Kai seem older, especially since he was so confident as captain of his ship. Then again, Arcus was king and he wasn't much older. His serious demeanor always made him seem more than a few years my senior.

"Indeed, but the most powerful among us have a duty to produce heirs, as you know. It is good to start young. You have seen how it is with me. I cannot have children and the succession is now uncertain."

Kai paused for several moments. "I will give the matter serious consideration, Your Majesty."

"Perhaps since your mother is no longer alive and your aunt has not found the right woman, I may be of assistance in finding you a bride."

His eyes widened. I stifled a laugh at his expression, relieved the conversation had lightened.

"You're most generous," he muttered, downing his drink.

The plates were cleared and dessert was served, tiny iced cakes and tarts filled with sweet berries and cream. In what I deemed a transparent attempt to ward off any further talk of nuptials, Kai carried the conversation, steering it into neutral territory. I pasted on an interested expression and tuned everyone out, mentally reviewing my plans.

"You have much on your mind," Prince Eiko said, leaning forward across the table and speaking in a low voice so as not to interrupt Kai's conversation with the queen.

I hoped the worry hadn't shown on my face.

He added, "You must be nervous about your trials."

"Yes, a little," I admitted, glad that I had a reasonable excuse for anxiety. "I'm sorry if I was inattentive."

He waved away the apology. "It's only natural. Anyone would be preoccupied on such a night. And it's difficult not knowing what to expect, isn't it?"

He glanced at the queen, who was still engaged in conversation with Kai, and leaned in further. "I can tell you a few things without breaking any oaths. If you like."

"Please," I said, wondering why he would want to help me. What did he have to gain?

He pressed his fingers together, reminding me a bit of Brother Thistle when he was about to give a lecture. "Each trial tests a different ability, so the first, second, and third trial are all quite different from each other. They're meant to push you to your limits so that only the strongest of Firebloods will have a chance of passing. However, strength of the gift does not guarantee success. There are other factors that come to bear on your success or failure."

"What kind of factors?" I asked.

"Some of them are physical, like endurance, agility, or skill.

Some things are mental, such as adaptability and perseverance. Your will, your decisions, can play a large role in the trials."

Suddenly, I noticed the table had fallen silent. I glanced up to see the queen watching Prince Eiko.

"You come very close to revealing too much, my dear," she said in silken tones. "She will find out more tomorrow, and that is soon enough, I think."

Prince Eiko sat back, looking chagrined. "Of course."

"Best of luck tomorrow, Ruby," Queen Nalani said as she rose to her feet. Prince Eiko, Kai, and I stood as well.

"Thank you, Your Majesty," I replied with a curtsy, when a question occurred to me. "Your Majesty, when you were telling me your history, you never mentioned what happened to the Frostbloods living in Sudesia. Perhaps next time, you can tell me more."

She smiled, but it was cold, as if it were ice and not fire that ran through her veins. "Why, child, I assumed you knew. When it was clear that my people in Tempesia were lost to me, I rounded up all the Frostbloods living in my kingdom. Some of them became indentured servants, like my loyal Renir." She gestured to one of the footmen standing against the wall and I blinked hard. How had I missed that? His eyes were a pale grayish blue, subtle but definitely the mark of a Frostblood.

"And the ones who refused to go into service?" I asked curiously, forcing myself not to stare.

She captured my gaze, her irises as cold and opaque as prison walls.

"I ordered my Fireblood masters to execute them all."

THIRTEEN

THAT NIGHT, I WAS PACING THE plush, richly patterned carpet in my room when a soft knock sounded at my door. I opened it to see Kai, still dressed, a cup in each hand. "May I come in?"

Conscious of the thin fabric of my nightgown, I crossed my arms over my chest and backed up. "I suppose."

"Can't sleep?" he asked, shutting the door with his foot.

I shrugged.

"Neither could I the night before my first trial." He held out a cup. "To ease your nerves."

"Is this tea or wine? I need to be sharp tomorrow."

"Which means you need sleep. Just a few drops."

I sighed and took the cup. He clinked his against mine. "To becoming a master."

"Are we toasting you or me?"

He grinned. "Both."

All was darkness outside the glow of my single candle. The emptiness pressed against us as if it wanted to swallow us whole. For all I knew, this night was my last, the last time I'd feel the comfort of a bed, the last time I'd dream my dreams and think about the person I cared for most in this world. I'd written a letter to Arcus after dinner, telling him things I'd never had the courage to say to his face. Hot tears had fallen, making a mess of the ink and sizzling tiny holes in the parchment. I hoped he'd forgive me. For that and for everything else.

I pushed the thoughts of Arcus away, at least as much as I could. He was never far from my mind.

"You're confident I'll pass, then?" I asked, my stomach knotting. I recognized the nerves—they were the same I'd felt every time I'd had to enter King Rasmus's arena.

He gave me a reproving look. "I wouldn't have wasted my time this week if I thought you couldn't pass."

Not as reassuring as I'd hoped, but maybe that was high praise from Kai. After all, he'd failed at least one of the tests.

"Did you pass the first trial?"

"Of course. I passed the first two trials, which is why I don't have to retake them." He took a drink and then stared at his cup, swirling it gently. I watched his dense lashes, several shades darker than his hair, cast shadows on his cheeks. He looked almost melancholy, which was so unusual for him that my heart squeezed a little.

I took another sip. “Do you ever consider how cruel the trials are? They’re risking the lives of anyone who isn’t strong enough. I see little difference between this and the Frost King’s arena.”

“The trials are a choice,” he said defensively. “No one is forced to take them. And there are ways out of the first trial for anyone who realizes they’re not strong enough to finish.” He snapped his mouth closed, as if realizing he’d said too much. “However, if you leave, you forfeit, and you’ll never be allowed to take them again.”

“Unless I bargain with the queen like you did. Oh, wait, you’re the exception to all rules.” I forced a smile.

“Indeed.” He lifted his goblet to me in acknowledgment, his lips curving, then drained it and set the goblet down. “Well, I suppose I should let you get some sleep. I don’t want to be the reason you’re fatigued on the most important day of your life.”

“Before you go, I have a favor to ask.” I went to my dressing table and picked up the rolled-up parchment. “If I don’t make it out of my trial, I’d like you to make sure this gets back to Tempesia.”

Kai frowned at the scroll. “To whom?”

“Arcus,” I said simply.

He frowned and didn’t move to take the letter.

“Just get it to him.” I pressed it into his hand. “It’s a last request. You do honor last requests here, don’t you?”

“We try.”

"Thank you." I paused. "I'd appreciate if you didn't read it."

He looked offended. "I wouldn't do that."

I nodded, feeling a little awkward, though I didn't know why. We stood in silence for a few moments more.

"You *will* pass tomorrow," he said, his eyes bright with warmth. "Just stay calm. Remember your training."

I tipped my cup, drank in a series of gulps, and offered it, empty, to Kai. "Thanks for the drink." Craving oblivion, I turned and crawled into bed to settle under the covers.

"Sleep well, little bird," he said, shutting the door with a quiet click.

The carriage wheels creaked in the predawn hush, depositing Kai and me at the school as sunrise bruised the sky. Master Dallr waited in the entryway. As we came closer, he held up one calloused palm to Kai, who halted beside me.

Kai took my hands briefly in his. He looked at Master Dallr and then bent to my ear. "Lava will burn the flesh off your bones—you or any Fireblood. Don't hesitate. Don't look back."

I looked at him sharply. My already elevated pulse sped up even more. Was he breaking his oath by telling me something about the trial? His gaze was dark, intense. I dipped my chin to show him I'd taken note. His fingers tightened before letting go. I turned and followed the Fireblood master without looking back. My stomach was a tight knot of nerves, but my mind was clear and determined.

Instead of entering the school, Master Dallr veered onto flagstones leading around the side of the building, then to a scrubby footpath that climbed a steep, rocky hill. As we crested it, the sun's rim peeked over the horizon, casting a pink glow over the undulating sea and the smudges of distant islands.

He gestured toward the shadowy bulk of a small building of gray stone. When we reached the inside, I saw a life-size statue of Sud holding a bowl of fire. The master knelt and pressed his forehead to the floor, and I did the same, mouthing a quick prayer. As he knelt, a chain slid from the collar of his robe and clunked against the floor. A black key hung from the end of it. The key to the library! My fingers itched to reach out and grab it.

But that would be far too obvious. I reminded myself I needed more than just the right book in my hands. I needed to conquer my powers as well. I wanted to become a master, not just for the sake of finding out how to destroy the Minax, but to prove I could do it when the time came.

He straightened and tucked the key back into his robe.

We left the temple and descended the hill where lava fields spread out below, barren and black with rough ridges like petrified waves. Plants grew from cracks and crevices, leafy ferns and saplings, bright green against the black. In the distance, a volcano spewed white smoke from its gray mouth, a dragon belching into the sky, vegetation clinging to its shoulders like bright green scales.

We reached the ruins of a stone wall. Black rock was pooled against and around it as if frozen in the act of trying to storm the walls. I followed Master Dallr through a broken archway—a remnant of the destroyed building—and continued for another minute or two. He stopped and gestured to the ground, then bowed low and turned away.

"I'm supposed to go in here?" I peered into an inky black hole, then looked up. Master Dallr was already several yards away. He didn't look back.

I slid in feetfirst, lowering myself slowly, palms grating against the sides of a narrow shaft. I lost control, sliding for a few seconds before I landed hard on my hands and knees. Kai's warning had put me on guard. I looked around quickly, sighing with relief that there was no lava in sight. Just torches lining the black stone walls of a tunnel, which tilted down into darkness.

The torchlight illuminated markings carved into the walls and ceiling: a swirl here, a diamond shape there, three curving lines underscored by a horizontal slash. I didn't know whether they were writing or art, but they did look familiar. I'd seen similar designs carved into the ice columns of Arcus's castle, most notably in the throne room. Come to think of it, I'd seen a few at Forwind Abbey, too. I'd figured they were common Frostblood motifs, something to do with Fors. How they made their way into a tunnel under the lava fields of the Sudesian capital, I had no idea.

Not far along, a wooden slab with the markings of a door blocked the tunnel, its bulk completely filling the space. A ladder hung a few feet before the door, leading up to a shaft above. That must be one of the ways out that Kai had mentioned. I ignored the ladder and pushed at the wood, then, when it didn't budge, put my ear close and knocked. It gave a hollow echo. I stood for a moment, calculating. I didn't think the test was supposed to be a great mystery. The door was made of wood. My gift was fire. It seemed logical I was meant to use it. Kai had said not to hesitate.

I burned through the door in less than a minute, careful to create a space only big enough to get through. I didn't want to exhaust myself unnecessarily.

I walked quickly down the passage past another ladder until a second slab of wood loomed before me in the darkness. A little thicker than the last. It took over a minute to burn through.

By the fourth door, I started to lose track of time. My breaths came faster. My limbs felt heavier.

I'd just burned through the sixth—much thicker—door when a loud grinding sound came from behind. The tunnel filled with heat. I turned to see a glowing ooze that changed shape as it slid down the incline behind me. So that's what Kai had meant when he told me lava would burn the flesh off a Fireblood's bones. My pulse jerked frantically. I hurried to the next door, this time burning the upper portion only before climbing through the gap, leaving the lower portion as a barrier against the lava. I might need some extra seconds later.

I arrived at the seventh door. It was maybe twice as thick as the previous one. The passage widened here, and a shaft of sunlight lit the space. Another ladder. It was far more tempting to climb now. But that wasn't an option.

I bent my attention to the door, pulling the heat from my

chest and sending it through my arms, fire exploding from my palms into the wood. It splintered and crackled. When the hole was large enough, I hauled myself through, trembling and winded, and looked back as I held myself suspended in the opening.

A pinpoint of glowing orange, still far, moved closer. I calculated that it must have crossed the barrier of the first, and perhaps the second door.

With a final glance at the ladder, I dropped to the floor and rushed on.

After a grueling battle with the eighth door, the lava felt close, the heat rising with each harsh, uneven breath. Fatigue weighted my arms. I shook it off, and pushed forward.

No ladder hung next to the ninth door, although a narrow opening punctured the stone ceiling, admitting buttery rays of light. A shadow passed over it. A master watching, perhaps. Or just a cloud passing over the sun.

The thick door yielded the dullest of thuds when I knocked on it. I took two short breaths and made a concentrated flame.

I groaned as I held the flame steady, eyes closed. All my will aimed into the wood.

Scorch marks blackened the door, but it was otherwise unharmed. I took a breath and tried again, recalling my training.

Focus, don't hold back, build the heat, let it burn. Hotter. Hotter. More.

My whole body trembled. I called up hot fear, burning hatred, the searing thirst for revenge. I allowed myself memories usually kept at bay: the night when the soldiers came to my village, their faces like nightmarish spirits in the glow of the burning buildings.

But when I pictured the face of the captain who killed my mother, another image came with it. Mother's body crumpling to the snow.

Pain lashed my heart. Like a candle burned down to its base, my fire sputtered.

No.

Focus.

Tired.

Heat.

Tired.

Exhaustion pulled at every muscle and sinew. My legs shook. I grabbed at the door to keep from falling.

Hissing came from behind. Fiery liquid poured through the opening in the eighth door, devouring the wood until only the upper edges remained. Lava pooled and oozed like a glowing oil spill.

Panic replenished my heat, like adding fresh coal to a forge. I poured my fire into the door and burned a few inches away, the edges blackening under my fire. When the depth of the hole reached about two feet, a tiny point of light appeared. I shoved my finger through it and felt a rush of elation.

The heat from the approaching lava suddenly singed the backs of my calves. Acting on instinct, I turned and threw my hands out, the way I would to control flames.

The lava stopped. Just stopped, as if an invisible barrier held it back. *But how?*

"Sage?" I whispered.

I waited for a vision of the golden-eyed woman who sometimes appeared to me. But I couldn't see her, nor hear her voice. Still, she must have intervened. Relief and gratitude brought another surge of strength.

I screamed as I poured the last bit of my heat into the door. The edges of the opening burst into flame, the space widening.

I pulled my legs up, away from the motionless lava, and wiggled feetfirst into the breach. As I hoisted myself through, my hips stuck in the narrow gap. I swore fiercely and braced my elbows on the sides, then a final heave ripped gashes into my tunic and leggings. My feet hit the ground. I looked back through the opening to see the lava moving again.

Two tunnels led downward to the left and right, but ahead, the passage rose. I ran up the incline, the torches blurring at the edges of my vision.

A minute later, I burst through into the sunlight. I collapsed onto the ground and saw that I was on the far side of the hill overlooking the school, the temple to Sud casting shadows in the morning sun.

I panted, lying on my back while clouds and seagulls cut white shapes into the blue. My head spun with relief—and just a touch of pride.

I'd passed the first Fireblood trial. I was one step closer to learning how to destroy the Minax.

Kai came to my room again that night. This time, he brought sweets: tiny iced cakes in a rainbow of colors. "To celebrate the passing of your first trial."

I carefully lifted a pink confection with a tiny chocolate leaf on top. I was still giddy that I'd passed. Everything seemed possible; suddenly, even the idea of mastering my gift and beating the Minax was within reach. The only thing tempering my euphoria was the knowledge that Sage must have intervened to help me. After all, who else could have saved me from death by lava at the last second? And if she intervened, I must have been in real trouble. She'd never helped me so directly before.

But I shoved the thought away. I wanted to bask in the elation of my win.

"Mmm, I love sweets," I said around a glorious mouthful of cake.

"I know," Kai said drily. "You were covered in powdered sugar the night we met." He smiled almost wistfully, as if that had happened years ago instead of weeks. "I had you pegged as a traitor to our people. Or at the very least, an opportunist who cared for nothing but your own ambition. Though the queen had sent me to recruit you, I didn't have much hope that you'd remain loyal."

I swallowed my bite. "I'm assuming you've changed your mind. Otherwise, it would be rude to mention that."

"I might have cause to reexamine my thinking." He seized a tiny cake and popped it into his mouth.

I dusted sugar from my fingertips, then selected another: white with blue piping. After eating a few more, I put a hand to my stomach. "I shouldn't have eaten so many. Or maybe I'm just getting nervous about the next trial."

He put the tray on a side table. "Climb in bed and I'll tuck you in."

I crossed my arms. "Again, I'm not a child."

"Well, you look like one at the moment. Could they have fit any more ruffles on this nightgown?"

I looked down. My nightgown was, indeed, covered in ruffles, one of which Kai flicked with an extended index finger. He transferred the touch to my chin and smiled. My cheeks heated. I turned away and crawled into bed. It seemed safer than standing in the candlelight in a semisheer nightgown. I didn't want him to leave yet. It was nice to have company to take the edge off my anxiety about the second trial.

"Tell me a story," I said with sudden inspiration. "Like you did on the ship."

He laughed. "I thought you didn't want to be treated like a child. You sound just like Aver." He came and sat on the edge of the bed. "What do you want to hear, then?"

"Continue the one you were telling. About the birth of the wind gods. Eurus had just been banished."

"Ah." He cleared his throat. "Well, Neb and Tempus barely had time to grieve for their son's betrayal when Neb found that she was expecting again. She gave birth to twins, Sud and Fors, who were equally matched in every way. As they grew, they loved to hunt. Cirrus would follow her younger siblings to make sure they weren't injured by the animals that had spread across the world. But she also felt sorry for the animals and often saved them, mending their cuts and pouring life back into their broken bodies."

"A convenient ability," I observed, covering another yawn.

"Indeed, and not just for the animals. Sometimes she healed her younger siblings from cuts and bruises and broken limbs. Sud and Fors were fearless and curious, getting into scrapes and risking themselves for the sheer joy of facing danger . . . much like someone in this room."

"You must be talking about yourself. I'm the soul of caution."

He chuckled. "As they explored the world, they found the broken dolls Eurus had discarded as a child. Together they fixed them and breathed life into them. They grew fascinated by these creatures, whom they called men and women. For a while, the twins worked in harmony to help people in small ways, teaching them how to hunt and cook the meat with fire."

"Mmm," I said. My eyes had fallen closed.

Kai stroked my hair—it felt so nice I didn't bat his hand away—and continued. "But Fors and Sud grew bored of watching people do the same things day after day, and decided to explore. They traveled east and found a young man who looked like them. He said he was their brother, Eurus, and that he was tired of living all alone."

I shivered and pulled the quilt higher over my shoulder.

"They brought Eurus back to their parents' dwelling, which

was built high in the clouds so that Neb could be close to her first daughter, the Sun.

" 'We have found our brother,' they said, 'and we want you to let him come home.' At first, Tempus refused, but the twins said, 'Do as we ask, or we will leave and never return.'

"So Neb and Tempus had no choice but to embrace their oldest son. In gratitude, Eurus wove palm fronds into fans and gave them to the twins. Fors used his fan to create the north wind and Sud created the south wind. And Cirrus joined them in a game that tumbled winds across the world and all four siblings laughed in great joy."

I smiled serenely, imagining myself as a wind god floating on the currents I'd made with my fan.

"But their games had caused havoc over the earth, creating typhoons and hurricanes and tornadoes. Sun looked down upon the people and saw that her siblings had destroyed simple homes and crops they had started to grow, and she shone a light on the destruction. And Cirrus saw what her sister, Sun, was showing her, and she told her other siblings to stop their game."

"Did they stop?" I asked drowsily. Grandmother had told me this story, but it was so long ago, I didn't recall the details.

"They did. All but Eurus. 'Why, those people are nothing but the dolls I broke as a child,' he said, laughing at their pathetic fragility. And he made wind after rushing wind and laughed as it swept people and animals into clouds of dust, wiping the land clean.

" 'You are cruel,' said Cirrus, shaking with rage, 'and you have no regard for life.'

" 'You are foolish and weak,' said Eurus, 'and you care too much for small, broken things.'

" 'I am stronger than you,' she said.

"Eurus said, 'Then let us see who will win a contest of strength.' "

Kai's warm hand cupped my shoulder. "Ruby?"

I tried to reply, but I was floating in the clouds. With one more stroke over my hair, his hand left me and I felt the bed move as he stood.

"Good night," he whispered.

That night, I was back in the Frost King's castle—in my old room with the heavy curtains, richly upholstered chairs, and the table piled with books in front of a darkened window. The room was lit by a single candle that sat on a table next to the bed. I slid out from under the covers, my feet landing on soft carpet. Strangely, the air was warm—scented with hibiscus and bougainvillea. I paused a moment, breathing in.

A book lay at my feet. As I picked it up, it fell open to a picture of a throne room that looked like one of Sister Pastel's illuminations at the abbey, painted with charcoal and scarlet and tints of cerulean blue. The throne was mostly black, with veins of red and vermilion running through it, and icy pillars all around. The walls were a mix of stone and crackling frost. A sapphire ring glinted on one armrest of the throne, while a ruby ring glinted on the other.

I closed the book and put it on the bed before leaving my room, breathing softly as I wandered the empty hallways.

"This way," a voice whispered. I followed it, my hands brushing the walls. Suddenly, I was no longer in the king's castle, but the queen's, the walls of black stone. I found myself at a set of double doors opening into a cavern with black pillars and sputtering torches, a throne in the center casting a dull red glow. I could feel its heat pressing against me, beckoning and warning, hinting at a power that could not be fully contained.

The fire throne.

It was so beautiful. Sud had created this, and I could feel the goddess's own heat searing the air. Hot bubbling lines of molten lava ran continuously through the black stone, small air bubbles forming and bursting, each tiny vein glowing. Could even a Fireblood bear to sit on that relentless heat?

It was hard to see the full shape of the throne in this light, but it looked somewhat irregular, the two armrests slightly uneven. I stepped closer and reached out, placing my hand on one arm. There was a long, breathy sigh.

My hand slid farther up the surface of the rock—it was hot, but not unbearable. My whole body warmed. I moved closer until my legs brushed the throne's base. Heat traveled up to my belly and into my chest, through my arms, and out my fingers, back into the throne. It felt as if I were part of it, drawing from its energy source and giving back in equal measure.

Suddenly, I sensed a pressure under my skin, and a consciousness that was not my own examining the feel of my form, curious and searching, like a bird that visits a newfound nest. I realized I'd been holding my breath, and exhaled a mouthful of air. I squeezed my eyes shut and tried to find the light inside myself, to expel the presence inside my skin.

"Ruby," a man's voice said. "What are you doing?"

My eyes flew open, but all I could see was a tall, shadowy figure, with only dim light coming through an open door. We were in a dusty storage room filled with broken baskets, sagging shelves, and piles of firewood.

"Where did the throne go?" I whispered.

The form moved closer, a warm hand finding mine. "You're not really awake, are you, Ruby? Come. I'll take you back to your room."

With those words, I felt the dark presence shift, felt its reluctance as it flowed out of me, leaving me limp and shaking.

FOURTEEN

A WOODEN BRIDGE WITH ROPE CABLES spanned two cliff faces. Lava poured from one cliff like a waterfall, gathering in a wide pool under the bridge before flowing away in a thin river that cut through the narrow canyon, meandering out of sight toward the northern edge of the island. In the center of the bridge, missing boards left a gap a couple of yards wide. A large glass cube sat over the gap.

I squinted, ignoring the elevated rush of my heart as I tried to figure out what it was and how it might relate to my second trial. I heard Kai swear under his breath and Master Dallr hiss at him to be silent.

The glass had a bluish sheen and was too thick to see through. I'd never seen—

I drew in a breath and stopped. Not glass. Ice.

Only a Frostblood could create ice in this warm climate—shape and craft it so carefully. And I hadn't seen any Frostbloods since coming here, aside from the queen's servant. Had he made this on her orders?

Kai appeared at my side, speaking quickly. "You can do this. You *are* ready. You just can't let yourself—"

"Silence," said Master Dallr. "Remove your shoes and stockings." I did so, dropping them beside the path. He motioned for me to approach the bridge.

"You see the chamber of ice," he said quietly.

I swallowed convulsively and nodded.

"The ice will hold if you remain still and calm. It's a test of restraint and endurance, control over your mind and body. Vital qualities in a master." He pulled a small hourglass from a pocket and held it up. "You must sit in the chamber for one hour, at which time, you will return here. If you move from that spot before I permit you to move, you will forfeit."

I turned to stare at the pool of lava below. My fingernails bit into my palms, frustration already raising my temperature. I had never been able to repress my heat under stressful conditions. Brother Thistle had warned me that I needed to learn. Why hadn't I listened?

"You may begin," said the master.

His face was a mask of indifference. How many young students had he watched die in tests like this? For a people with fire in their veins, it was such a cold way to measure its masters.

And this trial in particular—a test of my ability to deny my very nature—seemed devoid of pity.

I couldn't afford to get angry, not now. I closed my eyes and took a deep breath, then started toward the bridge.

"Stay calm," Kai instructed, grabbing my arm as I went to pass him. "Don't get upset, no matter what happens. Think only of controlling the beat of your heart, of keeping your skin cool. Deep breaths."

He pulled me tight against him. I had a moment, pressed to his chest, to ponder the irony of his advice. He counseled me not to grow warm, not to worry. Meanwhile, I could feel his chest rising and falling rapidly against my cheek, his overheated skin, his heart thudding in my ear. His warm lips pressed hard against my forehead, and then he let go.

I grasped the rope cables that ran like handles on both sides and stepped on the bridge. It was just wider than my shoulders but sturdy under my bare feet. I followed it until I reached the center. A small opening allowed access into the ice chamber. I climbed in and slowly sat, crossing my legs. I wouldn't look down.

Brother Thistle's lessons in mental control had never been so vital. Breath after breath, beat after beat of my heart, I sought the word he'd taught me and returned to it, trying to clear my mind. Without the freedom to coat myself in extra layers of warmth, I started to shiver.

Several minutes passed before I realized that my legs weren't just cold; they were growing damp.

The ice was melting.

My heart stuttered and pumped faster. My fingers tingled with pings of heat. I took several shuddering breaths. Calm. Cold. Slow. Slow. I thought of Arcus, his cool skin, his command of his gift. His lessons on control. I struggled to master my responses, not to panic.

Without deciding to, I looked down. Oh, Sud. Under the blur of ice, the orange of hot lava. How would this hold? How could it possibly—

Stop. Focus. I squeezed my eyes shut and returned to the task at hand: slowing my heart, my breathing. Keeping the heat at bay, ignoring the biting discomfort of the cold.

The minutes crawled.

When next I opened my eyes, I was sitting in a groove in the ice. My leggings were soaked. Still, I focused on the word, on not letting panic rule. The ice was melting quite slowly. If I could just keep myself as cool as possible, this would all be over and I would pass the test. I could do this.

That's when I felt it: a vibration. On the bridge, small, dark blurs made a skittering sound.

The miniscule spots rushed closer, growing in size.

Mice? Rats? Spiders, perhaps.

But no. Not spiders.

I'd seen an illustration of this creature in a book. It had eight legs, but a segmented tail rose and curled forward over its back with a stinger on the end. Its front legs widened into hard pincers that could sever the body of an insect in half. They were bright orange and glowed with heat.

My breath caught. Sudesian scorpions.

They came with terrible speed, flowing forward over the ropes and boards of the bridge. When they reached the ice, they would have nowhere to go but inside, inside the tiny space where I sat, where any increase in temperature would mean melting and death.

I started to struggle to my knees, then remembered Master Dallr's instruction. I could not move. If I left the chamber, I would forfeit.

Instead, I reached out, hoping this movement would not disqualify me, and sent bolts of fire at the shapes. When the first one burned, the nearby scorpions reared and changed direction. If anything, they moved faster now. I burned another, and another. Then realized my mistake. One of the rope cables caught fire.

I swore. How was I supposed to defend myself?

But of course I wasn't. I was supposed to sit here calmly as these stinging beasts swarmed over me, helpless on a block of cruel ice that would melt if I allowed my fear to get out of control.

"Sage," I called desperately. But I didn't hear her or see her. I was alone.

Even the presence of the Minax wouldn't be unwelcome now. I would use the darkness to burn those little creatures no matter where they ran, seeking out their tiny hearts with that warped but vivid certainty I always felt when I let the darkness rule. But there was nothing in my mind, no presence but my own.

Frantically, I searched for some defense. Brother Thistle's teachings...but I couldn't calm myself in these conditions. I could barely remember the mental practice. What was the word? I couldn't even remember the...

Something touched my knee and I lashed out unthinkingly with my fist. I screamed as pain lashed my thigh. The first scorpion had wasted no time in sinking its stinger into my skin.

I swore as another scorpion crawled up my back, hovering on my shoulder. I took a breath and tried to think. This was a test of self-control, so the test would be set up to punish me for movement and to reward stillness and calm. It stood to reason that if I remained still, they wouldn't sting. I tried to focus on breathing, but my breath came in sobs. All I could do was concentrate on keeping my mouth closed. If, Sud forbid, one of them touched my mouth...I shuddered in disgust.

More of the creatures poured into the space. They were small, not much bigger than my thumb, but they were fast and several of them grasped my skin experimentally in their razor-like pincers. I moaned, shaking with the effort of remaining still. The groove in the ice was deeper now. I was sitting in a puddle. How long before my movements, my fear and anguish, melted a hole that would drop me into the stew below?

But even though that was the greater threat, it was the scorpions that tormented me. Inside me, the heat was rising, my control slipping, my sanity unraveling. I was covered now. At least a dozen were in the chamber, scuttling and confused, crawling over me and over me in their desperation to find a way out. I breathed through my nose with shuddering breaths. When one attached itself to my neck, I jerked convulsively. They grew more agitated. Two more sank their stingers into my skin: one on my knee and another on my back.

Tears slid down my cheeks and hissed as they landed in the cold puddle below. I closed my eyes. *What a horrible way to die.*

I shook away the thought. The time had to be almost up. Just a few more minutes.

Some of the scorpions crawled out again, heading back the way they came. The fire I'd started on the rope deterred passage that way, but some of them chose the other rope. Finding no exit in the ice, they started to finally leave.

I allowed myself a sigh of relief.

And then the ice gave way.

The first sign was the puddle draining away into a tiny opening that let the water flow down and out, as if a cork had been removed from a stopper.

As the hole grew larger, I braced myself against the sides of the chamber with my arms, kneeling and widening my legs. Another scorpion stung the back of my hand, panicked by my movement, and then it fell, legs and tail moving with ponderous surprise, toward the lava below. The remaining creatures scuttled out of the chamber. All but one, which stayed tangled in my hair, its pincers driving into my scalp.

The hole widened. I used my fingers to carve handles into the sides of the chamber. I couldn't sit any longer. The floor would soon be altogether gone. I watched as the opening widened, widened. It was hypnotic to see the ice turn to liquid and drip helplessly into the lava. If I dropped, I hoped it wouldn't take me long to die. Since fire coursed through my veins, sinking into the lava would be like going home, in some way.

That's what I told myself.

"Hang on, Ruby!" a voice called.

Tears coursed down my face and dried instantly on my heated skin. "I'm sorry," I whispered. I wasn't sure whom I spoke to. The masters, the queen, Kai, Arcus, Brother Thistle. One or all of them. I'd failed them.

"Time!" a deep voice called. "Time!"

My head jerked to the right. Master Dallr stood at the edge of the bridge, holding the hourglass aloft.

I stared for a second. Disbelief, hope, elation. The hour was up.

"Ruby, come on!" Kai screamed. "Now!"

I gasped and flexed my arms, throwing myself through the gap in the misshapen, half-melted chamber. My feet hit the boards and I grabbed the rope on the unburnt side. I took a second to rip the last scorpion from my head, tearing out some of my hair with it, and threw it to the lava below. The fire on the rope had spread to the boards. The right side of the bridge was in flames.

I didn't fear the fire. I feared the supports would burn away before I reached the edge.

My foot landed on a charred board and sank through, yanking my arm as I held on to the rope. I hauled myself up and continued on, choosing each step carefully.

"Hurry," Kai called, his voice low and urgent. "Hurry!"

The bridge suddenly jerked and twisted. The whole right side detached from the cliff, the right-hand rope swinging uselessly. Only the rope on the left remained. I gripped tighter. I was still several yards from safety.

"Come *on*," Kai yelled.

I balanced on the narrow left support, pulling myself hand over hand along the rope. When I was a foot or two away from Kai's outstretched hand, the rope I was holding frayed and snapped. I pushed with my feet, vaulting toward him. As I reached the edge, he took my arm in a ruthless grip and threw himself backward. We landed on the flat cliff top, my feet dangling over the edge. Kai scrambled back farther and pulled me with him.

We stayed there, Kai on his back, panting, me half on top of him in an ungainly heap until Master Dallr offered his hand. He looked me over as he pulled me up. "Are you unharmed?"

I looked down at myself, gasping for breath. I was all in one piece. "Yes."

Kai stood, brushing bits of dirt and twigs off his clothes. I put my hands on my knees, my whole body trembling.

"Then come. We must return to the school to confer."

In a minute, I was recovered enough to trudge along the cliff path.

"A simple congratulations wouldn't kill him, would it?" I muttered.

Kai didn't speak for a minute. Finally, he said, "They probably need to discuss whether you passed."

I turned on him. "*Whether* I passed? I'm alive, aren't I? I didn't leave the chamber."

"It's not your fault," he said, his nostrils flaring. "It's mine. I helped you at the end. I grabbed your hand."

"If you hadn't, I'd have fallen. You weren't allowed?"

He shook his head. "If they think you wouldn't have made the edge on your own, they will consider it a failure."

My relief turned to horror. "So I might have failed?"

As the reality of that sank in, I knew I was no longer doing this solely for access to the masters' knowledge. I was doing this for me. Somewhere along the way, passing the trials had become a goal in its own right, a way to prove my strength and, in some way, my worth. I wanted this regardless of whatever else happened. I tried to push the feelings away, but there they were. Failure would not only devastate me with guilt because it would leave Tempesia at the mercy of the Minax, but the personal disappointment would cut me to my core.

The scorpion stings began to throb. I focused on the pain rather than the fear that I might have missed my chance, and all that meant for me, for Arcus, and for Tempesia.

We trudged down the hill in silence. The masters were far ahead on the lava fields now. When Kai and I neared the hill next to the school, I stumbled to a halt. The world spun and I found myself on my knees.

"Kai?" I said, blinking stars from my eyes.

"Mmm?" He was still walking away.

"Is the sting from a Sudesian scorpion poisonous?"

He halted abruptly. "Yes."

"Can you die of it?"

He turned. “Only if you’re stung a number of times.”

“How many times? Just for curiosity’s sake.” I closed my eyes against the spinning of the world.

“How many times were you stung?” he shouted, rushing to grab me under the arms as I toppled to the side. “Master Dallr asked if you were unharmed and you said you were fine!”

As he scooped me into his arms, my hand reached up to tug at his collar. The world was melting all around me, the sky blending with the land and swirling together like paints spilled onto parchment. I remembered an old song my mother used to sing when I was ill, and I sang a few bars as the colors behind my eyes blurred together and burst.

The pungent scents of healing herbs were so familiar that for a moment I was home in my village in our little hut, my mother’s soft hand on my forehead. When I opened my eyes, she looked different than I remembered—her features heavier, her hair darker.

No, it was the queen’s face, but blurred, as if seen through a fogged window. Still caught in the memory, I sang a few bars of the song. As I sank into sleep, I heard the next verse sung back to me in a soft alto.

When I woke again, I was alone in my room in Queen Nalani’s castle, sunlight slanting through a gap in the curtains.

I wiped the tears from my cheeks. I’d dreamed of her. Mother had held me in her arms and sang songs in Sudesian to soothe me.

I'd all but forgotten those songs. She'd stopped singing them when I was very young, speaking only in Tempesian for as long as I could remember. But some part of my mind had held on to the memory of that music, triggered when I slept here in her homeland.

Rising from bed made the scorpion bites throb angrily. My fingers and wrist were puffy and pink. Some sort of smelly unguent had been rubbed over the swollen skin, which must be the source of the strong herbal scents.

I pulled on calfskin boots and stood. A wave of dizziness hit. I was leaning awkwardly against the bed, wiping at a growing layer of sweat that beaded on my forehead and ran down my cheek, when the door opened.

A familiar mocking voice drawled, "What a relief. I was worried you might not recover your usual stupidity."

I tried to lift my head to glare at him, but if I didn't focus on balance, I might fall. I settled for making a shooing motion with one hand.

"Thank Sud you're just as foolish as ever," Kai said, coming closer. "I would hate the poison to have stolen that adorable quality of always choosing the option that guarantees the most risk and pain."

"I don't do that."

"No? Then how do you explain the fact that you're dressed in your training gear when you should be resting?"

"The third trial?" I said. "Or were you so busy with your wardrobe that you forgot?"

"The scorpions' poison made its way to your tongue, I see. As if it weren't acerbic enough already. Never fear, acerbity pleases the taste buds if it's cut by sweetness. Fortunately, your rosy lips are sweet enough to balance the bitterness of your words."

"Will you stop talking nonsense and help me back into bed?"

He raised his brows in mock surprise. "I hardly know which statement to address, the accusation that my compliments are nonsense, or the invitation into your bed." He slid his arm behind my back and took one elbow, maneuvering me toward the spot where I'd thrown back the covers. "The first one wounds, while the second entices. Such contradictions seem common for you. I wouldn't be surprised if you like to bite when you kiss."

His rambling set me on edge. I made sure to accidentally shove a hand against his face as I tumbled onto the mattress. He was almost too jovial, too teasing. As if he was trying to distract me by keeping up a steady patter.

"What are you trying to hide?" I squeezed my eyes shut against the room, which was moving like a ship in choppy waters.

It took him forever to answer. When he did, his voice was as somber as if someone had died. "I'm sorry, Ruby. They're conferring now, but it doesn't look good."

The breath left me in a rush. "No." I couldn't have failed the second trial. I couldn't have. If I didn't pass, I'd never gain access to the library, never learn the truth about the throne. I cringed thinking of all the ways I had failed.

I pushed back to my feet and stumbled from bed. "Where are they?"

"The throne room. But there's no sense—Ruby!"

I flung myself into the hallway and hurried to the throne room, leaning on the wall for support. I batted away Kai's hand when he tried to stop me. Finally, he gave up and followed.

Once I reached the room I saw that three masters faced Queen Nalani, who sat on her throne, grim and solemn. Master Dallr spoke in his confident baritone, and I caught the words "rules that must be upheld, no matter the student."

I blundered in, uncaring that all eyes swung to me, and stopped an inch from Master Dallr.

"I would like to speak in my defense," I said forcefully, trying not to weave as the room leaned a little to the left.

"This isn't a trial, Ruby," Master Dallr said impatiently, "this is a decision for the masters alone, which will be finalized in due course after we have a *private* discussion with the queen."

I balled my hands into fists and braced for the queen to berate me and tell me to leave, but when I looked up, Prince Eiko leaned over and whispered something in her ear. The queen's eyes met mine and held as she said, "You may stay."

I closed my eyes in relief. If there was any chance of stating my case, I wanted to be here to do it.

"This is highly irregular, Your Majesty," another master said. "If we let students interfere—"

Queen Nalani raised a palm to halt the master's argument and said pointedly to me, "But if you stay, you must be silent."

I bit my lip to keep from arguing and focused on staying upright while Master Dallr sighed in frustration. A second later, I felt Kai's warmth, one hand hovering at my back, one at my shoulder, presumably in case I decided to pitch forward onto my face. I wanted to tell him to stop rescuing me, especially while that was the very sticking point that was being argued, but the queen had ordered my silence. I settled for turning my head to glare, which earned me a raised eyebrow.

"As I was saying," Master Dallr continued, "if Prince Kai hadn't grabbed her arm at the last moment, she would have fallen. The nature of the trials forbids interference. It is in our codes, our sacred rules, which we have observed for generations. To have helped her means a breach of tradition."

"A breach of tradition," said Prince Eiko. "So this is the first time something like this has happened?"

"To my knowledge, yes."

"So, in fact, your codes and rules cannot tell you how to judge this unusual circumstance."

A vein beat a rapid tempo in Master Dallr's neck. "The code clearly prohibits the masters from interfering in the trials they judge."

"But there is no specific prohibition against a *student* interfering?" Prince Eiko said, his green eyes sparkling with triumph.

"Well...no."

Prince Eiko made a gesture that clearly said, *There you have it.*

"It sounds to me as if an exception has occurred," the queen said into the confused silence.

Kai's lips tickled my ear as he bent to whisper, "You see?" He was referring to his claim that he was the exception to all rules. My heart was pounding too fast to appreciate levity.

"You must be silent, too, young prince," Queen Nalani said to Kai.

He nodded in reply.

"The masters have always had the right to make this decision," Master Dallr argued hotly. "In this, we have always had autonomy."

He folded his hands and waited, as if he knew he'd just made the winning move.

The queen regarded him silently for several long seconds. Then she inclined her head. "You are quite correct, Master Dallr. It is not a sovereign's place to interfere in this judgment."

It was clear where this was going.

I broke my promise of silence, frustrated with the way my fists trembled at my sides. "I might have made it safely without Kai's help. No one can prove that I wouldn't have! Let me take the trial again and I won't argue, whatever the result."

"Be silent," the queen said coldly. "Prince Kai, she is clearly ill. Please take her back to her bedroom."

I looked at Prince Eiko, my whole body trembling, but he merely stared back with sympathy in his eyes. I didn't need sympathy, I needed a champion. A miracle. I turned to Master Dallr, even though I knew trying to convince him would do no good. His black chain with the key hung outside his robes, winking at me temptingly.

It didn't take much effort to lose my balance. I merely unlocked my knees and gave into the vertigo that was already making my head spin. As I fell, I made sure to dislodge Kai's hand from my back with a flailing elbow as I lurched headfirst toward Master Dallr. He had no choice but to catch me, which he did at the last second, just when I was convinced I would crack my head on the hard floor. He grunted as he lifted me into his arms. I grabbed his chain in a convulsive movement, then forced the rest of my body to go limp.

"Take her to her room," the queen said urgently. "I will send the healer."

"Of course, Your Majesty," he said, and strode from the room, the heat of frustration coming off him in waves.

As Master Dallr carried me down the tower steps, the jostling motion gave me the perfect cover to slide my hand along the chain to where a link held the key. With tight fingers, I melted the link, and the key came away in my hand.

When we reached my room, Kai opened the door and hovered as Master Dallr deposited me on the bed. I groaned and rolled over, sliding the key under my pillow. When Master Dallr noticed the loss, I hoped he wouldn't immediately know it was me who'd taken it.

A minute later, the master left as the healer came in and held pungent herbs under my nose. I feigned waking groggily, answered all his questions, and assured him and Kai that I just needed rest. When the door shut, I breathed a sigh of relief... only to have reality strike harder than a punch, burying me in layer after layer of regret.

If only I had controlled my reactions the way I was supposed to, the bridge wouldn't have caught fire and I would have made it back without any trouble. I still thought there was a chance I could have made the leap to safety without Kai's help—I had thrown myself forward, and even if I'd slid, there were rocks and branches I might have grabbed to stop my descent—but there was no way of knowing for sure. The masters had ruled that I'd failed, and the queen had agreed not to interfere. Which meant it was over.

I would never be a Fireblood master. I would never be able to match the gifts of Brother Thistle or Master Dallr. I would never be able to prove my worth to the queen. I hadn't realized until that moment how much I'd wanted that validation, how much I'd longed for the respect that would come with it. Most of all, I'd wanted to prove it to myself.

I wasn't strong enough to be a master and, for all I knew, that weakness could mean my defeat once I had to face the Minax. As much as my failure sickened me, there was nothing I could do to change that.

There was only one way to salvage some hope. I had to steal the book.

FIFTEEN

I KEPT THE KEY UNDER MY PILLOW until nightfall, when I'd have the best chance of stealing into the library undetected. After a few hours of rest, I was well enough to dress in dark clothing and slip through the corridors.

As I hid in the midnight shadows near the servants' entrance, waiting for the changing of the guard, an especially tall figure hurried toward the castle. It could only be Prince Eiko. Rumor had it he spent his evenings in the observatory, a tower mostly hidden by woods east of the castle.

He stopped, his chin rising, his head turning in my direction for a moment. I held my breath. Then he resumed his long-legged stride. I peered around the corner as the guards opened the creaking doors for him, making sure he disappeared into the castle. Two more guards arrived and the four began chatting. When their heads were turned away, I crept forward, taking a roundabout route and sticking to shadows as I picked my way through woods and over rocks and found the main road. From there, it was a straight route past the now familiar wharf.

The wharf wasn't ready to sleep. A tavern facing the road had its door propped open, spilling light and laughter and the reek of sweat into the night air. Sailors guffawed and argued, their rough accents familiar from my time on the ship. I was about to move on, when I caught sight of a familiar broad, sun-lined face. Jaro sat at one of the tables, his cheeks red with drink, his easy smile flashing as his companion spoke and gestured with his hands.

Jaro looked up, and for a second I thought he might have seen me, but then he took another slow sip. I moved on.

A minute later, I heard the clump of approaching footsteps. I spun around, my hands automatically heated and ready to fight.

Jaro chuckled and showed his palms. "I surrender."

I dropped my arms. "I didn't think you'd seen me."

"A good sailor is aware of any passing breeze." His grin was wide. "Even one from the north."

I just hoped he wouldn't ask me why I was passing by so late at night. "How is Aver?"

"Angry. I enrolled her in the school. She would prefer to be at sea with me. But I have a peace offering. I built her a small vessel she can sail around the island."

"On her own?"

"With a friend. As long as she watches the weather and tells me when she's going out."

"Am I considered a friend?"

"Of course, Ruby." He stuffed his hands in his baggy pockets and rocked back on his heels. "You don't even need to ask. If you want to sail, you can find me down at the seventh pier most days. Or here in the tavern at night." His smile widened. "And it's good to hear you speaking Sudesian. You learned quickly."

"I had a good teacher."

He made a dismissive gesture, but he looked pleased.

After we said our good-byes, I continued on until I reached the school. Sweat had beaded on my forehead, and my stomach roiled. The poison's effects hadn't left me entirely, but I ignored the discomfort. I needed to be back in the castle before dawn.

I crunched over the gravel drive and entered through the gate. No masters in sight. I crept through the school like a ghost, rolling each leather-clad foot from heel to toe.

The hallway was empty until I reached the black door of the library where two older masters dozed, one with her cheek pressed into her palm, the other with his head leaning against the door. Moonlight spilled in from the arcade of windows, and a single lantern burned from its perch on a hook.

Slowly, carefully, I lifted the lantern and walked it back outside, leaving it in the courtyard. I could barely see the guards in this light, but of course they could summon fire to brighten the scene at any given moment.

I needed to create a diversion.

I was considering lighting one of the straw-filled practice dummies, when a voice nearly startled me out of my skin.

"A little late to be practicing, isn't it?"

I spun around. A tall form stepped into a patch of moonlight.

"Prince Eiko," I said, hand to my chest where my heart was trying to break through. "What brings you here?"

The shadows shifted over his face. "I was going to ask you the same question."

I watched him warily. His eyes glittered green in the moonlight, but his posture was relaxed. He crossed his arms, waiting for me to speak.

Every excuse for being here would sound weak, but I had to tell him something. "I'd hoped to practice alone for a while. It's so peaceful here at night."

He paused for several too-loud beats of my heart. "I may not rule this island, but I do know what goes on here. In fact, I know more than most give me credit for." He took a step closer. "If you tell me what you need, perhaps I can help you."

I resisted the urge to step back, instead meeting his eyes squarely and trying to read the expression in them. What was he hinting at? And how could I question him without revealing something about myself? I had no reason to distrust him, but not enough reason to blurt out my secrets. It was like sparring blindfolded. "Even if I needed help, why should you want to offer it?"

"I think we might have a common interest."

I doubted that. I tried to buy time and to draw him out more. "Thank you for pleading my case with the masters."

His lip curled. "Master Dallr is a pompous—" He cleared his throat. "Well, that is neither here nor there. They seem to have made up their minds. Only the queen would be able to overturn their decision."

"But she won't. She said as much."

"She never has before." He paused before giving a frustrated little breath. "As much as you don't trust me, I don't trust you completely, either, Ruby. You need to meet me halfway. Tell me what you are doing here. Alone. At night. Dressed like a thief."

My heart stuttered and picked up speed. That was almost an accusation. "I'm dressed for practicing. Am I not allowed to be here?"

"I won't tell the queen, if that's what you mean."

That surprised me, the hint that he would protect me, even if it meant hiding something from his wife. He was trying to gain my trust, but I couldn't afford to make a mistake. I'd already made too many. This confusing dance was losing its appeal. Time was running out, I had a book to steal, and I was standing here trading riddles with the queen's consort.

"But it's only fair to warn you," he added, "it won't be easy to draw the guards from their post. If you're caught, you will have to explain yourself to the masters and to the queen. I don't think you want to have to do that. Do you?"

My hands fisted at my sides. I didn't like being pushed. "I told you, I came to practice."

He ignored that. "In only a few more days, you could have had legitimate access to everything here. But alas, you might have failed your second trial. So here you are now."

Fear fluttered in my stomach. If he accused me in front of the masters, it was his word against mine.

When I said nothing, his hand sliced the air angrily. "If you continue to waste time, you'll run out. When you realize that, come see me."

He turned and disappeared into the dark. It took several minutes for my breathing to return to normal. My mind raced with questions, but they would have to wait. The night was slipping away. I opened my palms, set the practice dummies alight, then ran into the darkened hallway. Pitching my voice lower, I called out, "Fire!" and waited.

The guards rustled into wakefulness, moving from their post to follow the light from the merrily crackling practice dummies. As they ran to the well for a bucket of water, I slid through the dark and up to the library door.

It took a second to unlock, and I was inside. The door scraped the floor as I closed it, reassuring me that no light would bleed into the hallway. I lit a fire in my palm, using it to light four lanterns hanging from hooks.

Bookshelves ran in two rows with a central aisle. Each shelf had a lectern—a shelf that jutted out at waist height—and benches faced the lecterns. The books were all chained so they could be consulted here, but not removed.

There were hundreds of books and scrolls piled on shelves. Fortunately, during my training I'd chatted with some of the masters and gleaned information that hopefully seemed innocuous, expressing a love of books and asking about the libraries in

Sudesia. Master Cendric had explained that there was a catalog, a master list of all books, and beside each title, a system of numbers and letters that marked a book's position on a shelf. I found the catalog easily, a narrow book laid open on a lectern near the door. I held up a lantern and drew my finger down the list, looking for Pernillius the Wise.

There. It was here! Excitement sizzled through me. I checked the shelf and lectern numbers and found the correct spot.

The book wasn't there. I double-checked the catalog, then the shelf. It wasn't where it should be.

I moved to the other shelves and yanked out book after book. I knew the school's routines by now, and I was running out of time. Before dawn, prayers would start, and the guards would change. That would be my only chance to leave. After that, the school would be too busy.

In my panic, I knocked my elbow against a shelf full of scrolls. Some of them fell to the floor. As I was picking them up, I saw the word *throne* on one and stopped to unfurl it. It looked like a schedule, with days and times. The title read, "Guard Schedule—Throne," and the dates were from just last week. But I hadn't seen a single master guarding Queen Nalani's throne room. Unless it was only at night...? No, the schedule on the scroll was round-the-clock.

Which suggested another possibility: Was there another throne room?

SIXTEEN

I SPENT THE NEXT DAY SEARCHING the castle for the throne of Sud, chasing my theory that there was another throne room hidden somewhere. I covered every square inch, aside from private bedchambers, and found nothing. As I stomped back to my room, I avoided eye contact with the courtiers and servants, filling the corridors and stairwells with the black cloud of my mood.

I'd made too many assumptions! Perhaps I had simply failed to notice the guards in Queen Nalani's throne room. The *throne* on the schedule could be a code for something else. I was so desperate for answers, I was conjuring them from thin air.

I didn't have the book. I hadn't passed my trials. I had no idea what my next step should be.

Tired and dejected, I asked Ada to have supper sent to my room, where I sat on the edge of the bed, leaning against one of the corner posts. I was almost desperate enough to approach Prince Eiko, to ask him what he'd meant about our so-called common interest, to risk telling him everything. At this point, any action, no matter how dangerous, would feel better than doing nothing.

Shortly after Ada dropped off a tray of food, Kai showed up. He was dressed in a loose white shirt, left open at the throat, and his usual dark breeches.

"Having a picnic?" Kai said as he motioned to the untouched supper tray I'd set on the end of my bed. "How pastoral. I've brought the most important part of any meal. The wine." He held up a bottle.

Wine felt too celebratory. "I'm fine with water."

He grimaced. "Very well. But I'm having wine."

"Suit yourself."

We sat on either side of the foot of my bed, taking sips. I was glad he had come. His presence gave me a focus outside of the doubt and confusion fogging my mind.

"So about tomorrow's trial," Kai said, twirling his goblet idly.

"Tomorrow's trial?" I sat up. "They're still letting you take yours even though I failed?"

I finally looked at him closely. How had I missed that Kai was bursting to tell me news? He radiated suppressed energy, practically vibrating with excitement.

His lip quirked. "Letting *us*. It seems the council was forced to have a change of heart."

After a frozen pause, I grabbed his sleeve with my free hand and shook him. "How? Why?"

He laughed delightedly. "All I know is that the queen has never interfered in the masters' decisions about the trials... until now. She went to the school this afternoon and, for reasons I can't even guess at, overrode their decision. She wants us to take our third trial! In my case, it'll be my second try." His eyes moved over my face and he chuckled again. "Are you sure you don't want wine? Should I fetch some brandy? You look as if you've had a shock."

I put my cup on the tray and took his shoulders in my hands. "We have another chance!"

My smile was so wide it felt like it was cracking my face in half. Just when I thought all hope was lost, the queen had turned everything around. I wanted to run and shout and pick handfuls of flowers from the castle gardens and weave them into garlands. I giggled at my own foolish thoughts. Hope was a beautiful thing.

Kai grinned back at me, his eyes warming appreciatively. "So this is what Ruby looks like when she's truly happy." He took my chin between thumb and forefinger, turning my face side to side, making a show of scrutinizing me. "I shall have to memorize this rare and lovely expression in case I never see it again."

I swatted his shoulder and twisted my face away, laughing. "I can't believe it."

"You can no longer refuse wine. I insist." He lifted the bottle, watching me as he filled my cup.

I took a sip, using the moment to calm my thoughts and

focus. Originally, I'd wanted to take the trials to gain admittance to the library so I could find the book. Now I knew the book wasn't there. Did I still have to take the final test?

Yes. If I couldn't steal the information, I'd have to earn legitimate access to it. Passing the trials was more important than ever. Once I took my vows, I would be trusted, and the masters would answer all my questions.

The third trial wouldn't be easy, though. Kai had failed it the first time, and he'd had years of training to prepare him. What were my chances without even a hint or two beforehand? My conscience nagged at me that knowing anything about what was to come was against the rules, but I discarded the inconvenient scruples. After all, I was doing this to defeat the Minax, not for selfish reasons. At least, that's what I told myself.

I flicked my eyes back up, catching Kai watching me with an inscrutable expression. "I suppose you're going to be miserly with details, as always?"

He took a sip before answering. "As it happens, I've decided I don't give a damn about the code of secrecy."

My eyes widened. "Really?"

"Your close call during the second trial has altered my perspective. I want to give you the best chance to win."

I found myself grinning again. "Then tell me everything."

"Yes, I'm anxious to share the details of my secret shame that I've guarded for two years." He smiled unconvincingly and took a few long gulps of wine, then picked up the bottle and splashed more into his goblet.

Mirth gone, I shoved the tray back to make room and sat next to him, my hand squeezing his upper arm. "Tell me. I won't judge."

He grimaced. "You say that now."

"Fireblood promise."

He chuckled. "There's no such thing."

I waited.

He sighed. "First of all, what I'm about to tell you probably won't help you. I'd assumed that each test is the same, but your second test was different than mine. So it stands to reason your third could be different as well."

"Go on."

"The third test is about obedience. That's all. Obedience. Nothing more. It's easy as long as you agree to do the thing the queen asks. Simple." His brows drew together and a look of pain passed over his face. "Or at least, that's what I was told by Master Dallr beforehand: 'Do whatever she asks, and you will pass.' So I resolved to obey her, no matter what."

"So the queen is present for the third trial?"

"She gives the orders and makes the final judgment."

I nodded. "So what did she tell you to do?"

He set the cup down and stood, pacing the carpet. "I was sent through underground tunnels similar to the ones in the first trial. The way is lighted with torches so there's no danger of getting lost. It's merely a long way, giving you plenty of time to grow nervous."

"You were nervous?"

"Of course." He gave me one of his *How foolish are you?* looks. "Do you think me inhuman?"

"No." I thought about how often I'd seen Kai scared. Never, at least not until my second trial. Not even when our ship could have ended up at the bottom of the sea. "Well, maybe sometimes."

"I *was* nervous. I knew of other students who had passed the first two trials and never returned from the third. And friends who had passed the test and weren't the same afterward."

"Maybe becoming a master changes people."

"So quickly, though?" He turned to face me, the candlelight bringing out the gold in his eyes and making his hair shine like polished bronze. "The change was almost immediate. I said good-bye to a friend that morning and a stranger returned to the school the next day."

"Oh."

He nodded. "So I knew it was something... big. Something difficult that would transform me or kill me. I was nervous."

I took a sip of water and he drank some more wine. He went to refill his glass, but I grabbed the bottle and tugged on it. "I need you to be sharp tomorrow, too. For me."

He paused and nodded, then put his goblet down on my dressing table and sat next to me. "I entered a chamber with a flow of lava running through the center. I stood on one side and someone else stood on the other. Someone I knew." He cleared his throat. "I soon realized that it was a childhood friend, Goran, who had... well, let's just say his weakness for gambling had led him to some activities that were rather... left of the law."

"He was a criminal."

"A thief, among other things. Tried and convicted several months prior. My other friends and I had mourned his foolishness in getting caught, and we'd drunk a toast to the memory of past exploits and moved on. Though we'd been close as children, I hadn't thought about him anymore at all, really. He'd left school a year prior and fallen in with a crowd of petty thieves and wastrels. It was his own fault, I figured. I no longer concerned myself over him."

"What did you have to do?"

Kai paused, then looked me straight in the eye. "The queen ordered me to execute him. Immediately."

My breath caught. "Just like that?"

"His life was to be sacrificed for the greater purpose of testing one of her precious masters. What more glorious way to die? She actually said that."

Anger made my lips tighten. "She's as bad as King Rasmus."

"No, no," he protested a little too quickly, "she was merely carrying out tradition. Master Dallr explained it all to me afterward. The final trial is about sacrificing something for the queen, showing that you choose loyalty to her over all others. The masters are the protection and the strength of Sudesia, et cetera. I understand it."

I suddenly felt very foreign, as if I would never comprehend Sudesian ways of thinking any more than I'd understood Tempesian ways. "What did you do?"

"Well, if I'd had the ability to manipulate lava as the queen does, I'd probably have used it. Much faster that way."

"She does?" I asked, blinking a little.

He spread his hands. "It's the mark of the royal family. Since I don't have that ability, I used my fire."

He paused, staring at the floor. I had an urge to take one of his hands and rub the back until his fingers unclenched.

"But then Goran screamed," he continued softly, "and the sound tore at me. He never had a very strong gift, and consequently, he had a weak resistance to heat. Enough fire to gain entry to school, yes, but it was obvious after a couple of years that he wasn't progressing. But without the designation of master, he couldn't claim his title or the rule of his parents' island. I think in retrospect his disappointment led him to his . . . other activities." He shrugged as if it didn't matter, but it was obvious to me that it did.

"So Goran didn't defend himself?" I asked.

"Well . . . he was chained."

I swallowed my disgust, though it was directed at the queen far more than at Kai. "Go on."

"I attacked him again. Again, he screamed. And then"—he inhaled sharply through his nose—"he started to beg. He told me his mother was ill—I don't know if it was true. But Marta had been kind to me after my own mother died. Goran said she depended on him and that's why he'd turned to thieving. He babbled on, rehashing memories of our childhood together: the time we'd stolen a fishing boat and been caught in a storm when we were twelve." His lips curved gently. "The boom had swung and knocked me out cold. Only Goran's proficiency with boats had saved us. He took me home before anyone knew I was gone, so I was fine. Yet he had taken a beating when he'd arrived home later. His father was not an understanding man. I'd made it home free and he'd..." He sucked in a breath. "Well, it worked. Every word stabbed at my heart. He'd been my close friend once and I couldn't hurt him any more. I just couldn't. I decided then that I didn't care about the test. Not enough to kill my old friend."

"So that's why you failed?"

"That's why, yes." He turned to me and I sensed his need for understanding, the need to tell this story. It was unusual for Kai to be serious, to show vulnerability. He might be comfortable with many emotions, but he'd never shown the softer part of himself, his secret shame, as he'd called it. It was a gift I didn't treat lightly.

He went on. "The queen warned me then that there are consequences to disobeying her command. She advised me to rethink my obstinacy and carry out her order. I refused. Three times she asked me to reconsider and I refused."

He lifted his empty goblet and splashed more wine into it. I didn't stop him this time.

"You see, I come from an old family, generations of Fireblood masters who ruled the same group of islands. We've been unwavering supporters of the Sudesian monarchy. There was no doubt that I would pass the trials, especially the test of obedience. When I passed my second trial, my father held a celebration that night, all our neighbors and nobles from the surrounding isles in attendance, including several princesses he would have been pleased to see me court. He was so convinced of my success; he gave me his ring that night." He held up his hand, displaying the ruby ring he'd lent me as proof of his Sudesian ancestry. "The ring worn by all Sudesian princes or princesses, even though I wouldn't actually rule until he was no longer able." He gave a choking laugh, his smile at odds with his shadowed eyes. "I had tears in my eyes as he put it on me, a symbol of my ancestry, my worthiness to continue his line. I lived to please him, to make him proud. And finally, I had done it."

He was quiet for a minute. The silence was complete. The castle slept peacefully, only a rising wind rattling the casements.

"What was the consequence the queen warned you about?" I prompted softly.

He blew out a breath and lounged back on his elbows, but his jaw was tense.

"I could have borne a lashing or a beating without complaint. But it wasn't me who paid the price. The queen took control of my family's island and gave it to one of the other masters, a prince's daughter from a tiny, outlying island who had just passed her trials. Her family had built ships for the queen."

"So . . . your father no longer rules."

"He and my sister and her daughter live on our home island, but in a small house far from the estate where I grew up. The clay on their land is so dense and rocky it yields barely enough wheat to last one season. I send them coin, but my father is proud and won't accept anything from me. So I have to give the money to my sister, who tells Father that her work as a tutor pays much better than it really does. I've offered her a place on my ship, but she won't leave him. His health has declined. No doubt that's my fault, too."

"You can't blame yourself for everything." I wished I could smooth the tight crease between his brows.

"I don't. I only blame myself for the things I'm responsible for, and that's plenty."

"So that's why you sail your merchant ship and occasionally indulge in a bit of piracy? To send money to your family?"

"Also because it's fun." He grinned at me, the same disarmingly roguish smile that had grown so familiar. "But I've been hoping to find a way to restore my family's name. And then, when I heard about you, I thought I'd found it. A nice fat offering"—I smacked his shoulder and he grinned—"in exchange for my second chance."

"She didn't want me as an offering. She thought I would fail. You said so yourself."

"Well, you've proven her wrong." He clinked his goblet to my cup of water and drank.

"So everything has unfolded according to your grand plan. Now, you just have to pass your third trial."

"Yes. I 'just' have to pass. And for that, you 'just' have to pass." The irony was clear. It wouldn't be "just" anything. He stared into his empty goblet. "But what horror will she unleash on you tomorrow, hmm? What atrocity will she demand of me? That's the part I didn't let myself think of when I came up with this brilliant plan."

"Is your test after mine, then? Assuming I pass?"

"I would guess so."

I pulled my knees up and rested my chin on them. I didn't know anyone in Sudesia, so there was no danger that the queen would make me hurt someone I cared about. But still. "I don't want to pass if it means killing someone. I've had to kill before and I made a vow to seek the light. . . ." I waved a hand. "Maybe that sounds fanciful—"

"It doesn't." He adjusted his body so that he was sitting sideways on one bent leg, his arm braced behind me as he leaned closer. "I could have closed my eyes to Goran's suffering and killed him. Afterward, sometimes I wished I had. When my family had to leave their lives, their identities, behind and move into a dilapidated hovel with a leaking roof, then I wished I'd been stronger."

"Cruelty isn't strength." As I said the words, I was reminded that Arcus had once said something similar after I'd run away and he'd found me in a blizzard. He'd said, "Tyranny is not strength." At the time, it had surprised me, the idea that the mysterious, ill-mannered Frostblood held an opinion in harmony with mine. The memory gave me a twist of homesickness.

I waited for Kai to agree, but he seemed occupied with letting his eyes rove over me. Warmth slowly spread across my skin and I was glad my heightened color wouldn't be visible in the dim light. It was confusing that I could think of Arcus in one moment and feel warmth for Kai the next. Arcus lived in my heart, but I didn't know when I'd see him again, or if there was any future for us. He had told me we had to let each other go a little, and I had tried to do that. Kai was here, and he was warm and charming and alluring, drawing me into his current. I looked at the floor, trying to sort through the confusing tangle of thoughts and feelings.

"A debate for another time, perhaps." He wound a lock of my hair around his fingers, seeming fascinated by the way the end curled. He brought it to his face and inhaled before tucking it back over my shoulder, his hands smoothing down my back. I shivered helplessly. "I've had too much wine to philosophize."

"You seem lucid enough to me," I replied lightly, though my heart had taken up an elevated rhythm at the stroke of his long fingers over my shoulder blades. "I hope you're not planning to use the claim of intoxication as an excuse to flirt."

"I never need an excuse to flirt—though I prefer to call it 'appreciating your allure'—any more than I need an excuse to breathe. And you are more intoxicating than wine, Lady Ruby."

I laughed to cover the way his words sent honey through my veins and how I had to make a concentrated effort to push the feeling away. "And you flirt almost as much as you breathe."

"You don't mind, though, do you?" he asked softly. "Not really."

"I wish you'd told me sooner about the third trial," I said quickly. Kai's smile grew. He knew I was changing the subject.

"You realize what would happen if the queen found out I revealed even the smallest detail of the trials? I'm sorry if it took a while before I trusted you enough to risk my life for you."

I let my breath out slowly. "You're right. I'm sorry. But, Kai... what do I do? If I can't do whatever she tells me to do, where does that leave you?"

"I don't know. But know this: There will be a price to pay if you don't pass. You won't walk away without losing something you care about."

"Maybe you shouldn't go, then. What if she decides to take my failure out on you?"

His hands cupped my shoulders and slid with careful purpose up my neck and into my hair, his thumbs stroking my cheeks, leaving trails of warmth over my skin. His gaze fell on me, dark and heavy, but his mouth quirked up on one side. "Are you saying you care about me?"

"Of course I do," I whispered, unwilling to lie after the way he'd opened up to me. "You're my friend."

"Just your friend?"

His head dipped slowly, slowly toward mine. I could have pushed him away.

I didn't.

Suddenly I couldn't breathe and I didn't care. I wanted the comfort—no, the excitement—of his kiss. I was tired of fighting the sense of ease I had in his company, the knowledge that we were so similar, so complementary. Our worlds weren't at odds. I wouldn't have to bury my nature, my very essence, in order to be with him. It could be so much easier than it had ever been with—

Thoughts fled as Kai's lips met mine. They were warm and firm, gentle but confident, pressing and moving with gentle abrasion, back and forth, sending sparks through the sensitive flesh that had suddenly become the center of my universe. His tongue came out to touch the crease where my lips met and my breath drew in sharply, my mouth opening. The electric joy of it lit something inside of me, and then I was struggling to get closer, my fingers diving into the thick, bright waves of his hair. He pulled me tighter against him, his chest a hard wall against my softer frame, his strong arms holding me securely, as if they didn't want to let go.

He pressed me back against the mattress, his weight making it dip, and his lips found their way to my throat. I moaned, and somehow that brought me to my senses.

"Wait, what are we doing?" I gasped.

"I didn't think I'd have to explain it," he murmured.

I pushed at his shoulder and he sat up immediately. We were both breathing hard, and he ran his hands through his hair to leave it comically spiked.

"You should go," I said.

"First," he said softly, reaching out to rub his thumb over my bottom lip, "what's your answer?"

All I could think about was the warmth of his touch, the way my lips tingled at the gentle contact.

"What was the question?" I asked, struggling through layers of feeling.

He gave a satisfied chuckle, and the dark sound seemed to trail invisible fingers against my skin. His voice was soft but challenging. "Am I just your friend?"

I shook my head, coming out of the sensual fog he'd woven around me. He waited, but my confusion kept me silent.

I did feel more for Kai than friendship. I couldn't deny it, but I wasn't ready to admit it to him. And no matter how hard I tried to let go of Arcus, thoughts and memories of him were always there. He was a part of me. I wasn't ready to let that go.

After a minute, Kai stood and went to the door.

"There will be reckonings, little bird," he said, turning in the doorway. "With the trials tomorrow, certainly. But after that, with me."

SEVENTEEN

THE NEXT MORNING, I JOLTED AWAKE with a racing heart. The nightmare faded so quickly that I could only grasp pieces of it. I'd been wandering dark hallways, crying out Arcus's name, and listening to him answer, each echoing repetition of my name coming from farther and farther away. I knew if I didn't reach him in time, he'd be lost to me forever. And the arms that reached out from the walls would drag me down into the deep, never to surface again.

I poured a glass of water from the pitcher on my nightstand and drank in agitated gulps, waiting for my heart to quiet. The nightmare and my third trial were jumbled together in my thoughts, as if the first was a bad omen for the second. I reminded myself I wasn't superstitious and dressed in my tunic and leggings, waiting for Kai to come to my door like usual.

When he didn't appear, I went to his room and found it empty. I called his name, as if he might materialize out of the ether, but there was nothing but lingering traces of soap and sandalwood. I stared at the meticulously tidy room, feeling lost. Kai had been with me on the way to each trial. Had the masters separated us on purpose?

I tried to shake off worry as I traveled alone to the school, my midsection tying itself in knots. I concentrated on my breathing, swallowing past a lump of fear in my throat. After what Kai had told me about his third trial, I wondered if taking it myself was worth it. He seemed to regard his decision not to kill his friend as a failure, but I viewed it as a show of character. He'd refused to become a murderer just to pass the trials. In his place, I would have done the same. It was only afterward that the consequences—the loss of his family's land and fortune—had made him doubt his choice. How would he fare this time?

If I failed the third trial, I'd have to leave Sudesia empty-handed. Even without the book, the knowledge of the masters could have helped me defeat the Minax; otherwise it would remain free. I had to weigh the cost of preserving my principles—following the path my mother and grandmother would have wanted me to take—against saving a kingdom.

I hoped the queen wouldn't ask me to kill. I'd had to make that choice in the arena, and I didn't want to make it again.

Master Dallr once again took me up the hill to the temple of

Sud, where I said a brief prayer. Then I followed a somber procession of masters trudging on foot over the barren lava fields in the general direction of Sud, the belching volcanic monster named after the goddess of the south wind. I kept looking back as I walked, hoping to see Kai loping behind us to catch up. He didn't appear.

We came to the ruin of walls, what might have once been a dwelling. Inside, a stairway led to underground tunnels. They sent me in alone.

Torches showed me the way, and as Kai had described, it felt like a long time before I arrived at the end: a wide, echoing chamber carved from black stone, a river of lava dividing the two sides like a bloody gash. My pulse played an irregular beat in my neck. A bead of sweat trickled from my hairline down my cheek.

The river was only a few feet across. With a running start, I could probably jump the distance. But I doubted that was the point.

Only the glow of lava lit the cavernous space. Then suddenly, there came a blinding flash of light. On the opposite bank of the river, two masters made fire blaze in their cupped hands, brightening their orange robes and giving them the appearance of living torches. Light and shadow trembled over their solemn faces.

In the center, between the masters, a figure materialized from the dark, her gold filigree crown shining with reflected firelight like an underground sun. She wore an orange-and-red gown that flared into a train, the edges cleverly sewn to mimic flames. Jewel-laden gold chains hung from her neck and wrists, and each of her fingers winked with rings. She moved gracefully, appearing almost to float over the coarse floor, a crimson fog filled with a swarm of glittering fireflies. She halted at the edge of the river.

"You stand at a crossroads," Queen Nalani said in a melodic, ringing voice. "Behind you, your lonely past. Born isolated and cut off from your people, you were forced to rely on your own strength, your own counsel, your own solitary power—your life as easily extinguished as a single candle. Your very survival is a triumph."

I swallowed. I'd expected her to say something by rote, but it sounded as if she'd composed the speech especially for me. Or perhaps she hadn't, and I just felt she had. Either way, I felt each word deeply, as if she had pulled thoughts and impressions from my very soul and spoken them aloud.

"Ahead of you, your future." She gestured to the masters. "The chance to join your strength with others, to live among those who would die for you, to be embraced by a tradition that is much greater than yourself, to join your fire with a conflagration, consuming your enemies even as your old self is consumed, laying down your petty striving and meager aspirations in favor of a larger cause."

She paused. Anticipation and dread wound my nerves tight. I became aware of my breath, which was coming too fast, and felt the pain of my nails biting into the tender flesh of my palms.

"Should you pass," she said, "you will become a Fireblood master. Once you cross that threshold, there is no returning to your previous existence. You will be altered, transformed—your old self discarded in favor of a stronger self. You will be born anew."

She gestured, and the masters extinguished their flames. The room was again lit only by the glow of lava.

"You have accomplished much," the queen continued, "but a vital step must be taken to reach the final prize. There is no improvement but through sacrifice, no gain but through loss. To form a new self, you must discard what is worn and broken. You must kill those parts of yourself that diminish you. And in so doing, you will rise higher than you imagined possible, become a vital facet of a priceless gem. You will join a legacy, one of the kingdom's most revered protectors, one of my most cherished servants." The firelight flickered. The queen's expression darkened. "But first, you must earn my trust."

She made a small gesture and the masters stepped back into the shadows in perfect accord, as if she held strings that controlled them.

"The test is simple: Obey me and pass. Deny me and fail. The choice is yours."

She moved to the side. The masters relit the fire in their hands and moved forward, a figure between them.

My heart sank. I had hoped for a different test of obedience that wouldn't involve anyone's death, but this was exactly as Kai had described. Some unfortunate prisoner was being hauled before me and the queen would order me to execute him. Could I do it? I'd killed before to save myself, but this was entirely different. This prisoner would be helpless, unable to fight back. Even if I was doing it to try to save Tempesia from the Minax, did that goal justify killing an innocent person? Was it worth becoming a murderer?

The glow from the masters' hands caught the prisoner's hair, which was like fire on its own: tawny chestnut and auburn with streaks of bright orange. I stared in shock and disbelief. He stared back at me, stony-faced and silent.

"Kai," I breathed. I immediately faced the queen and said very clearly, "No."

To my surprise, she showed no sign of anger at my defiance. Instead, her eyes fairly sparkled with enjoyment. "You haven't even received my order, child."

It didn't matter what the incentive was—what I could gain by passing her test, how hard it would be to find a way to defeat the Minax without the masters' help, or what she would do to me if I failed. I would not kill Kai. My heart hurt even thinking about it. I would figure out another way to destroy the Minax. I would search the rest of the school for the book; I would tell Prince Eiko my secrets and beg for his help.

I shook my head. "I won't touch him." As far as I was concerned, the trial was over. I wanted to turn my back and walk out. But I knew she wouldn't make it that easy.

She folded her arms, her rings making pinpoints of reflected light dance over the dark walls. "There are consequences to disobeying me, Ruby. I cannot condone dissension. Surely even a stranger to our customs understands this."

I closed my eyes, thinking of what a fool I'd been. I'd come to Sudesia too trustingly, just as Arcus had warned, sure that the

Fireblood queen would be better than King Rasmus. Instead, I'd found a ruler whose expectations of unquestioning obedience were only too familiar.

"Even still," I said firmly. "I won't hurt him."

She laughed, the sound echoing off the walls. My eyes snapped to Kai. He still looked serious, almost grim. He didn't, however, look scared.

"Then it's a good thing I don't wish you to harm him, isn't it?" She reached out and beckoned to Kai, who stepped forward. "On the contrary, what I wish for is an alliance that will benefit both of you. And me as well, of course. A union that will benefit the entire kingdom, and guarantee the uncontested succession of my throne. No need to look so worried, child." Her voice gentled—gentled! I'd never seen her as being capable of softness—and her expression was almost fond. "I have a feeling you won't mind what I'm asking of you."

A crease formed between my brows. "Your Majesty, I admit I'm confused. What do you wish me to do?"

"Prince Kai has already agreed," she said, "and you need to agree as well. How fortunate that to pass your trial, no blood need be spilled. Instead, we have cause for joy."

My teeth snapped together at the way she was drawing this out. Her barely suppressed delight was almost as frightening as her anger.

She took a step back and gestured to Kai, then me. "Prince Kai, I will not rob you of this moment. You may ask her yourself."

Kai was silent for a moment. Then he dropped down on one

knee. A strange enough sight, but with a few feet of lava between us, it was bizarre.

If the queen thought I was confused before—

"Ruby," Kai said in a strained voice that was a far cry from his usual lackadaisical tones, "I know I am far from worthy of you, but would you do me the great honor of consenting to be my wife?"

If the sky had rained fire, I would have been less shocked.

I turned to stone. At least, that's what it felt like. I didn't move, didn't breathe, didn't even blink for what felt like a full minute. Then Kai lifted a brow and the air rushed back into my lungs.

"You're not serious" was all I could manage.

He produced a winning, though forced, smile. "I assure you, the queen—that is, I—am quite serious. I'm asking for your hand in marriage."

"To . . . *you*," I said with heavy emphasis.

"Yes, that is why *I* am the one asking." Despite his blinding display of teeth, he spoke as if his jaw was too rigid to form words properly.

"To me." I said it carefully, as if testing out new words in a foreign language.

"Which is why it is *your* hand I'm asking for." Whatever patience he'd had seemed to be seeping away. Also, I noticed a rather unmistakable urgency in his expression. He shifted his eyes meaningfully toward the queen and raised a brow. I glanced at Queen Nalani and saw that her smile had faded.

"Surely it is not a complete surprise," she said coolly. "I

understand the two of you have grown quite close during your time together."

"I would hardly say..." I began, then noticed the subtle movement of Kai's jaw, as if he were grinding his teeth into paste. Suddenly, I remembered that this test was about complete obedience. If so, I was failing.

She was giving me a chance to pass the dreaded final trial—without bloodshed, without sacrificing the well-being of anyone I knew. Or anyone at all, for that matter. Kai had already agreed, which meant he had weighed options and decided this was safer than facing whatever would happen if he didn't comply. I didn't think for a moment this was his idea. His level of sincerity was that of a child who apologizes only because his mother is twisting his ear.

The queen's chin had risen, her eyes sharply assessing. Kai gave a surreptitious nod, his piercing gaze practically begging me to agree. I knew him well enough by now to trust him. We had no other choice. At least, not now. Not yet.

"I accept," I breathed, and then a rush of dizziness hit me and I had to widen my stance to stay upright. Even though I knew this was just a pretense, a temporary concession until we could find a way out, saying the words made it seem like a promise, permanent and irrevocable. I had the sensation of being trapped, of a prison cell closing with a resounding clang.

When I'd let myself daydream—and on rare occasions, I had—it had been Arcus's face I'd seen looking back at me as I recited my wedding vows. It had been his voice I'd heard whispering to me on our wedding night.

Marriage. The word alone made me dizzy.

Not that I would marry Kai. Not that I would ever be able to marry Arcus, either. Not that I knew for sure that I wanted to tie myself to anyone that way. I'd always thought I had years to figure that out. I resented being forced even to pretend that I was ready to bind myself to another for life.

The queen's smile returned and she clapped her hands together. "What a joyous day! Prince Eiko, you are brilliant."

I hadn't noticed the tall figure standing several feet behind her in the shadows. At her words, he stepped forward and took her extended hand in his own. In the flickering light, the planes and angles of his face looked mercilessly sharp. "You give me too much credit, my love." He bent and kissed her hand.

"You may thank Prince Eiko for the ease of your third trial," she said, giving him a fond look, "as well as his insistence that you had rightfully passed your second, and that it would be wrong to allow the masters to fail you. He was very persuasive, devising a solution that suits all parties."

I watched Prince Eiko's face, scouring it for clues, wondering again just what he was doing. He'd said he wanted to help me, and I hadn't had to make any life-and-death decisions today. He had spared me that. Perhaps, when looked at in that light, he *was* on my side. What his reasons might be, I couldn't imagine.

"But, Your Majesty," I said, unable to help myself, "it's hardly a test of obedience if we both want to agree." Of course, that was a lie, but I wanted to know why the queen had chosen this as our final test. She wouldn't have let Prince Eiko talk her into it if there was nothing in it for her.

"You could have refused," she said with a slight hooding of her eyes. "Your agreement shows me that you have truly left your old life in Tempesia behind. This is what I want, Ruby, for you to commit to your new life here. And you will have plenty of opportunities to pay tribute to me by producing children as heirs to my throne and our family name."

Kai choked and then turned that sound into a cough. I realized my mouth had dropped open. I closed it.

"Your Majesty," I began carefully, knowing that I might risk both Kai as well as myself if I angered the queen, "I thank you for this . . . astounding opportunity. But how could I, a commoner from Tempesia, provide your heirs? Kai is, after all, not related to you."

She put a hand to her chest. "How remiss of me. Ruby, my sweet girl, you still haven't a clue who you are, have you?"

I blinked at the sobriquet of *sweet girl* and said, "I believe I know quite well who I am." But the assertion came out hesitant. I'd had too many surprises to be sure of anything.

"You are my niece," she said, blinding me with her smile. "My own flesh and blood. Your mother was my dear younger sister."

EIGHTEEN

My vision narrowed and my voice sounded strangely wispy and distant. "That's not... possible."

I heard the scuff of feet and looked up to see that Kai had leaped over the lava. He put an arm behind my back and I leaned against him because it was either that or topple to the ground.

"Your Majesty, she has had an exhausting few days," he said, his hand on my shoulder as he looked at the queen. "With your kind permission, I'd like to escort her back to the castle."

"Indeed," she replied. "How can I find fault with a display of husbandly concern for your bride-to-be?"

He took my hands, but I resisted his efforts to pull me away. "My mother wasn't even a Fireblood." I hadn't made a conscious decision to speak, but I couldn't seem to keep the words in. "There's absolutely no way that I could be related to you. With all respect—"

Without warning, the queen's hands rose and a geyser of lava lifted from the river and came soaring at me. Kai jerked back, then started to move in front of me, but the lava stopped in midair, hovering over us like a frozen wave. In the breathless moment that followed, I realized that my own hands were raised, my palms aimed out.

I stole a look at the queen. She had an expression of terrible concentration. The muscles in her forearms flexed and the lava moved a few inches toward me. I groaned and focused on it, pushing at it with my mind the same way I would if I were manipulating fire. The wave twisted and roiled in the air before slamming back down into the river. Drops of lava sprayed through the air, sizzling audibly against stone and clothing. One drop landed on my arm, making me gasp with pain.

I stared, incredulous, at the queen. She had controlled the lava. She had tried to hurt us with it. And I—I...

"Do not tell me you are not my sister's daughter," the queen said, the triumph in her eyes nearly feral in its intensity. "She was the only other person alive who could bend lava to her will. I began to wonder when Master Dallr told me that he'd watched your first trial from the openings that lead to the surface, and he was certain you'd halted the flow of lava. However, I wasn't ready to believe. I thought of you as an outsider, someone I could use against the Frost King. I didn't allow myself to believe you were my niece until after the second trial. I visited you while you were delirious with poison. You sang a song that my mother used to sing."

"A Sudesian lullaby," I said weakly, remembering how I'd dreamed of my mother, then the queen, at my bedside. "Surely every child born here knows it."

"My sister and I made up our own verses, and you sang those, too. Only she would have known that song and must have sung it to you. That was the moment I could no longer deny the truth." Her eyes, dark and full of such intelligence and determination, held me spellbound. "You are my niece. And so, I have my heir."

She glanced at Kai. "Take Ruby home and make sure she rests." She turned and strode proudly to an opening on the other side of the lava stream, her skirts swishing like retreating flames, the masters following quickly at her heels. From somewhere in the dark, I heard her voice. "We will announce your engagement tomorrow. The wedding will take place in a week."

I didn't even realize the jagged sound I heard was my own breathing until Kai said, "Shh, Ruby. Come. We'll talk soon, but not here."

We stumbled back through the tunnels, or rather, I stumbled, and Kai kept me upright with a hand on my wrist. I wondered vaguely which alternate route the queen had taken and whether that way was more fitting, somehow, for royalty. Perhaps it was lined with fine carpets and trays of food were offered at intervals by attentive servants. If so, I should have gone that way, too. After all, I was her niece.

I giggled hysterically and Kai pulled me along a little faster. "Keep it together."

I pressed my free hand against my mouth and continued on.

Kai didn't speak until we stood in a veritable wasteland of black rock about halfway back to the school. And then, only because I pulled free and said, "Stop. Here. Talk."

"Not yet," he said irritably, reaching for me.

"Now."

"You look ready to swoon. I don't want to carry you all the way back to the school."

"I'm not some delicate court lady who swoons at everything. Do I look like I'm ready to faint?" It was a relief to bicker, to fall into our pattern of attack and defend. I could push away the shock of the revelations for a few more minutes.

"Yes."

I took several deep breaths. He wasn't wrong. I felt as if I'd been punched and pummeled, instead of passing the third trial so "easily," as the queen had said. "I don't even know where to start."

"Keep walking. I mean it when I say I don't have the strength to carry you. Not today."

"Then talk while we walk. There are things I need to know." I took a shuddering breath.

We continued on. Carrion birds wheeled overhead and a breeze scoured the plain with humid, salty air.

"I don't know all the details, but I'll tell you what I know," he began. "Queen Nalani's sister and her baby daughter disappeared seventeen years ago. No warning. They were just gone. Foul play was suspected, of course. Kidnapping, perhaps, for ransom. But no ransom demands ever came. King Tollak sent soldiers and spies all over Sudesia, Tempesia, and as far as the Coral Isles, but they found no trace of the princess or her baby.

"Princess Rota had grown up sailing, so eventually it was thought she could have taken a boat. One of the vessels was missing from the king's fleet of pleasure boats, and it was a tiny craft, small enough to be piloted by one person. Not large enough to travel outside the islands and definitely not capable of crossing the sea. Finally, with no other information, they had to accept that Rota and her daughter had been lost at sea. They held a funeral and mourned the lost princesses and that was that."

"You grew up hearing the stories, I suppose?" I pictured the princess and her daughter, but in my mind, they looked nothing like my mother and me.

"Of course. It was a great tragedy. Made greater when years passed and it became clear the queen could not have children. There are cousins, of course, and other relations to the royal family, but the succession isn't clear. The rules in Sudesia are complicated. Noble rank has often been awarded based on one's gift. And no one's gift, not even her close relatives', rivals the queen's. No one else in Sudesia has the ability to manipulate lava. No one could truly fill her shoes."

I tried to ignore the way my stomach was tying itself in knots, and just focused on putting one foot in front of the other. "I see how that ability is symbolic of the royal house, but does it really matter that much?"

"Of course it matters. Mount Sud erupts every decade or two, sometimes with little warning. Not to mention the smaller volcanoes and those on surrounding islands. The queen has saved hundreds, perhaps thousands, of lives. Her abilities allowed evacuations that wouldn't have been possible otherwise."

"She can do that? Stop eruptions?" I couldn't imagine any of the ladies of the Frost Court actually *doing* anything to help anyone, least of all something so dangerous.

"Perhaps not stop them, but slow the lava, at any rate, long enough to save many people. We've come to depend on that ability."

I trudged along silently for a few minutes. I couldn't wrap my head around these revelations, so I let my mind wander to safer topics. Perhaps I'd have to revise my assessment that Queen Nalani was just as bad as King Rasmus. She used her powers to save the lives of her subjects, while he had used his to instill fear and terror so he could expand his kingdom. He hadn't been beloved by anyone, aside from his brother. And perhaps Marella.

"So the queen has no heir," I finally prompted when I was ready to hear more.

"*Had* no heir," he corrected.

I stopped cold. "Wait a minute. This isn't a surprise to you, is it? You knew when you came to Tempesia?"

"I didn't know... but I did wonder. I heard the stories of the Fireblood girl who destroyed the throne and I contemplated the level of power required for such a feat. It was a reasonable theory."

"Did anyone else wonder if I could be the princess? Did the queen?"

"Perhaps she did, secretly. Maybe she didn't dare hope. We didn't discuss it. In any case, she decided you would be a valuable ally and sent me to . . . come to terms with you." He paused and added in a more subdued tone, "She trusted me for the task, despite my failure of the trials. I never once defied her or spoke against her, even after she took my family's island away."

I wanted to ask why he hadn't defied her, and if he'd wanted to. What did he wish he could have done? But I had other more pressing questions. "So you heard about the ball and decided to pretend you belonged there."

"It didn't take too much convincing to get the dignitary to let me go instead and to provide the necessary proof of my identity."

"You did look very at home at the ball."

"Not my first ball, I assure you. The only shock was when I saw you."

I jerked my head up to look at him. "Why was it a shock?"

"Well, you were practically coated in powdered sugar, for one thing. I'd expected you to have learned at least some basic manners."

I jabbed his middle with my elbow and he laughed as he pushed me away. "Actually, I saw the resemblance to your mother. There's a portrait of her in the queen's castle, painted when she was about your age, I would say."

"I never thought I looked much like her." Pain lashed through me. I wished so much that I could look at her right now, that she was here to discount these claims, to tell me what to do. How had she hidden her gift so well? Why hadn't she instructed me on how to master mine, and instead seemed nervous, almost ashamed, of my gift at times? And worst of all, if she'd been a Fireblood, *why* hadn't she defended herself when the soldiers came? I couldn't bear to think she had hidden a gift that could have saved her life. I couldn't bear it.

The obvious answer was that Mother hadn't been a Fireblood at all, which meant she *wasn't* the lost princess. She was just a simple healer who preferred solitude. My grandmother certainly hadn't been a queen. I could still remember every patch on her colorful cloak, which she'd repaired with whatever scrap of fabric was at hand as she traveled the world. She was an eccentric wanderer who blew in and out of our lives as the whim took her.

Relief washed away the pain and doubt. That was the simplest explanation. Resemblances happened all the time. It didn't have to mean anything. Let Kai think what he wanted. I knew the truth. They had made a mistake. I wanted to argue it out with him, but then he might have some counterargument that might make me doubt myself again.

And then my whole identity would go spinning into oblivion. I wasn't ready for that. Instead, I asked him how he'd managed to agree to the engagement when he'd left me late the previous night.

"They came for me this morning," he said, peering up at the cloudless blue sky. "Well before dawn. I'd barely slept because I was worried about our third trial. When Master Dallr brought me to the throne room, and the queen said I merely had to give her the right answer to a question, I was relieved. After all, I wouldn't have to hurt anyone I cared about."

"Until you found out she intended to foist a fate worse than death on you," I said, attempting a light tone.

"I don't know that it's worse than *death*. I did point out that my second chance was contingent upon you passing the trials and that you hadn't passed yours yet. She said, 'Her success depends on yours. You can both pass, or both fail. Your destinies are intertwined.' "

I gave a half laugh. "How you must have loved that. Being told I'm your destiny whether you like it or not."

"Then she asked if I would marry you, and I thought at first she was making a joke. But she had the same look in her eyes as she had when she ordered me to execute Goran. Utterly serious. So I said yes."

"So marriage to me is like an execution."

"Better than an execution, I hope." He grinned and waited, but when I didn't smile back he added, "It was unexpected. And I know you didn't expect it, either."

"No."

We were silent for a long time. The hill leading to the school came into view and he said casually, "Not that I hadn't considered the possibility. But I didn't think it would be so soon."

I stumbled and Kai righted me. I turned to face him. "What?"

He didn't quite meet my eyes. "It's not unthinkable. The idea of us being married."

"Not unthinkable. What a ringing endorsement."

"I'd considered it, that's all I'm saying. For a very distant future. After several hundred liaisons with—"

"A hundred other girls." I flapped a hand at him. "The only reason you considered marrying me is that you'd be sitting on the throne one day."

"Well, now that you mention it"—he rubbed his chin thoughtfully—"that would be a benefit."

"I'm glad you think this is funny."

His smile disappeared. "I don't, actually. I'm merely relieved the trials are over. You do realize that we'll both be initiated as Fireblood masters now? That's something to celebrate, surely."

"Is that before or after the ceremony that chains us to each other for eternity?"

He put a finger to his chin. "Probably after. It's going to be a busy week planning a wedding on such short notice."

My instinct was to hit him, but if I started, I might not stop. Kai had either lied or lied by omission about so many important things. How could I ever trust him again?

"I'm tempted never to speak to you again."

"That might make the wedding rather awkward."

I forced myself to take a deep breath and think reasonably. No matter what he said now, he was not the marrying type. "You must have a plan to avoid it."

"I don't have a plan."

"Well, make one." My temples began to throb.

"If you can think of something, by all means. My plan is to get my island back and give the queen lots of grandnieces and grandnephews in gratitude."

I wheeled on him. "I'll stab you in your sleep first."

"Now, that's a little extreme."

"Kai." I grabbed the lapels of his tunic. "Be serious for a minute. How are we going to get *out* of this?"

We had reached the foot of the hill. For once, he didn't complain that I was mussing his clothes. He just kept his hands by his sides and stared at me. "I don't know."

I let him go and we continued up the hill, my mind in turmoil. The queen had me cornered, and if there was one thing I hated, it was feeling trapped. I had come here to find a way to destroy the Minax I'd released, not to have my life upended. I'd seen the trials as a way to prove myself, to master my power, and to gain access to knowledge. I hadn't realized the cost. I knew I'd have to take vows to become a master, but I hadn't expected them to include wedding vows.

I also didn't know what to make of the fact that it had been I, not Sage, who had stopped the lava. If that were even true. I didn't know what to make of the lullaby. I didn't want to think about those things at all. I was feeling more and more like the queen's plaything. The walls were closing in and I needed to find a way out.

Kai seemed too willing to accept the queen's manipulations. I wanted him to be as angry as I was, and the fact that he wasn't made him seem like another adversary. I knew that wasn't fair, but I couldn't help it.

When we reached the carriage, I said, "I'm going to walk."

His voice held surprise. "It'll take you over an hour to walk back."

"Good," I said, turning away. "I need time alone."

NINETEEN

THE NEXT DAY, I STOOD ON THE queen's whitewashed stone balcony overlooking the castle grounds. The hum of an excited crowd floated up from an open area below. This was where the queen addressed her subjects during festivals or other formal occasions, and it seemed like the whole island had shown up for today's announcement.

My legs began to tremble with the urge to run, to escape their stares. It was nothing like the arena, I told myself. No one was howling for my death.

Behind me, the doors to the throne room had been flung wide, letting sea-salted air circulate among the chattering courtiers like an uninvited guest. The nobles stood in groups, peering at me from behind fans or openly staring with a mixture of doubt, shock, and fascination. I tried to look demure and royal, since that was my role today. But sometimes I couldn't resist staring one of them down until they shamefacedly looked away. After all, I outranked everyone but the queen—supposedly. And I was angry enough at the way I'd been backed into a corner to take advantage of that fact.

I knew I didn't look my best. I had dark circles under my eyes after a sleepless night. Every time I'd fallen asleep, I'd dreamed of the Minax hovering over me, its black tendrils reaching out to feather across my skin in a possessive caress. I'd jerked awake, staring wildly at the shadows gathered in the corners and wondering why it felt so real. After the third nightmare, I'd given up on sleep. I lit a candle and listened to the wind rattling the casement as I tried to come to terms with the queen's claim that my mother was her sister.

I couldn't accept it. It was impossible.

So I'd moved on to thinking about what I needed to do next: get through the initiation ceremony, which the queen had informed me was in two days. Then I could figure out how to destroy the Minax. *Then* focus on finding a way to escape the madness of this engagement to Kai. For now, I had to play the queen's game. This wasn't King Rasmus's arena, but I *was* here to perform.

Though, perversely, some part of me wanted these spectators to like me. No one here hated me for my gift. In fact, judging by many rapt and smiling faces, they seemed more than ready to embrace me as the lost heir. As I absorbed their unabashed approval, I was overwhelmed with painful longing. If things were different, this could have been the home I'd always wanted. For the first time, I contemplated how much it would hurt to leave Sudesia.

I smoothed clammy hands over my skirts. My gown had once belonged to the queen but had been altered to fit me. Embroidered roses, leaves, and vines trailed over the crimson fabric in a masterpiece of gold thread. Each stem sported perfect little thorns that looked so sharp, I was almost afraid to touch them lest they draw blood. A thick gold necklace had the appearance of lace. Several bracelets clanked together as I moved, and a gold filigree crown—a humbler version of the queen's—was pinned in my upswept hair.

Kai stood next to me wearing a doublet that matched my gown, red with gold thread. White cuffs peeked out at his wrists, and black breeches blended with polished black boots. A ruby earring winked from his ear. Queen Nalani and Prince Eiko stood to his right.

At the queen's signal, Kai squeezed my arm and drew me forward to the railing. Queen Nalani addressed the crowd. "My loyal Sudesians, seventeen years ago, I lost my younger sister. She left our kingdom with her infant daughter, never to return. I have been searching for my niece since that day. A few weeks ago, our loyal friend, Prince Kai of Isle Tuva, found my niece and brought her home."

She held out a hand to me and I curtsied as gracefully as I could. She smiled approvingly and turned back to the crowd.

"You may have heard the hardships she faced in Tempesia, how she was imprisoned, how she fought to survive in the Frost King's arena, and how she ultimately prevailed and melted their throne, the symbol of Frostblood tyranny. I am proud, so very proud and happy, to welcome my sister's child back home again and to reward her sacrifices. Not only has she returned, but I'm pleased to announce she has passed her trials and will be initiated as a master."

A cheer went up from the crowd.

The queen smiled beatifically. "I invite all of you to welcome her and to treat her with the same warmth and loyalty you would show to me. I present to you Princess Ruby Otrera Elatus, daughter of Rota, descendant of Tollak, and my dear niece and heir."

Another cheer erupted from the crowd. I flinched unconsciously. All those voices joining to create a buzz of noise that couldn't be shut out. I itched to put my hands over my ears.

Kai seemed to sense my discomfort. His hand came to my lower back, his shoulder pressed against mine. He leaned down and whispered in my ear. "Smile."

I took a shuddering breath and did as he said. The cheer swelled. I finally looked at the people, saw them as individuals rather than a mass of spectators. Babies were cradled in arms and small children sat on the shoulders of their parents to better see us. Some people waved colorful scarves. There was an air of real celebration. Joy. Something inside me softened and lightened. They were genuinely happy because of me, because of my presence, my existence. I blinked away moisture as the image blurred.

Then I saw a familiar face and my smile became wide and genuine. "There's Aver," I told Kai, waving frantically. "And Jaro!"

"I see them," he said in a kind but rather dampening voice that made me realize maybe a princess wasn't supposed to flap her hands in such an undignified manner. I settled for nodding and grinning at them instead.

"It is my greatest hope," the queen continued, "that our princess finds happiness in her new home, and that one day, she will rule in my place. To that end, she will need a partner who was raised in our ways, and who will guide her as she learns her new role. I am overjoyed to announce that I have given Prince Kai permission to ask for my niece's hand in marriage. And she has joyfully accepted."

As the crowd sent up yet another cheer, my eyes were drawn to the queen. She looked genuinely happy. No, not just happy. Elated.

No wonder they adored her. She was all beauty and strength, lovely strong features and perfect dark skin, her eyes and teeth gleaming with health, her crown sparkling gold in the sun. Her expression was a blend of affection and mischief as she said, "Prince Kai, give the people what they want. Give my beautiful niece a kiss."

"As my queen wishes," said Kai with a crooked grin, his hands curving about my waist as if we were preparing to dance a waltz. It wouldn't be our first kiss, but it made my heart jerk unpleasantly to think of this as being part of the performance. I shoved my misgivings aside to be sorted through later.

He raised a brow in silent question and I tipped my chin up in answer. He pulled me close and his warm lips met mine in a thorough kiss. Despite my nerves, my skin heated, my blood rushing in my veins. It seemed that he was showing the crowd that he meant it, that he wasn't unhappy about the marriage, that he wanted me for my own sake and not just for my crown. Well played, I thought dimly.

When he pulled back, I realized one of my hands had found its way to his nape. He turned back to the crowd, grinning at their jovial hurrahs.

As I came out of my stupor, my attention was drawn to a tall, hooded figure, clearly a man by his size, that moved against the crowd. While everyone else jostled to get closer to the balcony, he was carving a hurried path through the tightly packed bodies in an effort to get away. There was something fierce, almost desperate, about the movements.

I stared at his coarse cloak and hood. It was a warm day and most people were dressed lightly. There was no need for either. . . .

Someone screamed. Heads jerked toward the sound and shock rippled through the crowd. Kai stiffened and the queen leaned over the balcony for a better look. In the voice of a seasoned general, she ordered her guards below to calm the crowd. Meanwhile, the screams spread like a contagion, passing from one person to the next.

What was causing this reaction? The memory of the scorpions had me clutching my arms.

Then I saw it. The ground was turning white. Frost crystallized as it spread, a growing spiderweb of shining pinwheels that reached for each other with spiny tendrils, joining into a crocheted white blanket that covered the grassy slope. People behaved as if the ice were a deadly poison, slipping and falling and shoving each other out of the way in their desperation to retreat.

"Frostblood!" a woman screamed, and then the shout was taken up by the guards, who struggled to move toward the hooded figure everyone else was trying to escape.

"Don't hurt him!" I tried to shout, but my voice was hoarse with fear. I knew who it was now, I knew why he'd caught my eye, the familiar breadth of shoulders and the proud angle of his head. The thought of what these Firebloods would do to a Frostblood—*him* in particular—was terrifying. He was at the edge of the crowd and nearly to the wooded area that covered the hillside when the first guard reached him.

"No!" I cried.

Kai's hand fell on my shoulder. "Ruby, what—"

I turned and gripped his arms. "It's Arcus!"

The guards converged on him and he was lost from view.

TWENTY

ARCUS KNELT BEFORE THE QUEEN'S throne. Not that he'd had any choice in the matter. Guards surrounded him, two on each side and four at his back. He hadn't resisted, at least not since they'd steered him through the doors and pushed him to the floor. I had a dizzying recollection of the moment I'd first been made to kneel in front of King Rasmus, and the comparison made me sick to my stomach.

I stood inside the balcony doors, my heart trying to beat its way out of my chest. Kai stood a little farther in, his face inscrutable. The queen sat on her throne and Prince Eiko occupied the smaller throne next to hers.

They'd thrown Arcus's hood off, and I couldn't help worrying that he must feel exposed. When I'd first met him, he'd kept his scars covered at all times. When he'd been crowned king, he'd dispensed with the concealment, but what would it feel like to have his hood torn away by a group of hostile guards in a land that hated him?

However, he showed no signs of being cowed or embarrassed. His chin jutted high, his face blank but somehow radiating careless defiance. I'd never seen this side of him. If I didn't know him, I'd peg him as an outlaw, hauled before the queen for his heinous crimes. His worn and tattered hood covered a travel-stained blue tunic and loose black breeches in modest fabrics. There was nothing to indicate who he truly was.

"Who are you?" the queen asked in clipped, accented Tempesian. I stared hard at Kai, willing him to be silent. But my hopes were dashed when Arcus spoke.

"I am King Arelius Arkanus, son of Akur, ruler of Tempesia and the frost throne." His chin rose infinitesimally and his voice, deep as oceans, so dear and familiar, was at the same time so cold and distant that shivers traced my skin.

The courtiers, who had been muttering nervously, were stricken into sudden silence, as if an axe blade had severed all threads of sound. The air had been sucked from the room, and now it resided in the bursting lungs of twenty or so nobles who collectively held their breath.

"If you were any other Frostblood," the queen enunciated rigidly, "I would inquire what unfortunate mishap of fate had deposited you in the land of your enemies. But I must assume, as ruler of a land that has *murdered* my people"—her voice shook as she pounded her fist on the arm of the throne, then stood, rage suffusing her face, heat radiating from her whole body, until even members of the court gasped at the onslaught—"that you have come with some fatally misguided intention to harm myself or those close to me!"

"Harm you?" he said with angry confusion. "I came at your summons. I received a letter just after Ruby departed, demanding my presence here. It contained veiled threats that implied she would be in danger if I didn't come immediately."

"I sent no such letter!" she said impatiently.

"It bore your royal seal."

"Impossible! Can you produce this message?" She gestured to his cloak.

"I don't have it with me."

"How convenient."

"If harming you were my intention," said Arcus with icy calm, "would I not send an assassin? Why would I risk myself?"

"Indeed, if you are foolish enough to come willingly into my domain, you may be foolish enough to risk anything. Let me assure you, you have made a grievous mistake."

"I would agree, Queen Nalani, that I was a fool to come here," Arcus said. A muscle jerked in his jaw. His refusal to look at me spoke volumes. If he was merely angry, he might have glared or curled his lip. Instead, he stared stonily forward with a cool, metallic disdain. His expression bore no hint of his feelings, aside from that tiny muscle in his jaw that he couldn't control. He'd seen the announcement, the kiss—everything. I closed my eyes as a rush of regret surged from my throat to my stomach. He must be hurt and furious.

Then again, he knew me too well to think I would promise myself to someone else within weeks of parting from him. Even if his initial reaction had been shock, he would soon realize that I'd been maneuvered into this. He had to understand.

The courtiers seemed to realize that they needed, at some point, to breathe. The chatter started up again, quiet but fervent, until it sounded as if the throne room teemed with whispering mice.

"Get out, all of you!" the queen railed, waving a hand toward the door. The exiled court removed themselves in short order, the scrape of their feet sounding much like the scuttle of frightened rodents.

Only Kai and I remained. No one seemed to notice, anyway. Certainly not Queen Nalani or Arcus, who were locked in a battle of eye contact that neither was prepared to forfeit.

"How many?" the queen demanded.

Arcus waited. When no clarification followed, he asked, "How many what?"

"How many ships? How many ships and how many soldiers are en route to attack my kingdom?"

"None. None are on their way. I came on a single ship as *you* instructed. In your letter."

She scoffed. "You insult me." She stepped forward. "And I do not let insults go unanswered."

She pulled back and slapped him across the face with the

back of her hand, her rings slicing his cheek with thin ribbons that welled with blue blood.

"*No*," I cried, rushing forward and falling to my knees next to him. His head had barely moved when the queen struck him, but now he reared back as if my very nearness lashed him with a burning whip. He kept his head and eyes forward, not acknowledging me at all.

"Arcus," I breathed, and reached toward him. Could he really blame me for all this?

"Clearly there has been some . . . mistake," he said. "I will leave by dawn, and as compensation for my unwanted presence, I will leave behind many treasures from my kingdom, which I'd intended as gifts. I hope that will be acceptable to you."

"That will *not* be acceptable," the queen replied scathingly. "You will tell me how many ships and how many soldiers are on their way to invade my kingdom. Your crew will be questioned. And one of them will die every day that you do not reveal this information to me."

"There are no more ships," Arcus said, less calm now that she'd threatened his crew. "There is no planned invasion, no act of aggression of any kind. I came here virtually alone, with only enough sailors to crew the ship."

"Because of my letter, which I didn't write, and you cannot produce."

"Forget the letter," Arcus said angrily. "Clearly your seal was used without your consent." He turned his head to look at Kai with a narrowed, speculative expression.

Queen Nalani laughed bitterly. "My seal remains on my finger at all times." She held up her hand to show a heavy gold ring. "And what tale will you feed me next? That you had an irresistible impulse to explore? Perhaps you indulge a hobby as a cartographer and wished to fill out your maps? By all means, tell me. What nonsense do you expect me to swallow?" She resumed her seat, tilting her head to one side in a mocking imitation of an interested listener.

"Perhaps we could speak privately—"

"The only private audience you will enjoy with me will be in your prison cell, where I will employ some ancient but very effective means of extracting information from your lying Frostblood lips. These are my close and trusted family members: my husband, my niece, and her husband-to-be." I didn't miss how Arcus's eyes narrowed at the word *niece* and his nostrils flared at *husband-to-be*. "It does not get any more private than this."

"Then I respectfully decline to answer any more questions until you're willing to listen to reason."

"There is nothing respectful about denying me," she replied. The blood drained from my face as she continued. "Speak or die now. I may as well cut your invasion off at its quite literal head. I don't believe there is a clear heir to your throne, is there? Your death will throw your court into chaos. I'd like nothing more than to watch the wolves tear each other to pieces without the leader of their pack."

Arcus took a steadying breath. "My death could lead to the very thing you and I would both like to avoid."

"And what is that?"

"War."

"And who said I wished to avoid it?" Her voice and the expression in her eyes was so magnificent and terrible that I had to look away. "I relish the opportunity to avenge my fallen people. Bring war now or later. We are ready."

Her demeanor was so fierce, I wondered again if the Minax could be present and I was unable to sense it.

"That is brave talk," he replied, "but neither your navy nor your army is a match for my own. Not that it matters, as I have no wish to challenge you or your authority in your kingdom *in any way*. I merely wish to leave peacefully."

"The only way you'll leave here," she said, leaning forward, "is on a funeral boat that has been sent out to sea. And I wouldn't give any Frostblood that honor, least of all *you*."

"You seem to hold me responsible for the death of Firebloods in Tempesia. You must know that none died by my hand or my order during my first rule or my current one. It was my brother, Rasmus, who gave orders for the butchery of Firebloods in Tempesia. I am not Rasmus."

The queen made a show of glancing around. "Do you see him here? Shall I punish him instead?"

"My brother is dead," Arcus stated.

"Indeed. And so, the burden of reparations falls to you."

"Tell me what you need, then. What reparations will satisfy you?"

"Your death."

His mouth firmed. "Be reasonable."

"Your brother was not reasonable. Why is it required of me?"

"Because you're better than he was."

She threw her head back and laughed. "Now you truly do amuse me." She made a sharp gesture to the guards. "Take him to the prison. Lock him up in the smallest, most ill-favored cell you can find. Don't bother to clean it first."

"You're being completely unfair!" I cried, pushing to my feet. "He told you he's not responsible for the death of Firebloods and he's not lying. He rescued me from prison—"

"That's enough," the queen snapped.

"—and then he organized a rebellion that ended in his brother's death and the destruction of the throne. *With me.* He was my ally!"

"Enough," she said tightly, and then to the guards, "Take him."

"If you take him, take me, too." I put my wrists out to the guards, but I looked directly at the queen. "Shackle and chain me next to him. If you value me so little that you ignore my heartfelt plea for fairness, then I have no desire to be your heir or to serve as one of your masters. I hereby abdicate my right to succeed you as—"

"I said enough!" the queen all but screamed. "Do you think I won't put you in prison beside him?"

"I am quite sure you will!" I moved in front of Arcus, practically shouting in the queen's face now. "And I would rather be *there* than sworn to serve a monster like you. It would be no better than when I was King Rasmus's prisoner!"

Her hand pulled back and suddenly my face was turned to the side, my cheek burning as a ringing slap echoed through the room.

"My love," said Prince Eiko quietly, his tone clearly a gentle attempt to calm her.

"Don't touch her," Arcus snapped with a warning look at the queen.

Kai's hands settled on my shoulders, pulling me back against his chest. It might have been a protective gesture, but in my roiling fury, I interpreted it as an effort to silence me.

"No!" I said, elbowing him away. "Don't try to calm me or convince me that I should accept this. This is *wrong* and I won't stand for it."

The queen and I glared at each other, both of us breathing heavily, the heat in the room multiplying and swelling until I saw one of the guards wipe sweat from his brow.

Finally, the queen's brow relaxed, her lips lost their white-lipped compression, and a reluctant smile stretched across her face.

"If I had any remaining doubts that you are my sister's child," she said, something like admiration entering her eyes, "I would discard them now. You are most assuredly Rota's daughter."

"I won't let you hurt him," I said, trembling in reaction to her surprising change in mood.

She stared at Arcus, her gaze abstracted. Finally, she let out a long sigh. "Take him to the top of the north tower. I want six guards on him at all times. Kill him if he tries to escape." She turned to me. "I warn you, Ruby, when I decide what is to be done, even you will not stop me."

TWENTY-ONE

As I left the throne room, I encountered a group of courtiers. Two of the ladies stepped forward with curtsies, congratulating me on my upcoming marriage. I thanked them, feeling awkward and impatient. When I was finally free, I headed for the north tower, lifting my skirts to skip steps with impatient leaps. The requisite six guards were already in place in front of one of the doors in the short hallway. The closest two stepped together to block my way.

Time to act the princess. I produced a burning, haughty gaze, zeroing in on the younger of the two.

He blinked rapidly. "My apologies. You can't go in there."

I ratcheted my chin up. "I assure you, I can. The process is simple. You unlock the door, and I pass through it. Here, let me show you."

"Queen's orders," the other affirmed.

"Do you know who I am?" I put my index finger to my lower lip as if I'd forgotten my own identity and hoped they would fill me in.

They glanced at each other. "The princess."

I rewarded them with a broad smile. "Oh, you do know. Splendid." I did my best imitation of Marella's nonchalant hand gesture. Observing her in the Frost Court had proven useful more times than I could count. "Either unlock it for me or hand me the key. Whichever is faster. I can't stand here all day. Things to do. A wedding to plan. Have you heard?"

They looked at each other again, not sure how to deal with me. "Our congratulations, Your Highness."

"Thank you. Now, all I need is to deliver a quick message to our prisoner and then I'll be off and leave you to your duties."

"We would if we could," said the younger one. "But we were instructed not to let anyone pass."

I drew myself up. "Anyone? Are you saying that if Queen Nalani stood here and ordered you to let her by, you'd refuse?"

"Well, no," he said slowly. "No, of course not."

"Quite right." The sweet smile again. "I'm so glad you answered correctly. Anything else would have earned you a prison cell, and I can assure you it wouldn't be as comfortable as this one." I gestured to the door. "You understand, of course, the same applies to me as to the queen? I am what you call an exception to your rules." Kai wasn't the only one who could make that claim. "Think carefully before you answer. Your future depends on it."

"No one passes but the queen," said the older one, nervous but determined.

Heat flared from my chest outward. I walked closer to him, firmly setting my fingertip under his perfectly clean-shaven chin. He recoiled a little at my touch. He was a Fireblood, no doubt. His skin was warmer than someone without the gift. But not like mine. If I chose to, I could take out all of these guards. However, my freedom would be severely curtailed if I tried that. Persuasion with a dash of coercion was called for, not outright force.

"And if I tell you I disagree?" I asked. "Will you lay hands on me?" I pressed myself closer, letting my chest touch his. He stepped back a fraction, trapped by the door behind him.

"Of course not, my lady. Your Highness."

"I'd hate to tell my aunt . . . oh, I mean, the queen . . . how you put these rough hands"—I grabbed one of his clenched fists and lifted it to my cheek—"on my royal person. She wouldn't like that, would she?" I widened my eyes and blinked up at him.

His breathing stopped. Silence reigned. Finally, he let out a loud breath and stepped aside. "Keep your visit short." Mottled red had crept over his neck. Whether the blush was caused by desire or embarrassment or anger that I'd outmaneuvered him, I didn't know and it didn't matter. I'd won. I'd have to be quick, though. They might rush off to alert the queen.

He unlocked the door and I swept through, shutting it behind me.

Before I could speak, Arcus said, "Don't bother."

I leaned against the door, gathering my courage. After all the shocks he'd just endured, he was bound to take some of it out on me. "Oh, you'd like me to leave, then?"

"Say what you have to say and then leave. I have no wish to see you or your pretty husband."

So, this was how it was going to be. I looked at the ceiling, as if I might find a fresh supply of patience up there. "He's not my husband. I can explain—"

"'*To be*,' then. It's not worth debating. Or have you missed that? Someone to argue with?"

My teeth ground together. If he didn't want to listen to my explanations, so be it. "There are plenty of argumentative people here."

"Well, if you haven't come to argue, you've come to the wrong place."

I exhaled and looked closely at him for the first time since entering the room. He sat with his face turned away, but even the sight of his familiar profile made me dizzy with conflicting emotions: longing, pleasure, worry, guilt. "Do you think it's that easy to drive me away?"

"Nothing with you is easy. Ever."

Determined not to be drawn into the blowup he seemed to want, I glanced around the room. It was a good size, with all the trappings of a guest chamber: sturdy carved bed, two wingback chairs next to the window, tapestries and a worn but fine rug, a large stone fireplace with an empty grate, a heavy wardrobe and nightstand and dressing table. All in all, the queen had been generous in her choice of room. But the door was plated with steel, the window had bars over it, and I suspected the chimney was similarly barred inside. It was a fancy cell.

Arcus sat in one of the chairs, his face turned resolutely to the window. I moved forward and sat gingerly in the empty wingback. The familiar aura of cold that always surrounded him embraced me, and it was painfully sweet. *It's so good to see your face,* I wanted to say. *I've missed you so much.* I wanted to wrap my arms around him and beg him to wrap his arms around me and bask in the comfort and safety of his presence. My stomach clenched as I noticed that the cuts on his cheek had bled a little. I wanted to press a cloth to them and put salve on them and tell him I was sorry for the queen's abuse. But it was very clear he wouldn't allow me to do or say any of that. The tension in his body, from the cord standing out in his neck to the brutal set of his jaw, screamed rejection.

He spared me a glance, emanating hostility.

I swallowed, trying not to let hurt overwhelm me. After all, I knew exactly why he was angry.

"You saw the announcement," I said.

His chest rose and fell a few times before he said, deadpan, "Felicitations."

"Arcus, please. The engagement isn't—"

"If I'd had any worry until that moment that you were being held against your will, that kiss put my mind at ease. What a relief." The sarcasm was biting.

I took a steadying breath. "You said the message implied I was in danger?"

"As I said, I was foolish. One guess who was behind that letter." He kept his face turned to the window.

"You think Kai forged it?" I'd thought of that possibility, but I couldn't figure out a motive. "I'll find out, I promise you."

"What does it matter now? I must give him credit. Not only did he lure you here, he fooled me, too."

No, I couldn't believe Kai would do this. Even more stunning was the fact that Arcus had dropped everything for my sake. "I can't believe you came. To leave your court, your responsibilities, and travel all this way—"

"Really?" His brows drew together. "You don't think I'd care if you were in danger?"

"Of course I know you'd care. But you didn't have to come yourself. You could have sent someone to check on me."

"Who would I send in my place? Brother Thistle? He's getting rather long in the tooth to stage a rescue, don't you think? Or should I have sent my soldiers, perhaps members of my personal guard? Even if they'd shown no animosity to you before, that doesn't mean they'd be willing to lay down their lives for you in my absence. They could come back empty-handed with any made-up story of how a rescue was impossible and I'd never know the difference. There's no one I trust enough to send after you. I had to come myself."

His words warmed me like a great, crackling bonfire. "Who did you leave in charge?"

"Lord Ustathius, of course. He's more than capable and he has the court's trust."

"But what about the peace accords? It would have been a terrible time to—"

"*I know*," he broke in, finally meeting my eyes. For a second, I was startled by all that *blue*. Aside from the queen's servant, who had a paler shade, I hadn't seen vivid Frostblood eyes for weeks now, and they looked just as foreign and surprising to me as the impossibly pink flowers had looked when I'd first arrived in Sudesia. "Don't you think I know it was a terrible time to leave?"

"And to chase a Fireblood. I can just imagine the gossip."

He grimaced. "We had a cover story, of course. That the queen had agreed to talk with me, but only if I came in person."

"If only she *would* talk to you. If we can just get her to sign the peace accords, the provinces will follow suit."

"It didn't seem like the queen was all that eager to do what you asked." He gestured to my cheek, which must be fairly red, since it had started to throb. A flicker of something like regret sparked in his eyes before they shuttered.

"But you're here, aren't you, rather than in prison?" I said. "So I do have some influence."

He looked at me, his expression bleak. "Are you really the queen's niece?"

"They seem to think so." And I thanked Sud for my new identity, no matter whether I had any right to it. Without it, I would have no way to protect Arcus.

"You seemed comfortable enough in the role." He glanced

pointedly at my crown. "Almost as comfortable as you were in the arms of that fop."

"He's not a fop."

Arcus snorted.

"Well, Kai does love his wardrobe, I admit. But he's not so bad. You might like him if you gave him a chance."

He turned a look of complete incredulity on me. "You're many things, but I never thought you were deluded." He shook his head again, as if he couldn't believe it. "How do you happen to be a princess, anyway? I'm sure the Frost Court would enjoy the unlikely tale."

Despite the sarcasm, I knew he cared more than he wanted to admit. I briefly recounted the first trial when I'd stopped the flow of lava, and how, when I was delirious from scorpion poison, the queen had heard me singing her sister's version of a lullaby.

Though I spoke lightly about the whole thing, his brows drew together and he watched me with a penetrating gaze, his expression freezing as I described my brushes with death.

When I was done, he took a breath, making a noticeable effort to relax. "So you took the trials to gain access to the book, and instead you've gained a kingdom."

"I don't know about that. I'm not sure I'm willing to accept that I am her niece."

"It doesn't matter if you accept it. The queen believes it and has named you her heir. Your future is here now. Isn't it?"

A few weeks ago, I would have fallen all over myself reassuring him that wasn't true. But there was this awkward distance between us, and more important, I hadn't had time to process any of what I'd learned over the past few days. I said the one thing I was sure about. "My immediate plans haven't changed. I need to destroy the Minax." I stood and paced from the bed to the fireplace and back. "But first, I need to get you out of here. I'll speak to Queen Nalani when she's had time to calm down. She has to see reason."

"Don't bother."

I gasped. "Did you just say that?" Heat flared in my chest and my fingertips grew warm.

He put up a palm. "I only mean that speaking to her won't do any good. She conceded to you about my imprisonment because she saw that she was losing control of you. She retreated from a minor skirmish so she could amass her forces for a win. If she wants me dead, she won't be persuaded out of it."

"Then what do you suggest?"

"First of all, have you found the book?"

I hated to extinguish the hope in his eyes. "I broke into the masters' library, but it wasn't there. I don't know where else to look. After I become a master, I'll be able to ask them directly about the Minax. Or maybe there's another library or more books that could help."

"After you become a master. So you plan to go through with it?" His expression and tone were carefully blank.

"I have to. They won't tell me anything until I'm one of them."

"And what do you need to pledge to become one of them?"

I feigned nonchalance to cover my fears. "Undying loyalty to the queen. Complete subservience. My firstborn child."

"What?" he asked, startled.

"Oh, sorry, that last one comes with the marriage vows. She wants heirs." It was harder to be flippant about that last part. I rested my head against the chair back and closed my eyes. It was humiliating to realize how deftly the queen had maneuvered me. And I could only imagine what Arcus thought about me going along with this farce.

He was silent for a minute before asking, "And you've agreed to the marriage for the queen's sake? Or for your own?"

I shook my head, rolling it from side to side against the satiny brocade. "I agreed because I had to. The third trial was a test of obedience. I had to agree, or I'd fail the trials and lose my chance at finding a way to stop the Minax."

It was eerily silent. I opened my eyes as a gale-force sigh swept toward me like a cool breeze, stirring the loose hairs at my temples. He stabbed his fingers through his hair in a shaky gesture of relief. "The moment you saw me, those should have been the first words out of your mouth! When I was torturing myself with thoughts of you promising to love another for all eternity."

"You didn't let me say anything! You were snapping at me the moment I walked in! But honestly, did you think I'd jumped into an engagement within weeks of leaving you? You know me better than that."

He flopped back in the chair, his chest rising and falling on a deep breath. "Good *gods*, woman. You'll be the death of me."

"Don't say that." I touched his knee, and my hand was instantly imprisoned in his larger one. The cold was enticingly familiar. I treasured every goose bump that traveled up my arm.

"The kiss was real, though," he murmured after a minute, while his thumb traced the back of my hand.

"What?" I was lost in the pleasure of touching him again after so long.

"Your kiss wasn't fake. And you were too comfortable together for it to be your first."

"Oh." A frown pulled my brows together. How could I sum up my complicated relationship with Kai? I didn't even understand it myself. Suddenly, I felt both guilty and defensive. When I'd left Tempesia, Arcus had told me we had to let each other go. I had tried to do that and I hadn't been very successful.

"We've spent a great deal of time together training for the trials," I said simply. "And no, it wasn't the first." I hated hurting him, but I hated lying more.

He pulled back to sit with his hands on the chair's armrests. I drew my hand to my lap, hurt, even though I could understand his apparent rejection.

He spoke with quiet force. "I'm trying so hard to tell myself that it doesn't matter and that you and I hadn't made any promises. That clearly I felt something that you didn't and I fooled myself into thinking there was more." His eyes found mine, drowning me in shades of a cloudless summer sky. "But even though you never said exactly what you felt for me... Ruby," his voice broke a little on my name, "I truly believed there was more."

"There *is*," I said desperately, gutted by the pain I saw in his eyes.

"But so soon?" He blinked. "You just... found someone else?"

"It's not like that. It's... complicated." I threw up my hands, still struggling to put it all into words. "When I left, we knew it would never work between us. The court would never let it."

"*You* knew that. *You* were convinced. Not me."

I leaned forward angrily. "Well, you were fooling yourself, then. Because I did nothing but undercut you by being there and that is a fact, whether you choose to believe it or not."

"I still don't accept that."

"I didn't, either. Until they tried to kill you over it." I shivered at the memory. "Watching you almost die had a rather sobering effect on my daydreams."

His lips twisted. "I'll admit that the threat of death has a way of clarifying things."

I took a steadying breath. Whatever we had to sort out would have to wait. His life was at stake.

"Speaking of which, you're not exactly safe here. I will do anything I can to get you back on your ship."

His eyes swept me in a thorough perusal. "And what about you? Will you go through with a wedding that you don't even want? Or have you decided you do want it, after all?"

"I don't want it. I told you that. But the only thing I can think of right now is getting you out of here. I can barely breathe thinking of how much the queen hates you and what she might do."

He rubbed his hand over the beginning of a beard on his

chin. "I know the feeling. All I did after you left was think about you. Worry about you. Miss you." There was naked longing in his voice, and my heart leaped in response. "I couldn't bear it. Even if I'd received word that you were fine, I think I still would have come and tried to persuade you to come home."

"Home." I sat trembling in the chair, his words and tone affecting me more than I wanted, making me want to curl up and weep in his arms. "I don't even know where that is."

"You're my home," Arcus said softly.

I put a hand to my chest, pressing against the lump of pain that was gathering there. My whole body seemed caught in flame that was consuming me from the inside.

"I want to pull you into my arms more than anything," he said unevenly, "but I know if I do, I'll just end up begging you to leave here with me. No matter what the cost."

A knock sounded at the door. "Ruby?" Kai's voice was muffled by the thick steel. "You have one more minute."

I took a shuddering breath and dropped my hands. "We need to get you out of here."

"Find Marella," Arcus said, his resolution giving me strength.

"Marella?" I said in shock.

"She came with me."

"Oh, of course. I bet she's been attached to your side like a spare appendage since the day I left."

"Do I detect jealousy? I don't suppose you've forgotten that you're engaged."

I made an impatient motion and he continued.

"The ship is on the other side of the island, almost opposite to the main harbor." He described the small, hidden bay in detail, and how to spot it if I rounded the island in a boat, and what password to use to gain entry. "When you get there, Marella will assemble my crew and..." He trailed off, thinking. "She's been seasick for the entire journey, but she can still come up with a plan to get me out of this damn place."

"*I'll* get you out of here," I said, irritated by the implication that Marella was the only one who could strategize. "There's no way your crew can get past all the guards."

"Not without killing them, and I don't want to give the queen cause to retaliate. The last thing I want is to be at war with you on the opposing side."

"You don't want war at all. Neither do I."

"Ruby!" Kai called, knocking again. "I'm coming in."

"One minute, Kai!" I tossed back, not missing how Arcus flinched as I said Kai's name. His jaw was tight, his eyes aimed resolutely at the rug, his hands on his knees. He had already started freezing me out again.

"I'll have them give you ointment for your cuts," I said, standing.

His lips twisted, making the scar on his lip whiten a little, which made me long to touch it. "They're nothing. Don't fuss."

But I think he liked that I fussed, just a little. I stood and stepped forward, bending down to kiss his hair, but he stiffened.

"Don't. I don't think I can . . ." He didn't finish, but I understood. It would just make things more difficult for both of us if he had to leave without me.

"All right," I whispered. I stood there for a moment, breathing his familiar scent, then stepped back.

He looked up with a small smile, and even though it was just a subtle curve of his lips, amusement reached his eyes, and that made all the difference. It felt like a ray of sunshine on my soul.

"Far be it for me to argue with Ruby Otrera, destroyer of thrones, secret princess, and who knows what else? You've never failed, yet."

"And don't you forget it."

The door opened. Kai cleared his throat meaningfully, and Arcus turned back to the window, shutting out everything but his own private thoughts. I stepped from the room.

As the guard relocked the door, I was filled with nearly frightening resolve: I would take my initiation vows, find the book, and free Arcus.

I would free him if it took my own life to do it.

TWENTY-TWO

IN THE DARKEST HOURS OF NIGHT, I snuck out of the castle by the servants' entrance, used the guards' shift change to slip past, and hurried to the wharf. I checked the tavern first, and when I didn't find Jaro there, I headed to the seventh pier. A few sailors lingered, some working on their boats, some sitting in small groups drinking. Jaro sat alone, legs folded under him on the dock as he repaired a frayed coil of rope.

"Don't you ever get enough of that?" I teased. "Canoodling with ropes?"

He grinned and looked up. "This is what I do when I can't sleep." He nodded to the east. "I feel a storm brewing—a day or two off, but still, it makes me edgy."

I hesitated briefly, then told him what I needed. Jaro knew

the exact bay I'd described, but when I told him he had to keep the trip a secret, his eyes narrowed.

"Why?"

Water lapped at the docks in a soothing rhythm. "The less you know, the better."

"Does Prince Kai know about this?"

"No, and you can't tell him. I'm meeting someone and Kai won't like it."

Jaro folded his arms. "I'm not taking you unless you tell me who you're going to meet."

I took a breath. This was a huge leap of faith, but something told me Jaro could be trusted. I lowered my voice and whispered the essential facts.

He stood and glared, gesturing angrily. "What you ask is treason!"

"Shh." I glanced around nervously. "I wouldn't involve you if there were any other choice. I'm trying to prevent a war. Don't you think that's a good enough reason to bend the rules?"

"Bend them? You mean to break them into tiny pieces and set them ablaze!"

"True. But only to prevent a much larger catastrophe. Do you want to see your kingdom go to war with Tempesia? I can help prevent that. I just need your help this one last time and I won't ask again."

His lips were pressed so tightly together, they'd almost disappeared. He grimaced and looked away. Then he sighed heavily, his shoulders sagging, and my tense muscles unwound. I knew he was going to agree.

Without speaking, he threw off the lines of a small boat that bobbed against the dock. The smell of fish overpowered my senses as we pushed off. He piloted the tiny, single-sail craft in his effortless way, his beefy hands wrapped lightly over the tiller, while I watched the ambient light of cooking fires and lanterns casting moving reflections on the breakers. The moon played hide-and-seek behind clouds, flitting out now and again to lay bands of silver over the waves and shore.

On the eastern side of the island, Jaro steered the boat into the small, forest-wrapped harbor where an anchored ship threw its shadow over the moonlit water. Our little craft sidled up to the massive hull.

"Gamut," I said just above a whisper. It was the password Arcus had given me, and it warmed my soul that it happened to be the name of one of my favorite people: the healer monk from Forwind Abbey.

"Who is it?" a voice whispered back.

"Tell Marella that Ruby is here to see her."

Quiet footsteps led away, and then back. "Come aboard."

A rope ladder knocked against the hull. I climbed to the deck. No lanterns were lit. Moonlight picked at the dark spines of the masts and the horizontal ribs of the yards, the furled sails bound tight like muscle on bone.

The planking rumbled with the approach of running feet.

I spun around just before a small whirlwind collided with my stomach.

"Oof." My hand came out automatically and landed on a tangle of braids. Two thickly lashed eyes blinked up at me above a mouthful of white teeth.

"Kaitryn?" It was little more than a gasp.

The girl's excited voice chirped out of the dark as she stepped back. "Hooray! We've got you! Now we can sail home again!"

"What—"

"Not that I mind living on the ship. Square meals and my own hammock. But now that we got you, I suppose we'll be leaving."

"But how did you end up on this ship?"

"After I saw you, I started thinking about what you said, how I might find life on a ship better than life on the streets. There was a call for ship's boys or girls on the docks at Tevros. I didn't think I'd get a spot, but somehow Lady Marella—the one who was choosing us—thought I looked more trustworthy than the rest."

"And was she right?"

She planted her small fists on her hips. "I haven't stolen anything since I've been on board, and there are plenty of marks to choose from. There are barons and warriors aboard, did you know? Anyway, I listen at the captain's door sometimes and that's how I knew we were coming to get you."

A quiet "hmph" came from somewhere in the dark. "Kaitryn, I don't know how you can hear anything when you're always talking." There was a swish of skirts and the blur of a slim figure moving closer.

"Doreena?"

"It's me, Lady Ruby."

I stepped forward and hugged her, forgetting about my heat until she gasped. I let her go quickly. "Sorry. I'm just so surprised to see you! What are you doing here?"

"When King Arkanus was rounding up some warriors to come along, I heard word of it and begged him to let me come, too. I wanted to do everything I could to help you."

I laughed delightedly. "I can't believe it. How is your adventure so far?"

"I don't like the storms, but the rest I've become accustomed to. I'm so glad to see you're well."

"I am, but I need to speak to Marella. Where is she?"

"She's sick," said Kaitryn. "We're not to wake her."

I turned to Doreena. "It's true," she confirmed. "It's best we don't bother her."

"It doesn't matter if she's ill," I said. "I need to talk to her."

Doreena hesitated, then nodded and gestured toward the steps leading to the cabins. "Second door."

As I crossed the deck and took the stairs down to the cabins, the calm swells of the bay nudged the hull, making the planking creak softly. I knocked on the door of the second cabin and, when I heard no reply, turned the knob and stepped in. As I crossed the threshold, a clench of prickly nausea rippled through me. Most likely just a memory of my first hours on Kai's ship when I'd been too sick to see straight. This cabin was similar, after all: bed bolted to the floor, table, chest, wardrobe, washbasin, oil lamp turned low. It was dim enough that it took a second to notice the slight bump of a motionless figure lying on her back in the bed, her face chalky and angular.

"Marella," I said in horror. "What happened to you?"

She chuckled, but it was a wan imitation of her usual breezy laugh. "Nice to see you, too, Ruby."

"Oh, I'm sorry. Of course it's good to see you, Marella. And I'm so grateful you came all this way for me."

"I've lost some weight, haven't I?"

"I heard you were ill, but..." I moved to the bedside. Her cheeks were sunken, her waxen skin oiled with a sheen of sweat. Her lovely wheat-gold hair was lank and plastered to her head.

She swallowed and gestured to the pitcher. I poured some water and she took the cup and drank. "Thank you. Ugh, I'm so parched all the time." She gave me the empty cup and I returned it to the table. "Sea travel disagrees with me. Violently."

"My seasickness only lasted a day. I didn't know it could be this bad. Shouldn't it improve now that you're anchored?"

"Who knows?" Her eyelids fluttered as she tried and failed to open them all the way. "Distract me from my boredom, Ruby. I've been cooped up here for weeks. Tell me about Sudesia. Is it everything you've ever dreamed it would be?"

"In some ways, I suppose. The island is more beautiful than I imagined. But nothing else has gone as expected." I gave a brief account of my efforts to become a Fireblood master, including the part about stopping the lava in the first trial. I played nervously with the hem of my tunic, feeling strangely shy as I said, "And from that, they seem to think I'm the queen's lost niece. If you can credit the idea of me being royalty."

She closed her eyes and shook her head with a low laugh. "Of course you are. Because you weren't special enough already."

She sounded bitter, which stung. I couldn't help but feel a little defensive. "It's not as if I've been rewarded for my gifts before. Not in Tempesia, at least."

"No, not at all," she said drily. "Only with the infatuation of two kings."

I inhaled sharply. Now she sounded . . . jealous. "I didn't know you felt that way. You know I never wanted Rasmus to—"

"Stop, Ruby. You don't need to defend yourself. I don't really feel that way. I mean, I didn't. Maybe only to a small degree, but I never blamed you." She moaned as if in pain. "These past weeks . . . I'm finding myself dwelling . . ." She put her fingertips to her temples and pressed. "I just . . . I'm not myself."

"Marella, we need to get you some help." I leaned forward urgently. "A healer. Medicine."

She laughed, a bit more like her old self, but cut with bitterness. "No healer can help me."

My stomach flipped with worry. "Why do you say that?"

"Hmm? Oh, I only mean I can't get help here. Hostile territory and all that."

"You need to get home, then." I scrubbed my hands over my face. When Arcus had said Marella was seasick, I'd had no way of knowing she'd be this ill. Clearly he'd overestimated what she was capable of right now. She was barely lucid. "Unfortunately, Arcus has been captured and the queen seems rather reluctant to let him go."

"He was captured?" She huffed. "Well, of course he was. He couldn't stay away from you, could he?"

My cheeks warmed. "Frost doesn't show up in these parts too often anymore. You'd have thought a plague had just been unleashed."

Her lips curved. "I'm sorry I missed that." She paused, staring dully at me. "You're the only person who makes him do that, you know. Lose his temper. He never does with me. Or anyone else for that matter."

She made it sound like I brought out the worst in him. While she brought out... something better, at least.

When I didn't reply, she asked, "Where is he now?"

"In the north tower of the castle. I don't know what the queen will do to him. She's convinced he has a fleet of Tempesian warships bearing down on her."

"That's what we should have done. Brought some warships. Made her think twice about defying us."

"How can you say that? You never wanted Firebloods to be hurt."

She waved her hand and I cringed at how bony it appeared. "Don't listen to me. I hardly know what I'm saying."

I heard the frustration and the hint of shame. Marella, for all her pretty smiles and fancy gowns, was as tough as tempered steel. She prided herself on it. This illness must feel like the worst kind of weakness. Concern and pity were not emotions I'd ever felt for her, but I felt them now.

Her lids fluttered. I sat on the chair next to the bed and went to take her hand, but she drew it away.

"When I get Arcus back to the ship," I said, "can you haul anchor and get away from here?"

"We'll be gone before you can blink."

TWENTY-THREE

THE QUEEN SENT A MESSAGE TO SUMMON me first thing the next morning. My heart took up a rhythm somewhere between panic and terror. Had she heard about my nighttime visit to the ship? But no, there was no way I could have been followed. And if she had somehow found out, she wouldn't have waited until morning to confront me. Perhaps she just meant to chastise me for daring to visit her captive the day before.

The moment I left my room, Kai's door opened, as if a sixth sense told him I was passing by. He fell into step beside me.

"Do you realize," he asked, "that tomorrow we'll be Fireblood masters?" A smile lit his face, so wide and genuine that I couldn't help but return it. He gestured with his hands as he spoke, all fizzing energy and excitement. "I have the perfect place to celebrate tonight. A little tavern on the wharf. It gets a bit rough after midnight, but don't worry, half the people there are former crewmates who will back us in a fight. The ale is surprisingly..." In lieu of a description, he kissed the tips of his fingers to show his appreciation. "And the music is—"

"I'm sorry, Kai, but I can't. I'd love to, but I need to rest tonight."

I hated to say no, but there was too much at stake to consider carousing in a tavern with Kai. As soon as I took my vows as a master, I had to find out the location of the book. Once that was accomplished, I could focus on breaking Arcus out of the north tower and getting him safely onto his ship. If I was lucky enough to have the book in hand by that point, I would go with him.

"Rest?" he scoffed, not seeming to notice my abstraction. "Please. You—"

"Really, Kai," I said, gently but firmly, to prevent a lengthy argument. "I mean it."

As we stepped into the dim stairwell, he idly created a ball of flame in his hand, the warm light carving shadows under his brows and cheekbones. I sensed a thread of hurt hidden under the surface, and I felt an urge to comfort him. But what could I say without revealing the plans I needed to hide?

"Hmm." He gave a careless shrug. "After our initiation, then. You can't argue we deserve a celebration."

"Sounds...perfect." At least that wasn't a lie. It did sound perfect. I just wouldn't be here to join him.

Maybe he heard the longing in my voice. He gave me a

sidelong look and said, "I know you probably don't feel like celebrating. You're worried about him."

I stopped. "You mean Arcus? You don't have to dance around it, you know." And yet, I couldn't meet his eyes.

He extinguished the flame with a snap. "Maybe I'd prefer not to say the bastard's name."

"He's never done anything to you." I resumed my descent of the stairs.

He caught up to me and put a hand over his heart, gazing skyward dramatically. "Except steal your affection."

How I hoped that gesture wasn't genuine. The thought of hurting Kai made me sick. Covering my worry, I slid him a mocking glance. "Are you sure you should be covering your heart? Maybe you should cover your coin purse instead."

"How insulting. But perhaps you're right." A mischievous smile curved his sculpted lips. "There are some things I value more than my heart."

"I don't even want to guess what part of your anatomy you're referring to."

He laughed heartily, and I relaxed, glad my attempt to diffuse the tension had worked.

He took my hand and tucked it into the crook of his elbow as we reached the south tower. A few courtiers passed, looking at us curiously and whispering as we disappeared around a corner. I could only imagine the gossip we inspired. At least no one was sending me hateful glances or trying to trip me as I passed. This wasn't the Frost Court.

"I just want you to be happy," Kai said with a note of sincerity that touched my heart. "As I am right now, knowing we've passed our trials. And instead, you're moping over your Frostblood... *friend*." His tone had taken on a bitter tinge.

I was sure he'd intended to use a different word. His censure raised my ire. "Forgive me for having feelings."

"Oh, you never have to apologize for that. Only for the fact that they aren't for your betrothed." He looked down at me, making a woeful expression. "I'll have to find a way to ease the pain." He sounded so tragic that I had a moment of panic, until he added meditatively, "Perhaps the soft arms and softer bosom of a tavern wench... or two... will provide the necessary cure for my melancholy."

I made a dismissive sound to hide my relief. "The day you suffer from melancholy is the day I become quiet and biddable."

"So, never."

I grinned. "Precisely."

We climbed the tower stairs and reached the throne room doors. I turned to Kai, suddenly nervous. "You don't think she'd execute me in there, do you?"

"No, she would definitely take you out on the balcony for that. She wouldn't risk blood on the tapestries."

"Funny." I flapped a hand in a "later" gesture and entered the room. The Frostblood servant I'd seen before lifted a tapestry to reveal a door tucked into a corner of the wall behind the throne. To my surprise, the door led to an anteroom, where the queen waited. The space was small but inviting, with upholstered divans, large pillows scattered over the floor, and stained glass windows that tinted the sunlight. Lanterns with elaborately worked metal covers sat on polished tables in dark wood.

I sat across from the queen, my expression smooth, my hands loosely clasped, everything about me screaming *dutiful princess and niece.*

If I'd thought there was a chance of convincing her to let Arcus go, I would have argued until my throat was raw. But pleading or arguing would only make her suspicious of my intentions. Besides, I didn't think I could plead his case without losing my temper when she inevitably refused.

It was vital that I keep my wits during this meeting. If I lost the queen's trust, she might decide to have me guarded or followed, which could hamper my search for the book. If she suspected I was planning to break Arcus out, she could increase the guards on his room, or move him to the prison. I needed her to think I had come to accept her word as law.

As we made small talk over tea, her attitude was more conciliatory than I'd expected. However, a calculated retreat could precede an attack.

"How do you like my little sanctuary?" she asked, taking a delicate sip.

"It's lovely," I replied.

She smiled, smoothing the edge of a velvet cushion. "Prince Eiko and I often spend an hour or two here after we are finished with the demands of the day. When he hasn't disappeared onto the tower roof to observe the stars, that is."

"Oh yes, I remember you saying he had an observatory." I had a sudden memory of Lord Ustathius berating Marella for spending her nights on the roof looking at the stars. I wondered if the queen took exception to her consort's pastime.

"Indeed. He stays up many nights watching the moon and planets and stars, charting their movements and making maps. It is his passion and I appreciate that, even though it means he often sleeps during the day when I am occupied with matters of state."

I reached out and picked up my teacup, taking a small sip. The mood was more mellow than I was used to with the queen. I realized this was the first time we'd been alone together. I found myself asking a question I hadn't had the courage to voice before. "What was your sister like when she was young?"

Her brows rose in surprise. "Why do you want to know? I was under the impression you were still unsure about your heritage."

"I'd like to know if your sister sounds anything like the mother I knew."

She nodded. "You remind me of her in some ways."

My heart squeezed, even as I told myself I might not be who she thought I was. Still, I couldn't help but ask, "How?"

"You are... idealistic. Passionate." Her lips curved. "I, too, am passionate. As you may have noticed." Her eyes twinkled with mirth and I smiled in response. "But in a different way. I am passionate about large things: my islands, my kingdom, my people as a whole. I was raised to ask myself what is best for them. What will benefit the greatest number of people? These questions have allowed me to make difficult decisions time and time again. I need to make judgments that hurt people sometimes." Her smile fell away. "I need to be brutal."

I saw the proof in her eyes. They were hard as polished granite—dark and cold, despite her inner fire. Languidly, she reached out and lit the lantern on the table next to her with her fingertips, the light shining prettily through the filigree cover.

"Your mother," she said, returning her gaze to me, "she cared for small things. Things I was taught to see as insignificant: an injured bird, a lame horse, a peasant child carrying too heavy a load. I chastised her for it. I told her that if anything happened to me, she would have to rule, that if she didn't harden her heart, the throne would break her."

"So you believe that the throne was—"

She added, "Not the throne literally, you understand. The responsibility. The crown and all that comes with it." But I noticed she didn't meet my eyes. Did she know about the curse?

"Is that why she left? She didn't think she could rule if it came down to it?"

"I don't think she left for that reason, though I can't be sure. I've pondered this question for years, you see. The only thing I can recall that gave some clue to her state of mind was a comment she made when you were first born. She said... she said she'd had a vision. A woman with golden eyes had come to her in a dream and warned her that you were in danger remaining here. When I questioned her about it later, she made light of it and would tell me no more. She never confided in you? I'd hoped you could illuminate her reasons for leaving."

"She told me nothing." Not about Sudesia, nor the fact that she was royalty. Nothing about Sage, who had come to her in a dream the same way she'd come to me in visions. I tried not to feel anger at the thought of all she'd kept from me.

Assuming that I really was Queen Nalani's niece. My mother wasn't a Fireblood. I would have known if she was. Still, it was hard not to be drawn in by the queen's certainty.

Queen Nalani sighed. "You were only about a year old when she left. It was something of a scandal when she wouldn't reveal who your father was. But Rota had no reason to take you from us. I was furious with her. It was a betrayal of her identity, of our parents. Of me."

"Your parents." I didn't know why I hadn't thought of it before. "If your sister was my mother, then your mother would be my grandmother."

Her brows arched upward. "Do you wish to know more about Queen Pirra?"

"No. Well, yes. I knew my grandmother—my mother's mother. But her name was Lucina. She helped my mother with healing sometimes and came to visit often."

"That's not possible."

I grew insistent. "She brought me books, told me stories—even about you. She taught me to use my gift, even when my mother disapproved. She died when I was nine. Could . . . could your mother have known where we were? Could she have visited us in secret?"

"I meant it's not possible that the woman you knew was your

grandmother." She set her cup down. "My mother died five years after Rota left, when you would have been six years old. I was there when the pyre was lit. I saw her return to flame."

I stared at the flickering lantern, thinking. A Fireblood funeral sounded so different from the short, cold one my mother and I had for Grandmother when we'd heard of her death. The memory brought me up short. I'd never seen Grandmother's body. Mother had received a message from a distant cousin that Grandmother had died while visiting them. Not that it mattered. If Queen Pirra had died when I was six, she couldn't have been Lucina, who died three years later.

"But still," I reasoned, "this is proof that I'm not your niece. My maternal grandmother was not your mother."

"It only means that your mother lied to you. Perhaps Rota felt guilty that she had taken you from your family, so she created a false one."

"She wouldn't have lied to me."

"She lied to you all your life. You didn't even know she was a Fireblood. You don't even know your name."

My head snapped up. "What's my—I mean, your niece's—name?"

"Your name is Lali. It means 'Ruby' in the old tongue."

I could only stare.

She sat back, her lip twitching up on one side. "Now you see why I wondered about you from the first."

"It still doesn't make sense," I said quietly. "My mother's skin was cool compared to mine."

"Rota had exceptional control of her gift. She could suppress her heat."

"Even in her sleep? She used to cuddle next to me for warmth on the coldest nights. I'm telling you, *it doesn't make sense.* She didn't use her fire to defend me when the soldiers came! She would have done anything to defend me. I know that much."

Queen Nalani shook her head. "That I cannot explain. So much of this is still unknown, and will never be known. It eats at me, Ruby. I hate not knowing why she left. I wish I could talk to her just one more time."

"I wish that, too," I said hoarsely. How I'd wished that. More times than I could count.

"Can you begin to understand how her disappearance tore at me? She didn't trust me enough to tell me where she was going. For a short time, I even suspected her of treason. Our father died of grief within months—she was always his favorite. Then I had to take the throne. In the midst of all that, some of the outlying islands rebelled and I wondered if she was behind the uprising, if she had played the reluctant princess when she really wanted to be queen. But there was no trace of her. Nothing."

I shook my head, unable to cast my mother in the light of power-hungry usurper. I didn't understand how Queen Nalani could ever have suspected that. It was almost as if she hadn't known my mother at all. Or maybe *I* hadn't.

Either way, her grief was real. I could see it in the tightness around her eyes, the brittle slant of her mouth. For the first time, I experienced a flutter of pity for the proud queen.

As she caught me staring, her gaze hardened. "So, I'm sure you'll understand why trust is such a delicate and precious thing to me, Ruby. It's important to me that when I ask you a question, you answer honestly."

Nervous heat flooded my veins. "You can ask me anything." Whether I would answer honestly was another matter. I couldn't reveal anything about my plans.

"My soldiers have combed the island twice over and can't find the Frostblood ship. I want you to tell me where it is."

The blunt words cleaved the veneer of warm reminiscences like an axe. "How would I know that?"

"Come, now. You spoke alone with the king for a quarter of an hour. Surely he told you things. He trusts you, does he not?"

I took another sip of tea, concentrating hard on keeping my hand steady. "Not with everything."

"But he did trust you with that."

Always be aware of your surroundings. Never let yourself be maneuvered onto dangerous ground. Who had told me that? Brother Thistle? Kai?

Arcus. After backing me into a fish pond. The memory came fresh and vivid. I could still feel the lily pads brushing against my skin, feel my fury as he stood, untouched and superior, on dry ground.

Well, clearly I hadn't learned. The queen had softened me up, made me lower my defenses by sharing fond memories of my mother, and then backed me into quicksand. When cornered, there was no choice but to attack.

"If you expected me to interrogate your prisoner, why did you send Kai to drag me away?"

"I sent him for your protection," she replied smoothly.

"I doubt that. You know the king is no danger to me."

"I know no such thing. His brother—"

"He's nothing like his brother. I wish you'd believe me."

She took another sip of tea. "You may believe what you're saying is true. Tell me this, then. How many ships are on their way?"

"No more ships. There's only the one."

"Why did the king come himself? Why risk the journey? He wouldn't come on a simple scouting mission."

"As he told you, it wasn't a scouting mission. He thought I was in danger. He came for me." I swallowed past the lump in my throat.

She put her cup down with a rattle. "The Frostblood king. Came all the way here. For you."

"Kai tried to tell you how much he cares for me when we first arrived in your court. I know it might sound far-fetched, but—"

"He had no reason to think you were in danger. There was no time for me to send him any message. So, what drew him here?" Her hand cut the air in an angry gesture. "Did he plan to kill me? Although he could simply have hired an assassin..." She shook her head. "If what he says is true and he received a letter, he could have sent messengers to procure my confirmation first."

"He did send a messenger ship to invite you to diplomatic talks. It never returned home."

She sat back, pinning me with a steely-eyed glare. "The

masters who guard the strait know better than to let a Tempesian ship through."

Outrage tightened my hands into fists. "So they destroyed it? The people on that ship were trying to help achieve peace."

She lifted a shoulder and let it fall, as if one ship full of Tempesians was of little consequence. She leaned forward in her chair. "I couldn't save the Firebloods who died under Rasmus's bloody rule, but I will avenge them."

Steel bands wrapped around my lungs, squeezing. "What do you mean?"

She pinned me with her eyes, as if deciding in this exact moment whether or not to trust me. "We've been building ships, training soldiers. Recruiting men and women from the outlying islands. In a few months' time, we'll start by destroying their navy. Then when the Frostbloods are scrambling, we'll be ready to invade."

A tremor ripped through my body. Her plans to attack by sea were one thing, but a land invasion would be suicide. I couldn't help but think back to King Rasmus, who had also taken foolish risks in his military campaigns.

"The king must have heard of my plans somehow," she continued, "and he decided to strike first. I just cannot figure out why he came himself."

"You are so, so wrong about this," I said hoarsely. "Talk to the king. Not an interrogation. Just speak to him. Discuss this as the rational people that you are. He would *never* do what you're saying. He has no desire to conquer you or anyone else."

She watched me keenly. "He hasn't told you anything, then." She sagged backward into the chair ever so slightly. "I think you are telling me the truth. You know nothing."

I leaned forward urgently. "I know that he would never do what you're suggesting."

She swept my assertions away with one manicured hand. "You are no use to me in this. I am disappointed. I must find another way to discover his plans, starting by questioning the king himself." She nodded, as if she'd asked and answered a question in her mind. "After your initiation, I will persuade him to see reason."

My blood heated further. "You're not listening to me. I don't want—"

"You may go, Ruby. I will see you tomorrow."

Gripped with anger at her cool dismissal, I spoke before I could consider my words. "Maybe. Maybe not."

Her head turned slowly, tension straining her jaw. "What precisely do you mean, child?"

I couldn't let my temper get the better of me. I needed to negotiate. What did I have to bargain with?

She believed I was the princess. That was leverage.

"Who am I to you?" I demanded.

She swept me with an irritated glance. "You are my niece. My heir."

"I assume you have much to teach me and many things you want me to do in my new role. You want me to be willing to do those things, don't you? You want me to be loyal, but you also want that loyalty to be genuine. Am I wrong?"

"You're not wrong," she admitted.

"So when you talk of interrogating Arcus, how do you think I'm going to respond? He's been my steadfast ally, whether you want to acknowledge it or not. When you threaten him, it makes me want to defy you."

She stared at me thoughtfully for a few beats. "Let me ask you this, Ruby. Who am I to *you*?"

"I—you're the queen." The title of "aunt" seemed far too cozy for the stone-hearted ruler sitting across from me.

"*The* queen," she emphasized. "Am I *your* queen? Will you pledge your life to me at tomorrow's initiation? I wonder if you harbor some doubts about where your loyalty belongs. In fact, I am starting to have some doubts of my own."

I was nearing another patch of quicksand. "Isn't that natural? To doubt?"

"Certainly. But that doesn't make it desirable. Not in one of my masters. Not when the kingdom might be on the brink of war. Not in my heir. So, who, I ask again, am I to you?"

I wanted to say that I would never fight in her war. But she held Arcus's life in her hands. She could hurt me all she liked, but I wouldn't let her take her wrath out on him. Rebellion was a luxury I couldn't afford.

"You are my queen," I forced out.

"Then stop pushing me." The words came as a low-voiced warning.

Her face remained smooth and controlled, but her nostrils flared, her eyes gleaming with fathoms of dormant embers ready to combust. Beneath her polished veneer, a cauldron of tempestuous power. I had a moment of startled recognition. Her emotions were like mine: quick, fervent, near the surface. Perhaps she had trouble controlling them, too. A part of me felt a kinship with her, whether I liked it or not.

"If you'll excuse me," she said in a lighter tone, "I have much to do before the wedding. Be ready for the seamstress. She will come this afternoon to measure you for your wedding gown."

As I rose and curtsied, my hands curled into fists. Once the initiation was over, she would turn her attentions to Arcus. She'd all but said she planned to torture him for information tomorrow. I couldn't keep waiting and watching. I needed to act.

As I strode angrily from the anteroom, I noticed the Frostblood servant standing sentinel in the throne room, his back against the wall next to the fireplace.

A spurt of indignation heated my skin further. The queen must have chosen that spot deliberately. A punishment for being a Frostblood, no doubt. How uncomfortable it must be for him, standing for long periods so close to that blazing heat. He let nothing show on his face, though. He'd had years to perfect that blank look. At least twice as many years as I'd been alive, from the look of the harsh creases in the finely drawn map of his skin.

I approached him slowly, still deciding how to play this. I needed him to trust me.

"You know the Frost King is a captive in this castle." I left a moment of silence for him to fill.

He kept his eyes aimed at the wall behind me. "Yes, Your Highness."

His voice was as rusty as an iron bucket left in the rain. Did no one ever talk to him? My heart contracted in a brief pulse of sympathy. It had been like that in Blackcreek Prison when Captain Drake first captured me. I could have melted into the stone floor or frozen to the iron bars of the cell, becoming just another fixture in the prison, and it wouldn't have mattered.

"I have a theory," I said. "The tunnels under the lava fields—they were created by Frostblood servants, weren't they?"

He swallowed but didn't speak.

"I saw some carvings in the walls during my first trial. Frostblood symbols I've seen on pillars in the king's castle. Now, why would the Fireblood masters of Sudesia carve Frostblood symbols into their tunnels?"

He didn't even blink. I tried not to be impatient, praying I wasn't wasting my time.

"They wouldn't, of course," I answered myself. "Which means Frostbloods were there. I think they dug those tunnels and left marks on them, something that was precious, a tribute or an act of rebellion. Most of them died, didn't they? The heat. The lava. So many ways for a Frostblood to suffer despite all that thick, frozen skin. The king has burn scars. I bet you have some, too."

One of his hands twitched, a butterfly's wing of movement. A tiny, telling reaction.

"There aren't many Frostbloods left here, are there?" I asked.

He shook his head.

"I bet it was you who made the container of ice for my second trial. Suspended on a bridge? Is that right?"

He nodded.

"Do you know the tunnels?" If he could navigate for me, we might be able to use them to get Arcus back to his ship. "The queen plans to interrogate the king and I don't think she'll be gentle about it."

He shook his head, his lips pressing together until they turned white.

Encouraged, I went on. "You don't know King Arkanus, but I can tell you that he is a good king. A good person. He doesn't deserve what Queen Nalani plans to do to him." No reaction. I tried a different tack. "Have you ever been to Tempesia? Most of it is covered in snow for more than half the year. In the north, they barely have a summer at all. There are festivals in the mountains to celebrate the snow. Frostblood craftsmen create magnificent sculptures out of ice. I know the king would take you on his ship. You could live among your own people."

His eyes held longing, but he shook his head once again.

I sighed in frustration. "What's your name?"

"Broderik."

"Broderik, are you a Frostblood or not? The king has no one to help him but me, and I can't do it alone."

I watched him, waiting. I was about to give up, when he gave a hesitant nod. My heart leaped. "If you can tell me anything, anything at all that might—"

"She plans to move him after the initiation," he whispered.

I had to lean in to hear him. "He'll be transferred to the prison tomorrow morning. I overheard her telling her personal guard."

Panic gripped my chest. "Tomorrow?"

"Yes."

So she'd already been planning to move him to the prison for interrogation before I'd even spoken to her. Questioning me must have been an afterthought, or a way of gaining information. Either way, this meant her plans for him were firmly in place.

"Don't you know anything that could help?" I asked. "If you don't know the way through the tunnels, is there anyone else who does?"

He hesitated before saying in a rush, "The only people who use the tunnels are the masters. And sometimes Prince Eiko. But there's no sense asking any of them." His eyes darted to the corner and back to me, widening. "Go. She's coming."

He returned to his blank-faced stare.

The door to the anteroom started to open. I slipped from the throne room.

There was no doubt where I had to go next. If Prince Eiko sometimes used the tunnels, perhaps he had a map. Queen Nalani had said that the prince slept late in the mornings.

A perfect time to search his observatory.

TWENTY-FOUR

I VAULTED UP THE OBSERVATORY tower stairs and entered the room at the top, narrowing my eyes against the sudden brightness. The round room was well lit by three tall windows and crowded with tables, bookshelves, nautical instruments, and metal contraptions I had no name for. I swept toward the nearest bookshelf, which also held rolled-up maps.

I had another reason for searching the observatory. Ever since my failed mission in the library, the whereabouts of the book had played on my mind. Prince Eiko had intercepted me the night I'd broken in. He'd known I was looking for something and certainly seemed to know more than he was saying. If he had the book, where better to store it than among a hundred other volumes in a tower used only by him?

I traced my fingers over the spines of books, then pulled scrolls from their perch on the shelves, unrolling and tossing them aside one by one. There was nothing neat or methodical about this. Prince Eiko would know his inner sanctum had been ransacked, but I had no time to be careful.

"Can I help you with something?" an amused voice asked.

I jumped and whirled, recovering my composure with a glare. "You startled me."

Prince Eiko sat on a chair tucked into the shadows between an armoire and a painted screen, making him almost indiscernible at first glance.

"It's *my* observatory," he pointed out.

I cleared my throat, opting to be blunt. He had shown me in small ways that he wanted to gain my trust. I hoped I wasn't wrong about him. "When you followed me to the school that night, you told me to come see you when I realized my time had run out. I'm out of time."

"You were looking at my bookshelf rather hopefully," he remarked.

"There's a book I need. And I have a theory you might have it." I wasn't ready to tell him I needed a map of the tunnels. Telling him about the book would be a safer way to gauge whether he was willing to help me.

He didn't even ask which book. He just pointed. "Bottom shelf, far right, behind the volume on ocean currents of the Vast Sea."

I hadn't expected him to tell me so easily. Hiding my surprise, I bent and found the book.

The Creation of the Thrones stood out in gold letters on the black leather cover. I touched the spine with reverence, lifting the book gingerly and placing it on the table. Elation and relief made my hands tremble.

"You had it this whole time," I breathed, opening to the first page.

"For a while, anyway. Long enough to translate the old tongue and understand most of its contents. The masters have the knowledge, but they do nothing with it." He paused, as if deciding whether or not to go on. "They don't care if my wife is taken over by a curse. They only care about the power the throne gives her."

"So the throne *is* on Sere!" Triumph surged through me. In my dream, the throne had been in an underground cavern. Once again I wondered if Sage was sending me visions. "Does the queen know?"

"No. She believes it was destroyed in the last eruption. Only the masters—and I—know the truth. Shortly after Rota disappeared, their father, King Tollak, died and there was an uprising on some of the islands. The masters saw that series of tragedies as a sign that the curse was awakening in the throne. The curse has periods of dormancy and activity, according to the book. At any rate, when a volcanic eruption occurred within months of Nalani being crowned, the masters saw an opportunity to hide the throne, to claim it had been destroyed. In truth, the castle was destroyed, but the throne remained. As there seemed no way of destroying it, the best they could do was hide the throne, hoping the distance would protect the queen."

"Is that all in the book? Or did the masters tell you?"

He shook his head. "The book is ancient, and the masters are an outrageously secretive lot. No, I confess I found out by accident. Years ago, while using the tunnels between the observatory and the castle, I sometimes noticed a master or two passing by. One day, I followed. I saw the cavern where they keep the throne and the guard who is always posted."

"You're convinced the curse is affecting the queen?"

"I am. I noticed changes in Nalani when King Rasmus took the throne in Tempesia. Her understandable grief and anger at his massacring Firebloods could have accounted for the changes, but I began to grow nervous. I started actively trying to find out more. Finally, I stole the book."

"Are her veins black? That's a sure sign of possession."

He came forward, close to the other side of the table, and gestured to the book. "A black vein is a sign of *full* possession by the Minax, but the creature exercises a lesser influence on people outside its immediate vicinity. Even with the throne hidden at a distance from the castle, the curse affects the queen, although the changes in behavior are less obvious. At first, I didn't want to see the signs, but when she had Frostbloods executed—" He broke off. His expression darkened. "That is not the woman I married."

"And now she's planning a war she can't win. That's exactly the kind of thing the Minax craves. Death and chaos and all the lovely grief that follows." All this time the Minax had been right under my nose.

"May I show you something?" Eiko reached forward and

flipped through the book, pointing when he found the page he sought. "There."

An illustration showed two indistinct figures, one throwing fire and one throwing ice, the two streams meeting in the center to form a blue-white flame directed at a dark, orange-veined throne.

"A Fireblood and a Frostblood creating frostfire. Destroying the throne of Sud."

He turned to the next page. The throne was gone. In its place was an oval outlined in black, a malevolent pair of eyes staring out of it. Even the illustration was enough to make the back of my neck prickle.

"The Minax," he said calmly. "Trapped in a remaining shard of the throne. I've translated the ancient Sudesian and the instructions are quite specific: The shard must be at least as large as an ancient Sudesian coin." He opened a small wooden box and produced a gold coin, which was not much larger than modern Tempesian ones. "A smaller stone would risk its escape."

"But how could anyone know this?"

"Well, Pernillius devoted his life to recording the prophecies of Dru. She was—"

"A prophetess, I know. I understand enough. We need to destroy the throne with frostfire but keep the Minax trapped in a shard of the throne. And then what? A friend of mine in Tempesia found something that indicates a Minax can destroy another. Could I use the shard to kill the other Minax?"

"Only one who can master or control the Minax can use one against the other. What was the phrasing in the book?"

He flipped a few pages and translated. "'Only shadow can create shadow. Only shadow can move shadow. Only shadow can destroy shadow.' It seems we cannot destroy the 'shadow' in the throne without the other one. The best option is to trap the Minax in the shard and remove it from the island completely."

"And who is going to do that?"

"You, I hope. On the ship of your friend the king, if he is willing?"

I nodded. Arcus would surely agree once he knew that removing the curse from the queen's island might be our best chance to prevent a war. If the queen was free of the Minax, she might change her position on Frostbloods. And I needed to take the shard back to Tempesia to destroy the frost Minax.

"We'll need to get him back to his ship once the throne is destroyed," I said. "I hear you know the tunnels well?"

"As well as the masters themselves."

Some question lingered at the back of my mind. I turned the page to the illumination of frostfire destroying the throne, then stared, narrow-eyed, at Prince Eiko. "What a happy coincidence that the two people you needed to make frostfire ended up in Sudesia."

"Not such a coincidence," he admitted hesitantly. "I suspected you had royal blood after hearing that you melted the throne of Fors. You see, Pernillius believed only the gifts of two people of royal blood can make frostfire. When Nalani sent Prince Kai to recruit you, I suggested to him that if it turned out your situation in the Frost Court was unsafe, he should bring you here and I would smooth things over with the queen."

"Lucky for you that I was in danger, then."

"It wasn't luck so much as probability. It was likely that you *would* be in danger. The Frost Court isn't known for its acceptance of Firebloods. To put it mildly."

"What about Arcus? The mysterious letter implying I was in danger?"

"I sent the letter to lure him here, instructing Kai to have it delivered before he left port and only if he was bringing you to Sudesia. He had no idea of the letter's contents, so do not blame him. I gambled that you were the princess and, if so, I needed the king to come here so you could destroy the throne together. There was certainly no way Nalani would see past the Minax's influence. She'd never agree to combine her fire with your king's frost."

"You lured him here to possible torture and death. Did you ever think about that?" I stared at him, the flames in my heart burning hotter.

He leaned in urgently. "I've done everything I could to protect him, as I have with you! I instructed the scouts to avoid the eastern edge of the island, creating false reports that it had already been searched. I assumed his ship was most likely to find a hiding place there. I've kept Nalani from questioning him until now. But you must understand, the risks to him were secondary to my goal. I did all this to protect my wife. I love her more than anything."

This was too much. If what he was saying were true, it meant I *did* have royal blood, because Arcus and I had created frostfire when we'd melted the throne of Fors. If the book was right, I really was the queen's niece. "You couldn't just tell me all this from the beginning? You let me take the trials—risk my life—for nothing!"

"Not for nothing. Your training has made you stronger. And I needed the trials to reveal whether you were truly the princess."

I pulled from his grasp and looked down at the book, forcing myself to take a moment to think. I hated being manipulated. I hated lies and subterfuge. He'd not only risked my life by letting me take the trials, he'd put Arcus in danger, too. My emotions were raw. My chest hurt, as if my very heart were bruised. I felt like a fool for not seeing through him.

I lifted my head and looked at Prince Eiko. He was watching me anxiously, one hand clutching an oval pendant that hung from his neck on a silver chain. As his thumb caressed the smooth ivory, I saw that it was a miniature of Queen Nalani, her distinctive features replicated with tiny, delicate brushstrokes. My heart gave a little squeeze. He wore an image of his wife around his neck. There was nothing deliberate about his nervous gesture, his hold on this small likeness that gave him comfort. It was clear that he truly did love her.

I let out a long sigh and asked myself one question: What wouldn't I do to protect Arcus? I could hardly blame Prince Eiko for doing what I would have done in his shoes. Besides, we had a common goal. I needed the Minax to destroy the other one, and he needed to get rid of it.

"When?" I asked. Prince Eiko looked confused, so I added, "When do we melt the throne?"

He blinked and his lips curved in a tentative smile full of warmth and gratitude. "As soon as possible."

"Arcus is being transferred to the prison tomorrow after the initiation. We don't have much time."

His face lost color. "If she's sending him to the prison . . ."

"I'm assuming she means to interrogate him."

"That's not the worst of it." He looked disturbed. "I heard her saying . . . she wants to send a message to the Frost Court. She has spoken of how the king's death would plunge Tempesia into chaos. If she plans to send him to the prison already, that means she intends to carry out her plans sooner than I thought."

I couldn't breathe. It felt as if someone had grabbed my throat and squeezed. "*No*," I whispered. "She'll kill him?"

"She doesn't make idle threats."

The blood abandoned my limbs, making my legs weak. Somehow, I had to get him out immediately. I picked up the book and turned toward the door.

"Ruby, wait! We must plan."

I closed my eyes and halted. For a second, he'd reminded me of Brother Thistle when he'd warned me not to take unnecessary risks.

"You're right," I said through numb lips. "The initiation ceremony tomorrow . . ." I no longer needed to take my vows to keep the queen's trust or to access the knowledge of the book. And saving Arcus was far more important than becoming a Fireblood master—no matter how much I'd longed to gain their acceptance. But what would be the consequences to Kai? Would the queen still allow him to go through with the initiation if I didn't show up? Would she revoke his rights to his title and land? Would she take her disappointment and anger out on him?

I had no choice but to hope that she wouldn't. I had to trust that the queen was honorable enough to keep her word.

Prince Eiko picked up on the idea immediately. "The masters will be there, as well as the queen. The throne should be unguarded. That *is* our best chance."

TWENTY-FIVE

MORNING CREPT IN FURTIVELY, A burglar skulking behind black storm clouds. The ocean had darkened to the gray of dirty bathwater, the whitecaps like leftover soap foam. Treetops genuflected to the sky and branches snapped off and sailed away like poplar fluff. Rain lashed the island in horizontal sheets, raging in from the east.

It was the morning of my initiation.

I dressed in my leggings and tunic, then covered those with the clothing provided, accepting Ada's help to put on the loose-sleeved orange silk robe covered in golden embroidery. Metal wrist guards were embossed with the shape of licking flames. Silk ribbons secured a satin cloak around my neck.

If anyone saw me, they'd think I was fully prepared to pledge my life to the queen today.

Ada smoothed my hair back and wound it in a simple knot. My face in the mirror appeared stark, almost lifeless, the bones protruding more than usual. My pupils were small in the meager light, leaving amber-gold irises below thick, dark lashes.

A princess? No. I looked like a terrified warrior before her first battle.

So many things could go wrong. If any one of the moving parts of our plan went awry, it would throw the rest into chaos.

Kai appeared in the open doorway as Ada disappeared.

"Ready?" he asked, everything about him from his bright hair, rich-toned skin, and engaging grin adding sunshine to the gray day. He was dressed like me, though his tunic hugged the muscles of his shoulders and chest a little more lovingly than mine, and his polished black knee boots added a touch of style.

"You're early," I pointed out. But I had expected him to be early. Counted on it, in fact.

He jerked his head toward the hallway. "Carriage is waiting."

I sat at my dressing table to pull on my calfskin boots. When I stood, I made a show of stumbling, stepping hard on the hem of my cloak. The stitches I'd pre-loosened gave way with a gratifyingly loud rip. Half of the cloak's collar fell at an odd angle against my shoulder. I cursed and scowled at it.

Kai chuckled and shook his head in wonderment, stepping close to inspect the damage. "Did you just trip over nothing? Surely you will be the clumsiest master ever to take the vows."

His elegant fingers explored the delicate fabric. "Quite a tear. But I don't suppose they'll reject you for it. The masters don't worry much over sartorial concerns."

I quirked a brow. "You'll be wasted as a Fireblood master, then."

He grinned. "I don't have to wear the robes all the time, little bird."

He hadn't called me by that nickname since the night we kissed. The reminder brought heat to my chest. He was standing very close. I could feel the heat of his body and smell the scent of his skin. To avoid whatever was brewing in his warm, intent eyes, I untied my cloak and folded it over my arm. "I'll get Ada to mend this. It won't take a minute. You go on without me."

His face flickered with annoyance. "I'm capable of waiting for a few minutes."

"No, I'm nervous enough as it is without you tapping your foot in the hallway. Plus, I have to find Ada and . . . it might take longer than a few minutes. I'll meet you at the school."

I swept into the hallway and he fell into step beside me. I avoided his eyes, sensing his growing consternation and not wanting to give myself away. The urge to blurt out the truth was gaining force with every second. I hated keeping things from him, but I'd thought about this all night and decided not to involve him in Arcus's escape, not to mention the highly punishable act of melting the throne of Sud. The queen might forgive her own husband for his treason, but Kai was merely a well-liked and useful courtier who already had past strikes against him. I didn't want him to lose all he'd worked for, not for my sake.

I'd shared my fears with Prince Eiko, and he had sworn to do everything in his power to protect Kai from any backlash when I didn't attend the initiation ceremony. He was sure the queen would see reason, and that she would uphold her promises to Kai.

"Ruby," Kai said softly, touching my shoulder with three fingers as we reached the bottom of the tower stairs. I drew to a halt. "Is everything all right?"

I took a steadying breath and forced a smile. "Everything is fine. I just want to look perfect for the initiation ceremony."

"Far be it from me to criticize you for attention to your wardrobe." His voice softened. "You're sure nothing is wrong? This is a big step. I'd be lying if I didn't admit I was terrified, too. But the benefits of taking the vows outweigh the sacrifice of some of our freedoms."

"I know," I said, staring resolutely at his chest so I didn't have to see his concern. I was so close to breaking down I could feel the confession forming on my tongue. No matter how I reasoned that Kai would be fine, I couldn't help a surge of worry on his behalf. And lying was a poor way of repaying everything he'd done for me.

He hesitated before adding, "You know you have to go through with it now, don't you? She expects it, especially from you. It would be dangerous to refuse."

"I just want to get my cloak mended." I forced myself to meet his eyes.

"All right." He stared at me for another few seconds, then lifted my chin with his index finger and warned, "But if you're late, I'll make you pay for drinks at the tavern later."

“Deal,” I said, wishing again that I didn’t have to lie.

I waved him off with a smile, my gut twisting with guilt and nerves. For all I knew, it could be the last time I saw him.

The realization sent shock waves through my body. It would hurt me far more than I wanted to admit to myself. I would miss him fiercely.

I watched until he moved out of sight, imprinting his bright hair and the lean athleticism of his movements into my memory. When he was gone, I allowed myself a moment to stare at the empty doorway, my chest aching.

With a cleansing breath, I shoved the feelings away. There was no time to spare. I threw the cloak into a corner and raced toward the north tower.

When I reached the hallway at the top, I slowed, relieved to see Prince Eiko already there. Two guards waited outside of Arcus’s door instead of the requisite six. When they saw me, they wore twin expressions of confusion.

“Princess Ruby,” Prince Eiko said with feigned surprise. “I just sent the other guards to attend you at your ceremony, as the queen requested.” His act was entirely unconvincing to my ears. I would warn him later never to consider a career on the stage.

“I came back for something.” We hadn’t exactly rehearsed the details of this part. “You didn’t give me...” I stepped closer to one guard, unable to think of anything I might need from the queen’s consort.

“Ah, yes,” he said, making a show of reaching under his cloak. “I assume you mean this?” With his free hand, he grabbed the guard's halberd and tossed it away, while with the other he pulled out a dagger in a lightning movement, putting it to the guard's throat. I did the same thing with my guard, though my dagger came from my sleeve. We *had* rehearsed this part.

"Open the door," I ordered, staring into the furious eyes of the guard.

"No," he said clearly, his jaw defiantly squared.

"You get points for loyalty." I pushed the blade to his skin. "I'm sure you'll get special recognition for that at your funeral." I made a motion as if to draw the edge across his throat, hoping he wouldn't notice the blade was ceremonial and as dull as a butter knife.

His eyes rounded. "I'll be dismissed if I allow you in."

"I assure you," Prince Eiko said, "the blame will be all mine. I give you my word you won't suffer for this."

The guards glanced at each other out of the corners of their eyes, then my guard motioned to the other, who produced a key and unlocked the door.

"Ah-ah," I cautioned when my guard twitched. "Stay still until I tell you to move."

As the door swung open, Arcus's voice came low and resonant, sending a shiver across my skin. "Is this my cue that I've overstayed my welcome?"

He grinned at me from the doorway. Despite the tension in my chest, I smiled back.

"On the contrary," answered Eiko lightly, "my wife would like you to stay. But I think you'll find our plans preferable."

Arcus looked surprised to see Prince Eiko, but he deftly

moved into the hallway out of the way of the guards, and we pushed them inside the room, keeping our blades raised.

Prince Eiko said, "You have no other key, I take it? Be honest, or my promise to protect you from consequences is void."

"No other key," one said sullenly, and the other nodded.

"Your breastplate and helm," I said with an impatient motion to the taller guard. When he handed them to me, I gave them to Arcus. "Put these on."

"Sorry about this," Prince Eiko said to the guards in a cheerful tone. "Someone will no doubt release you soon. Until then..." He put a finger to his lips in a shushing motion. He locked them in and dropped the key into a pocket.

Arcus slid the helm on and was buckling the leather breastplate as we swept down the hallway. I handed him the halberd I'd picked up off the floor.

I gave the prince a sideways look as he passed me at the stairs. "You enjoyed that too much."

"Intrigue is rather invigorating. I don't know why I don't engage in it more often."

"Thank you for getting me out," Arcus said quietly from close behind me. "Is my crew involved?"

I shook my head. "Marella was in no condition to plan anything, and the crew isn't big enough to face all the guards. You can thank Prince Eiko for this. He gave orders so that most of the guards were otherwise occupied."

"A well-executed plan, which I appreciate. But why is the prince helping us?"

"We have a common goal." I met his eyes and lowered my voice. "To melt the throne and trap the Minax. I need your help for that part."

"Of course." He cleared his throat and said only slightly louder, "Thank you, Prince Eiko."

"It's you who will be helping me," Prince Eiko said. "I'll breathe easier when the curse is far away."

As we reached the bottom of the stairs, I reminded Arcus quietly, "Don't let anyone see your eyes." Frostblood eyes would stand out like bluebells in a bed of daisies. Luckily the helm with its horizontal eye openings around the narrow nose guard left the upper half of his face in partial shadow.

Arcus stuck close to the wall while Prince Eiko and I stayed on the outside so anyone passing wouldn't sense the waves of cold coming off his skin. His gift became harder to control in times of stress.

One of the courtiers came around a corner, a heavyset woman dressed in a turquoise gown covered with tiny white ribbons. As she saw us, she smiled and curtsied, blocking our way. "Prince Eiko, shouldn't the princess be on her way to the initiation at the school? I'm on my way there now."

Prince Eiko cleared his throat. "We'll be along shortly, of course. I merely wished to . . . well, now, Lady Zini, you're spoiling my surprise. I had planned to give the princess a piece of jewelry for the occasion—an heirloom from the royal vault."

She clapped her hands in delight. "What a splendid idea! I look forward to seeing you wearing it later, Princess."

Eiko bent his tall form in a bow. "If you'll excuse us."

We left the curious lady behind. Arcus and I followed Prince Eiko along the colonnade of arched windows that ran between the towers, nodding at anyone we passed and praying they didn't engage us in conversation.

I breathed a sigh of relief when we reached the south tower.

"Hurry," Eiko whispered, finally showing signs of strain as we moved through the empty entrance hall to a servants' door, which opened to a dark stairwell leading down. "There's a hidden entrance to the tunnels down here."

When we reached the musty lower level, he passed a few doors and opened one to a dusty storage room filled with empty barrels and empty baskets. The prince slid a shelf away from the wall. A hidden door lurked behind it.

He moved into the dim space and we followed. The torches were spaced far apart, with chunks of near darkness in between. Our footsteps echoed against the rock. As we went deeper in, the air thickened and heated. I listened with concern as Arcus's breath grew labored.

More tunnels branched off at random intervals, but Eiko didn't hesitate as he led us along. I tried to memorize the path, but after innumerable twists and turns, all the squiggly lines of my mental map blurred together.

Now that we were safe from listening ears, I told Arcus what I knew about the throne, how Prince Eiko was convinced it was influencing the queen, how the book said the throne could be melted with frostfire, how the Minax could be contained by a small shard.

"And if Brother Thistle is right," I concluded, "then the shard containing the fire Minax could be the key to destroying the frost Minax."

Eventually, the tunnel opened into a vast cavern. Black pillars stretched from floor to ceiling, disappearing as they exceeded the reach of light from wall-mounted torches. In the center of the room, a large, blocky object glinted with pulsing veins of orange.

The throne of Sud.

Its presence dominated the air, commanded the flow of blood in my veins. Its power beat against me like great black raven wings, soft and swift and irrefutable. When I'd encountered the frost throne, I'd felt a sense of awe mixed with repulsion. Now, the awe was there in full measure, but without the counterbalance of aversion. Instead, I trembled with the need to prostrate myself, to swear allegiance, to serve.

My knees turned to water. I locked them to keep from crumpling to the floor. Arcus stood close, his hand briefly touching my elbow in support, but I was too overcome to respond.

I exhaled, long and slow. A corresponding intake of breath came from the throne, as if the sacrifice of air from my lungs provided the first full, satisfying breath it had taken in an age. I knew from experience that no one could hear the Minax but me.

A whispering started, a silky caress. *I have waited. I have waited. You are here. You are here.*

The fire Minax tugged at something inside me, as if a thread connected a spot behind my rib cage to the consciousness in the throne. How I longed to rush forward and fling myself against it like an insect against a lit window. *Yes, I'm here,* I thought, then shook myself. I was aware of the Minax in the same way one is aware of a gentle rain pattering over the roof. The whispers rustled in my mind, persuading rather than demanding. A ceaseless backdrop of chatter.

You are here, you are here, come closer, come to me.

It took vigilant effort not to obey. I put my head against the bumpy rock wall and closed my eyes. I counted to one hundred in Sudesian—anything to keep my mind busy, to drown out the compulsion to move closer to the voice.

"We have very little time," Prince Eiko reminded me sharply.

I struggled to regain focus. By now, the Fireblood masters would have realized I was late for the initiation ceremony. They might be searching. If they found us, not only would we lose our chance of destroying the throne, but Arcus would face recapture. If the queen had decided to execute him, I didn't know if I could stop her.

We had to work fast and get him back to his ship. I might even be able to leave with him. *If* we could melt the throne. *If* the book was right that a shard would contain the Minax.

A shiver ripped through me as I finally realized the odds against us.

"Ruby, are you ready?" Arcus asked, leaning close. I nodded. We moved toward the throne in tandem.

I knew the exact moment the fire Minax noticed Arcus's presence.

Frostblood! The bloodthirsty cry echoed in my mind. I clapped my hands over my ears.

Even Arcus seemed to sense it. He recoiled, the sudden jolt and catch of his muscles making him tremble slightly, as if he were an arrow shot into the ground.

I spoke softly, because the throne was on edge, its consciousness straining toward Arcus the way a dog tugs at the end of its leash when it sees a nice fat rabbit nearby. Everything in me wanted to soften the Minax's craving, to appease it. With my voice, if not my actions.

Kill him, kill him, the throne chanted.

"Stop it," I whispered to the throne. "You don't need his death. You have the blood of all the Frostblood servants who made these tunnels."

Not enough, never enough, the throne chanted. *Powerful beyond measure. His frost vastly strong. His death would be a feast. Yours for the killing, Daughter of Darkness. To make you strong beyond measure, your fire and your dark. Unmatched power. Incendiary power. Bliss.*

I turned my back on it angrily, my whole body shaking with the effort of separating its desires from my own.

"Arcus," I said, trying to reclaim myself, to reassert my identity. "Remember the shard must be no smaller than a coin."

The Minax screamed, a howling excoriation of the quiet places in my mind, like a gale-force wind that scrapes mountains bare. I covered my ears, but the sound was inside me, shearing my nerve endings and stabbing through my veins. My shoulder bashed the rough wall as I tried to escape. Then arms came around me.

"Ruby, I'm here. You're not alone. We have to do this." The low rumble of Arcus's voice soothed me. I grabbed his collar and held on as the scream faded.

"It wants..." I shook my head, eyes wide but unseeing, as if the sound had stolen all other senses.

"Don't listen to it," he said, pulling my attention back with his commanding tone. "Listen to me. You can do this. *We* can." He held me tight for a few seconds, his cold lips pressing firm kisses to the top of my head, brushing the pulse at my temple, gliding across my cheek.

Everything else faded as the mindless pleasure of feeling his cool lips took every ounce of my attention. It had been so long since we'd touched like this. I realized in that moment how scared I'd been that he would never hold me again. Layers of distance between us fell away, melted by his hands curved tenderly over my shoulders, the gentle brush of lips on my forehead. I wanted to burrow into the comfort he offered and live there for a while, cherished and protected.

The reassuring scent of his skin calmed me, and I drew strength from his size, from his natural self-assurance, from his steadfast belief in me. When I felt ready, I nodded and pushed him away, straightening.

"Let's get it done," I said, all calm resolution on the outside, while my insides quaked with nerves.

"If you melt the rock completely, you will free it," Prince Eiko warned. "You must leave a portion intact."

Do not trust him. Do not trust him, said the Minax. *This throne is yours for the taking. Our union will bring you extraordinary power. Embrace me.*

"I know," I replied to Prince Eiko, shoving the voice away. "Arcus, I'm not... myself right now. I may... I may lose track of the size of the shard."

His eyes were shadowed, but I felt their intensity. "I'll tell you when to stop."

We moved forward until we stood about two arm lengths from the throne. Close enough to attack, but far enough that I couldn't touch it. I knew instinctively that physical contact with the throne was dangerous for me. The frost Minax had been an invasion, an insidious voice in my head. The fire Minax felt like an extension of self. A universe where I could happily dwell forever.

I shuddered.

It was my enemy. My enemy.

I began with a stream of fire, a simple blast of pure orange flame directed at the line where the seat and back met—what I thought of as its heart. Arcus welded a ribbon of ice to my fire. The fire and frost curled together, two separate strands that merged into one writhing cataract, flowing like a torrent of glistening blue-white water, sinuous and elegant. Blue sparks flared from the column like shooting stars before winking out. I shut my eyes against the blinding light—so bright, it filtered through my eyelids. The room suddenly felt cooler. Like a summer day when a cloud moves over the sun.

The Minax thrashed in agony, its voice grating like knives dragged over chain mail. *Cold, cold, hate it! Stop him! Kill him!*

I felt its burning, stinging, unbearable hurt as my own.

"Ruby," Arcus said sharply, "look at me."

I couldn't. Couldn't answer, couldn't even shake my head. I couldn't do anything but throw out fire, and I could barely do that. Pain, so much pain. Any more of this and I would—

"*Ruby*. Look. At. Me."

Somehow, my muscles obeyed and my head turned. When I opened my eyes, circles of white danced over my vision as if I'd stared directly into the sun. I blinked hard until I could see. Arcus's pupils were pinpoints, his irises bleached almost white by the reflection of the strange, bright fire. He scrutinized me, searching my eyes, then my wrists. I realized he was searching me for signs of possession.

I turned back to check our progress. The throne wept lava, now reduced to a misshapen blob about half its original size. I gritted my teeth, maintaining the flow. My limbs shook with fatigue. It felt as if I were destroying myself.

"You can do this," Arcus said, his confidence bolstering mine.

I shut my eyes again. More fire, more pain. Time crawled.

When I opened my eyes, I saw our progress was too slow. I was shaky and exhausted and the throne was still only half-melted. Lava oozed from it in rivulets, sliding toward the edges of the room.

In a moment of inspiration, I used my gift to gather the lava on the floor, lifting it and forcing it back toward the throne. The lava joined the frostfire, bursting with blue-white light and heating to a painful degree. Arcus gasped. There was a shuffle as he changed position, backing up to put a few inches more distance between himself and the lava. The throne melted faster, its outline flattening and shrinking. My fire was nearly spent. I closed my eyes to focus, hoping my last shreds of endurance would be enough.

A shift. A change. The Minax's pain turned to anticipation. Excitement. Its prison was melting. Its tether had nearly snapped.

So close.

"Stop, Ruby, stop!" Arcus put shaking hands on my shoulders, leaning heavily on me as he brought me back to myself. "It's done."

I reined in my fire. A rogue wave of relief knocked my legs out from under me. Arcus was as unsteady as I was, and I brought him down with me. We stayed on our knees, breathing heavily. One of his arms went around my waist and he pulled me against him, my back against his chest.

So close to freedom, the Minax raged. *True vessel...please...*

Its grief was so acute, I lifted my hand to comply, to try to melt the small, flat shard of rock that sat where the throne had been. Arcus caught my hand in his own and gently pulled my arm down.

"It's done, Ruby."

I shuddered.

Then, pulled by an unbearably strong compulsion, I broke free of his hold and picked up the shard. It was smaller than my palm and felt like the kind of smooth stone you'd find in a riverbed.

A sharp sensation of extreme heat flooded my arm and eased into numbness. My head spun, and then nothing hurt at all. I was suddenly floating. Incandescent. I held the shard to my cheek. It was as smooth as silk. Soft as fur. It caressed me like a mother's hand.

True vessel, it said. Its voice was my voice. Its thoughts, my thoughts. Finally, it breathed. *Alone for so long. Now we will be one.*

This is what I'd come to Sudesia to find. Suddenly I knew that this was the real reason I'd trained and bled and tested my limits with the Fireblood masters. For this moment.

The shard was swept from my hand. It fell to the floor, bouncing and tumbling end over end until it settled, glistening black, into the shallow indentation where the throne had been. I screeched and dove after it. A viselike grip wrapped around my upper arm.

"Don't touch it!"

There was a strange, animal keening. It took me a second to realize it came from my own throat. I struggled against Arcus's restraining hand, heat building in my chest. I needed to burn him—anything to make him let me go.

The Minax was still trapped in that shard and I needed it. I needed the Minax with me. Part of me. Forever.

I threw myself forward. His arms clamped tighter and I was lifted off the floor, my feet kicking ineffectually. I put my head forward, preparing to slam the back of it into his face, when his voice rumbled at my ear.

"Ruby. Please. Remember who you are. Who I am."

His arms were cold around me. Heat came off me in waves. I heard the unevenness of his breathing. This place, my heat, the lava—it must have been so uncomfortable for him. It was this awareness of him that made me come back to myself.

I sucked in a breath and let out a sob. My muscles went slack.

Arcus exhaled and relaxed. "Come away from it." He led me away from the shard. I could still see it from the corner of my eye. It winked invitingly, illuminated by the glow of lava just inches away.

Prince Eiko moved forward and scooped up the shard in a handkerchief, depositing it in a pocket.

Arcus took my face in his hands, the cold from his fingers steadying me, the familiar blue of his eyes seizing my gaze and holding it, tethering me to him. To reality.

"It's all right," he said soothingly, but I could tell from the underlying tension in his voice that it wasn't. "We have to leave."

Under normal circumstances, I would've taken action. Offered options. Given orders. But I couldn't think. Everything was hazy and blunted, the only clear thought that I wanted to get the shard back.

As we moved toward the exit, Prince Eiko led the way. "I will take you to a branch that leads to the eastern side of the island where Ruby said the ship is hidden."

But as we neared the doorway, a silhouette blocked the opening.

TWENTY-SIX

THE FIGURE STROLLED FORWARD, removing a huge black shawl that fell to the floor. Torchlight shimmered over wheat-gold hair and tinted her white gown with an angry light, making her look both celestial and terrifying. Shadows hollowed out her sunken cheeks. She still looked gaunt, but much stronger than I'd remembered from my visit to the ship.

"Marella?" I murmured in amazement.

I glanced at Arcus. He looked shocked, then furious. "I don't know what you think you're doing here, but this isn't a party, for Tempus's sake. Get out of here before—"

"You always underestimate me," she broke in, sounding

irritated. "You do realize that just because I dress well doesn't mean I'm a featherbrain?"

"Marella, this is not the time," I warned. Then, because I couldn't help myself, I asked, "How did you even get here?"

"Through the tunnels, of course. I had a guide who knew the location of the throne. My own personal shadow." Though her words made no sense, her tone was relaxed and smooth, as if we all sat at a grand table for a court dinner. "Now, where is the shard? Ah, yes. I sense the tall one has it. Prince... Eiko, is it? If you'd just hand that to me, I'd be much obliged." She waltzed up to him and held her palm out.

He regarded her in stunned silence.

"I don't want to hurt you," Marella explained. "But if you don't hand over the shard, I'll have to."

"Marella," I said desperately, "what are you doing?"

"I want the shard," she said slowly, as if talking to a simpleton. She beckoned to Prince Eiko.

"I'm not giving it to you," he snapped, clearly outraged by this confusing turn of events.

She dropped her hand. "Well, I suppose it's as good a time as any to test my new abilities."

She closed her eyes and dark tendrils flowed from her pale hair. A gossamer shadow took form in the air above her. First, its shoulders bristled with protrusions that appeared to be jagged icicles, with similar pointed shapes forming a crown on its head. Then there were hints of a humanlike upper body.

Dread sank talons into my fast-beating heart.

Somehow, the frost Minax was here.

As it hovered in the air, it whispered in a sibilant language I couldn't decipher, though I could hear the fire Minax answering in the same tongue.

Both of them. Here. No!

Then, to my utter horror, Marella spoke in the same language, as easy and familiar as friends gossiping over tea.

A wash of ice settled at the base of my spine. Arcus was suddenly in front of me.

Terror elongated Prince Eiko's face, accentuating the bones in his cheeks. "What—"

Marella fluttered a hand at the hovering shadow. "I'm sorry, how rude of me. You don't understand its language. The Minax said 'Give us the shard.' " She held her hand out again, palm up. "I hope you're more willing now."

We all stared helplessly. The Minax wasn't something you could fight with frost or fire. It was made of mist and midnight.

"No," Prince Eiko said shakily.

The shadow creature flowed toward him, its obsidian tendrils disappearing into his hands, which had come up to ward it off. His eyes widened and he jerked a couple of times before reaching, puppetlike, into his pocket and pulling out the shard. He extended his arm and dropped it into Marella's outstretched palm.

She flashed a smile, as sparkling as a sunlit waterfall and as infectious as typhoid, the one I'd seen charm a roomful of courtiers. "Thank you."

The shadow creature left Prince Eiko's body and floated toward me. Arcus sent out a blast of frost that went right through its transparent form.

True vessel, it begged, drawing nearer. I shrank back instinctively.

"Return to me," Marella commanded, and the frost Minax flowed back into her instantly.

"Marella," Arcus said, sounding horrified, "how long has that... thing... been part of you?"

"It wasn't easy," she said softly. "I had to find it in Tevros. Convince it to choose me as its next host when the previous one—rather conveniently, mind you—died in a brawl over a game of dice. And then there was hiding my... condition... on the ship. Luckily, seasickness is an excellent cover for Minax possession." Her breathy laugh raised a fresh crop of goose bumps on my arms. "That's why I had to stay in my poorly lit cabin most of the time. I couldn't let you see my veins. Also, I truly did feel ill at times, and then I had these strange visions.... I think I saw you, Ruby. In the Fireblood school, and once when you were in a cave or something. There was fire and lava. Did you see me? On the ship?"

"I think so," I answered, feeling sick. I'd seen someone on a ship. It must have been Marella, or rather the frost Minax that was somehow still connected to me, sending me images she was seeing.

She nodded. "Most people who are possessed don't survive longer than a week, but I'm stronger than most people." She glanced at Arcus. "Sometimes at night I sent the Minax into one of your sailors for a few hours to give myself a rest. If you heard someone screaming with nightmares, that would be why."

A razor-sharp chill skittered over my body, raising every tiny hair on my arms and the back of my neck.

"You're mad," Arcus breathed.

"Not mad. Tired. Tired of having to behave like a ninny to fulfill my father's expectations for what a lady should be. Tired of being underestimated by you and the court. Tired of being passed over. Tired of pretending to be so much less than I am."

"What are you planning to do?" I asked.

She moved gracefully toward Arcus, whose whole body tensed.

"Arcus, you're going to step away from Ruby," she instructed with a small, chilling smile.

"No," he said firmly.

She moved closer. "You're going to move away from her now."

"No!" He lifted a hand to stop her approach.

She stopped inches away. "If you hurt me, if you knock me out, the Minax will merely be free to do as it wishes. You know what follows. Death. Pain. Madness. It will inhabit whomever it chooses and you will have no control over it. I, however, control it perfectly. As you have seen. And by the way, Prince Eiko can stop right now or he will be the first to die!"

She swiveled suddenly, catching Prince Eiko just feet behind her.

"Get back to the wall," she ordered.

The prince moved to the wall, the rage in his eyes spitting green fire.

"I don't need you, Arcus, or you, Prince," she said with a flap of her hand. "You can both leave."

They didn't move.

"I can see you're not taking me seriously." Her jaw hardened. She pointed at Prince Eiko and the Minax seeped into the air again, then flowed into his body. This time, he gave an earsplitting shriek of agony that echoed off the cavern walls. He dropped to his knees.

I sensed the exultation of the Minax, both of them, as they absorbed the joy of his suffering.

Marella said, "Return to me," and the shadow arced toward her and disappeared into her veins. "Now that you know what I'm capable of, I suggest you leave. Or should I just kill you?"

Prince Eiko grabbed the wall and hauled himself to his feet, then turned to face Marella again.

"Go, Prince Eiko," I said pleadingly.

"I brought you here. I won't leave you." He brought his hands up, palms tilted at Marella to attack. She watched him, poised. A snake about to strike.

"You can't fight this with fire, Prince Eiko," I said. "Please, go now."

The corner of Marella's mouth twitched up, as if she enjoyed his indecision.

"Just go," I repeated. "Please!" Hearing the urgency in my voice, he backed toward the door and, with a reluctant glance, left the cavern.

"Now you, Arcus," she said calmly, tilting her pert chin toward the entrance.

He shook his head. "Only if Ruby leaves with me."

Marella closed her eyes, and the Minax came for him, its onyx talons outstretched. He put up his forearm to block. I waited for that sickening moment when the tendrils would penetrate his skin.

Instead, it recoiled visibly, jerking back as if rebounding off an invisible barrier.

Not that one, it whispered, shaken. I felt its revulsion and pain. Shock rippled through me.

Marella's eyes were narrowed to slits as she examined Arcus, who stood with his arm still raised as he watched the Minax return to her.

She shuddered as it disappeared into her fingers. "I guess I'll have to let you stay for now. But I think I'll close that opening, in case anyone else decides to join us."

Her arm shot forward and frost surged out to strike the ceiling with the force of a battering ram. A deluge of rock shook the floor, clogging the opening. When the ground stopped trembling, she smiled, self-satisfied. "Didn't think I could do that, did you? The Minax lends me power."

Arcus and I shared a brief look. She truly was unstable. Weeks of possession by the Minax had tangled the threads of her mind.

"I've dreamed of this day for so long." She smiled benignly. "To reunite them both. I can hardly believe I've done it."

"Why would you want to?" I asked, wondering if her reasons would make any sense to me.

"The frost Minax and fire Minax are like twins. Not only did the frost Minax feel the constriction of its own bonds, it could feel the pain of its twin in the fire throne. The fire Minax was isolated here, kept from its true host, the queen. The best it could achieve was a partial bond, blocked by rock and castle stone. How do you think that felt, Ruby?"

The bond had been strong enough for the queen to execute any Frostbloods who didn't agree to servitude. I couldn't imagine what a full bond would look like.

Marella's eyes were shrouded by shadows, but somehow they managed to glow with a restless fervor—nearly fanaticism—that terrified me almost more than the Minax.

"I could hear it," she continued. "The Minax speaking to me from the frost throne. My mother's family worshipped Eurus, the creator of the Minax, though I only found out after her death. My father wouldn't let me speak to her when she took ill, probably because he knew she'd tell me secrets about the Minax before she died. But I'll never know for sure, will I? Thanks to his small-minded fear of power."

"Small-minded fear?" I breathed with disbelief. She spoke as if exposure to the Minax were no great risk.

"Don't you want the power to control your own life, your own destiny? Having authority over others only makes that easier. I was groomed to marry a king. But when it became clear that would never happen, I was forced to come up with an alternate plan. I *will* rule. Just not at anyone's side. I have a much more powerful ally than any king."

"Who?" I asked.

"It's time for you to find out. Come here, Ruby."

"No," I said. "I know how hard it is to resist the Minax, but don't let it control you. Don't let it win!"

"I'm the one who has won." She opened her hand to show the black shard resting on her milk-white palm. It seemed to absorb the light, making everything around it dim and colorless. "Let me see how well you resist now, Ruby."

"Give me the shard, Marella," said Arcus in a low, persuasive voice. "Whatever you think—"

With decisive speed, she dashed the shard against the floor and crushed it under her heel.

The sharp crack was followed by wisps of obsidian mist rising from the shard's remains. The tendrils coalesced into a roughly humanlike shape. Rising from its brow were several curved points that moved sinuously, like flames. A crown of fire. The fire Minax.

The inky creature gathered itself and twitched toward me.

Arcus moved to block its path. The creature changed direction and slipped around him and behind me, flowing into the nape of my neck like a splash of hot water. I clapped my palm over the vulnerable skin, but the Minax had already seeped in, taking hold, curving into the dark, hidden spaces of my mind and clinging like a bat to a cave's ceiling.

We are one, the Minax said—or was it I who spoke? It didn't matter. In seconds, I'd forgotten who I'd been and what I'd wanted. I was whole in a way I'd never been before. I experienced the relief of no longer fighting something inevitable. Fear left my body in an exhalation and loosening of limbs.

I met Marella's eyes and she smiled. I felt peaceful suddenly. She and I were in tune with each other. Her plans were no longer a mystery to me. If I hadn't been fighting so hard against my connection with the Minax, I would have known her intentions sooner. Now all that was left was a final joining, to touch my twin for the first time in a thousand years. It could have been a million. Or yesterday. When the separation was over, it would no longer matter.

I moved toward her, arm extended, hand seeking.

The Frost King—Arcus—caught me around the waist and I cried out, hating his very nature, his touch. His essence repelled me, made me writhe and want to leave the safe and perfect shell of the Fireblood girl Ruby—the Daughter of Darkness who had come to free me.

"Ruby!" he said sharply, and I pushed at him, lashed out with hands and feet, drew in breath to wield my fire. His arms tightened like cold steel bands pinning my arms to my sides. I focused on expelling him with a flash of heat over my skin. If I had to burn in order to escape him, I would.

But while he held me, she—Marella, host to my twin—came forward. Her hand sought and found mine. As our flesh touched, cold to warm, my twin and I reached our shadow fingers through our hosts' skin and touched as well.

A wavelike pulse rippled out into the air, shuddering through the walls, drawing cracks on the stone floor, shearing through sections of the ceiling and pulling down rocks into shivering piles of rubble. The Frostblood was thrown off his feet.

From our linked hands came a bubble of light that swirled and grew larger until a lozenge of blinding white spun between us. All that was left was the recitation of words of power that would complete the ritual. We said them in unison, old words no longer remembered, an ancient tongue only spoken by gods. Saying the words was a joy because it meant we were no longer alone, we had found each other and would soon be reunited with our creator. We would never be alone again.

The Frostblood—Arcus—surged to his feet. A gash on his head leaked blue liquid, the lifeblood of his frail mortal body, and I noted that weakness in case I needed to attack.

"What is that?" he demanded, staring, the white of the portal reflected in his wide-open eyes.

We didn't respond. We didn't need to. We didn't answer to him.

The portal steadied, its borders stabilizing. My twin and I stepped back, our arms falling to our sides.

Moments later, a figure strode through the shining portal, his skin too bright, glowing like moonlight and sunlight and crushed pearls, smelling of spring buds and the wind of eastern storms.

"Who brought me here?" The voice of the east wind was resonant, immense, and implacable.

"We did," we said.

"And where is my vessel? The mortal body that will host my essence so that I might remain in this world?" he asked.

We lifted our arms to point at the Frostblood man.

"An imperfect vessel," said our master. "He is bleeding."

"There is a Fireblood prince in the tunnels," I offered humbly, hoping that Prince Eiko was still there. I was shivering now in all my human limbs, and in my shadow self as well. To risk his displeasure was to risk great suffering. We had no power over him. We had learned that unmistakably when he put us in the thrones and we'd begged for freedom, for mercy, and found none.

The god of the east wind turned to the tunnels and a bolt of purple light shot from his hands, making us cower and cover our heads with our arms and whine in fear. His light scorched. To let it touch us would be anguish.

The rocks that blocked the tunnel entrance were blown into a cloud of choking dust. When the debris settled, not one, but two figures emerged, their mouths covered by their sleeves.

"Ruby?" one called. Kai. He had hair like a summer sunset. He came closer, waving at the dust that clouded his vision. He froze in shock as he caught sight of Eurus, a being made of glowing light. "What—"

The other figure who followed was tall and dark, his eyes the green of wet leaves. Prince Eiko. He had brought the Fireblood and the Frostblood to destroy my throne.

"There are two of you," our god Eurus said, his skin too bright to look at. "And I only need one. Who shall be my vessel?"

Neither spoke.

"You, then," said Eurus, pointing at the bright-haired Fireblood prince—Kai—and I felt a strange bolt of something unpleasant. Some unwelcome human feeling. Fear for another's safety. It was my host who made us feel this unpleasant thing. We didn't want him to hurt Prince Kai with the hair of glowing coals and the eyes of golden brown.

Eurus moved toward the mortal.

"Wait!" The sound had come from my own mortal throat. The part of me that was still Ruby had surprised me, taking control. "Take the other one." I spoke without wanting to, without thinking, and then trembled in fear of the god's wrath.

But Eurus was merciful for once in an age, and he changed direction and slid into the other body, the tall man. Prince Eiko's green eyes turned white for a moment as the light entered his thin body, then returned to normal.

Eurus-Eiko turned to the sunset-haired man. His expression spoke his intentions clearly. Our god had no use for Kai and so he would get rid of him.

We struggled with ourselves, the Daughter of Darkness trying to assert her consciousness.

"Kai!" Ruby's will once again took control of our voice. "Go! Run!"

Kai shook his head, his gaze flinty as it latched on to Prince Eiko—Eurus. "You are no longer Prince Eiko. Are you?"

"Eiko is gone," said Eurus.

"Then I don't have to worry about hurting him," said Kai. The bend of his knees, his wide-legged stance and posture all screamed his intention to fight.

"Kai, no!" I called out.

Fear had brought me partially back to myself, but the Minax struggled for dominance, bathing my mind in a cocktail of sweet numbness and a sense of futility. *What does any of it matter?* the thoughts said. *Everything is fine.*

I forced myself to focus on Kai and Arcus, on memories of my mother and grandmother, finding the parts of myself that feared and cared and hurt. I rejected the floating joy the Minax offered and grabbed at thoughts of affection, empathy—even grief. Every second was a power struggle between myself and the Minax. I phased in and out of awareness as a separate entity.

I was pulled from my self-absorption as fire flew from Eurus's fists, or rather it was Prince Eiko's fire coming from fists he no longer controlled. The attack caught Kai off guard, throwing him backward. He slid across the floor for several feet before coming to a stop. I took a step toward him, relieved when I saw his chest rise and fall.

"Leave him," said Eurus. "He is of no consequence."

I jerked to a halt. Arcus had moved beside me. Eurus's gaze sharpened on him. If he meant to do to him what he'd done to Kai...

Fear broke through the remaining mist in my mind.

I'm Ruby, I thought, beating away the velvety layers of numbness wrapped around me, wresting my identity from the mind of the Minax. *I'm in control.*

I must have spoken aloud, because Eiko—Eurus—smiled condescendingly. "You are no longer merely a simple Fireblood girl. You are something more now. And though you will not live long enough to see the final triumph that comes from your sacrifice, your life will be given for a greater purpose. You will serve as host for the Minax as we travel to the Gate of Light. And when my Minax destroy the sentinels, I will break the bars that keep the Gate closed, so the rest of my living shadows will pour from where Cirrus trapped them in the Obscurum. So, you see? You're not dying in vain. You'll be remembered by the gods."

"As the one who helped you unleash the Minax on the world?" I asked, more fully myself for the moment. "That's not how I want to be remembered."

His green eyes narrowed, but his smile widened. "Somehow you've retained more than a little of yourself, haven't you? Remarkable. The Minax chose a strong host."

The Minax inside me grew excited, murmuring something about a *true vessel* and *Daughter of Darkness*, and though I was careful not to form the words with my lips, I sensed that Eurus could hear its voice anyway.

He lifted a brow. "Are you certain, pet?"

The Minax eagerly answered *yes*, and then the heart-shaped scar near my left ear burned. I clapped my fingers over it, but Eurus stepped closer, grasped my wrist, and drew my hand firmly away. His eyes met mine, and even in the dim light, they looked brighter green than ever. "There is only one person on this earth my Minax would mark this way." His eyes seemed to glow.

"You are my daughter."

TWENTY-SEVEN

I HEARD ARCUS'S SHARP INHALATION. If it hadn't been for the Minax half in control of my limbs, I'd have staggered. The moment was an echo of the queen's revelation that I was her niece, but far less welcome. And my mind was still hazed with the Minax's thoughts—chaotic and disordered, always striving to regain control. I wanted to refute Eurus's claim, but I couldn't even manage to open my mouth.

"Not truly my daughter." Eurus's satisfaction gleamed from Prince Eiko's green eyes. "Not blood of my blood. My interfering mother, Neb, had long since forbade dalliances with fair mortals, I'm afraid. But your mother, the Sudesian princess, she was possessed by the Minax while you grew in her womb."

"That's a lie." I'd meant to shout the denial, but the words emerged in a trembling whisper. I wanted to use my fire to attack him. I wanted to run. But my arms hung limp at my sides. It was as if I were made of stone and could only watch and listen, helpless to stop the words coming from his smiling mouth.

Eurus crossed his arms over his chest in a way that was eerily similar to what Eiko might have done. "Though I could not interfere with mortals, I have always had the ability to communicate with the two Minax I'd trapped in the frost and fire thrones. I decided on a small experiment: a mingling of the shadows with fire to create the first in a possible new race. A Child of Darkness."

"No," I whispered. My worst fear was coming true.

"I told the Minax to leave its host, the Fire King at that time, and inhabit his younger daughter, Princess Rota, who happened to be expecting a child." He smirked at the memory. "An infant in a mother's womb surrounded by the essence of the Minax, day in, day out. Things looked promising for a while after you came howling into the world. By the Minax's account, you were a demonic little thing, with the characteristic quick temper of a Fireblood princess. But your mother didn't seem to mind. She was tender and endlessly patient, barely showing signs that she'd been possessed for months. And when you were born, she shook off the Minax like a dog shaking off water."

At the mention of my mother, a pang of grief pierced my heart, and then the power of the Minax eased the hurt back into numbness.

Eurus tilted his head to the side. "She was a problem. She kept soothing all your discontent into patience and your fury into love. Your darkness had no chance to grow. I decided to get rid of her, but before I could act, Rota took you away, somewhere far enough that the Minax could no longer sense her. I suspect Sage assisted her somehow. I have a few scores to settle with Cirrus's favored mortal when I find her."

I sensed the Minax rattling around in my mind, but it had grown almost placid, as if Eurus were telling it a bedtime story and it was soothed. I felt its leap of recognition when he mentioned my mother. Horror was laying siege to my body—thickening my throat, forcing beads of sweat to my forehead, twisting my stomach—but the Minax's influence blocked the feelings from taking hold. I was trapped in a strange, echoing limbo between my own agonized reactions and the Minax's numb indifference.

"But why did you want to create a Child of Darkness at all?" I asked hoarsely, half-lost in my inner battle.

"Why, the Child of Darkness was to be the first one. The first of a new race of Nightbloods. I want to create my own people, people who are strong enough to host the Minax permanently, people who will do my bidding. My living nightmares will leave the Obscurum and possess mortals . . . and I'll rule the shadows. After all, Sud created Firebloods, and Fors"—he gestured to Arcus, who emanated deadly cold on my left—"made his walking icicles. It was my turn. I set out to create humans filled with the very essence of darkness. Nightbloods."

A wisp of fear penetrated my mental haze. My first night on the ship, I'd dreamed of a creature with shadow arms spreading wide, as if the night itself longed to embrace me. My nightmare was coming true.

Eurus's eyes glittered, his pupils dilated wide—little windows into a pitiless, obsessive mind. "But instead of creating my own people, the Minax scampered from person to person, using them up like an otter with a pile of clamshells, cracking them open and sucking out the meat before discarding them."

"You weren't creating. You were destroying. Taking away identity and free will."

"Bah! Mortals would do far better if they relinquished control. You make a hash of everything anyway. You warred with each other before Frostbloods and Firebloods were created. The gods have merely made the conflicts more entertaining."

Arcus made an angry sound. I turned to him with a warning look.

"And now that I have you," Eurus continued, "the first successful Nightblood, the very thing I've wanted to create for a millennium, I can make more of you. You have shown me that sending the Minax to possess an unborn child is the only way to create a vessel that can accommodate one indefinitely. I'll form a people who will conquer both Frostbloods and Firebloods—or kill them all off, for all I care—and rule the mortal world." Ice ran down my spine as he rubbed his hand over his chin and added thoughtfully, "I haven't decided whether to let the rest of the mortals live. The ones without any powers are so dreary. But I suppose they're useful in their own way. Serfs. Servants. Chattel. What have you."

My pulse surged, my hands clammy. I didn't know what I felt. The Minax held the barrier between body and mind.

"They do have their uses," Marella said, moving closer to Eurus, hands loosely clasped, her white gown and gaunt frame making her appear frail and pure. "And if you prize drive and ambition, I've proven myself to you time and time again."

He turned his head and looked her over. "You're a pretty little thing, aren't you? A bit starved, but rather fetching in a wasted sort of way."

"Lady Marella," she said, offering her hand as if she was meeting him at court. He continued to stare. After a moment, she let her arm fall back to her side.

"I suppose I have you to thank for all this?" he asked sardonically.

"Yes." She lifted her chin. "And I expect you to recognize that you couldn't have done it without me."

He chortled. "You *expect* it, do you? And what do you expect in return? Currently I'm offering your continued ability to draw breath."

"You want to storm the Gate of Light and liberate the rest of the Minax. I've helped you already by opening the portal to bring you here. Both Minax are here for the taking, so they can fight the sentinels that guard the Gate. In return, I would like you to gift me with Nightblood powers so that I can be a bridge between gods and mortals for you. You need someone who understands the Minax, who can communicate with them when you return to your own realm. If you give me the power to rule the Minax, carrying out your orders, I will be your mortal queen—your faithful servant—forever."

"Please," said Eurus, clearly enjoying her speech. "Tell me more of what you think I need, Lady Ghost."

My muscles were coiled with nervous tension as I watched the tall stolen body of Eiko face the frail body of my one-time friend. Why she thought she could bargain with the god of the east wind was beyond me. The Marella I knew wouldn't have been so foolishly daring. The Minax must have ruined her judgment, twisted her mind so that everything she was saying seemed reasonable. I wanted to shake some sense into her.

But this wasn't the time for sudden moves. I spoke evenly, trying to make her see reason. "You surely don't want what you're asking for, Marella. Imagine what the world would be like, this place you're envisioning with the Minax possessing mortals and controlling them. Look at what it makes them do."

"The whole point is that I'll be controlling the Minax, so *I'll* get to decide what they do. Someone needs to make sure they don't just wipe out all the mortals with their hunger. I've shown that I can control the frost Minax. I'll be able to control the others, too."

"You really think you can do that?" I asked, the urgency of my emotions breaking through the Minax's hold. "That anyone can fully control them?"

"Any misgivings I might have had were burned away over the past few weeks. In time, you'll see my side of things." Her eyes narrowed. "Stop fighting the Minax, Ruby, and let it do its work. You'll feel better for it."

The Minax rushed to the forefront of my mind, overwhelming me. I felt myself losing touch with my thoughts, my identity. Then Arcus's hand touched my back, the cold shocking me into awareness again.

Eurus watched all this, amused. "A delightful fantasy, Lady Skin and Bones. But you are not a Nightblood. You wouldn't last a day in the Obscurum, not like my Ruby."

My reply was quiet but fervent. "I'm not *your* anything."

In an abrupt change of mood, his eyes darkened. "Your protests bore me. Time to leave."

My muscles locked. "I'm not going anywhere with you."

Arcus edged in front of me.

"Yes, my dear, you are. We're going to the Gate of Light to release the rest of my beloved Minax—and I need a Nightblood alongside me. Haven't you been paying attention? Please tell me I didn't sire a dullard."

"I'm not going with you. Anywhere. Ever."

His lip curled. "You're in that rebellious phase of adolescence. How tedious."

He reached out for my hand, and Arcus slammed his forearm across Eurus's wrist. Eurus cried out, his eyes startled, his body bent at the waist. "This experience of human pain," he said breathlessly. "I didn't miss it."

With a deep breath, he straightened up again. His eyes were dark green and full of murder. "Normally, I'd make you die slowly for that, you bastard spawn of Fors." He spat the name of the god of the north wind, his hatred clear. "But I don't have all my usual talents in this mortal form. I'll have to settle for using the powers in this borrowed body." He whipped his arm back, fire coiling in his palm, but Arcus was faster. He sent a massive beam of frost at Eurus's chest, which lifted and threw him across the room. Eurus moaned and tried to stand, staring with fury at his uncooperative human legs.

The Minax quivered in reaction to Eurus's pain, freeing my mind a little. I focused on Eurus. I'd spent most of my fire melting the throne, but I summoned what was left to bathe the god of the east wind in flames.

I threw a quick glance at Kai to make sure he was still safe; a slight movement showed that he was waking. As I turned back, cold fingers wrapped around my wrist, sharp nails digging into my skin. Marella yanked my arm down and punched me, her fist landing on my shoulder as I twisted automatically to avoid the blow. I gasped and staggered, amazed at the strength in her skinny arms.

From the corner of my eye, I saw Eurus attack Arcus with twin blazes that curved together and met in a swirling column. Arcus dodged and countered with ice that knocked Eurus off balance.

"You're not ruining this for me, Ruby," Marella snarled near my ear. "You've ruined everything else."

She aimed at my feet, coating them in a layer of ice that crawled up my ankles to my calves. I sent out a pulse of heat to my lower limbs and kicked free, but before I could regain my balance, she'd hit me with a bolt to the stomach, making me double over and fall to my knees.

"You'll do as you're told," Marella said, spraying my bent back with a barrage of ice arrows that cut through the robe and silk tunic. Hot blood welled in the gashes and spilled down my back. "You will cooperate in every way or be gutted like a fish, and I will find some other willing host for the fire Minax. Do you understand?"

"Not sure that Eurus agrees I'm expendable," I replied, snapping out a whip of flame that caught her around the neck before hissing away.

She gasped and clutched her throat. "I'll kill you."

"Try." I stood and snapped at her with another fire whip that made her stumble back. The Minax reveled in the fight, pushing my conscious thoughts to the fuzzy edges. Elation coursed through me in blissful waves. I could hear Eurus and Arcus brawling several yards away, but my interest in the outcome faded. The scene lost color. Torches flickered white instead of orange. The lava from the melted throne flowed in light gray ribbons toward the corners of the room. I could see Marella's heart in her chest, a white pulse of energy that begged to be targeted.

"I can see your heart, too, Ruby," she said with a flare of cold purpose in her eyes. "And I can read your every thought. The Minax is in control, which means you aren't."

Imitating my previous move, she lashed me with an icy whip. I spun to avoid the brunt of it, and it shattered against my shoulder. "My gift is stronger now," she said, loosing a current of frigid air filled with stinging needles of ice. Several landed on my cheek, slicing the skin.

"So is mine," I replied with arrows of fire.

She blocked, batting them down with her forearms. "But you're tired. You're not yourself."

She was right. I was something far, far more dangerous. I wasn't the girl I'd been a year ago: Ruby, the helpless Fireblood peasant, victim of the Frost King's soldiers. I was Princess Ruby, heir to the Sudesian throne, Nightblood daughter of a twisted and bloodthirsty god. Nothing could or would stop me.

My chest expanded with a surge of fire, the Minax's possession refilling the well of heat I'd depleted. My mind sharpened, sped up, everything laid out in excruciating detail. I could use the one gift that only the queen and I had. The power to control lava.

Reaching deep for a final burst of energy, I called up the lava from the corners of the room, the bubbling remains of the throne, and I drew the strands together, pulling the gathered mass of liquid up behind Marella in a wave. The heat was blistering. The lava unstoppable. Killing her would be the easiest thing I'd ever done.

My hands hovered, ready to bring molten death down on her. Time stilled.

Images flashed.

The arena.

Gravnach—the Frostblood champion who'd regularly engaged in torture before he killed his opponents. First, an image of him sawing at my little finger as I screamed, then him convulsing on the ground, his blue blood leaking from his mouth.

Captain Drake, his blade poised over me. Then his lifeless body. His wife and daughter watching.

Rasmus, murderous, trying to suffocate me with his ice in his throne room. Then a later version of Rasmus, his eyes wide with surprise as the Minax filled him one last time, using up the last of his energy, severing the connection between spirit and body.

Arcus facing me in the arena as Kane, when I'd almost killed him. Arcus in the Frost King's throne room, shaking in my arms as I held him, muttering his brother's name.

Kai shoving me against the brick wall of the alley outside the tavern, demanding to know why I'd almost killed a man for no reason. The school courtyard. Kai holding me gently, telling me not to fight my emotions.

Then I saw Sage, clear as if she stood in front of me, her gold eyes burning into mine, beaming a message straight into my mind. *Not her.*

And somehow, I immediately understood. I was fighting the wrong opponent. This wasn't the arena. Marella was not my enemy. If I killed her, I would have lost myself to the Minax. And I would never, never fully come back from that.

Be, Sage said. *Be you.*

Clarity was instant and cataclysmic. I was Eurus's creation. The Minax had known it almost from the time I'd first seen the frost throne. It had recognized a kindred spirit and known I belonged with it. I was a Nightblood.

I was also a Fireblood. Kai had tried to explain that I fought my emotions too much, that my internal struggle diminished my power. My fear of losing control held me back from realizing my full potential.

I had to trust that some basic part of me was good, and let myself be fully Nightblood, fully Fireblood—just for this moment—both merciless and passionate, and know that my mother's love had provided a foundation that would never let me stray too far from my true self.

I threw the lava back, watching the bright glow of it slosh against the wall, making sure it settled once again.

Then I focused on the Minax inside of me, concentrating on my connection to it, letting it merge with me, putting up no resistance. When my mind synced completely with its darkness, I expelled it from my body with the force of my will. Pain cleaved my head and I lost my vision, but I didn't allow myself to lose focus.

For a moment, both Minax seemed startled. I knew everything they felt and heard their every thought. They had longed to be together for an eternity, trapped and separated from each other and from their kind. But they were used to being in control, not being controlled.

I forced the fire Minax to pull the frost Minax from the shell of Marella's body, its shadow arms wrapping around the essence of its twin and yanking it out. I heard Marella's gasp and cry. I heard her body hit the floor. Dimly, I listened to another fight nearby. Arcus's grunt of pain, and Eurus's malevolent laughter.

I bent every fragment of awareness on the fire Minax, controlling its movements, forcing it to drain energy from the other

Minax, to turn its vast hunger on its twin. The frost Minax screamed and fought back, threatening and begging. I showed no mercy. The frost Minax had caused war, genocide, and murder in Tempesia. Never again. Its time was over.

It spat a torrent of ancient words I didn't understand, though I sensed the general meaning. A curse, a vow of revenge, a wish for my suffering. As the frost Minax spouted invective, I forced the fire Minax to snuff out its last spark of life.

As the echoes faded, the fire Minax hovered there, confused, filled with extra energy stolen from its twin. It struggled with something deep and irrevocable, something unfamiliar that confused it. The confusion turned to anger. I called it back to me before it could take its anger out on anyone else.

Return to me.

I staggered as the Minax, doubled in power, slammed through the barrier of skin.

Be silent, I told it. *Sleep.*

It railed and fought. I repeated the order. It whimpered, an inhuman keening, and finally, reluctantly, curled up in a corner of my mind and went silent.

The room pulsed with quiet.

The pounding in my head eased. Blood prickled behind my eyes, and I opened them. The room came into focus.

Arcus was covered in rivulets of shining blue blood, still standing, tense and angry. With surprise, I noticed Kai, breathing hard but alert next to him, his hair mussed, his robes burnt, his hands raised to defend.

They faced Eurus, who stood some yards away near the spinning portal.

For a moment, I wondered why they'd all stopped fighting. Then I noticed that Eurus held Marella in his arms. A human shield. Her white gown trailed to the floor like a sparkling waterfall, one limp arm also hanging down. Her honey-rich hair had come loose from its pins and spilled over his arms. Her face was bone white, her eyes closed.

My heart lurched to see her so still. "Is she dead?"

Eurus's gaze shifted to me, then back to Arcus. "Make any sudden moves, and she will be."

"Leave her," said Arcus roughly. "You don't need her."

"I do need her. To make sure you don't attack again. The death of my Minax has weakened my bond with this frail mortal body. If I had my own powers, our battle would have turned out very differently."

"If you weren't hiding behind an unconscious girl," Kai chimed in, his roughened voice lacking its usual verve, "things would end very quickly."

"Hence my reluctance to put her down," Eurus conceded. He kept his eyes on Arcus, but turned his head to me. "Ruby, you'll come with us."

I clenched my fists. "No."

"Then I'll kill this Frostblood girl," he threatened. "Snapping her neck will be like breaking the stem of a flower." He glanced down at Marella, then refocused on me. "I'll leave her here if you come with me."

I started forward. Arcus's arm snaked around my waist, hauling me back against him.

"Ruby won't trade her life for Marella's." He bent to whisper in my ear. "Don't trust him. He could just take you both—kill you both."

"Put Marella down and then I'll consider it," I said firmly.

A look of stark rage contorted Eurus's features into a frightening mask. "So your friends can kill me? I don't think so."

I recoiled, my heart kicking at my ribs. Just as quickly, his face smoothed back into amusement. "Unfortunately, I'm in no position to force you. Alas, even gods must retreat when confined in inconveniently breakable bodies. However, denying me now will cause you... deep regret in the future. You have already destroyed one of my Minax. I will consider waiving your punishment if you cooperate now."

"I'm not going." As Arcus had said, there was no way to know Eurus wouldn't kill Marella the second I complied. And if I went with him, he'd have the Minax, too, which he needed to open the Gate of Light. He would hold all the cards.

The portal contracted. His nostrils flared. "As you wish. I'll be back for you." He grinned, Eiko's green eyes glinting with a god's haughty malevolence. His attention shifted back to Arcus and Kai, who stood tense and ready. I noticed for the first time that Eurus was bloodied and battered, breathing heavily. His legs trembled. Arcus and Kai had given him a beating. The thought gave me a moment of satisfaction before he spoke again.

"This Frostblood lady won't last more than a few hours as a

host for the remaining Minax, poor thing." There was no sympathy in Eurus's tone. Only amusement. "Why don't you keep my creature, my daughter? Consider it training—a lesson to prepare you for your future."

The blood drained from my face. He was going to leave the Minax with me. I was hosting the creature, and I had nowhere to trap it. No way to destroy it.

Eurus grinned fiercely. "Until next time, Ruby."

He turned and leaped into the portal with Marella in his arms. I rushed forward, trying to grab her at the last second, but before I could touch her, the light flickered and contracted to a pinpoint. A rushing noise filled the air, a sucking hiss that echoed off the stone walls and faded into silence as the light disappeared.

The silence didn't last. The floor shook with another tremor. Pebbles rained down from the ceiling, covering my face and arms with a layer of gray dust. I rubbed it from my lashes, opening my eyes at the sound of someone coughing.

Across the wide space, a few feet inside the doorway to the tunnels, Queen Nalani and Master Dallr stood side by side, staring in confusion.

After a stunned pause, the queen demanded, "What have you done with my husband?"

TWENTY-EIGHT

MASTER DALLR STRODE FORWARD, his orange robes swirling around his feet. Several masters filed in after him, the torchlight glinting off their wrist guards. They all wore ceremonial garb, obviously straight from the initiation. Queen Nalani followed slowly, her hand pressed to the wall for support.

"What is the meaning of this?" she demanded.

Master Dallr looked furious. "A guard reported seeing frost and fire within the tunnels. Explain yourselves!"

I shook with exhaustion. My body felt strangely cold. The throne, Marella, the fight, Eurus—they had taken everything out of me.

Kai stood straight, but his skin was coated in sweat, his

breathing still uneven. Arcus was made of stone, his expression flat and empty. He watched the queen, waiting for her next move.

My heart sank, inching toward despair. What hope did we have that she'd let Arcus go? None. The Minax, grief-hungry, stirred in the back of my mind. I tried to ignore the feelings.

Focus on each moment, I told myself. *Make sure Arcus is safe and then rest.*

Master Dallr took in the scene, staring at the spot where the throne used to be. "The throne of Sud is gone. What treason is this?"

The queen stared at the empty central area, her hand still braced against the wall. I was shocked to notice a tremor run through her. She was normally the embodiment of strength.

"We did what we had to do," I said shakily. "Prince Eiko wanted to protect the queen. The curse was gaining strength—corrupting the queen."

"The curse?" Queen Nalani frowned. "What is the girl speaking of, Dallr?"

"Eiko had no right!" Master Dallr said harshly to me. "He had no right to destroy the throne that gives the queen her power."

The queen put a hand to her chest and rubbed, as if easing a pain there. Her keen gaze swept the room and landed on Master Dallr, fixing on him like an archer taking aim. "So you lied to me about the throne's destruction. You hid the throne here. You hid it from me."

Dallr hung his head. "Yes, Your Majesty. But it was for your own protection, a necessity once we realized the curse was active.

Had you known the throne was still on Sere, you would have insisted on using it. This way, you had the benefit of the throne's power—but we kept the curse controlled."

"The danger of the curse outweighed the benefit of the throne!" I said.

Dallr's lip curled. "The throne was safely contained here where the curse could not affect the queen. Now look at her. She's weak."

It was true. She leaned heavily against the wall, her expression haunted. Perhaps the absence of the throne caused a deep emotional rift, or maybe the separation was affecting her physically. She reminded me of Rasmus after the frost throne was destroyed—grieving for the Minax he thought he couldn't live without. But Nalani hadn't even known that the Minax was present. She was yearning for something she'd never known she'd had. She clearly felt the loss just the same.

"You're wrong." I fought to sound calm, to not show the anger that swirled inside me. "It's the removal of the curse that's making her feel sick. She'll get better now that it's gone."

I could only hope that were true.

Dallr ignored me. "You will have to answer for these crimes. All of you." Without turning his head, he ordered, "Take the king back to the north tower."

The masters moved forward toward Arcus. Ignoring my exhaustion, I bent my knees, widened my stance, and raised my fists.

Master Dallr barked a command and the masters halted. To

me, he said with forced patience, "Be sensible, Princess Ruby. Don't make this harder on yourself."

"Ruby," said the queen, bringing my gaze to her. Her voice sounded faint; she looked tired and strained. "Where is my husband?" No one had answered her before.

I swallowed and stepped closer. "Your Majesty—Queen Nalani—I'm sorry. Your husband is gone."

"He was here a moment ago." She looked around as if expecting him to step out from behind a pillar. Her voice sounded thin, her face crumpling like a child's as she searched the room with frightened eyes. "This is not the least bit amusing."

My breath came shorter, dread settling in my belly. This was going to crush her, especially now when she was feeling the absence of the Minax so acutely. "We... have much to tell you."

"Then tell me!" she demanded hoarsely.

I pushed myself to recount the events of the last two days, including my search for the book, and my conversation with Prince Eiko, when he'd told me his suspicions about the throne's influence. Then, haltingly, I described the destruction of the throne, Marella's betrayal, and the portal that opened to the realm of the gods. I left out the revelation that I was a Nightblood, that I held the Minax now. I wasn't sure what her reaction would be if she knew it was so near.

I stumbled a little as I told her what happened to her husband. "Then Eurus... the... god of the east wind, entered through the portal and... and took over Prince Eiko's body. He—"

The queen held up a palm. She was shaking her head, her

expression more haunted than ever. “You expect me to believe this, Ruby. Surely this can’t be true.”

“You saw it yourself. I know you did.”

“I saw a bright light.” She lifted her chin proudly. “It could have been . . . a reflection of fire.”

“You want to deny it because you can’t make sense of it, but you saw it happen. Prince Kai can verify it.” I didn’t offer Arcus’s testimony, because I knew she wouldn’t accept his word on anything.

“It’s true, Your Majesty,” Kai said, his voice still rough. “When I was searching the castle for Ruby after the initiation, Prince Eiko found me. He was frantic, saying that he’d been expelled from a secret throne room by a Frostblood woman, and that Ruby and the Frost King were in danger. I followed him back, and there we saw the god of the east wind . . .” Kai swallowed hard. “He took over Prince Eiko’s body. He blasted me with fire and I was knocked out. I woke as Eurus tried to take Ruby through the portal. We had no choice but to fight him. Then he used the Frostblood woman as a shield so we couldn’t attack. He left through the portal as . . . as you came in.”

The queen’s eyes fluttered closed and she bent forward at the waist. Master Dallr held her up, his expression murderous.

“I’m sorry, Your Majesty,” Kai said softly, so much pain in his voice that my heart contracted. “I’ve failed you. I should have protected him.”

I shook my head. There was nothing he could have done. But

Kai wasn't looking at me, he was staring at the floor, locked in self-recrimination.

"Does he live?" the queen asked hoarsely. "Is he still alive somewhere?"

"We don't know for sure." I couldn't bear to tell her that Eurus had said that Prince Eiko was gone. Maybe there was some small chance of rescuing him. I wouldn't take away her hope.

"I feel weak," she said plaintively. "I... I feel sick. I need... I need Eiko. I need... something. Something feels wrong." Her voice rose. "The... the voice that calms me is gone." She moaned, the sound echoing off the ceiling, multiplying her pain. The words were shredded, desperate, begging.

I moved closer to her slowly, trying to block out Master Dallr's hostility. I was careful not to touch the queen in case contact with my skin would alert her to the presence of the Minax inside me. "It was the curse in the throne," I said softly. "The voice in your head was the Minax, urging you to... to war and acts of hatred."

"It eased my pain," she cried, almost keening the words. "It made me strong."

We were all silent for a moment. I looked down, not wanting to see the naked vulnerability on the queen's face. It seemed wrong there, somehow.

"And where is the curse—the Minax—now?" she begged.

I hesitated, looking at Arcus briefly for his opinion on what to tell her. He shook his head almost imperceptibly.

"One of the Minax was destroyed," I said. "Eurus plans to

use the other to open the Gate of Light, and unleash the rest of the Minax trapped behind it." Both statements were technically true, if misleading. "I'm sorry, Your Majesty," I said again, not knowing what else to say. I didn't even know if she was capable of understanding what I said.

However, Master Dallr looked shocked. I stared hard at him. He couldn't deny this was a threat to his queen and kingdom, something the masters should help us deal with instead of blocking our attempts. That was, if he chose to believe me.

"You must go after Prince Eiko," Queen Nalani said, quietly raising her eyes to Kai's. Then she said more firmly, "You will go after him. And you must stop this . . . this monster."

"I will," Kai said simply. "Immediately."

"I'll go, too," I said.

"And I," said Arcus.

Master Dallr looked at him with loathing. "You will go nowhere."

I glanced around the room. There were four masters in addition to the queen and Master Dallr. Kai was a master now, too, I realized with a shock. He would be obliged to fight against Arcus and me. And if we did fight, the Minax that lay dormant in my mind could wake and I could lose control. It was too great a risk.

"You must allow it, Your Majesty," I said urgently. "If we don't stop Eurus, he'll open the Gate of Light, and countless shadow creatures with the ability to control people will spill over the earth, possessing and killing people. And we're the only ones who can stop it."

"Why?" she asked. "Why only you?"

"I'm..." I glanced at Arcus and he nodded. "I'm what Eurus calls a Nightblood. I have some ability to control the Minax. But I need Arcus and Kai with me. If we have any hope of retrieving Prince Eiko, we have to use every weapon at our disposal."

The queen glanced at Arcus, as if struggling to understand how he—the enemy—had become vital to the rescue of her husband. At least, I hoped those were her thoughts.

I turned to Master Dallr. "You must know how dangerous Eurus is, and that we need to act quickly."

"The masters have never lost our connection to ancient knowledge," he replied. "It's now a question of which steps to take to avert this disaster."

I sighed my relief. I'd been afraid that they'd continue to fight against us.

"Have you considered that Eurus hopes you will follow him?" Master Dallr said. "He could be luring you into a trap."

"All the more reason for both the king and me to be there," Kai jumped in. "Our combined power will give us the best chance of success. And we'll both guard Ruby with our lives."

I looked at him with surprise. He was arguing on Arcus's behalf?

The queen looked down for a moment, touching her wedding band lightly before squaring her shoulders. When she spoke, her voice was still weak—but the old note of determination had returned. "I have been entrusted by birth with the responsibility of caring for an entire kingdom. When King Rasmus took the frost throne, I was helpless to stop the massacre of my people. We were caught unprepared. Not enough ships. Not enough weapons or soldiers. Unable to fight."

She stared at Arcus, and my heart lodged in my throat. She was going to throw him in prison, question him, kill him. She would do all the things she'd threatened and more, taking her rage and pain out on him. My whole body was filled with bated breath.

"I will not be responsible for another massacre," she said, a fierce light shining in her dark eyes. "I will not stand by as tragedy unfolds." She turned to me. "If you, my niece, tell me that you must go, then I must place my trust in you . . . and you will go."

I let out the breath. "Thank you."

"You will all go, then. And you will take Master Dallr and a contingent of masters with you."

Arcus cleared his throat. "Respectfully, Your Majesty, even if my crew accepts the presence of Fireblood masters, the enmity between our people goes back too far. I'm afraid we have a long way to go before Sudesians adjust to a cordial relationship with Tempesians, and vice versa. Though, to be clear, I very much hope our kingdoms will be allies again."

"Allies or not, my masters are going," she declared. "Rest assured they'll behave with admirable self-control. See that your crew does the same."

"We could take two ships," Kai suggested. "The Fireblood masters could travel on mine. As my ship is faster, I'll take Ruby with me. The king and the Frostblood crew can follow in theirs."

Arcus made a quiet sound, a low growl deep in his throat. "Ruby will be with me. That is not negotiable."

The queen's eyes narrowed. "You will do what is best for the mission."

"Then we'll take one ship," Kai conceded. "And we'll combine our crews."

She gestured to the door. "Go, then. Take all the supplies you need."

My throat was tight. "Thank you for your faith in us."

She turned her gaze on Arcus. "I will hold you responsible if my husband and my niece are not safely returned."

"I would feel the same in your position, Your Majesty," he replied. "I would tear the world apart if someone took Ruby from me."

She gave him a long, considering look. Their eyes held, some message passing between them.

She leaned into Master Dallr and whispered into his ear. He nodded and led her carefully, step by step, to the doorway. She looked as if she'd aged by decades. The loss of the Minax had ripped something important from her.

I wondered if she'd ever be herself again, or if some essential part was lost forever.

A chill ran through me. Is that how I would look one day?

What would be left of me once I finally found a way to destroy the Minax I held in my heart?

TWENTY-NINE

"YOU MIGHT AS WELL WRAP ME IN sailcloth and dump me over the side," Jaro moaned, gesturing past the railing to endless rolling waves. "Those Frostbloods will be the death of me!"

"All they want is to be given berths, same as the Sudesian sailors," I said in a placating tone. A northeastern breeze grabbed my words and threw them back at me. Even the wind was arguing tonight. "Surely you can find room in the forecastle."

"But I'll have to put them right *next* to each other," he cried, oblivious to the attentive ears of the crew, keeping busy at their newly assigned tasks on the main deck. "They'll kill each other!"

I reached up and patted one of his hands, both of which were fisted in his already thin hair, one frustrated tug away from ripping out strands he could ill afford to lose. "You'll find a way, Jaro. You always do."

His shoulders slumped as he dropped his arms. "The prince can pay me double my usual wage for this trip."

"I'm sure you can negotiate some extra pay with the captain." I had no idea if that was true. I'd been telling everyone what they wanted to hear, walking on eggshells strewn over a tightrope for the past day. I was weak and hungry and could barely see straight, my eyes nearly crossing from exhaustion.

After leaving the cavern, Kai and I had accompanied Arcus to his ship. Kai had inspected the vessel thoroughly and quickly declared it too old, too slow, and in need of several repairs. After a certain amount of bickering, bribing, begging, and grudging compromise, we'd all agreed to take Kai's ship with a combined crew of Sudesian and Tempesian sailors, along with a half dozen Fireblood masters, as decreed by the queen. The Sudesian sailors had only agreed to crew a ship alongside Frostbloods after we'd informed them that Kai would captain the ship.

Aver and Kaitryn already showed signs of becoming fast friends, leaping and scuttling along the lines like demented spiders. Jaro bellowed cautionary remarks at the ship's girls, which earned him nothing but impish grins.

The storm that had gusted in the day before had blown itself out just as quickly. The *Errant Princess* had been hastily crewed and outfitted and we'd left port at dawn. The jewel-green island had disappeared in a gray haze.

Kai had set a course for Tempesia. We hoped Brother Thistle

would be able to help us interpret the more cryptic passages of *The Creation of the Thrones*, which I'd retrieved from Prince Eiko's observatory. Perhaps some hint, something hidden in the illuminations or in the symbols on some of the pages, would lead us to the Gate of Light.

Spyglasses were currently fixed on the horizon, though even the last streaks of sunset were fading. I was eager to curl up in whatever hammock or pile of sailcloth would serve as my bed. More permanent accommodations could be sorted out tomorrow.

"So, this is what perdition is like," a low rumble said, followed by the sensation of cold. I shivered and turned to lean my back against the railing. Arcus and I hadn't had a moment alone together in the rush to organize the voyage—not that we were alone now with the crew all over. Still, it was a relief to have a moment to soak up his presence.

"Ocean cruise not to your liking?" I asked, shaking my head to surrender my tangled hair to the wind's questing fingers. My braid had come undone hours ago and I hadn't bothered to repair it.

Arcus laid an arm along the railing and moved closer than what could be called, even by the most indifferent of observers, a polite distance. In his court, he'd been careful not to engage in physical displays unless we were alone. I couldn't help but wonder if he was staking his claim on me.

My eyes were drawn to Kai, who stood on the quarterdeck, his eyes narrowed thoughtfully, hair charmingly mussed by the wind. How did he feel being back at sea only a day after taking his vows as master? Relieved? Disappointed? Indifferent? It was hard to tell. Despite his open-book exterior, he hid much behind that charismatic mask.

"Not when half the crew wants to kill the other half," Arcus said, answering my earlier question.

I turned back to him and smiled, suddenly filled with gratitude that he was safe. The queen had gone from planning to imprison, interrogate, and possibly kill him, to letting him go. That change of heart was proof, to my mind, that she had been under the influence of the Minax, and was no longer. Now the Minax was my burden to bear, but so far, I only felt its presence as a distant throb, like a toothache that comes and goes.

I was also glad, I realized with a surprised jolt, not to have taken my vows as a master. I wasn't sure until that moment how I really felt about it. I'd wanted the approval of the masters, the inclusion into their ranks, but I didn't want the restrictions of pledging my life to the queen. It was good to know I still belonged to myself.

No matter what happened, I had this journey to spend with Arcus and I would savor it. I would store up each memory like a treasured gem strung on a chain. I hoped the warmth of those remembrances would help me to master the Minax when it woke. And when the time came to use my newfound Nightblood powers.

"The Frostbloods don't want to *kill* the Firebloods," I corrected, wrapping my hand around his arm. He covered my hand with his in a cool caress. "They just want to dump them overboard to see if they can swim. It's more sporting that way. At least, that's what I heard a few of your crewmembers saying."

Arcus closed his eyes briefly. "It'll be a miracle if everyone survives as far as land."

"Well, we've already witnessed a few miracles...or events that are equally impossible. What's one more?"

He leaned in, his voice lowering to an intimate volume. "We haven't been alone until now, so I haven't had a chance to ask. How are you doing?" His free hand lifted and his knuckle traced a path along my cheek. "You've been remarkably calm in the wake of some shocking revelations."

I considered answering flippantly, but this was Arcus. He would persist until I told him the truth.

"Shaken," I admitted. "Terrified. Determined."

I looked up at him. The lanterns had been lit, casting a glow over the deck and brushing half his face in gold. He nodded slowly, but looked worried. In what started as a comforting gesture, I put a hand to his shoulder, feeling the hard muscle underneath the soft, dark shirt. The V-shaped collar exposed the bit of chest below his collarbone. Unable to help myself, I slid a hand to that enticing triangle sprinkled with hair. A pulse of coolness met my fingers, but it was as pleasant as heat. Better. Because it was from him.

Then somehow I was in his arms, struggling to get closer to the cold, hard wall of his chest. His arms bound me so tightly I feared being snapped in half. I laughed breathlessly.

"I missed you so much after you left," he muttered, burying his nose against my neck. "I was so worried."

"I missed you, too." I had. I hadn't realized how much until I'd seen him again.

"Next time you go, take me with you."

I laughed again, tempted to point out that that might not always be practical. But the thought of practicality was sobering. Nothing had changed between us. Or if anything, matters had grown more complicated. He was still king of Tempesia, but now, against all odds, I was heir to the Sudesian throne. I should push him away. Tell him it would never work. The same reservations I'd had before should still be there, multiplied tenfold.

Only none of that would matter if we didn't stop Eurus from releasing the Minax from the Obscurum. That was the difference. That was what had changed. When you don't know if there's a tomorrow, you realize quickly what matters most. I couldn't afford to waste another moment with him.

As he loosened his hold, I squeezed him harder, telling him without words that his feelings for me were not one-sided. His lips rested against my hair and I breathed his scent, which was both calming and exciting at the same time. Finally, he set me back slightly. "I'm making you cold. You're shivering."

"That's not from cold." I lifted a brow and added boldly, "It's the feel of you that makes me shiver." I smiled when he shivered in response.

A lantern was extinguished, then another. I realized we should go our separate ways, say good night. But I wasn't ready.

"We haven't talked about Marella," I ventured. "She was a friend to us both."

His jaw squared and he looked away. "I can't even let myself think about what she tried to do. It merely makes me want to kill her myself."

"I can't believe I didn't see it. When I visited her on your ship, I was so worried about her." I paused. "You must be worried about her still." He'd known her all his life.

My feelings about Marella were complicated. She had been an ally against King Rasmus, then a friend, then a betrayer. I wondered if she'd known what she was doing when she first hosted the Minax. It had used her to get to its twin and Eurus. She had become a victim in the end. Whatever she had done, she didn't deserve to die for it. I admitted to myself then that I wanted to find and rescue Marella, too, if we could.

"I can't help but regret what happened to her," Arcus said finally, echoing my thoughts as he sometimes did. "But I'm far more worried about you. Are you . . . can you feel its presence?"

We had to be very careful to hide my secret on the ship. If word got out to the crew that a Minax was on board, it would be pandemonium. I knew the superstitions of sailors, and this would horrify even the most skeptical of souls.

"Not so much." I wondered how to describe it. "It's . . . dormant, I suppose is the best word. I know it's there but barely."

"Good," he said, wrapping an arm around my back and pulling me close. "I hope it stays that way."

"Me too."

"And how do you feel about . . . what Eurus said?"

"That I'm a Nightblood?" Even the word chilled me. Night was too vast, too inevitable. You could light a candle and hide, but you could never fight it. And I carried it in my veins. I rubbed my upper arms to warm them and tried to hide my fear. "I don't want to believe it. Part of me hopes it's not true, even though there are signs it is. The mark. The way I can host the creature without feeling sick. My ability to control the Minax to the degree that one destroyed the other."

"You are remarkable," he whispered. "I hope you know that. The things you've done. The things you've had to face."

I didn't feel remarkable. At the moment, I felt small and scared. Unequal to everything that I'd have to do, without a clear picture of what that even was. And tired. So tired.

So I leaned more heavily on him as I said, "But even though I don't want to believe it, well . . . I have to face the truth. I am the"—I lowered my voice—"Child of Darkness."

"I don't believe that," he said with quiet vehemence. "At least, I don't believe it's something evil. If that's what you are, then it's not bad. Because everything about you is just as it should be."

I chuckled, surprised. "I thought you said I rush into danger and take unnecessary risks. You told me I was selfish."

"I was the selfish one. I just wanted you to stay. But if you hadn't come here, we'd never have discovered how to destroy the Minax."

"We don't know how to destroy the other one, unfortunately."

"Have you . . . tried?"

"You mean . . . just by willing it to die? No. I . . . I don't think that would work."

I was terrified that if I reached out mentally, it would wake again. I still didn't know how or why it was dormant. It had occurred to me that if the Minax did share human traits as Brother Thistle had once implied, that the creature could actually be grieving for its dead sibling. It had yearned for its twin for years—centuries. On the other hand, grief and death were fuel for the Minax. That could be making it stronger.

As usual, when I dwelled on the Minax too much, my spirits sank. Arcus sensed the shift and pulled me tighter. The feel of his strength surrounding me was a balm on my soul. I closed my eyes and leaned my head against his chest.

The sound of a throat clearing made me jerk back reflexively. "Sorry," Kai said softly as he came into the lantern light, "I didn't mean to scare you."

"I'm a little jumpy for some reason," I replied with a smile. For a second, I felt awkward, guilty about being wrapped in Arcus's embrace when Kai and I had kissed—and not a chaste peck, either—just a few days ago. I still had all the warm feelings of friendship for Kai, and a few nebulous ones that might be more than friendship. But once I'd seen Arcus again, it had clarified things for me. I just hadn't had a chance to put them into words yet.

I watched Kai's face for signs of bitterness or jealousy, but there were none, so I allowed myself to relax.

"Can't imagine why," he quipped. His teasing was reassuring.

"So do you think you can get us to Tempesia in record time?" I asked.

"Of course." His expression was so delightfully arrogant, I almost wanted to laugh.

Kai cleared his throat again. "Do you have a moment?"

Arcus's arm slid away from me. "Excuse me, I'd better go make sure my crew hasn't taken the best berths. Or been forced to sleep in the brig." He strode off in the direction of the hatch, and I watched him go, glad that he'd tactfully left me alone with Kai without showing any animosity toward him.

Kai moved to lean on the railing beside me, a careful distance away, and tilted his head. "How are you, little bird?"

I was glad he used my nickname, another sign that he wasn't upset with me. "Mostly I'm just tired. I feel worse for the queen. She seemed so... broken."

"She seemed stronger when I visited her before we left. You didn't want to come with me, if you recall."

"I feel so guilty. As if I betrayed her."

"For trying to save her? That *is* ridiculous. What happened after was not your fault." He sighed. "I keep wondering, though, whether Prince Eiko is alive. Do you think his mind is in there somewhere?"

"I truly don't know." Eurus probably wasn't like the Minax, who shared the space in your mind. A wind god would have far more power than his creation, and he seemed to have no scruples about snuffing out insignificant lives to suit his convenience. "We need to be prepared for the worst."

"Except the worst keeps getting... worse."

I chuckled. "We couldn't have prepared for Eurus."

As I said the name, a puff of wind came from the east, filling the sails to bursting before dying off.

"I'll remember not to say that name again," I whispered, rubbing the goose bumps on my arms.

"I'd appreciate that," Kai replied softly.

I took a deep breath and looked down. "I'm sorry I didn't tell you the real reason I came to Sudesia. I should have trusted you."

I lifted my head slowly, scared of what I might see on his face. Anger? Hurt? Contempt? That would be worst of all.

But what I saw in his eyes, golden in the lantern light and a little wide, was something warm and open. Sympathy. Understanding. Something harder to identify. As he caught me watching him, his eyelids fell to half mast, and his mouth quirked in that typical teasing smile that warmed me by degrees until I couldn't help but return the look.

My spirits, I realized, had lifted somewhere above the mainmast. "Do you forgive me?"

"I suppose I must," he said, flicking an invisible piece of lint from his pristine black doublet. "Normally I would hold a grudge for such an offense. But one might say, Princess Ruby, without exaggeration, that you are an exception to all rules."

"Glad you recognize that. Finally."

"Exceptions must stick together." He reached out and squeezed my shoulder, his expression conveying support and affection, but his hand lingering a little too long. It seemed our whole complicated history was contained in that gesture.

His eyes went to the sailors on watch. "Well, it looks like everything is in hand. I'm going to my cabin to sleep like the dead."

"Must be nice to have a cabin."

"Would you prefer to sleep there?" he asked quickly.

I lifted a brow.

"Alone, if you're so inclined." Mischief danced in his eyes.

I snorted. "Thank you, but I think you've made enough sacrifices. Taking on this crew, for instance. You'll need a quiet space to get away from all the arguing."

"We'll find you a cabin tomorrow. One of my officers can bunk with the crew. But for tonight—"

"I'll sleep on the deck if that's all that's available."

"There's a hammock in steerage if you don't mind bedding down among crates and barrels. You won't be disturbed. I'm thinking you might like some time alone."

Something sweet closed my throat. I was touched. "Very thoughtful, Kai. Thank you."

He nodded and left, his gait adjusting to the roll of the waves without a flicker of difficulty. Like he was part of the ship.

I turned and rested my elbows on the railing, staring down to where the sea churned—nearly invisible in the dark. In a few minutes, I wouldn't be able to see the water at all. But I'd know it was there because of the way it heaved us up and dropped us down, gentle now, but subject to the whims of the winds. In a matter of hours or even minutes, the swells could turn from calm to violent.

It was like the Minax. I couldn't see it, but I knew it was there. I sensed it more now that I had no one and nothing to distract me. Would it remain passive and allow me to direct it? Or would it take its cue from a vengeful wind god and dash me to pieces against the rocks of its hate? I had no choice but to try to weather it, to hold the wheel tight, to fight to stay on course.

It wasn't only me who counted on my ability to remain in control. The entire world would suffer if I didn't. When I thought of it that way, I couldn't breathe. Couldn't think.

I gripped the railing and stared down at the deepening gloom.

I was darkness. There was nothing to be gained by denying it. My best chance lay in treating this new ability the way I'd always treated my fire—as part of me. Fear of my fire had ruled me when I'd had no control over it. Darkness, like fire, was a gift I could master.

A gust brushed my hair to the side and I turned toward it. It smelled of harvest, of wheat being bound into sheaths, of fallen leaves and crisp pine. The stray breeze had come from the west. I smiled. Cirrus was sending a message of support. I held my hand out, catching the scented air in my palm.

Just as suddenly, a vicious gust cut across the deck, snapping the sails. An east wind, threatening rain. Air swirled around me, pulling the breath from my lungs and wrapping my hair around my upper arms like binding ropes.

The wind twisted away. The sails fell slack.

I shoved my hair back and rubbed the chill from my arms. The air smelled of smoke and blood, of army camps and battlefields.

A wordless message from Eurus, as clear as if it were written in the stars: Prepare for war.

ACKNOWLEDGMENTS

I'm so grateful for the guidance, patience, and steadfast encouragement from Deirdre Jones and Kheryn Callender at Little, Brown. Cheers to the amazing LBYR team: Annie McDonnell, Sasha Illingworth, Angela Taldone, Virginia Lawther, Emilie Polster, Stefanie Hoffman, Jane Lee, and especially Kristina Pisciotta for putting up with my many questions. Hats off to Megan Tingley, Jackie Engel, and Alvina Ling. Big thanks to Dominique Delmas at Hachette Canada!

To Emily Kitchin at Hodder & Stoughton, thank you from the bottom of my heart for being so patient and helpful in the home stretch! Huge thanks to Fleur Clarke, Becca Mundy, and Natalie Chen!

Hugs to everyone at New Leaf Literary, especially my brilliant agent, Suzie Townsend, and to Sara Stricker, Kathleen Ortiz, Pouya Shahbazian, Mia Roman, and Hilary Pecheone.

Endless gratitude to friends found through RWA, starting with Nicki Pau Preto, who found me first—lucky me! Tightest hugs to the Lady Seals: Anabel, Brooke, Crystal, Guida, and Sarah. So grateful for the Pitch Wars Table of Trust, especially early readers Jennifer Hawkins, Mary Ann Marlowe, Mara Rutherford, Nikki Roberti, Kelly Siskind, Summer Spence, Ron Walters, and Kristin B. Wright.

Alexa Donne, thank you for your perceptive insights! Morgan Rhodes, Eve Silver, Lori M. Lee, and Julie Kagawa, thank you for being wise and generous! Thanks to my coworkers at ECL: the Library Warriors. Deep appreciation to early readers Lauren Kennedy, Sabrina Chiasson, and Isabelle Hanson. Hugs to the 2017 Debuts!

Love and thanks to my super-supportive family: Matt, Nancy, Dan, Erik, Mark, Fred, Donna, Heather, Jill, Todd, Zoe, and Quinton. All my love to Nicklas, Aleksander, and Lukas! You are my sunshines. Dearest Darren, thank you is not enough. I love you.

Last, but not least, thank you to readers. Your support and enthusiasm inspire me!